The gun is pointi
gets a lucky grab
leverage to grab th
animal brain goes

Make no mistak
lethal techniques a..
in those terms. The danger of the situation has
kicked him up to a level beyond conscious thought.
The Watcher can't command his muscles – not to
battle reflex – because it is halfway across the world
in America and no signal moves that fast. So here's
the thing, Adrien: there's no one to blame but
yourself. It's your *shuto* that flows out to its target on
the cervical vertebrae, passing through and crushing
the trachea en route. You don't stop yourself. It's
your power. It's your ki. *You* are the killer.

Yet it's the Watcher who grips this moment in
pleasure and shakes it, like a wolf.

Tricia Sullivan is a young American sf writer now living in London. Her first novel, *Lethe*, was heralded as 'spectacular' (*Locus*) and 'awe-inspiring' (Ian McDonald), and she has been acclaimed as 'One of the finest new talents in the field' (David Brin).

By the same author

Lethe
Dreaming in Smoke

Tricia Sullivan

SOMEONE TO
WATCH OVER ME

MILLENNIUM

A Millennium Paperback

First published in Great Britain by Millennium in 1997
This paperback edition published in 1998 by Millennium,
a division of Orion Books Ltd,
Orion House, 5 Upper St Martin's Lane,
London WC2H 9EA

A CIP catalogue record for this book
is available from the British Library.

ISBN: 0 75281 638 1

Typeset by Deltatype Ltd, Birkenhead, Merseyside
Printed and bound in Great Britain by
Clays Ltd, St Ives Plc

For my parents,
with love and admiration.

ACKNOWLEDGEMENTS

This book was a real bitch to write. I would like to offer heartfelt thanks to Mic Cheetham, for extra touches like that supersonic predawn reading of the first draft, and for just generally holding my hand while I thrashed.

Anne Lesley Groell has provided humor and buckets of patience, both much appreciated. Steve Morris revolutionized my thinking about martial arts, some of which is (inadequately) reflected here. Dan Sullivan kindly explained technical matters, and I'm indebted to Mark Rudolph for medical information and vulgar e-mail. Thanks also to Caroline Oakley, Jonathan Karp, Ray Roberts, and especially Russ Galen – about whom too much to tell here.

Quid pro quo, Shaka. And you're in big trouble.

Finally, to my family and friends: you know who you are, but you may not know how much your support means. It means a lot. Cheers.

Deus in camera obscura

I ride tandem with the random
Things don't run the way I planned them

Peter Gabriel

One

He was on the wrong train and he had to get off. As he crawled from his seat, grappling for the door amid the scramble of passengers, he was seized by the conviction that there was no such thing as *the world* except insofar as it was defined by his personal and specific pain. The world was turning all to smoke and aquarelles, whereas his pain was as precise and ruthless as a panther. His pain, in fact, was carving out its own identity, a private timestrand, snarling and obscene. It was athletic, gifted – bewildering – so that when the train whirled away he was left swaying on the platform while his senses, one by one, crunched down toward singularity, eliminating the world and admitting nothing but – you guessed it – pain.

This probably meant he was about to pass out.

Voices; shuffling bodies. Fearful of collapsing in public, he checked his thoughts: agony is vulgar. Tamed by discipline. Think about something else. Zagreb. The conductor said Zagreb. Luckily he still had his bag. Better keep moving. Find a hotel. If any bones were broken, they weren't important ones. He would buy drugs, sleep for one day, and then on to New York. There, if still coughing blood, hospital.

He was moving unsteadily toward a welter of kiosks. Embarrassment was surely called for. Or anger. Or fear. But at the moment he was strictly into feeling sorry for himself. The Watcher had abandoned him; his role now would be merely to slither away and lick his wounds. He had been put in his place. No one would care what he did anymore, so why keep up pretenses? He permitted himself the luxury of limping.

Peripherally he noticed that an adolescent boy outside the newsstand was giving him the eye. Glancing once, he took in the characteristic pattern of facial pierces that identified the kid as a bootleg wire-seller, and veered away. He had left his own bootlegging career years ago. Now he had enough money to use any commercial wire on the market: he could afford to buy a six-hour Tantric orgasm *and* the illegal subroutine that would remove the urge to book a flight on the Concorde afterward; but he didn't use wires. He had a lot of problems, but addiction to pleasure wasn't one of them.

He staggered toward the Hotel Esplanade.

Preoccupied with his physical condition, he failed to notice the doorman until the latter stretched out an arm stiff as a toll barrier, his language-neutral howdareyou expression barely masking the glee that evidently accompanied the act of repelling intruders. There was a torrent of words in Croatian. In the middle of this obloquy he began coughing and had to hawk and spit right at the doorman's feet. A clumsy kick was aimed at him but he dodged it without effort.

He abandoned the idea of entering the hotel and shuffled off in hope of finding a taxi. He noticed that a thin stream of blood, diverted by his left eyebrow, was tracking down his face and dripping on his shirt.

There weren't enough taxis lined up to cope with the crowd. It was just occurring to him that if he had to stand and wait he would probably faint, when he saw this girl at the far end of the row of cabs. She leaned against her car smoking a cigarette and watching the throng approach. The car was either parked or broken down, a fragile-looking doorless affair, piebald with rust. She had presence, or he was giddy with pain, or both, because he made an effort to stop gasping and dragging his right leg. Her leather jacket and old trainers were stained, but the way she inhabited them made their condition immaterial. He wondered if the bruises on his face were visible yet. He gritted his teeth and told himself to beat the two businessmen who were also bearing down on the girl, conversing in rapid Chinese. Picking up his feet, he shouldered past them, muttering, 'Discourteous occidental fuck coming through.' He flung himself ahead, falling with a wheeze on the hood of the car. Clutching his midsection, he lowered his head toward the gutter and loosed a long cough; he could feel her eyes on him so he swallowed the warm, foul admixture of bodily fluids and tried to straighten up.

She put out her cigarette delicately against the rusted iron and pushed herself off the car with one movement, coming toward him with the smoke flying out of her nostrils and her dark hair lifting off her face and her cinematic eyes fixed on him so that he no longer wanted to move. He flashed the thoughts: She is an angel. She will save me.

She did not look pleased. She shouted something in Croatian, and he saw her waving at the two Chinese over his head. He shut his eyes against new insurrections in his chest, leg, kidneys and head and found some money in the pocket of his jeans. He thrust it toward her, but she was still tearing strips out of him by the tone of her voice.

'No Croatian,' he groaned. 'Hotel. Hotel. Just take me to a fucking hotel. Please.'

He straightened, coaxing down a wave of nausea. His head pounded. When he thought he was fully upright, he opened his eyes. She was not beautiful, not even close, but she was ... she was ...

'You need hospital, not the hotel,' she said. She looked at the money, and then back at him, as if she could not reconcile the two. 'Get in.'

He folded himself into the car. 'No hospital. Hotel.'

She started the car. He stared at the dashboard, which moved closer and then farther away.

'Which hotel?'

'Good hotel. Money hotel.'

She pulled out into traffic. 'No respectable hotel wants

you, like this. They will throw you out, the concierge. Anyway, you don't need the car in city center.'

'Your English is very good.'

'Thank you.' She took a sharp turn and he had to grab the door frame to keep from sliding out.

'We could go to your place,' he said. 'You could nurse me back to health and I could ...' It was odd, but he was forgetting how to speak. He knew the words, but the correct movements of the tongue and jaw were suddenly mysterious. He closed his eyes again.

'Protect me from crazy foreigners who fall on my car?' She was laughing; that would normally be a good sign but something told him she was still a long way from flirting with him. 'I will take you to hotel where all Americans stay.'

'Oh, no ... please.' His words were becoming syrupy. 'You wouldn't do that to me. Can't you take me somewhere quiet, where I won't be bothered?'

'You have no reservation? Not good. I do what I can.'

He heard the engine blast into a lower gear as they began to ascend into the residential districts, but he must have lost consciousness after that because the next thing he knew the car had stopped and she was shaking him.

'We are here. Are you getting out? If you don't get out now, I take you to hospital and they must deal with you.'

'I'm getting out.' He did it gingerly, then leaned back through the place where the door should be and proffered some more money.

'You already paid me too much. You paid five times the fare.' She seemed to be struggling to keep a straight face.

'Will you wait for me, then? I still need you. This place is small: it might be full. I'll be right back.' Without waiting for an answer, he hobbled into the hotel and tossed an ax card on the counter before the oiled and unfriendly clerk. He filled in the registration card and came up with some cash for tips. The clerk was saying something about no rooms, sir, you are a disgrace to this hotel, leave at once before I call security. He turned the registration card over and wrote: '3 large steel bowls. Cotton. Syringes. Vodka. Scissors. Adhesive tape. Penicillin.'

He glanced up, thinking, and glimpsed himself in the mirror behind the reception desk. His green eyes were bloodshot. His white braids were caked with some unpleasant substance, and instead of sticking out from his head at all angles as they were meant to, some of them were clumped into an unsightly mat. His dark skin had a green cast, like an old statue. His upper lip was swollen and furry with dried blood.

The clerk fumbled with the phone. The only word he understood was 'Milicija' – police.

He put the pen down and tugged the cord out of the phone.

'Get me a room,' he said, 'before I jump over this desk and redecorate you. Police. Ha. You make me laugh.' He coughed. 'Take the ax card. There's plenty of money on it.'

He returned his attention to the list. 'One dozen red roses. Ice. Clean white sheet torn in strips 18" × 3". Latex gloves.'

He thought a second and then added: 'Sewing kit.'

Horror and disbelief were wrestling with one another on the clerk's face. The ax card was handed back to him. His balance had been noted; he saw the clerk swallow.

'Can you read this?' He passed over the list. The clerk frowned.

'Yes, but, sir, you wish to see doctor. We cannot allow you inside like this.'

'No.' He put his palm down over the list. 'No doctor. No disturb. You understand? I want quiet and I want rest.' When he picked his hand up there was money beneath it. The clerk looked at it as though afraid to touch it. But the key was given to him, the bell was rung, the bag was taken. He was tempted to follow the bellboy upstairs and collapse, but instead he pocketed the key and went outside. Her car was still there. He got in.

'Look,' he said, turning to her with effort. 'My name is Adrien Reyes. I know I don't look so good, but I can't go to the hospital. I just need to get some medicine. Can you *please* take me somewhere I can get good drugs. Morphine, Valium, something like that.'

'Why can't you go to hospital? I am not drug dealer. Adrien.'

He ground his teeth. 'I'll pay you anything you want, but don't ask me questions. Just take me somewhere I can get drugs. What do I look like, the police?' He reached into his sock and pulled out a roll of hundred dollar bills but fumbled as he tried to remove the rubber band. He was starting to feel sick again.

She turned on the engine.

'Get out,' she said. 'Go to your room.'

He was afraid he would start crying because he really didn't have a Plan B this time. He didn't want to drink himself into oblivion as he'd done on the train. But she took the money out of his hand, peeled off three bills, and gave him the rest back.

'I'll be back in one hour, two hours,' she said. 'Wipe blood off seat, please.'

Two

In the room he took off his clothes and sponged himself down as best he could. He had decided a shower would hurt too much and he wasn't sure he could get out of the bathtub once in. He bloodied three washcloths even though he made an effort not to break any scabs. The hotel provided a robe, and as he was trying to put it on, two bellboys showed up carrying the various items he'd requested. He made them clear off a table and drag it closer to the bed and bring extra towels and stack them in readiness, and then he shooed them out. He gave himself a shot of penicillin in the ass.

From his bag he removed a handheld wand powered by batteries. He switched it on and scanned his own skull. He didn't really believe he was under anybody's surveillance, but he'd been around HIT too long not to take precautions. While he was unconscious, Max might have planted him with any number of nasty things. There were devices to simply track his movements; devices to interfere with his transmissions to and from C; devices to fuck with his perceptions in their own right. But the only plant that registered on the detector was his own, and he ran his hand over the bump behind his ear where his battery was nestled against the bone of his skull to be sure there were no fresh incisions.

He was clean. He lay down on the outside of the bedspread and closed his eyes, for the first time succumbing to something like relief. But he was not to be alone for long.

As unpleasant as it was to be in Adrien's body at this moment, it was not to be expected that C would miss any of this. Indeed, when he closed his eyes he could feel C was there, come to witness and explore his exhaustion and pain.

9

The knottings of his mind turned all to silk under C's touch. The Watcher with its whitewhite divine hands cupped his brain and, even now, made everything somehow all right.

It was asking for his memories of the train journey, vague and jumbled as they were; it had no shame about the fact that it had deserted him during the beating, leaving him to wake afterward on a train somewhere south of Moscow from a sleep he'd mistaken for death. In that time, alone with the blood, the bruises, the betrayal – and yes, the guilt for that was part of it too – he had decided to leave C. This was not the first time he'd made such a decision, only to find himself unwilling or unable to part from the Watcher at the moment of truth; yet this time was different. This time he had not only killed for C, he had nearly died for it.

Forgive me, Adrien – what happened in Moscow was my fault. I'll have Max's head, the pretender. We'll bring him down. We'll get I and then show him for the lowlife he is—

I won't do this anymore, he told C. Let me go.

But we're so close! So close to I, and then we'll both be working on a new level. You and I can be free of the satellites, Max's cowboy signal-jamming – no one will touch us. If you'll only trust me, the way you used to ...

The idea made him want to cry. Nothing was like it used to be. Once upon a time C had taken Adrien to the edges of himself and showed him how to be more. Simply by the act of Watching, simply by drinking his life, C had brought him meaning. Now it was no longer content to Watch, or even to guide. These days it insinuated itself into his very core, so that everything Adrien did was really about C and its nameless seething need for this thing called I, this tiny, hotly contested piece of Human Interface Technology.

Even now, while C superficially pretended to soothe him, it probed for details, questing through the sediment of the past few days' recollections. He knew he was being used but, too exhausted to resist, he could only sit back while C stirred the remnants of his memories, making them blend and swirl hypnotically until they melted him into something like sleep.

C says: *Time to review the incident. See what went wrong.*

He is drawn back into the middle of it, momentarily disoriented with respect to both time and place. Disordered sensations fly out of memory: smoke and the reek of gun oil; blood on blackened snow, the distant sirens—

Please, I'm in no condition for this. Let me sleep.

It means nothing in the street, C admonishes. *As a martial artist you should know. Whether you're hung over, sick, whatever … in the street it means nothing.*

Yeah, the street. The Northern Lights, wheeling overhead like some fucking lunar invasion while Max's army of believers stalk Adrien down the snow-clad avenues, his breath coming in liquid chunks from bronchitis and one broken rib. There is no way he can escape but he will not accept this, so he kicks open a door, held only by a rusted padlock, ducks inside and throws himself flat on his belly. Knees stained red and armpits jungly with fear, he presses his face to the icy hell of the floor. It's freezing and the abandoned slaughterhouse has an ingrown stench of sour garbage, dead meat and loathing – should have been knocked down in the nineties and made into a mall but it's still here as if preserved for posterity, a shell with brown leaks frozen gleaming on the walls and half the ground-floor windows shattered. Strangely, there is a freshly drilled hole in the plaster wall, through which a bundle of electric cables passes and snakes up to the ceiling, where it disappears into another hole.

C observes: *These details are unimportant. Center yourself. What happened next?*

Where did the fucking kid go? The kid must have been in on it. The taste of metal in his mouth: a trap. Outside the April snow is everywhere, melting sound to blurred globules so that he can hear nothing of his enemies. The Watcher waits, present to his senses but light as an insect; it heightens his perceptions as he tries to put together what's happening all too fast here.

Who could be working in this building? A construction crew? But where is their equipment?

Your mind is undisciplined, C rebukes, impatient that he should dwell on irrelevant details. *Give the memory up to me and I will order it for you.*

He halts the flow to fire accusations back at the Watcher: How could you let it get so out of hand? This was all your idea. You begged me to get you this thing I. You said your contacts in the Deep were reliable. But what good were you while I was up to my eyeballs in my own blood?

Believe me, I had no way of foreseeing that Max would get wind of this. We were so close. Maybe something can still be salvaged—

I don't want to salvage something of it. Whatever I is, it's not worth killing for. I don't like what I'm becoming. I don't like what *you're* becoming.

I understand. If you'll just give me your memories, I can make it all go away for you. That's what you want, isn't it?

No. No: don't try to take my memories.

The guilt is for me to bear, not you.

You only want to take the guilt away so you can make me do it again, and again, as many times as you need it. You can't have my memory. I remember what happened now. I remember everything perfectly.

You will give it to me, Adrien. If you don't it will haunt you. Don't you understand that I'm responsible for you now? There's no need for you to suffer any of this. That's what I'm here for. The judgment calls, the moral complexities – those are for me to deal with. All I need from you is your body.

He tries to struggle against this idea. He's never been able to comprehend how C can make everything sound so reasonable, so *normal,* when it isn't.

If you'll just let go of the memories, I'll release your endorphins and you'll feel better, I promise.

C will, too: it knows his brain chemistry better than he does. He's grinding his teeth, wondering how long he can resist the temptation to surrender, when the girl knocks on the door and brings him back to consciousness.

C retreated. He had to get up to let the girl in and that took a while; she pushed inside impatiently and handed him several small plastic bags.

'What's your name?' Opening one bag, sniffing.

'Sabina.' She handed him two small, sealed bottles. 'I have no needles.'

'So this won't turn out to be, like, rat poison or anything, will it? Because I can't read the label.'

She ignored his playful tone. 'It's pain killer but not addicting. Morphine is not so good you have to be careful with it so I brought you this too.'

He shivered with pain while she measured and administered the shot.

'Please don't take offense, but I may pass out anyway.' He groped for adhesive tape, but she had already picked it up.

'I do it,' she said, pulling on the latex gloves with what he felt was a shade too much relish. But he submitted. He had already decided to trust her. It was the kind of call you had to be able to make. You couldn't be on guard against everyone.

She began to tape his ribs and tears sprang into his eyes. The nausea returned, yet even though he gasped and clutched at the arms of the chair she continued taping, impassive.

He said, 'So, maybe you could tell me some jokes, to keep me from puking.'

'Puke away.' She handed him one of the steel basins.

Startled, he gulped back his sickness. 'Have I done something to offend you or is this just, like, normal Zagreb taxi-driver bedside manner?'

'You want me to be sympathetic? But I am sure you deserve this.'

'Oh, really?' He was so startled that he forgot how much it hurt for a few seconds – until she wound another length of tape around him so hard his teeth sang.

'Obviously you are in the dirty business, a person who has

13

no self-respect. The people who do this, they do not pick on innocent citizens. Therefore, you have done something to deserve.'

'How do you know I'm not a victim of random violence?'

'Why don't you go to hospital? Why do you rip out phone when the concierge tries to call police?'

She continued working and he attempted an abortive inhalation that ended in a choking cough, the products of which spattered unpleasantly into the basin. It felt like tugging on a heavy rope of pain that extended to the bottom of both lungs.

'Who asked you, anyway?' he said dispiritedly.

'Is free service provided with drugs.' She smirked.

'Yeah … speaking of which, this shit isn't working. I need morphine.'

'So you make a habit of this, then? Morphine every time, yes?'

'Sabina – shut up.'

She got up and tossed back a couple shots of vodka before offering him the bottle. Then she lit a cigarette, took a few drags, and gave it to him to hold while she lifted the robe off his right leg. She blanched. He didn't look down, didn't want to see the gouge again, so he kept his eyes on her face. She had fatigue circles beneath her eyes, and her front teeth were slightly crooked.

She sounded slightly kinder: 'Adrien, I don't know. Infection is so easy. You need doctor for this …'

'Some morphine, then just stitch it up. You can sew, right? Any fool can sew.'

'You must be crazy. Here.' She swallowed another mouthful of vodka, shook out one of the pills from a little bag and put it on his tongue, then handed him the bottle. The alcohol almost made him gag, but once it was down he enjoyed the burn.

'We will wait a little while,' she said, and blew a smoke ring. 'Give it time to take effect.'

14

But it wasn't long before he started to phase in and out of himself: fatigue or medication, he couldn't tell.

'Come on,' he murmured. 'Tell me a story. Tell me about yourself.'

She didn't look at him, but she began to speak. Either the drug was very fast, or she was speaking Croatian. She paced back and forth across the room, leaving him slumped in the armchair surrounded by bloody cotton. She spoke quietly but rapidly, apparently not to him at all. Then her syllables began to elongate, and she was singing, half under her breath, an enigmatic little tune full of steep angles and odd Middle-Eastern semi-tones. His eyelids began to droop. He flew away on the song, thinking, it isn't exactly sad, but it's old, very old.

He roused briefly later, and he could feel the bumps of stitches on his leg. She had turned off the light, but he managed to locate what he hoped were the morphine tablets and swallowed one. The bed was occupied. He could hear her breathing, slow and steady. With an effort, he levered himself out of the chair and into the bed. If he woke her, she gave no sign. Obscurely comforted, he dozed off again, mind swarming in all directions at the solid darkness.

With the pain gone, he could put his memories together on his own terms. Adrift in a zone where he could think but could not move, he began to reassemble the events in Russia that had gotten him so fucked up. He had to go back to the beginning, while C's purpose and guidance had still been strong: while he had still been on top of the situation.

It isn't the first time Adrien has gone to Moscow to exchange information he doesn't understand with people he doesn't know, but it's the first time C's ever felt like a buzz saw idling inside his body, thrumming all his nerves. He's supposed to be picking up something identified only as I. C is being even more secretive than usual, but it doesn't take a genius to add up Moscow and the Watcher's uncharacteristic tension and conclude that I is the latest HIT candy to come out of the Deep.

If C is nervous, Adrien is probably in trouble already. He never questions the terms of C's arrangements; it's safer not to know too much. To do his job effectively – to survive, even – he's learned to switch off his mind and let the body decide his actions.

When he arrives, C has already laid the groundwork. C's contact meets Adrien perfectly on schedule in front of a certain ladies' underwear store. He takes Adrien to a make-shift mall arcade where the wire-dealers stand in velvet-curtained booths, displaying their licenses like hairdressers; you can walk in depressed and walk out happy, even if you do feel compelled to grab for a particular brand of breakfast cereal in the supermarket for the next three weeks. His contact goes to the back of the arcade, past the whirring and ringing slot machines that never seem to go out of style in this town, and beckons him into a private booth. Adrien tries not to laugh. 'Nikolai' can't be more than twelve, and he is plainly nervous as he whispers the information he's come to share. He's chewing bubblegum, for godsake. Adrien would pat the kid on the head and walk out but C comes into him and when C is in his body he isn't required to think.

Entranced, clinging to the edge of sleep, Adrien remembered the Watcher crackling with anticipation and then delight.

Through his eyes it reads the specs included in the data kit. He doesn't understand the data, but he can see that this I is some kind of new plant. Surprise surprise.

While they negotiate, Adrien is busy keeping lookout through the parting of the curtain. He can pick out all the types: the ones who want sex, the ones who want faith, the thrill-seekers, the already-jaded. He can pick out which are designers scoping the market for new ideas. He can recognize the bootleggers because they are the best-dressed; and he can see who here might know more about HIT than the average mark. He indexes them all, deciding who might be a threat; who might be some other Watcher's trans, spying on his deal;

who might be from Nikolai's camp; or from the Deep itself – you simply can't be too paranoid in Moscow these days.

This is why not everything C says through him survives in his memory: because he isn't all that conscious of saying it in the first place. But he remembers the kid going on about moral duty.

'We don't understand the full implications of this technology,' he says to C. 'Now that I has been developed, it should be taken to the University and field-tested there. It's too soon to allow it on the market – any market.'

And C, what does C say?

Field-tested? On what? Monkeys? Convicts? Political prisoners? No. I will do my own field test.

Something to that effect.

'You must be careful,' persists the boy. 'We don't know what will occur when we place the patterns into the receptacle. You may not get the result you hope for.'

'Life,' C says in Adrien's voice, 'by definition is transformation. With all of your technical skill to build such a tool, you are too young to understand what it means.'

That burns the kid: even through the haze of his own ignorance Adrien can see it. The rest of the conversation is conducted in the frost of the boy's hauteur. The pick-up site is decided. The time is set. C slips away, back to its own body, or to some other signal wave and some other plot – none of which he wants to know about. Adrien goes to the men's room and when he returns, Nikolai is gone.

He's eager to finish this business. He hopes that once he obtains for C the plant it covets so much, things will be normal again between them and C will retreat to its proper place in the scheme of things. The nature of the plant which makes C a Watcher and Adrien a trans, or mere vessel, means that he ought not to feel C's emotions even though it can feel his. However, C has become adept at creeping feedback into the link: that's how it speaks to him, directs him – manipulates him. Now it seems he is also becoming privy to what C is feeling, and he doesn't like it much.

He tries to rest in his hotel, aware that his spring head cold is turning into something worse – not surprising considering that the city is suffocating beneath an unseasonable excess of snow, with the sky promising more. When C is in your head you never think: this isn't fun anymore. You never think: I want to go home. You stay focused – you have to. So he makes himself get up, stretch, and mentally prepare for the pick-up of the plant I. He does not allow himself to think yet of the flight home; it would be bad luck.

The meeting place is in front of a building in a kind of industrial park, deserted after hours except for some activity around the new tv station nearby. Nikolai is standing in the shadows behind an ornamental planter stuffed with evergreens. Adrien is surprised that the same person would show himself twice, and he suddenly wonders if he's dealing with the Deep after all. They're simply too smooth to use a mere boy as their main conduit in a transaction.

He walks up to the kid, holds out his hand, and a small package drops into it. Adrien starts to open the package but the little shit dodges to one side and vanishes, at which time Adrien's heart starts pounding and he knows it's all wrong.

He lunges forward, ducking around the planter and looking for the kid's tracks, but the snow has been carefully cleared away for the previous day's business. Columns and boxes containing dense evergreens make a kind of maze out of the colonnade in front of the building; he weaves among them, fast and quiet, ears tuned for any scuffling noise, any breathing: nothing. Shit. C in his skull is urging: *get out, get out fast*. He wonders what the Watcher knows that he doesn't, but he's too well-trained to stop and think about it. He pockets I, turns, and begins to jog back toward the car he was instructed to leave six blocks away. The silent buildings rise to either side, shadowing the narrow street. All is still.

He feels the hairs on the back of his neck stand up.

Max's army is here. The Deep's PR executive relies on a combination of misinformation and intimidation to do his job: for this Max needs a small army of followers, so he's printed one. Every one of them is wired with a little 'voice of Max' that endlessly massages his or her subconscious mind with Maxisms: his philosophy, his tastes, his sense of humor – whatever that is. Alas, this reduces their fighting effectiveness, but it makes them eerie as hell to deal with. Adrien has encountered them before, but never in quite such unfavorable circumstances.

Without a sound they start appearing in doorways, up and down the street, one by one until there are about thirty of them: men in big WWI coats with rifles. Their costumes must reflect some recent historical enthusiasm of Max's, because the last Adrien heard, Max's army was decked out as a band of Tibetan monks with sub-machine guns. Here in the snow among shadows cast by golden streetlights, their presentation is so theatrical that he knows right away they don't necessarily want him dead. It is as if making an impression of strength is more important than actually felling him, which could be done with a single bullet from a dark window.

Yet the spectacle captures his attention: he almost misses the shadow that grows at his feet. Someone's right behind him. He spins, his blood sparking with familiar chemical response, hands floating into position. There are two assailants, both big – Adrien's only hope is that they might be so big they've never bothered to learn to fight. One has a pistol in his left hand; Adrien charges inside the arm's radius and deflects it to one side, shoving the gunman into his partner, who stumbles and is kept out of the way momentarily. Adrien is already closing. Too late he realizes that the knee strike he directed into the body will fail, dulled by the thickness of the coat, but his hammerfist comes down more or less on target, missing the bridge of the nose but connecting with a cheekbone. Twisting the gun hand as he steps in, Adrien tries a leg sweep, but this guy is heavy and his upper body is too strong for Adrien to easily unbalance him. The gun goes off somewhere past his right ear; he slips on the snow and almost goes down himself. The other guy wades in and grabs him around the waist, picking him up. Adrien twists like a cat and

19

pummels the man's face repeatedly with his fists and elbows until he is released.

The gun is pointing at his head. He throws himself on the ground, skidding into his opponent's knees, and the gun goes off twice into the snow behind him. His enemy lands on top of him, knocking the wind out of Adrien and snapping a rib. Adrien rolls over, gets a lucky grab in an eyesocket and uses that leverage to grab the hair, jerking the head back. He scrambles to his knees, stretching his struggling opponent across his body, and his animal brain goes for the kill.

Make no mistake: he could do a number of non-lethal techniques at this point but he's not thinking in those terms. The danger of the situation has kicked him up into a whole new level, a level beyond conscious thought. The Watcher can't command his muscles – not to battle reflex – because it is halfway across the world in America and no signal moves that fast. So here's the thing, Adrien: there's no one to blame but yourself. It's your *shuto* that flows out to its target to the focal point on the cervical vertebrae, passing through and crushing the trachea en route. You don't stop yourself. It's your power. It's your ki. *You* are the killer.

Yet it's C who grips this moment in pleasure and shakes it, like a wolf.

He shoves the man, gurgling and twitching, out of the way just as the other guy blunders toward him, his face a mask of blood. Adrien takes him out with one booted foot to the temple. The whole fight has lasted maybe twenty seconds; there is no time to ponder the consequences of what he has done. Clutching his side where the rib is swinging in directions it shouldn't be, he scrambles to his feet and flees. Playful gunshots sprinkle from above as he half runs, half skates down the street, the army falling in behind him like revenants from deep snow graves. Bullets to the left, bullets to the right, hopscotching, the rhythm of the sound like a Tchaikovsky waltz.

C, reacting to the shock of the ambush, shoots an excess of adrenaline through him as he runs, but Adrien is thinking about the kill strike. The Russian's throat was cushioned by a scarf and part of a fur collar, but not enough to save him. Adrien can still feel the hard-soft quality of cartilage imprinted on the edge of his hand. He can feel the shape inscribed in time and space by the blow: perfect execution – literally. He can still hear the last wordless utterings of the doomed mouth as he pushes the dying man away...

Stop it! Pay attention!

Snow flies up in disciplined puffs after every bullet. He skids into an alley beside the deserted building; C spots the sagging door and drives at him until he kicks it in, slams it and bars it on the inside. C must be crazy: he's trapped now. If he'd kept running he might have made it to the car.

Lying on the floor of the slaughterhouse, *moritori te salutamus*.

He listens to the wheeze in his own chest, trying not to think about the fact that C got off on the act of Adrien killing. He can barely breathe – feels like that rib's been shoved right into his fucking *lung* – he can't think of a way to escape, and the cold is slowing his thinking. As he reconstructs this memory once more, he again sees the gray wires leading up into the abandoned building; and again C deflects his attention away from speculating about them. His memory keeps returning to this time here on the floor, but in the scope of the night's events it is a moment that means nothing. It's peculiar where the imagination can choose to fix its attention.

It's a momentary respite, anyway. When the Molotov cocktail comes curving through the window right over his head, he knows it's just a taunt, a cat and mouse drawing-out of the fun; but even so it works, dumping filthy glass on his back and sending him catapulting through a different door, out into the snow again. Right where they want him. He picks up his feet and again begins to run: Adrien can run, yes. He can run and he can fight, only in this remembered cold it is all pain—

—He only wanted to sleep in the hotel in Croatia. But C had

no intention of letting him off so easily: it was hooked on his memory and wouldn't let go. The reliving went on and on, the whole débâcle like an evil little movie nipping the edges of dream—

—He comes around a corner and perceives the narrow slit of the barrel and the bluish gleam of a face behind, too far away for him to grab the rifle but close enough to blot out the sight of everything that is not gun. Dead end.

He sheds his own emotion like a second skin and goes into the moment bare and empty. Some prescience that only comes in battle takes him down, releasing his legs into a skid beneath the gun barrel. His feet slam into the guy's knees and he catches hold of the barrel as it points toward him, using the leverage to pull his opponent over on top of him. The rifle is no use as a gun now, but here it comes to choke him: he tucks his chin and uses his hands just enough to keep the barrel off his neck. He has his opponent between his legs and tries to soften him up with foot strikes to the kidneys, but it feels like the other guy is wearing body armor.

Peripherally Adrien sees he's in a narrow space between a dumpster and a wall: the alley leads on unlit toward the next street, maybe an escape. His opponent's ki is strong. He has dark eyes and pale skin – Adrien's opposite – and he makes hissing noises of concentration as he realizes a bit late that the American might be on the bottom, but that the bottom is the position of advantage for a good groundfighter. Given enough time, Adrien will get a lock on this guy; but he doesn't have time, and who knows when the next Faithful Soldier will come around the corner and blow his brains out while he's stuck under this one.

He can hear sirens from the next street over. The Russian is chanting something under his breath, but whatever Hymn to Max it may be, Adrien can't understand the words. He's thankful for small graces. Frustrated by his failures to choke Adrien out, the soldier tosses the rifle aside and reaches into his coat. Adrien seizes his wrist, snaps his right leg over his opponent's left shoulder, and squeezes, pressing his shin against the carotid artery.

Unconsciousness follows in seconds.

They're coming. Shouts and splashes of color reflected on snow.

He disengages and gets to his feet once again. C notices the gun lying in the lax hand; Adrien bends, picks it up, and points it at the head, between the closed eyes with their long, dark lashes. This is how murderers feel, he thinks.

Yes, C sings in his mind. *Do it. I want to see what it is like if you do it on purpose.*

Lights; footsteps; dogs on chains to his left. To his right, a snowmobile. Shouts and more sirens.

He drops the pistol and raises his hands in surrender, too horrified at what he has almost done to even think of running anymore. He finds himself staring at the face of the man who seems to be sleeping in the snow. He is trembling all over.

—He stifled a sob, half-asleep in Croatia. His mouth worked—

He hears Max's voice behind him, laughing. C flees his mind.

'You're not ready to steal from me yet, Adrien, if you can't even bring yourself to kill.'

Then Max is gone, and the police are screaming at him in Russian—

—With an unerring instinct for anticipating what Adrien's thinking and doing, C now tuned in to Adrien, sweating in the hotel bed, just as he was recalling the moment in Moscow when the Watcher panicked and left him to cope, fleeing to the safety of its distant anonymity. There had been no first-hand sharing of torture for the Watcher; no, sir. It was easier to sweep in afterward to take his memory of the event. He couldn't stop it from reading his memory, but he could keep C from inducing him to forget what happened in the blue-lit sub-basement of the jail. As he relived the scene he held on to it, refusing to let it dissolve in the current of C's Watching—

* * *

—Arrested in Moscow: now there's something to write home to the Bronx about. It must be a slow night at the precinct, because there are no other prisoners in the chill jail and the place is creepily quiet except for the sound effects of the play session the cops are having with Adrien, who is hanging upside down with his head four feet above the concrete floor. Eventually Max sweeps in and sits on a metal stool, nodding his head like an opera-goer keeping time. Five or six uniformed cops flee the room at a flick of his wrist; they stand in the hallway looking lugubrious and Russian and slightly worried. Three of Max's soldiers march in after him and take off their coats.

'Max!' Adrien coughs, almost choking on his own sputum. 'Please, Max, get me out of here.'

Max frowns and Adrien gets an impression of eyes so deep-set they are invisible, and a mouth as pink as a newborn's bottom. It's not that Adrien would ever trust him – calling Max a snake would insult an innocent species – yet he pleads in hope of being shown mercy by the Deep. This mythic entity lives mostly in rumors among trans like Adrien and their acquisitive Watchers, ever eager for the newest wrinkle in Human Interface Technology. If anyone out there understands how the Deep really works, they aren't talking. All Adrien's sure of is that the Deep is a kind of network. It conceives the plants that let C possess his body – and this presumably includes I, or why would Max be getting involved? The Deep is so elusive, it's said that even people who are at the very nexus of it don't always know it themselves.

Except Max. Max knows exactly what he's doing. If the Deep is a traveling circus hailing from nowhere in particular and staying in town just long enough to baffle everybody who uses the tech, then Max is its barker, a bit of a freak himself but the closest thing you can get to a reliable contact in the milieu of unlicensed HIT. In the real world, he's made his fortune selling wires which impart religious feeling. Max regularly dines with the chairmen of multinationals who use his ecstatic states to advertise their products; he yachts with cardinals; yet here he is in a Moscow jail late at night, smoking Marlboros and looking like there's no place he'd rather be.

'Would you like to tell me about this evening, C?'

Thump.

'Or would it please you more if I hurt your boy lover?'

(He was sobbing a little, in his sleep. C fed on his memories, his shame.)

'C ... gone,' he manages to gasp. 'I don't know ... anything.'

'Left you to die, has it? C is a heartless creature, Adrien – I probably know more about your Watcher than you do, believe it or not. But I have no intention of being cruel. Brutal, but never cruel. Now, I'm sure you can remember what this is that you think you bought.' He holds up a tiny glittering vial, squints through it at the light. Adrien, swinging from a hook on the ceiling, vomits.

'Clean that up, Boris,' Max says idly. One of the men beating him sullenly kicks Adrien in the already-ruined ribs before stalking off. 'Adrien?'

'It was ... a clean deal, Max, I sw—'

'Boris' comes back carrying something shiny. A knife – or a machete. Max shakes his head at Adrien's answer and clicks his tongue.

'It's too bad you never took an interest in matters of faith. I have a nice piece of Jainist thought I've been thinking of selling to Mercedes-Benz for their new marketing campaign. Of course, you'd need to be open to the idea of reincarnation. If you cooperate with me, I'll give you a free sample. Honest injun.'

'I don't do wires. I'm ... fucked up ... enough.'

Boris begins a bass drone: 'Hail Max, who does fuck up the enemy—'

Max cuts him off. 'I'm not interested in your protests of sincerity. Tell me everything you know about your so-called *deal*. Do it fast. I'm losing patience with this charade. C, you're a coward not to be here.' He laughs, the upside-down image of his body swaying in Adrien's vision as if seen

25

underwater, and the room spins. The cops don't seem to be hanging around anymore.

Shit it's a knife all right but why is Boris looking at his head like that? Is *scalping* the flavor of the week in this town?

'It's pretty,' Boris says. The expression on his face would best be described as rapturous. 'Max, can I?'

Adrien stammers, 'A-all I know is the name I. I met my contact, I saw design specs but I ... I didn't understand them. It's a plant of some kind. It's part organic, that's all I know. Max, you know C wouldn't let me in on any real information – in case I'm caught, which I have been, so ...'

'So give you some milk and cookies and send you home to bed? I don't think so.'

'As far as I know it was a clean deal,' Adrien insists.

In Croatia, C absorbed the recollection. If the Watcher had stayed with him in the jail, it would have had to endure his every sensation. Although his memories were blurry and sometimes skipped around, by removing itself in time C could control its level of involvement, taking only the cognitive threads and weeding out some of the pain and fear. Some, but not all: Adrien's not a computer, and the color of his agony bleeds into every thought and perception by association.

'Clean deal, my friend? Didn't you think it was strange, Adrien, that so many *armed men* showed up afterward?' Max's voice begins to ascend in pitch. He's hopping around like a Mexican jumping bean. 'Didn't you think it was strange that your *contact* didn't stick around to make sure you were satisfied?'

Let me guess. Through his half-sleep Adrien directed his words at C. *Nikolai stole the plant from the Deep and sold it to me. I get to take the fallout. Lucky guy that I always am.*

C gave away nothing in the mental tone of its answer. *Maybe.*

Max stops in his tracks, bends over, and peers into Adrien's face. In a low, singsong voice he says, 'You killed one of my men, Adrien. To my men, I *am* God. They've got the *Max* wire. That lays on me certain *responsibilities*.'

Adrien shudders.

Max whispers, 'Do you think you're going to walk out of here tonight? Do you think C can protect you?'

Right about now it's occurring to Adrien that he hasn't seen anyone in a uniform recently, doesn't read enough Russian to know for sure if this is actually a state jail ... duh...

That sinking feeling.

'And of course, at the moment it's you, not your Watcher, hanging stark naked by one foot from the ceiling – soaking wet—' Max stands back.

Splash! and Adrien's blindsided by a bucket of icy water. The window is cranked open, admitting the long winter.

'—with all that excessive head-wound blood pouring all over your face.'

The knife, at least, is artfully quick and all things considered not as painful as it might have been. He attempts unsuccessfully to detach his consciousness from his scalp.

'You can't have it for free, C,' Max is cackling. 'I don't know what you think you're playing at, but when you send your most visible trans into my territory, you should assume I'm going to have him followed. Now, Adrien, with regard to this toy you've been so kind as to bring me. Do you have any idea what it is?'

Shaking his head, eyes closed. Bile.

'Are you quite sure? It's chilly in here, isn't it? Boris, ask him if he's sure.'

A cigarette lighter held within centimeters of his scrotum. The smell of burning hair. Someone screaming.

'That should keep your sperm count down, my friend. Well. Enough, Boris. You're just a dumb brute, aren't you, Adrien? Tell me about the seller. I have a traitor to cope with.'

The idea that anything should happen in the Deep without Max's knowledge goes a ways toward explaining why Max is so upset. But at the moment Adrien's trapped in the pages of a comic book that thinks it's reality: a few smacks from the tuff boys bring him around when his mind wanders. And the Russian wind. Adrien shivers so hard he bites his tongue. The fact that the blood is rushing to his head and flowing right out again doesn't improve his concentration.

'I'm waiting, Adrien.'

Surely he will pass out eventually? He makes bets with himself as to when.

'I see you're having difficulty speaking. Can you tell me the gender of the person who sold you I?'

He contrives to nod.

'Was it male? Don't strain yourself now. A simple grunt or monosyllable will do.'

He nods again.

'Ah. Twenty questions. Physical description. What did he look like, Adrien? Blond? Dark? Tall? Hm?'

'J-j—just a k-k-. Id. Kid.'

'A kid.' Long drag on cigarette.

Max's soldiers are standing back a little from him now. He isn't sure if this is good or bad. Probably no one wants to be too close to him in case he actually dies.

'How old?'

'Eungghh.'

Now would be a good time to lose consciousness.

Nope. Can't seem to manage it.

'Fool! What use are you to me if you're brain-dead?' Max turns to his men and snaps something in Russian; then, in a very gentle voice: 'How old? When you say "kid" I assume you mean younger than twenty? Yes. Interesting. As young as fifteen, maybe? Really? Maybe even younger? Maybe as young as twelve or thirteen? Well … did he have dark brown hair, blue eyes?'

Easyeasy. Nod nod.

'And now for his name. What name did he give you, Adrien?'

No, José. Sorry, but the tongue won't …

'Nggai. Nnggugai.' Sorry, Nikolai, but for all I know you set me up.

28

Max's eyes glitter.

'OK, Adrien. I need for you to listen, baby. Are you listening? Good. I want you to remember every word I'm saying so when your Watcher reels you in and puts on the Bandaids there won't be any misunderstandings about why I'm letting you go. Tell C that we have I. Say that your little friend Nikolai is known to me and there's no way anybody can get to him behind my back again. C, are you listening? Cross me again, and not only will Adrien die, but so will every other trans you've ever had. I'll storm you and hunt you down. Don't play with me.'

Adrien has no memory of the rest. He doesn't remember Max's order to cut him down, or anything else that happened before the train. He remembers only the river of his own blood, and the cold cold cold like the premonitory breath of a Nordic hell, and cries coming from his mouth that really should belong to a seagull—

'I think you should wake up now.'

Sabina's words hooked him and fished him out of his trance.

Three

Even before he opened his eyes, he could feel that he was soaked in sweat, and the pain in all its complexity returned like an obnoxious party acquaintance you thought you eluded appearing suddenly at your elbow, drink in hand. His strangled cries still echoed in his mind but he knew that here, in this room, he had only been whimpering. C was gone.

Sabina had pulled the armchair over to the window and was sitting in a gauzy, wonderful sunlight, watching him. It was a child's pose, heels drawn up against haunches and chin resting on one knee. In one hand she was twirling a long-stemmed red rose. In the sun her eyes were robin's egg blue. He thought she looked satisfied with herself, and he trembled in sudden apprehension. He couldn't possibly have – not with the morphine—?

'Did we ... forgive me, Sabina, but did we have sex last night?'

She laughed, and her tone said, *you have got to be kidding*.

He let out a sigh of relief that segued into a fit of coughing. At least C hadn't gotten *that* out of him.

'So – Adrien,' she said as he spat blood into a tissue. 'Who the hell are you?'

He rubbed his eyes. 'I'm not myself. Well, I'm not usually myself.'

She didn't get it, or, if she did, she didn't think it was funny. Adrien dragged himself to the other side of the bed, within reach of the various medications arrayed on the table. He wondered whether she had slept nude and restrained himself from sniffing the sheets. It was depressing to think how long he had gone without. Shakily he prepared another injection of penicillin.

'Downstairs, they all think you are dangerous criminal but they are too greedy to call police. They are charging you triple rate for this room.'

'I'm not dangerous for anyone but myself,' he said. 'If I'm paying triple, can I at least get some room service?'

'I order breakfast.' She picked up the phone.

'I don't eat breakfast. Order lunch.'

After a spate of Croatian directed at the receiver, Sabina hung up and said, 'So probably you wish me not to ask questions. Right?'

'Right.' Now she was getting the idea. Maybe—

'But ... is greatly interesting. I have never seen ... mutilation? like this one before, even in movies.'

'What?'

'Designs cut on your head.'

'What designs?' He struggled to sit up, but there was no mirror opposite the bed.

'Like eye, on top of your head. Don't worry, I cleaned it. Your hair will cover most scars.'

Adrien levered himself out of bed and hobbled into the bathroom, where he tried to find what she was talking about in the mirror. All he could see was a mass of blood-coated, tangled white hair half in and half out of its braids. Almost as an afterthought, he closed the door, pissed, and returned naked to the main room. He wondered if it took effort for her to appear to be neither looking at nor avoiding looking at his body. He was inexpressibly weary as he crawled back under the blankets.

'Fucking Max.'

'Yes, who is Max? And who is C?'

'I talked in my sleep? Shit shit shit. Well, never mind.'

She came over and sat down on the edge of the bed, placing a cool hand on his forehead.

'Yes, well, I will ask no questions. Probably I ask too many questions, I get killed, right?'

'Very funny.'

'I am not trying to be funny.'

31

He closed his eyes. There was a long silence, and a slight breeze brought in fresh air and the sounds of the street below. Afterward, he would wonder what made him do it. All he had to do was lie here, rest, get better. There was no need to start talking to this Croatian girl. Not about HIT anyway. He didn't have to explain himself to anyone. But...

'Sabina, you've never shared your head, have you?'

'Ah ...' a long, low, exhalation. She was catching on.

'You didn't guess?'

'I don't know much about it. If you are saying what I think you are saying, I only know rumors.' She paused. 'Is it true someone can feel, inside you?'

'Yeah, it's true.'

'You don't like it.'

He grunted. 'How did you guess?'

'Why? Why do you do if you don't like it?'

Good fucking question. He said, 'When you first start carrying, it seems like a simple deal. Almost too good to be true. They tell you all you have to do is live your life. It's not like you're being broadcast, it's private between you and one Watcher.'

His hand plucked idly at pills on the cotton blanket. He knew he should stop himself, but the drugs gave him an excuse not to. His voice sounded hoarse, scarcely his own.

'So technically it really shouldn't affect you. Like, you don't even notice anything on a conscious level, but you do get ... well, you do get a feeling of *meaning*. Like, the Watcher using you stimulates the part of you that ... you know. Believes in some purpose. Anyway, you get paid really well, and I guess since I knew my Watcher wanted to get something out of my life, I started to live more ... intensely. Take more risks. Like, use my life, not like sitting in front of the tv when I could be experiencing something real.'

It was impossible to convey the sort of quality that C had brought to every second of time, simply by *being* there. The idea that what he did at any given moment of the day could actually *matter* to anyone acted as a powerful motivator not to waste his life.

'After a while I found myself talking to … the Watcher.' He had almost used the pronoun 'it' but he didn't want to have to explain about the fact that he didn't know the identity of the person who shared his head; he didn't want to have to think about why they both preferred it that way. He suppressed a cough, feeling his face flush with the effort.

'And then, one day, the Watcher talked back.'

He stopped. He was pretty sure C wasn't there, but all the same he'd never verbalized this shit before. He was scaring himself a little.

'Like God,' Sabina said.

'What?' he opened his eyes, startled. For a second he'd forgotten she was there.

'You go through life talking to God, but what do you do if, one day, God talks back?'

What he'd meant but didn't want to say in so many words was that first C learned how to ride a cognitive signal back to him while it was receiving his realtime data, which had been just an intermediate step en route to actually getting deep inside his mind and, later, controlling him. Like God? No. Not really …

'Look.' He'd caught himself, guts trembling wetly on the verge of spilling. He *had* to shut up. Too much had been said already and now he found himself scrambling back from the edge of saying more. 'It's nice of you to keep me company. Especially considering your opinion of my … job.'

She shrugged. 'I think is wrong, but you have your reasons. I assume.'

He could sense more questions crowding behind her words and tried to deflect the conversation to another avenue.

'You know,' he laughed, 'I've always been able to talk to cab drivers, but this is way beyond the call of duty.'

Amusement trembled in her voice.

'Is not cab, my car. You made mistake.'

'But you picked me up anyway ... what were you doing in the taxi lane?'

'The sound there is good.'

'*What?*'

'I was going to record what-you-call-it? Ambient noise. The trains, the crowds, there is good echo in that spot and I wanted it.'

'You wanted to record *noises*?'

'Right.'

'Um ... why?'

'You will laugh.'

'Me? Laugh at you? Not likely.' He'd reminded himself of his own sins again. He felt like shit. His leg was hot; she'd been right about infection, surely. He wanted her to keep talking, just to take his mind off it.

'Never mind,' he said. 'Last night you made it clear you think I'm a lowlife. Why should you tell me anything?' He shut his eyes again.

'I am composer.'

'No shit? What do you play?'

'Nothing, really. Well, everything. I am not instrumental-ist, I compose.'

'You write music.'

'Yeah, sometimes. Right now, I experiment.'

'With ambient noise? Is it like, you know, like perform-ance art, avant-garde stuff?'

'No! Not really. Yesterday was part of experiment.'

He opened one eye: something had just occurred to him. 'Am I an experiment?'

Someone knocked on the door. Sabina got up and answered. He heard a brief exchange in Croatian; then she wheeled in the food trolley and shut the door without admitting the bellhop.

'Are you experiment?' She gestured for him to sit up. 'I don't think so. I am my experiment, and you wandered into it.'

She had ordered him soup: invalid food. He took the steaming bowl from her gingerly, wondering at what point, precisely, his show had become her show. The soup was spicy and he sipped slowly, watching her over the rim. She climbed onto the foot of the bed, sitting Indian-style with a plate balanced on her knees, and began shovelling in pasta. For some time she concentrated solely on the food, not seeming to notice his scrutiny at all. When at last she glanced up and caught the expression on his face, she shrugged, swallowed, and said, 'I was hungry. Yesterday I forgot to eat.'

'But it *is* music, right? When you say you're a composer.'

'Yes, is music.'

'Do you ... do you perform this music? Or do you make recordings, or what?'

'Composition and act of performing are the same thing. One is not object of other. Yes, I make recordings. But I don't sell very many, if your question means this.'

'I see. Why not?'

She shrugged. 'I think I am too weird for them.'

It's always cute when girls think they're weird. It's almost never true, in Adrien's experience. You want weird, he thought. I'll give you weird.

'For example, thing you have in your head.' Her eyes bored into him. 'Thing that you don't want to talk about. I think it is sad that only the criminals use, or government for the espionage – military things, whatever they do. People use for pornography I guess, right, but this is stupid. Never mind pornography, we could have real understanding. I would like to compose music that uses that little chip, just senses, like you said. I would compose everything: sound, touch, smell, and give it to audience to feel exactly as I felt. You understand what I'm saying?'

'I guess,' he said warily. It sounded so sweet: use the plant to share music. His ribs ached. If only everybody wanted to make music, he wouldn't need the morphine at all.

'I think you don't understand,' she said gently. 'You are stuck in the underworld, yes?'

'Underworld?' He started to laugh – then he caught her

35

eye and understood what she'd meant to say. If Sabina had heard of the Deep then there was no pretending It didn't exist. 'You mean the underground? The Deep? What do you know about that?'

'The Deep, yes maybe that's how you say in English. I hear some stories, that's where your technology comes from, but they say is very dangerous.' She searched his face, then added, 'What do I know? Never mind. It doesn't matter.'

But she was only pretending not to care. He could almost hear the gears clicking and spinning in her mind. She reminded Adrien of himself when he first learned about HIT: curious – and stupid. The sunlight in the room faded, brightened, faded, brightened and stayed as clouds scudded by outside. They finished eating in silence, and he grew drowsy again; he was glad to let her stack the plates and sweep crumbs off the bedspread. He watched her moving around the room. She had the gift of being almost silent with apparently no effort at all. She caught him staring and smiled. A sudden, unbearable yearning flowed into him – fuck acting tough. There was so much he was missing.

'What would you do,' Adrien said, 'if you suddenly realized that a big, elaborate trap had been constructed around you and was about to close down on you, but right before catching you, the maker of the trap wanted you to perceive it. The maker wanted to know you knew.'

'Is this question?' she laughed.

'Yeah – I don't know – the question is, when you're in a trap every action you can take has been foreseen and accounted for, right?'

'It depends on the trap.'

'It's a strong trap. Clever.' In fact, it was so clever he couldn't even be sure it was there. He felt like Wonder Woman in her invisible plane, flying along and then suddenly glancing down and seeing the ocean glozing miles below because the plane doesn't appear to have *any floor*. When you've got to that point, you'd better *hope* the invisible thing is real, because if it ain't … well, you're not

Wonder Woman anymore, you're Wile E. Coyote running out into thin air, just about to realize you've gone off a cliff fifty yards back – shit, this morphine is good stuff.

She was gazing at him thoughtfully.

'Never mind. I can't explain, really, anyway. It's just this feeling I have.'

She sat down on the bed and stroked the folds of the spread idly. 'The humans allow their imagination to be used against them. We feel despair too easily. Animal doesn't have this problem.'

'So I should think like an animal?'

'I don't know what *you* should do. I know the animal in trap will bite off his own leg to be free—'

'I'd have to bite off my own head.'

'Well, if you want to be funny—'

'No! I'm not being funny at all, Sabi—'

'Because how can I give you the good advice anyway, you don't tell me what's going on.'

'Actually, I think your advice *is* good. I'm just scared to do it.'

She reached over and placed her empty plate on the trolley, her brow wrinkling. 'Have you ever had conversation with someone and you are sure they are only using you to convince themselves of their own idea, what they already think?'

He flushed. 'Am I doing that?'

'I would say, Adrien, people place not enough value on fear. Always I am hearing all this nonsense about conquering your fear, overcoming the inhibitions. I mean, you *should* be afraid. People who are not afraid have their eyes closed. Fear helps us survive.'

'But you just said ... never mind.' He couldn't keep track of this conversation. He emitted a mighty yawn and his chest rattled.

'You see? You dismiss me.'

'No, I don't, it's just – Sabina, I wish I could tell you everything. Someday, when this is all over, I'll tell you. I

37

promise. We'll sit in a café and I'll tell you what's really going on, but you won't believe it. You'll think I'm joking.'

'When it's over? When *what* is over?'

'This. I'm going to stop. I really am.'

Sabina stood up and checked his temperature again with her palm. 'You should have doctor. Dressings must be changed, and I don't know about your leg. I should call someone—'

He caught her hand. His eyes were growing heavy but he made himself hold onto her. 'No. You stay. Please.'

She looked down on him. 'You are crazy if you think I can help you.'

He closed his eyes, smiling. 'Yes.'

He could feel her puzzled stare.

He must have slept then until dark, because he remembered nothing until he half woke from a fevered nightmare to find Sabina in bed beside him, naked. He had a thunderous erection and a headache all the way to the roots of his teeth. He could hear rain hitting the windows, and her breath was in his ear. Her warm arms encircled him.

'Shh. Don't be afraid.' Her lips moved against his neck.

He wanted to speak but he was not yet awake, and he found himself grabbing at her, pulling her towards him and rolling over to mount her at the same time. She was already wet, and her muscles clasped him when he slid into her. Time and sensation had wound around one another in that peculiar way they sometimes can on the threshold of awareness, and the pleasure of this first penetration was long and exquisite.

But somewhere, in a dark room, C was Watching. Like a god. Or a lecher. And straight old-fashioned fucking didn't seem to be enough of a turn on for it, not tonight. For when Adrien opened his eyes, Sabina in the semidarkness was not as she should be. She was a horror of shadow and light projected on his mindstage: C was overriding his very senses with perceptions of its own choosing.

The body beneath him was wasted, skin mottled with yellow imperfections and wrinkled with age and disease. It shuddered and twitched, beyond the control of its owner: a brittle husk with dry breasts like collapsed balloons flattened over thin ribs, bony pubis almost hairless. The rubbery cunt sucked him like death itself.

The face was a hybrid of flesh and medical mechanism: wires grew from its scalp like hairs and tubes filled its nose and throat, causing its mouth to be pulled back in a permanent, toothless grin. Black eyes glittered sightlessly, empty caverns never visited by humans.

Swift on the heels of this impression came C's thoughts: *yes, you see? It can be like this for us, this is what it is*
no C, please—

He didn't know what was happening, but he knew he didn't want to do this – not anymore, not with the remote monster crawling around in his mind, eating him, engorging itself on his organs. Why, *why* was C torturing him this way? For despite his revulsion, his body kept moving ...
you want, you want don't deny it I felt it

for a second maybe but no, no that wasn't. nono

Even as he began to get control of his body, to shudder and draw away, the apparition faded and Sabina was herself again. Her heat was all around him and he threw himself at her, trying to negate what the Watcher had just done to him.

Was C jealous of Sabina? Why would it try to destroy their lovemaking, to torment him, when it was C who could be the recipient of every sensation?

He heard himself gasping and Sabina moved with him, skin sliding on smooth skin. She held fast to him, apparently unaware of what just happened. Her hands locked behind his neck; she pulled his head down so that their faces were a breath apart.

Everything became very slow.

Her eyes were shadowed but he knew there was healing in them. By being human and nothing more, by staking out these moments in time that belonged only to them, to

Adrien and Sabina, she could save him. From the Watcher, from HIT. From himself. Tears of relief came into his eyes. She was pure. There was no other word. Everything that was not Sabina erased itself and he was grateful for this and he went slower and she was still with him.

He could feel the music in her then, it was something contagious that came up from her and wrapped around his spine and glistened on her lips where all else was shadowed. Something was happening. It was the same as the rush of wings and the temporal perfection of a flock of cranes taking flight from dark water, turning as one in the sky. Sabina was a window to some other place, she was letting him pass through like light, and he let go into perfect thoughtlessness.

His lips moved; he breathed her name; and again Sabina turned into something terrible and he clutched a desiccated, twitching corpse in his arms.

Adrien, I'm here, don't you see? I'm with you and we can be togeth—

no I said please not to pull that string leave me

He heard himself making choking noises as if to vomit the Watcher out of his system, but instead his penis was pulling rhythmically, ejaculating like a machine. He turned his face away in disgust.

Sabina twisted with thwarted pleasure beneath him. Disappointment – or was it alarm?

'I'm sorry,' he whispered into her neck, feeling his tears collect against her flesh. 'I didn't. I have to stop. Stop it. Get out. I can't do it anymore.'

His ribs ached; he wanted to scrub out the inside of his body with steel wool and burn the blood and shit that was thus purged; he wanted to be sick at least but he was too exhausted to do even this. He tried to lift himself a little, to look into her eyes as he'd been doing for that single moment, before …

She was wriggling away from him; she was out of bed, a white shadow stooping to pick up clothes off the floor and talking to herself rapidly in Croatian. Still dazed, he watched her pull on clothes, drop her jacket with a jangle of keys, pick it up, drop it, and finally throw it over her shoulder and snatching up her shoes cross to the door. She wrenched it open and stood there silhouetted in the hall light.

'Adrien, I wish you luck. Whatever is wrong with you—' She fell silent, drew breath as if to start again, and abruptly closed the door. He could hear her receding footfalls.

It's too bad you scared her, C whispered. *She was rather delicious.*

He groped in the dark for a needle but when he found it he threw it across the room and fell face down on the mattress, small and large pain bombing his anatomy again.

* * *

I, of course, am 'it'. In the game of tag we call identity, I am always on the run.

Adrien and I are linked, thalamus to thalamus, so that whenever I wish it, his world becomes my world. His consciousness is expressed in terms of a rhythm, a pulsing wave that originates in the intralaminar nucleus and sweeps his brain every 12.5-thousandth of a second, triggering the sensory cells of his cerebral cortex to fire a return wave back to the thalamus. The patterns of synchrony among groups of cells, recorded as a sequence of neural firings expressed in time, determine the shape of his consciousness, including image, sound, smell, and – with a little finesse – all the emotional and cognitive baggage that can be harnessed to the so-called physical. It is this return wave on which I eavesdrop. The tiny transceiver in his brain digitizes the wave and, with the aid of a small battery implanted behind his ear and powered off his body's excess metabolic heat, transmits the signal to me via LEO satellite, where it is received by my thalamus and interpreted by my brain as being indistinguishable from the real thing.

This last bit took some work to achieve because no two

minds are alike, and I had to learn to compensate for the differences between us much the way one learns another's language. It also took me some time to figure out how to ride a signal back to him without completely jamming his perception of being in his own body. For when I'm Watching Adrien, I have no sense of *being* anything but Adrien: as far as my brain is concerned, I *am* him. However, the last thing we would want would be for Adrien to inhabit *me* – O no, we wouldn't want that at all. I rely on my anonymity to keep control of him, and he knows nothing of my physical condition – or didn't, until very recently. No, I prefer to express myself in cognitive terms.

Not that 'cognition' is anything more than a convenient term for jazzed-up, self-referenced perception. As someone who spends almost every moment cognating, I can state categorically that, starved of perception, the mind does some very weird things. Of course, when your perceptions lie to you (as Adrien's perceptions lie so sweetly to me all the time, letting me pretend to be something I'm not) things are not quite right either. All I want is the integration of mind with body, something most people take for granted.

Hence my need of Adrien. Other trans can be my hands and eyes in the world; others can conduct my business – and now more than ever, there is plenty of it to conduct if I'm to pull off the *pièce de résistance* of a lifetime's struggle…

But Adrien is different. He's the one I need; he's the one I'm going to *become*. Even if I have to die; because death is coming anyway.

He's right about being in a trap. He's mine. One way or another I'll have him, and it won't be coercion, either.

He'll want it.

Four

Rain was falling. Sabina wasn't certain of the time: it was one of those slow hours of fading night when anything that can be imagined seems possible and habits of thought break down and the world is all strange and dense with potential.

Exultation came in surges. When it ebbed she felt tired and guilty. When it flowed, she could scarcely contain herself. Something had happened. Something finally had happened to her. Instead of getting in the car and driving home she began to walk, alone on the quiet streets.

You fool, she said to herself with every stride. You fool you fool you stupid stupid fool you *fool* ... He was a criminal – not a very successful one, to judge by his injuries – and she was a composer. She might imagine herself radical and daring but she spent most of her life at a computer – or a piano, that symbol of civilization, of finer things. What was she thinking, going to bed with a man whose enemies communicated with him by carving messages in his scalp?

Warm semen trickled out of her and she rallied. She argued with herself. A piano was more than a bourgeois item of furniture. How many nights, sitting at hers, had she found herself trembling and disturbed by it – and it was not the case that she didn't understand physical danger, either, because she did. But a piano was also a dangerous thing. Lamplight, seduced by the polished black wood, caressed curves whose gleaming belied the fact that most of the light simply vanished. The piano took in light and never released it. The piano released sound, which by some mystery could also be music, itself locationless and seemingly dimension-less. Music was ineffable, extraordinary – even, to her, metaphysical. Yet it came out of a thing made of wire and wood.

What had come out of Adrien as he coupled with her?

Sperm. She laughed slightly. For a day at least she would carry his smell with her, however she washed. What might this mean? If it had been just sex she could have said, 'Ah, it was just sex.' But it wasn't just sex.

Sometimes she thought she suffered from a lack of courage. She had determined that by composing she would live a life free of pointless habits: she would use the material of her time on earth as a basis for exploration, not stagnation. But in the necessity to make enough money to survive and keep up payments on her equipment, she'd all but forgotten about the experiment and had become caught up in the frenzy to produce. In the past three years she once had been offered a government grant to compose something for a Young Artists CD, but she'd defiantly spent the money and hadn't written anything; she didn't know why. There would be no more grants after that. For free she had done a computer-generated soundtrack for the film of a friend of a friend. This had brought in offers of work on soundtracks for Japanese softporn. Three weeks mixing saccharine mood music had driven her to Prague and into a revolting soul band where she played bass until Kyoto stopped e-mailing her with assignments.

Ah, well. What was money, anyway? Money couldn't bring back the dead, or reverse time. So one had to find other ways of distracting oneself from the bad things in life. Recently, subsisting on what small savings she had, she had been trying to write something serious. Something real. But she was stuck. She was too facile at bullshit and too easily drawn to the cerebral, the ironic, the post-anti-postmodern ultimate lack of commitment to any one idea. Her ears were jaded. And therefore everything she did sounded like shit, and she needed to do something that wasn't a lie. So she spent her time recording raw sound and waiting for inspiration. Until two days ago, when she took her microphone and cigarettes to catch the echoes at the train station.

Meeting Adrien had certainly shaken her out of herself. With his white hair and dark skin he was like some weird negative version of her, and as he staggered around Zagreb bleeding and coughing, it seemed to her that he looked like she felt – sometimes, anyway. But the resemblance ended there. He inhabited his body like an animal; and at the same time he was crying out to escape it. He offered up vulnerability and then at the last second substituted danger instead. He was a riptide.

She should have had more sense than to pick him up.

She didn't consider herself a suitable saving angel and anyway unlicensed HIT was too much of an unknown quantity to risk playing with. Some said it was a superficial, trendy pursuit, a way for the rich and bored to act out their affectations and kinks. Others said it was a way into reality. But the truth about the Deep and its renegade technology was lost in legends propagated by wire-users, who rhapsodized about 'real HIT' when they tried to imagine the Next Level. No one Sabina knew had actually met anyone who'd used unlicensed HIT, so everything she knew about it she'd heard fourth- or fifth-hand.

Until Adrien. He did have a quality about him that seemed to reify the idea of the Deep as something secret and transcendent ... and perilous. It was as if he'd been thumbed by magic, rained over with a sheath of invisible hope that made the air around him surge even when he wasn't moving. Whatever was on the other side of him was a thing with teeth and claws. It had scared her. But it was real, and it couldn't be explained. This combination of qualities – the unexplainable and the real – worked on her like a drug.

Of course, she could be sublimating. Women did it all the time: tried to engage in important work only to toss it away when some interesting specimen came along and aroused their primal feelings. It was stupid to think that, by getting involved with Adrien and his strange, possibly cruel HIT practices, she could somehow unlock her own creativity.

It was stupid.

The sky was a steel color. She turned and headed back toward her car, reluctant because she knew she would stand for a long time outside the hotel, looking up at the window where he was.

Five

He woke to sounds of dying animals, which he eventually deduced must have come from his own mouth. In his sleep his head had rolled back over the edge of the mattress, filling with blood until it ached enough to wake him; but when in the middle of a self-pitying cry he opened his eyes and tried to move, he couldn't. It was light outside. The room was upside down, an empty syringe and some cotton wool cast on the floor between table and door. There was also a brown leather billfold splayed on the carpet. His queasy mind took some time registering the significance of this; then, carefully, he turned over and looked again.

The wallet was not his.

He probed for C, but he was alone. If he inched forward on his belly he could just stretch out his arm and pluck the wallet off the floor without breaking his stitches or falling off the bed. He attempted this cautiously, snagging it but releasing a fit of coughing in his effort. The mucus was Technicolor.

There were some bills inside, most of which he had given Sabina himself. There was a national identity card-cum-driver's license, a bank card, and a couple of receipts with names and phone numbers scrawled on the back. There was one snapshot: a slender, rather gangling teenaged girl with long, dark hair hugging a drooling Doberman and flanked by two beneficently smiling elderly persons. He flipped back to the driver's license and remarked, 'The … Lazarich … family portrait.' The thought of Sabina's parents (grandparents?), childhood and especially her faithful dog depressed him instantly. He resisted the impulse to hurl the object across the room and instead got out of bed, running

47

his hands over the bumps and knottings on his head. He pitched like a leaky rowboat when he walked.

Outside it was raining. He stood at the window looking out on the narrow street with its immaculate houses and shops, and when he realized what lay ahead – what *must* lie ahead – one sliver of a larger terror shrieked through him. He quelled it as a matter of habit.

Although C wasn't there, he spoke to it. Practicing.

'You can't have me. I won't give permission anymore.'

In his own voice he sought evidence of the strength he was going to need, but he couldn't find it, so he went into the bathroom and threw up. Then he got ready to check out.

He took a cab to Sabina's street. She lived, essentially, in a slum. By Adrien's New York standards, the houses didn't look too bad, and certainly the area didn't strike him as *dangerous*, but against the prosperity of the rest of Zagreb, the neighborhood was a sad disgrace. Well, he thought: she's an artist. What can you expect? He spotted the husk of her car parked at an angle on the sidewalk a short distance from the house in question.

The red door opened only after a prolonged spate of knocking. Darkness and the cloying odor of weed groped out into the street, and an orange-haired boy with severe acne and listless eyes held up one hand against the intrusion of light, the smoke drifting between his fingers and into his hair like hunting dragons. He blinked continually.

'May I speak to Sabina Lazarich, please?' Adrien said in Croatian he'd learned in the cab. He fiddled with the handheld and listened intently to the boy's response, which was one laconic word: 'Work.'

Adrien consulted the digital translator and thumbed in the direction of the street.

'Car,' he pronounced carefully, attempting to argue. 'Sabina car is there.'

The reply was rapid, complex, and beyond his ken altogether. He tried asking the kid to slow down but was ignored. Eventually, the youth turned his back on Adrien and drifted into the house leaving the door open, still talking and gesturing intermittently. Adrien followed him into the front hall and up a long, steep flight of stairs. The house was overly warm and stuffy, and the stair treads hadn't been swept for some time. Adrien held his breath and told himself that he would not cough. The effort made him light-headed.

They stopped at a closed door. The boy knocked twice before seizing the knob and pushing it open. He gestured for Adrien to step inside; Adrien remained on the threshold but looked in. The room was small, banked wall to wall with computer equipment, musical keyboards, speakers and other miscellany of sound recording. The windows had been covered with black plastic bags and the only light came from the computer monitor and the rectangle of illumination presented by the open door. Sabina sat with her back to the door, her head engulfed in enormous headphones, playing a keyboard silently while the levels on the monitor jumped and twitched. She must have perceived the change in the light because she stopped playing but did not turn. She pulled the headphones down so that they hung around her neck while the boy addressed her.

Without moving her head she replied in Croatian: briefly, quietly and, Adrien thought, without emotion. He wished he could see her face. The boy left; Adrien shut the door. Sabina turned and he held out the wallet. She stood up and took it, placing it on top of a speaker without looking at it. Then she half turned away, twisting the cord of the headphones around one index finger. He realized she was nervous.

'I'm sorry about the other night,' he said. 'I was feverish or … something. I meant no disrespect.'

He could see she hadn't expected him to say that. He wondered what she had expected. What she thought had happened between them. He stared at her, and behind his eyes C stared at her, and suddenly the room felt crowded.

She lit a cigarette. The silence had grown so long that he said, 'So this is where you compose your music.'

Stupid. Stupid. He sounded like some loser in a bar. But the sight of the equipment had relieved one of his anxieties: it proved she really was a composer. She had been telling the truth about herself.

In the silence he could pick up the thin sparkle of static from the headphones around her neck, but Sabina ignored it. She was so guarded he could scarcely believe she had sat cross-legged on his bed licking spaghetti sauce off her fingers and laughing. Still less could he convince himself that he'd held her warm and living body against him, breathed her breath, and as he watched her defenses wheel and snap into place in the S of her cigarette smoke and the soft but perceptible tapping of her boot toe (*I'm busy, I've got things to do, can you fuck off and die now please*) he felt suddenly like he was drowning, and he didn't know if this feeling came from within him or from C, but—

'What are you supposed to be, Adrien?'

'I'm sorry?'

'You heard me. What are you? What was in bed with me last night?'

Oh shit. 'I'm really sorry, I don't know what hap—'

'What do you want?' She sounded aggrieved.

To get away from C, to let the exposed brain go dark and acquire cobwebs, to push Sabina up against that speaker and *have* her. To receive some guarantee of laughing about all this someday, but he could say none of these things. None of them was part of C's plan for him.

'You see?' she said at length. 'Where is the point of talking? I opened up to you, and you – you – you say nothing back.' She turned and adjusted something on the amplifier. 'I think you should go now.'

He didn't want to go. He wanted to stay. C rumbled some kind of warning but he had actually *forgotten* about C and he said, 'A whore.'

'What?' She spun on one heel. Her eyes sparked.

'You want to know what I am. I am a whore. Satisfied?'

Her expression settled, balancing in the long curve of her mouth. Her arms stretched down at her sides, drawing slightly away from her body, and the cigarette burned there, ignored. He thought: she believes this whole thing is sexy.

'Tell me more,' she said. 'Tell me what happened to you last night.'

In her gaze now there was no warmth or compassion. There was, instead, a distant hunger, and behind that, the intellect working silently.

'I can't.'

Sweat in the deep lines of his hand: headline, heartline, lifeline, the line of Fate.

'I have taken care of you, I have talked to you, I have told you about myself. I have made love with you—' (here he felt his neck muscles relax when she didn't say fuck) '—which was very strange, and you can't tell me anything. You know I'm interested in nature of experience, don't you? You must realize, if I could hear some piece of music through other person's ears, it would be, it would be as – I can't think of word – powerful? as going to some other planet. The music I make, it must be only mine. It *is* me. It is nothing else, no one else. But. You! You know what I cannot know. You could hear the music of another person, yes? And you will tell me nothing!'

Adrien's hand went involuntarily to his head, which contained nothing but C's stunned silence. Into this vacuum he said, 'I can't. I can't believe what I'm hearing. Sabina. It doesn't work that way. You don't do this for an hour, or a day. It isn't *art*. It's like – it's like – it isn't like anything.' He stepped forward, seized her hand with the cigarette and brought it to his lips, sucking furiously. Of course he began to cough then. She let go of the butt and slid away, out of reach.

'Sabina, look at me. Do you – no. You have *no idea* what it's like. You have no idea.'

51

Her voice, soft and angled with that accent, out of the black shapes of recording equipment: 'So tell me.'

'No.' The fucking morphine. Why did he ever start talking?

'Why not?'

'Because.'

'Adrien.'

'Goddamnit are you stupid? Because it's dangerous. Because it's bad for you. Because the less you know the safer you are.'

'I don't want to *deal* it. I just want to know. What it's like.'

Maybe it was her persistence, her aggression hiding in that gentle low voice; maybe it was C, inside him, leaning toward Sabina with a kind of heat – no – more than that, it was his frustration at being unable to articulate, to convey even the slightest—

He took two steps forward and pressed the lit cigarette into the smooth skin of the inside of her forearm. She gasped and he let her slap his face; when she brought her arm to her mouth it was all he could do to stay there within the radiance of her body's heat and look at the tears starting up in her eyes.

'You don't like that? You don't get off on that, Sabina?' New York came through in the shape of his vowels. 'Then don't ask any more questions. 'Cause that's what it's about. Closest approximation I can give you.'

He turned and left the room without a backward glance. There could be no other way. C wanted a piece of Sabina, but he wasn't going to let it happen. No one was going to get Sabina, and after he got away from C he—

On the front steps he cut off his own thoughts ruthlessly. Whatever he thought, C would know instantly. So he couldn't think.

He tossed the cigarette onto the street. The wind caught it, and it rolled away.

Six

He had to pick up a flight to Frankfurt before he could continue on to Tokyo, and so he did go to a doctor for the bronchitis and forced himself to rest an extra day. He was awake for part of the long flight, but he scrupulously avoided thinking about where he was going or what he was doing. In his mind he ran through every kata he knew; he replayed fights; he evoked the lost discipline of his life before C, hoping to find some shred of himself still untouched by it, even if only in memory. He drew the walls of the dojo: its dimensions, its floorboards, the irregular shape of the makiwara where hands striking it had altered it like water on stone. He reconstructed the Japanese characters on the wall paintings, forcing his mind to comply with him – forcing himself to turn away from the lure of C.

He couldn't stop C from coming into his head. But he had to stop responding to it. This had all gone much too far.

If only he had stopped fucking around back when he was a kid, had stayed with the karate and not succumbed to the thrills of the street – then he never would have met C. Then his mind would be his own, and his body as well. The latter, thankfully, was taking care of itself, and except for lingering stiffness and a bone-deep ache throughout his torso, he was on his way to physical recovery.

But as he entered the HIT labs at Seiroka hospital, C woke up inside him and began to protest. Under different circumstances, it might have struck him as funny that he had walked into an institution that would like nothing better than to take his head apart – literally and metaphorically – to study the long-term effects of being a full-fledged trans. Because of the hugely profitable free market in Moscow, the street was way ahead of government in its ability to apply HIT. Adrien's life was made possible because the Deep functioned as yet outside the law, and because the Russian government turned a blind eye on the wildly inventive products that surfaced in the Muscovite market. The Deep's technology was exploding too fast to be kept up with, for the Deep could think fast and in every direction.

Besides, no government had yet devised a way to sidestep the human rights problem of experimenting with trans technology on human beings except in cases of medical need; the Deep had no such qualms.

Adrien was nervous just being here among some of the world's foremost HIT experts, as if they would guess by sight what he really was and drag him off to some inner chamber where he'd be dissected. For this and other reasons, C was bloody furious that he'd come within a mile of Seiroka HIT. Throughout his attempts at conversation with the staff of the Human Interface Technology Lab, it was standing within his throat and filling his head with sharp *pinging* noises that startled him repeatedly. His Japanese was only a little better than his Croatian, and he soon found himself propelled backward into a narrow hallway outside the lab, talking to a sweaty American student named Steinmetz and a nurse.

'I'm trying to find Dr Yoshimura. Mitsuko Yoshimura. She's a senior researcher here. She knows who I am, Adrien Reyes.'

'Mm-hmm.' Steinmetz said something to the nurse, who shook her head and gave Adrien a piercing look. She answered Steinmetz rapidly and with some feeling.

'She *was* on staff here,' Steinmetz said with an air of congratulation, 'but she's recently retired. Lives on Maui, apparently.' He added, 'They all miss her.'

Adrien didn't have to fake the crestfallen expression. 'She saved my mother's life,' he lied. 'Many years ago. She was the only doctor in the world who could treat the problem. I am visiting Tokyo and I wanted to thank her on behalf of my entire family. I wish I could have thanked her personally, but I am happy that she has retired. She deserves to have a good life.'

He had spoken slowly and clearly for the benefit of the nurse; Steinmetz was looking at him sidelong. C inserted the smell of dead mammals into his awareness.

'Come wis me,' the nurse said, inclining her head and smiling. 'I give you address, you send her card?'

Adrien bowed and followed her. Steinmetz turned away, already thinking about something else.

*　*　*

I should have seen this coming. I knew he was unhappy, but I never thought he'd actually take this 'escape' so far. This wouldn't have happened if I'd had him to myself in Zagreb; if only the Croatian girl hadn't started in with him, making him feel like a moral failure and going on about music and art as if life isn't really about fighting for every inch of survival – what can she know about suffering and compromise, half-baked youth that she is?

I must stay calm. I kept myself under control so carefully, doing the groundwork in softening Adrien to receive me, so that when all was ready we could share I. My brief lapses into passion have been disastrous. I has been snatched from my reach, and he's going to leave: two major wrinkles in the master plan. Suddenly I find myself forced to make fast decisions, ones whose consequences I can imagine only dimly.

I will have to work with Max. I had hoped to avoid this, but he has the plant now. I left him contact information in the Deep, through which I can pass with virtually no trace; his response indicates he's willing to do a deal. He's even stopped crowing. Now that he's had a chance to calm down, now that he knows he's dealing with a piece of tech

55

beyond the workings of his shallow public relations mind, Max needs me.

And I need something, too. Or rather, some*one*. I thought it would be Adrien, but now it seems I can't rely on him. I want him. I have always wanted him. But where one method fails, another appears.

When they had sex, Adrien and the girl, he regained that intensity I first discovered in him. She brought it out the way rain brings out the color in autumn leaves. There must be something useful in that.

I shouldn't be thinking what I'm thinking.

She is wrong about HIT: totally wrong. HIT is not about art, it's about life. Still, she said some things that suggest her mind may be almost big enough for my purposes.

I don't want to want Sabina.

But do we ever have a choice about what or whom we desire?

*　*　*

He found that he could numb his mind by studying patterns, and this seemed to lull C, keeping the Watcher away and giving him breathing space. At the moment he was paying attention to the uneven, Mandelbrotian rhythm of the grinning heat as it shuffled across his shoulders: sunlightshade, sunlight　　　shade because the trees with their leonine shadows tossed outrageously in the wind, leaves trembling pizzicato and branches swimming in slow time. The pattern was impossible to predict and made him want to sleep. The wind too was hot but not piercingly so, lacking the aggression of light. After all, light was that same phenomenon which, focused and controlled, could bore smoking holes in leaves and slice bone on the operating table. Light, as if it knew what Adrien was up to, had already begun to rivet him, pinning him to the earth and making him sweat as he breathed the stale-piss odor of sugarcane in the fields below and, caught on a crosswind, the complementary smell of horse. The horse shed was located on the lowest point of the property, perched near the edge of a steep decline on a broad shelf that was big enough to accommodate a paddock as well as a driveway. To get to the house itself you had to climb a long flight of stairs, and to get to the garden beyond you had to ascend yet again, so that the garden, the roof of the house, and the horse paddock were all strewn at your feet like steps, each casually askew. Farther down the volcano was the bustling town of Makawao, and farther up was a riot of trees and meadows that finally terminated in the bare nipple of earth with its grey, crumbling interior that was Haleakala.

Adrien stood still, feeling the leaf-shadows haunt his back and trying not to think of the music suggested by their movements, for he had thought too much of music since leaving Sabina. The sun also visited the small woman kneeling between the tomato plants: it was aligned with the row, in fact, and cast a broad beam on her. The reflection off her white tennis shirt was not unlike the soft and potent aura of gold. She wore a straw hat and her back was turned toward him. He watched her work until her head turned fractionally and she saw him. She got to her feet, dusting herself down economically.

'Weeds,' she said. 'I can't keep up with them, no matter how often I'm out here.'

She walked toward him carrying a clump of the offenders in one gloved hand. Her face hadn't changed in two years: she was tanned nut-brown, and the wrinkles around her eyes and mouth were charming, adding character to an otherwise bland and unreadable face.

'Eugene told you I called?'

She nodded, tipping back her hat to look up at him. She frowned. 'What have you done to yourself?'

'Long story.'

Her head swivelled slowly from side to side as she let out a long breath, her eyes moving assessingly over his body

57

and returning to his face. 'I remember when you first got the hair,' she said, making spiky gestures with one hand around her own head. 'I told you you'd have women in heat coming out of the woodwork for you. Do you remember what you said?'

He did, but preferred not to discuss it. He frowned, which she interpreted as meaning he didn't remember, so she continued, 'You said, "I don't want to be admired – I want to be feared."'

She was studying him, gauging his reaction. He realized that, like any opponent, she was looking for a show of weakness. Rapidly, almost subconsciously, he calculated what he would lose by letting her take up the mentor role, or was it the mother role? Too much, he feared.

'I haven't come to repent,' Adrien said, meeting her gaze. 'Mitsuko, I want to hire you.'

'Adrien.' Her tone said it all: you foolish boy. What can you be thinking. I'm not. I don't. Not anymore.

The moment of contention had passed, but now he could feel the Watcher inside him, like a moth beating its wings within a jar. Mitsuko began to walk toward the house, tossing the weeds on the compost heap as she passed. In the horse paddock below, a slim man led a pony out of the shed. Mounted on the pony was a tiny girl wearing a bicycle helmet. As they descended, the roof of the house blocked the view of the paddock.

'How did you find me here?'

'Asked for you at the hospital. Your colleagues wish you'd never left; they send their regards. They really miss you. You were the best.'

'Yes, I was. But I'm retired now. I have kids to raise, tomatoes to grow.'

'But you haven't stopped entirely, have you? They told me you still sometimes consult on special cases.'

'Who told you that?' A sharpness there, a small fault in her armor.

'Just something I heard.' So he had guessed right. He

maintained nonchalance in his tone. They had reached the steps and she went down ahead of him. Looking down on the top of her hat, he wondered what it would be like to see through people's skulls, right into their brains.

'I need something done.'

'Go to the hospital.'

'Mitsuko, you know as well as I do no hospital's going to even know what I've got, much less how to deal with it.'

'OK, you want me to scrub down my kitchen table and cut you open with my husband's electric drill?' They stepped onto the deck of her house, and she opened the screen door and left it open for him to follow. It was dark inside.

Adrien said nothing. Mitsuko took off her gloves and hat and opened the refrigerator, rummaging among glass bottles that chimed and clattered.

'Hmm,' she said eventually. 'Who told you to come to me?'

'I knew. From two years ago, when you cleared up the problem I was having.'

'That was a software glitch. Now you're talking about surgery. Why don't you go to the person who planted in the first place?'

'I'd need C's cooperation to do that, and I can't get it. My Watcher's getting really strange and violent.'

'You got this far, didn't you? Surely C knows what you're up to.' She selected a bottle of pink juice and poured two glasses, handing him one.

'C is at this moment torturing me with images of what will happen to me, you, and everything I ever loved right down to my pet goldfish, if I go through with this.'

'Thanks. Glad you came to see me. Drink your juice and get the hell out.'

'Mitsuko, wait. You can't allow yourself to be intimidated by that, and neither can I.'

Mitsuko looked him over in a manner that suggested she was not impressed by what she saw.

'Adrien, how can I make you understand? The unlicensed HIT scene is like one of those giant fungi that take up thousands of acres. You don't even know it's there because all you see are these funny little mushrooms that pop up every so often. Now imagine that this fungus is malevolent. You pick off one mushroom and the rest of it gets pissed off – the entire state of Ohio, say, picks up and attacks you. Why don't I want to have anything to do with you? Because you, Adrien, are a mushroom of the Deep.'

'That's cute,' he allowed, wondering how many times she would have to score off him before she would settle down to business. 'So what is C in your analogy? – if you're so worried about the ramifications of helping one small mushroom.'

'I don't think you know what you're up against with C. You've been allowed to see only what C wants you to know. For example, let me ask you this: is C a man or a woman?'

'I don't know.'

'There you go. You only know what C lets you in on. The newer generations of computers allow a Watcher to manage multiple trans, keeping each one available on a different frequency-shifting code, and switching back and forth at will. Most Watchers, to my knowledge, only want one or at most two trans, but taken to its theoretical limits, the technology permits many more inputs than that. A being that pushes the envelope of HIT would have many limbs, more like a Hindu deity than a human. I hear things, even here in Hawaii. And I think C is the perfect example of just such a being.'

'A *being*? That sounds a little goofy, Mitsuko.'

'Think about it this way, then. *You* are a part of C. Your Watcher can draw on you, use you, inflect its existence with the flavor of Adrien Reyes. The kind of seeing that a Watcher does isn't a simple matter of subject and object. It's a form of being. There's that word again – see, it's hard to even talk about it. This isn't a notion of identity that has words or concepts from any known culture. That's what makes someone like C so difficult to understand, much less predict.'

'OK,' he said slowly, 'but what does this have to do with me?'

'It means that if I take out your plant and C gets pissed off, there could be repercussions neither of us can foresee.'

'But Mitsuko, I'm not asking this because I'm bored and I want to take up a new career. I'm asking it because whatever's happening to C – whatever it's becoming, I don't like it. I don't like the idea of being absorbed into it. C has no respect for right and wrong anymore. I know that sounds old-fashioned, but everyone has their limits, even me.'

Mitsuko said, 'I might be more sympathetic if I didn't see a guy who basically gets to go around seeing the world, getting in and out of trouble and making vast amounts of money. I mean, yeah, I can see you've been beaten up once too often. But I still think you need to work this out with C. I'm not prepared to cross a Watcher. It's simply too dangerous.'

'I'm not going to take no for an answer.'

'Adrien, you have nothing I want. Money I don't need; I have Eugene, I have kids, I have land, I have everything I want.'

'Except your work.'

'I told you, I no longer need it.'

'Bullshit! It's a crime, you out here growing tomatoes! Whatever tripe you've fed to your colleagues and family, saying you needed to leave the field, you needed a more well-rounded life, raise the kids and all that shit – maybe they're buying it, but I'm not. It takes a coward to know one, Mitsuko. Were you threatened, is that it? You can tell me. I mean, I'm like occupying a prominent position on the shitlists of at least one or two international crime lords, so it's not like I can't relate.'

He took a long swallow of tart heterogeneous juice.

There was a chuckle in her voice. 'I forgot how melodramatic you were. I ought to ask you where the hell you get off. I ought to tell you where your plant really belongs, because it isn't in your head. But you're so ignorant, you make me laugh. Come here.'

She led him to the front of the house, through cool rooms with white walls and bare floors, to a picture window overlooking the paddock. Memories of his third grade teacher percolated in him as she pointed wordlessly to a sling chair by the window. The Watcher was hanging eagerly on Mitsuko's every movement, but Mitsuko said nothing at first, staring out the window at the small girl on the horse, circling slowly around the paddock with the man alongside, his head tilted up toward the child.

'Is that Eugene?'

'You know,' Mitsuko said, 'I never liked *Frankenstein* much. Did you? I thought it was unnecessarily sensational.'

'I never saw any of those movies.'

She looked like she was trying not to laugh and he wondered why. She said, 'What is it you think this is all about?'

'You mean, being a trans?' He shifted. These rhetorical questions. Mitsuko was going to wield her intellect against him unfairly – he could sense it.

'Why are you a trans, why do trans exist, what is going on here in the world if this is happening?'

'I don't know why they exist,' he said slowly. 'And I don't really know what's going on in the world. For me, all I know is, I don't want to be one anymore, for personal reasons.'

Mitsuko frowned. 'For personal reasons? You're using your stupidity to run from the truth.'

'And you're using your intelligence to run from the truth. I don't need you to lecture me, Mitsuko. I can imagine your objections. It's a sick technology – right? What's the world coming to? Et cetera. You object. And that's why you're hiding out up here. Or so you say.'

'You have no conception of what it is you're involved in. Do you think it was easy for me to walk away from the situation at Seiroka HIT? I'm not just talking about the money, I'm talking about the opportunities for using this technology to frame a window onto consciousness. Forget theory, forget computers, forget the whole mind-body problem.' Mitsuko gestured emphatically with her small, practical hands. Adrien liked how, when she got excited, the slightest of Japanese accents came through her polished West-Coast American. 'Those are shadows on the wall of the cave – I'm talking about looking human consciousness full in the face and being able to pinpoint what is actually there.'

Her nostrils were flaring as she spoke and Adrien found himself leaning forward unconsciously.

'But you quit,' he prompted, fascinated.

'My grandfather's family came from Nagasaki. All my life I've read accounts of the people who built the thing, made the decision to drop it, all that shit. I won't bore you with an exegesis on the bomb. I tried to understand it for a long time, and I couldn't. I still can't. Yet imagine my surprise when government people started coming to *my* project, started offering contracts for me and my colleagues to work on HIT for military purposes. For espionage. For politics.'

'It's not the same thing as a nuclear weapon,' Adrien said. 'People aren't being murdered, there's no wholesale destruction – I mean, not like in a war, it's not the same.'

She said nothing for a minute. It bothered him that she was obviously making a concerted effort to speak on his level. 'It's never enough for us to understand something, is it? It's always necessary to tamper with it. So with physics, so with genetics, so with the brain. We're a race of tinkerers, messing around with things until something goes boom, and then we run screaming for anything that can make us forget what we've done.'

'Look, uh, Mitsuko, I just don't think it's like you make it out to be. I mean, you're saying you quit because you couldn't condone what's being done with HIT, is that it?'

'In a nutshell, yeah.'

'But if you don't figure it out, someone else will.'

'Yeah, maybe. But not me. I don't want to be the one. Maybe it's crazy but that's the way I feel. So you see, I'm not jiving you when I say I'm out. I'm not interested. Life is too short; I had to make my decision.'

Her profile was toward him: she was watching the scene in the paddock below. Eugene stepped away from the pony, and the little girl kicked mightily, her legs beating on the saddle skirts. The pony obligingly shifted into a trot. The child began to post.

'That's my personal choice,' Mitsuko added, turning to face him. 'You could call it a cop-out or you could say I decided to grow up. Have you?'

'What do you mean?'

'You know what I mean. You can't come here with your hat in your hand pretending like I don't know what you've been into all this time.'

'I've been a trans. I'm not the only one,' he said defensively. He should have expected something like this from Mitsuko. She was obsessed with morality even if she did not always practice it.

'No. Lots of trans are just glorified sex toys. Party animals. Your rep when I first met you was the holy terror of Western Europe.'

He said, 'Don't you understand? That's C. It's what my Watcher wants. Why do you think I want to get out?'

He was watching the child kicking the horse violently, legs slapping saddle leather and making no apparent impression on the animal. Eventually it broke into a half-hearted canter. Mitsuko was flaming him.

'Oh, I get it. "The devil made me do it" – right? Don't you ever think, Adrien? You're a criminal. Don't make faces. What is this urge in you to dominate, this aggression? Do you think because the Watcher's pulling the strings that you aren't somehow doing what you're doing? Do you think this karate of yours is cartoon violence, Saturday morning tv?'

Adrien took a long breath. To his surprise, he found there were tears in his eyes. He cleared his throat.

'The Deep has something called I. It's semi-organic, it requires no satellites, and my Watcher wants it. C doesn't care that there's only one prototype in the entire world, that it's never been tested except by computer model. I had to kill for it, and even then I didn't get it. *Max Niagarin* doesn't even know what it is.'

Her face was expressionless except for a slight tic near her mouth.

'Mitsuko, C wants to use this plant on me. Don't ask me how I know – I just know. And I think – I'm afraid – it'll be a way for me to be *controlled*, not just Watched. You can't imagine what it's like. It's not enough for C just to Watch. It'll never be enough.'

Adrien steepled his hands and rested them on his knees, resting his chin on his fingertips and looking up at her. He was trembling.

'I want off the satellites. I don't want C to be able to find me, to control me, to fuck with my head. I just want you to open me up and take out the plant. Period. No more. I don't think that's unreasonable – do you?'

'I can save your ass – but why should I? When have you ever done the right thing? It seems to me all of a sudden things are getting a little too real for you. All of a sudden it isn't pretend anymore, right?'

'Look, I'm at your mercy here. Will you do it or not?' For the first time it had occurred to him that she really might say no.

She turned toward the window again. Eugene reached up and mopped sweat off his brow as the child and pony broke into a canter, dust swirling up in the bright wind.

'There would have to be conditions. I can't endanger my family, and I don't want to get between you and C.'

'I don't think I'm being followed. I'm supposed to be too scared to even think of playing any tricks.'

'And you *are* scared.'

'I'm concerned, yeah.'

'Bullshit, you're pissing scared. You want it deprogrammed? That's not so hard to do. No surgery involved; I could do it here. I can change the codes so your Watcher can't reach you.'

'It's not enough. Someone else could tap in. Or C could break the code.'

'Well, have you ever thought of just taking the auxiliary battery out? You can't transmit very far without signal amplification.'

'Mitsuko, haven't you been listening? It's not transmitting that worries me. It's *receiving*.'

'You actually want a hole in your head, then? Take home the plant in a mayonnaise jar like a kid with his tonsils?'

'*You* can have the plant, Mitsuko. It's not new, but it's top of the line. It should still be some use. For personal research.'

He saw her smile begin, check, and go still.

'They're easier to put in than to take out, you know. I'll need support staff. An operating theater, nurses ...'

* * *

There is a feeling here on Maui of a little too much joy: a dangerous happiness that skates the limits of sanity. Adrien on the beach near Paia looking at the sunset cloudscapes, solid enough to tread on – a highway to some night of meaning where yes fairy tales can come true, it can happen to you ...

Adrien is wary.

I sit listening to his mind. The ocean pulse softens the edges of music that with the smells of marijuana and burgers spills from the back door of a nearby restaurant. The day has gone silver with age. Arms of darkening land bend and stretch toward the horizon like faded dancers. They have lent their color to the sky: the transaction troubles young Adrien. However giddy and sensual the island's bright fruits and tumbled landscapes may be, that they can engage in trade with this sky, this Atlantis of fabulous ever-morphing, pinkly laughing, nuanced yet titanic cloud architecture, seems inconceivable. It's as if the daylit world by giving over its powers to this fantastic display has somehow compromised its own logic. It's as if Something from Somewhere Else is calling, and if the rest of the world has sense to stop its ears, Maui is stoned and smiling: nodding and listening, listening –

Or maybe that's just his own Existential Crisis talking.

For it's true: the symptoms all point to an EC, that root canal of the soul (which phantom-like eludes the questing knife of reason that would dig it out and kill it to prevent pain to the host: oh, the soul resists to the end). The hunted soul, in fact, has been known to hide, migrate, disguise itself, and play dead – anything to prevent the cauterizing of its own life source, and while the soul resists, the knife cuts deeper and deeper and the pain becomes a fine-tuned madness. Adrien's soul is presently lurking in his hands clasped loosely-almost-hopelessly on his lap, con-spicuous by their idleness. Calloused, scarred, lumpy with knuckle calcification caused by *makiwara* training, the fixity of his hands now betrays the paralysis he feels within. There they are, vulnerable, huddled together as if for solace even though Paia Beach offers no threats, only gentle waves and soft wind. When he realizes this, perforce his hands separate, dig into the sand and convulse, gripping a substance that leaks out and disintegrates.

There are other signs as well. His eyes, for example, have a fugitive stillness about them. They don't really look at anything, but they not-look in a practiced way, as if hoping that the soldiers of the enemy will pass by on that long wartime train platform – let them harass the cloaked and starving mothers with their dog-eyed children, for these at least have faith and biology in their favor while he faces the Existential Crisis with nothing but his skin, and even that no longer intact.

The nights are the worst. On Maui the sky comes down, a field of lances all pointed at him out of a thick and cloying blackness. The EC whuffles its hot breath in his ears and no drug he can take will banish it. The only thing that saves Adrien in the night is the thought of the operating room Mitsuko is going to book and staff; one of these nights he will walk in bearing the burden of my consciousness, and walk out a free man – whatever he thinks that is.

Adrien.

He feels me there, realizes I've been Watching all along: he shakes his head; he writhes; but he can't make me be quiet.

Adrien, you can't do this. We've come so far together. Adrien.

In a low voice he says, 'I'll pay you back the money. I'll move to Montana and live in a shack. But I can't go on this way.'

You won't have to. Everything's going to change. If you'll only trust me – Adrien, I need you. I can't live without you.

I let him feel how I feel; how the thought of losing him shakes me to the pith.

'The killing. And what you did when I was with Sabina. It's not on. You have no respect for boundaries.'

I'm sorry. I'll learn. I promise. Don't you see – we're explorers. We're pioneers. We have to make our own way. These problems, they're not important enough to throw away the work we're doing together.

'Maybe you're the explorer. But I've seen enough.'

Those things that upset you – I'll never do them again. I never meant to hurt you.

I can feel him turning it all over in his mind, trying to find the geometry of the situation: trying to find the balance. He holds his skull in his hands and squeezes: we both feel the bones shift.

What he feels could be called guilt, although I'd prefer to

call it something else. Because he owes me the whole shape of his adult life. If not for me he'd probably be in jail right now, or addicted to wires or drugs – or all three. He thought very little of himself when I first encountered him. He was desperate to be rescued.

When I found him he was a runner for a wire outfit operating out of the Bronx. It was standard stuff: Sex, Power, Delusions of Grandeur. Most of it was the same as the commercially available wires you could get legally, only of course it was bootleg. No ads to compel you to buy products to make rich America richer. You could get canned experiences anytime without fear of spending addiction, and in the end everybody knew that it was cheaper to buy a bootlegged feeling than to get the 'free' stuff which you'd pay for the rest of your life through flashbacks that would make you drool over Haägen-Dazs or black thigh-high boots or the latest model of smartcar until you succumbed and bought.

All Adrien had to do was handle security, which consisted of looking tough and getting into scuffles from time to time when things went wrong. He'd trained in the martial arts since childhood, and with the new laws cutting off the supply of handgun ammunition, he could hold his ground in almost any situation.

When Tomaj, one of my other trans, ran into him by chance one day, he had just dispatched the entire comple-ment of a rival posse except for two pit bulls which had cornered him in a stairway – not the sort of opponents that Okinawa goju-ryu, or even Gracie jiu-jutsu, prepares you to deal with. Being an animal lover, Tomaj had managed to charm the stupid creatures, and Adrien owed us one. He was a cynical-yet-clueless street kid, typical except for the fact that, unlike most of his ilk, he wasn't fronting when it came to his fighting ability: in fact, he had such a surfeit of talent that he didn't seem to know what to do with it.

He understood the implications of the HIT implant that would make him a trans about as well as the average person: he thought of it as a glorified wire, an electro-chemical activator. Something a little less binding than marriage and a little more serious than a long-term tripwire. Should I have disclosed more? Maybe. But I thought I was giving as good as I got.

In those days he was a willing vessel. He was looking for guidance, the filling of a void whose depth he'd only begun to imagine; and I found much in him to develop. I found much to teach. Intimacy is a weak word for what's grown between us. He may not know me as well as I know him, but I have left my footprints on his soul. He has grown, whether he realizes it or not; he has feelings for me that he doesn't want articulated even to himself.

It's dark now on the beach. The waves are faintly luminous; the breeze is turning cooler. He's at the limits of his ability to think. I've overloaded him.

'Please, C. Leave me alone. Let me think for myself. Please go now.'

If I go, what will he decide? He is disgusted; ashamed; guilty. He doesn't want the weight of me, but doesn't he understand—

'Go, C! *GO!!* GET OUT!' He leaps to his feet, roaring out the words, and runs into the sea. I feel the waves against his legs, his body flowing like wild horses, the tears swelling his throat – and I pull myself away. Back to neutral space, to the six walls of my own head, to my icons and video links and all the stiffness of the machinery that's supposed to be enough.

Seven

Four days after his visit with Mitsuko, his new cellphone rang.

'Mitsuko?'

'Adrien. It's Tomaj. Don't hang up!'

He'd been about to, but what was the point? C had apparently plucked the number right out of his head, even though he'd made an effort not to memorize it.

'It's no big thing, I just want to talk. How you feeling? How's the leg?'

'Oh, it's just dandy, Tomaj. Just dan-dee.'

'Don't you be getting mad at *me*. I didn't do it to you.'

'No. C did. Why the hell are you calling me on the phone? You could crawl straight into my brain, C.'

'Adrien, don't be such a prick,' Tomaj said. 'C's not here. I'm calling you for myself. We *used* to be friends, remember?'

Adrien took a deep breath. 'I got nothing against you. My problem is with C.'

'I know. I know. I just wanted to say, I understand what you're doing.'

Warily: 'You do?'

'I never figured you for somebody who'd be in the scene that long. I'd have given you a year, maybe, before you split. You don't *need* it bad enough.'

'What about you? You've been with C longer than I have.'

'C and I, we have an understanding. Both of us are getting something out of this arrangement. And I don't fight C. There's no reason to.'

Adrien said, 'C didn't put you up to this? This isn't a trick?'

'No. C doesn't accept what you're doing. But I do. I thought you should hear that from somebody who understands the position you're in.'

'Yeah. Bye, Tomaj.'

He turned off the phone. He felt moved, and fought the feeling. He had reached the point where he no longer trusted anyone, where even if Tomaj was for real, Adrien wasn't at liberty to turn to him for even the shadow of a friendship. He had to find a different way to live.

Later that same day, Mitsuko called.

'Tonight,' she said. 'Two a.m. Come in the emergency room entrance and say you have a migraine.'

After he hung up the phone C stabbed him in the eyes. It said, *You do have a migraine.*

The emergency room nurse led him into an examining room, took the usual readings, and left him waiting. C had been thrusting noises and smells into his consciousness to show its anger; reminding him of every shame and fear he'd ever experienced; trying to break down his resolve. But when Mitsuko came in, suddenly C changed tactics. It began to speak, slowly. Deliberately.

I've lost you. I've failed.

Mitsuko took a look at Adrien's face and bit off what she was going to say. She waited.

I tried to be the bridge you wanted between body and spirit, the god-who-looks-on – but by crossing over into you, all I've succeeded in doing is teaching you that you have no boundaries. What an incredible idea: that one should have no boundaries! It gives me hope. That one could go anywhere, be anything. That the self should be quiet and surrender to greater forces. What could be better than to discover we are not doomed by biology to be alone?

But if this notion excites me, it scares you. Satellites connect you to the vast interior tracts of another being, one who (you're beginning to grasp) has a different moral code and a different physical configuration from your own. Fear of my difference interferes with your body, with me. With us. You can't deal with the idea that there are spaces inside you larger than you can understand.

'Are you sure?' Mitsuko said, closing the door.

He nodded.

Adrien, this is very sad for you.

'OK. But when you walk out of here this morning, I'm calling up some people I know at CalTech. I'm turning the plant over to them.'

Adrien was startled. 'I thought you intended to take it apart yourself.'

'First of all, I'm a surgeon, not an engineer. I can't do this sort of work myself. Secondly, I don't want to have the thing around here, which brings me to the fact that I'm hiring security for my family. I have no interest in getting caught up in some kind of vendetta with these guys from the Deep, or whoever it is you're mixed up with.'

'I understand.'

'The government will be on to you, Adrien. I'll tell CalTech no more than I have to, but those university guys are in tight with the NSA – they get big funding from the government so they have to talk. The Secret Service can track you down if they want to. They can file charges against you.'

'I'm not worried about that. I just want to get this over with. Whatever happens then, I'll deal with it.'

'Because I don't want to have to worry every time I put my key in the ignition, is my car going to blow up. Or are they going to do something to my daughter. You understand this, don't you?'

'Do what you have to do. Protect yourself. I don't care. Tell the local cops about me if you want. Tell them whatever you want. I really don't care.'

She folded her arms across her chest, shifting her weight

to one hip. 'Adrien, what are you going to do after this? Do you have a plan?'

'No.'

Oh, I get it. You won't even formulate a plan, will you? Because you're afraid of what I'll do to you. You're afraid I'll send another trans after you. If this is the way you want to play it, we'll play it your way. You dishonor me with this mistrust and suspicion. But I will survive.

Mitsuko was still looking at him.

'All right, then,' she said at length. 'Get on the gurney. If anyone asks you, you're having a PET scan for migraine and that's all you know, OK? Let's do it.'

He was ashamed because he was trembling and sweating. To make matters worse, C had adopted the voice of his own mother to sing an old tune, softly. Like a lullaby.

We'll meet again / Don't know where / Don't know when...

Afterward it was like Sesame Street. He wandered outside to the blue sky and palms and pastel cars of the hospital parking lot. The world seemed such a simple, delightful place. Probably it was just that he wasn't thinking.

Mitsuko had found someone to drive Adrien back to Paia – a bearded, blond giant wearing only a sari and jelly sandals who called himself Wave 7 and drove a tiny, left-for-dead lavender Geo. Wave used both sides of the road indiscriminately and plied the horn like a *Jeopardy* contestant, yelling 'Peace!' every time he nearly collided with a person or thing.

Adrien's body was completely limp. He shared a joint with Wave; it had no effect. How could it? He was already lucid and empty. When Wave stopped at a health-food store to buy watermelons, Adrien stood at the cold drinks case and perused the choices. He was thirsty but had no preference. He listened idly to Wave chat with a tubby, fifty-something man: something about an ad-free limited-edition wire the guy had just spent the price of a small car on.

'You know,' Wave was saying, 'that kind is like McDonald's, even if it is ad-free. I only use the ones personally blessed by Shivadashi herself.'

'It's not for me,' the fat guy replied. 'Haven't used 'em since I was in corporate finance in New York, years ago. Anything to escape that job. No, this is for my girlfriend.'

'You should get her off them,' Wave said piously.

'Yeah, right? Tell me something. Why won't women sleep with you without being loaded on these things? I mean, what's the point of having sex with someone if you're going to use a wire to substitute some movie star? What guy can compete with that?'

'Huh.'

'They pull that shit with you? Women, I mean?'

'No-o...'

'I guess I'm just old-fashioned. *Hey!*'

Adrien started and looked over. The fat guy was scowling at him. Wave passed his hands over the watermelons as if trying to sense them without touching them.

'You OK, bud? Letting out all the cold air, there.'

He took a drink and closed the case.

'Just picked him up from the hospital,' Wave said. 'Lobotomy.'

'*Oh...*'

Wave laughed. 'Just kidding. Adrien, you coming?'

Adrien said, 'Take me to the beach.'

'Mitsuko said—'

'Take me to the beach.'

He sat in the shade from midday until sunset. Sometimes he got up and walked around. There was nothing to do, and no reason to do it. He fell asleep on the sand and woke in the morning when a dog sniffed him. The next day he did nothing. Didn't eat. Why should he?

The phone rang about fifty times. He looked at it.

His skin blackened.

Really, although he was in no position to verbalize it, there was no reason for Adrien to live. He had poured his entire self into the relationship with C. Now that the plant was gone, everything in the world seemed to be outside Adrien. There was no inside at all. He felt like a zero-dimensional object, a *point*. and for godsake what was that?

Pain is better than nothing. Fear is better than nothing.

Late in the second night, in the dark hours when people usually die, Adrien got up. His body had become the very definition of a shadow. He could only sense himself indirectly, through observing how the air and sand displaced themselves to accommodate his physical presence.

Slowly, of their own volition, his hands curled into fists. He had a fleeting awareness of his diaphragm, and with this came a fear of feeling and he almost retreated; but he was filling with energy in spite of himself. His body was breathing for him. It aligned itself: his weight fell naturally on the balls of his feet, and suddenly inside everything came on line. It was like somebody had closed a circuit: he could feel the live wire connecting sole to fist, passing through legs and pelvis and up the curve of the spine through the shoulder and out. He was ready to attack; but he moved slowly, his entire body deep in thought. It knew what it intended to do. For karate is a way of thinking with the body, and Adrien's body was at last coming out of its stupor.

The right foot felt its way forward in the sand, planting into sanchin stance as he took in air, cycled it through his system and as he stepped brought his fists out to block; the whole body flexed and tightened on the imaginary impact – just *then*, making a lightning bolt of controlled force as his diaphragm pushed the air out.

It was the first move of Sanchin kata. Just in this manner, feeling everything, he went on. It was coming to him without conscious effort. The kata drew him down into his own body; endowed him with substance; reified him. Through karate, Adrien had a chance of touching his own genius – in every other respect, of course, he was as fucked as ever – for genius in martial arts comes not from intellect, but from the connecting of the mental concept to the electric tree of reflex arc, of instinct. As in any formal system, the principles of karate form the basis of a kind of language; but it's a language of muscle fiber and nerve impulse. It draws power from the animalian brains that lurk beneath the cortex like the many layers of Troy: the city of the mind rebuilt each time over the ruins of its evolutionary predecessor. Make the right connections between new and old brains, and you'll move like an animal and think like a human.

Adrien was performing kata, which looks like a dance but contains inside every move and twitch countless hidden applications for fighting, countless ways to turn a given moment to advantage. The signal to noise ratio of a kata is high, whereas a fight is almost all noise. Kata teaches the conversion of noise to signal – your signal, the one you use to control the outcome in battle. Adrien's body, so long the object of conflict between C and him, was now wholly his own. With the kata he reclaimed it. He performed Sanchin in the darkness, again and again, gaining momentum each time; when the joggers came out in the cirrus dawn, he was still doing it. Those who passed by saw slow, simple movements; formality; repetition.

Adrien, inside the kata, saw the fight he was going to win.

Eight

Tomaj typed the letter on the subway, balancing the slender laptop on his clenched knees. Although it was rush hour, he took up two orange seats – few people were willing to squeeze too close to a six-foot-four black man wearing a ski jacket fifteen years out of style, which might have concealed any number of weapons or even explosives. He was oblivious to his effect on the other commuters, hunched over the computer with lips parted slightly in concentration and a thoughtful frown wrinkling not only his forehead, but a fair bit of his clean-shaven pate as well. A fluorescent butterfly tattoo jigged slightly as the pulse beat in his temple. He was waiting for the words to come.

'Dear Sabina,' he typed, and then deleted 'Dear'. That's better.

> Sabina,
> I can't stop thinking about you. I'm sorry for what happened. I had to act that way. I was being observed. But everything's different now.

Here Tomaj paused, feeling for the right threads. He felt like a nineteenth-century spiritualist practicing automatic writing. Words like ghosts floated through the ether to lodge in his fingertips and dance.

> Do you remember what you said, about having to compose the world? In a way this is what
> I do. It's because of this that what happened, happened.

Tomaj pursed his lips. Bad syntax, but it would have to

stay. It was characteristic of Adrien, almost genuine.

> I'm better now. I'm not the same.
> I want to explain. I want to see you.
> Can you come

And here the train plunged underground. The flow diminished to a trickle and vanished. He had lost contact. He tried not to be alarmed. There was a simple explanation: the electronic link had been broken. He was used to it: more and more these days, he was left to his own devices, abandoned to complete assignments with no support. He didn't mind improvising, but he missed that warm you'll-never-walk-alone glow of C's presence. The Watcher didn't always have time for him, nowadays.

He frowned at the screen and rubbed his head, murmuring to himself. The letter had to be sent today. Tomaj could guess what the gist of it should be, but he didn't know if he could finish it properly on his own. It was hard to do that. Think like Adrien.

> Can you come to NY? I'm enclosing an open ticket.
> If you don't want to see me, come and be a
> tourist anyway. But you do want to see me, don't
> you? I'll be at the airport if you call me.
>
> Please come. I promise it won't be anything weird.

Tomaj typed 'Love', deleted it, skipped three lines and typed 'Adrien'. The train stopped, disgorged passengers at 50th Street, and went on. Tomaj re-read the letter, resisting the impulse to alter the goofy, ineloquent prose. He addressed the FedEx waybill as C had instructed him, scrawled a signature above Adrien's name on the printout and slipped the letter, tickets, and a wad of cash into the package.

He got off at Times Square, drifting up into sunlight with

that familiar feeling of not knowing what the fuck is going on. New York, of course, is melting: Tomaj could feel it under his feet when he climbed the stairs from the train. Dirt is the only thing saving the city from complete liquidity. There is so much dirt in New York City that it's easy to underestimate its power and overlook the truth: only on careful scrutiny does one come to realize that the dirt is in *control*. Tomaj believed it was once a sort of bonus substance, entropy's grubby fingerprint blown in on the sheering winds and deposited by the collective energies of the parasites who live here. Once it was a modest thing. But night after night, day after day, dirt has insinuated itself into the town's concrete steel and plastic guts until, overnight, it achieved critical mass to become no alluvial bonus, but *the* fabric of the city, the very glue holding the whole shebang together. Everything else is slowly melting around and beneath the dirt. Tomaj fancied that the skyscrapers would be the first to go, wavering like jell-o towers in the regard of sun and wind until they finally would bend too far and topple, oozing sensuously into NY harbor. One or two might remain north and south, lovely fangs bowing to each other hopelessly across the gulf of the Village as geology became destiny and left in place of gorgeous, bedrock-planted spires the urban equivalent of mud and wattle huts, and these only in direct correlation to their degree of filth. For gallant dirt is not subject to meltdown. Dirt will remain, chuckling in the dark.

By the time he'd found a FedEx drop, he was late. He sprinted east and arrived at the restaurant sweating. Once inside he hauled off his jacket and thrust it at the hostess, who disappeared beneath a flood of orange nylon. He could smell Max already.

Wearing an avocado suit and orange shirt, Max Niagarin was waiting for him at a window table. He leaped up and threw his arms out genially as if to embrace Tomaj.

'Tomaj, you son of a bitch!'

Max was skinny, bald, and wore a paint-job for hair that

was expensively crafted to suggest a resemblance to an early 70s' Ken doll. Tomaj ducked to one side and patted Max on the head. Surprisingly, the 'hair' was not sticky, but his hand came away smelling odd. His nostrils flared.

'What the hell are you wearing, Max?'

Max smirked. 'Convict: For Men. Like it?'

'It's very – god it smells like cat piss, Max.'

They sat down. Max's gestures were all birdlike, presto to Tomaj's andante, and today he was wound up like a mechanical novelty chicken. As soon as Tomaj was sitting, Max began patting himself down until finally he reached into his breast pocket and pulled out a small lavender cut-glass amphora, which he set on the table between them.

'Is there a genie in it?' Tomaj quipped, but Max's brows were knitted with affected care. His voice dropped half an octave.

'I was surprised to get a message from C. I thought it was all over between us. Would you like to explain to me why it is you want my help so badly?'

That was not a question he was able to answer, and anyway he'd be damned if he let Max take control of the tempo of this conversation. Tomaj let his eyes unfocus, picking up a water glass to buy time and gazing at the jumbled silvery light and haunt-green glisten of lime captured in the brown circle of his hand. He let his gaze rove until it fixed on the air beyond their table, where a dense column of sunlight angled into the restaurant, mead-yellow and salted with rising motes of dust. He tried to pick out one speck of dust and follow its progress – Brownian motion it was called, he remembered – but to him the patterns were slippery like cartoon characters and less readable, and every time he managed to track one flake of skin or hair or whatever dust really was, it vanished to be replaced by others, which danced in its place the way a sympathetic crowd gathers to hide a fugitive from pursuers. Now you see it; now you don't.

'You don't need to know why,' Tomaj said finally, wishing C would show up.

Max's eyes were very pale. He indicated the glass jar. 'I suppose you think I'm the bad guy just because I interfered with Adrien.'

Tomaj had never been more clueless, but he reminded himself that Max had no way of knowing C wasn't with him right now, so if he relaxed and took his time he might still be able to pull this off. He raised one eyebrow in a practiced manner and did not look at the amphora.

'I'm not thrilled about it. About what you did to Adrien. But I try to keep an open mind.'

Max shifted severally in his seat, a wooden marionette with too many conflicting strings. 'You must understand that there is more to this story than you know. I have many things to protect, and Adrien is an amateur. Don't judge me yet.'

C limped into his mind and hovered there for a moment. He reached out for the Watcher, felt it struggle to focus ... and then everything he should do and say became suddenly clear.

'I strongly suspect, Max, that you and your people don't understand this plant. I don't think you even know whether it works.'

A look of alertness came over Max. 'I'm sure we can agree that the Deep is a bit of a no-man's land. Even I don't know *everything* that happens in it – if I did, there's no way you'd have gotten within a hundred miles of something like I.'

'You had no right to interfere.'

'On the contrary. It's my job to protect the interests of the Deep. It is not in our interest to have I floating around out of control, and if there's a leak in the Deep letting tech like this get out, why of course I'm going to plug it. End of that story.'

'You admit, then,' Tomaj asked for himself, caught up in things, 'that you didn't have control of I from the beginning?'

Max laughed. 'Do you want to play with me, or do you want to do business?'

C clamped down on Tomaj and said tersely, 'I want the prototype. I'll pay.'

Max waved this aside. 'If you would ... volunteer ... what you know about this *Nikolai*, I might be in a position to give you a piece of the game.'

C was incredibly happy at this. Something about the fact that Max didn't know everything about Nikolai set C all alight.

'You were wise, of course, to keep Adrien ignorant,' Max continued. 'I could have cracked him like an egg. But we're wasting our energies. Let's be on the same side, C. I can cut you in on the profits, provided you tell me the source of **I**.'

'I'm not interested in the profits. I just want the prototype.'

'Don't be absurd. If **I** does what the specs say it does—'

'—we could sell it to every world leader on the planet provided we could build enough of them. Starting with someplace like – I don't know. India? Anyway, assassination would become a thing of the past. We could tap the same market as cryogenics if we could get the cost down. And what about you, Max, and your army? You could have more than a bunch of tin soldiers going around believing your philosophy. You could have *yourself*, multiplied, for ever after ... I guess you've thought of that, too?'

Max's eyes sparkled. 'That's only the beginning, angel. When I think of the impli—'

'I don't want to discuss that now,' C cut him off in Tomaj's deep voice. Tomaj was disappointed because **I** was sounding pretty fucking intense ... 'I'm only interested in the prototype.'

'But why? What good is it to you – unless you intend to poach the design from me, and I know you're too smart to try to do that, because you know I'd have to hunt you down wherever you are and have you and all your loved ones killed—'

He paused for breath and in Tomaj's voice C said, 'It's nothing like that. It's a matter of *mortality*. My own. Max, do I have to spell it out for you? I *need* it.'

'Whoa, mama!' Max cried and shot back in his seat. 'This changes things considerably.'

Tomaj had the feeling of being in a room with people who are sharing an inside joke. What did C mean about its own mortality? It always made him uneasy to dwell on the idea that C was actually some grubby *person* in a room somewhere, like the funny little wizard behind the curtains of the Emerald City.

Max produced some papers and passed them across to Tomaj. They were mostly technical diagrams. C scanned them rapidly.

In a calm tone Tomaj continued. 'I will provide the test subject. You'll have supervised access to the results. But you must agree to keep this quiet.'

Max nodded. 'Naturally. Others know we've quarrelled, but not why.'

'I'd like to keep it that way. Have you discovered how the thing works?' C used Tomaj's eyes on Max, knowing that they were soft and deep and could inspire confession even in enemies.

The waiter came over and stood there.

'Coffee,' Tomaj said without moving his eyes.

Max proceeded to interrogate the waiter about various dishes, all the while engaged in ritual staring with Tomaj. The Russian was visibly excited by what C had said about mortality, whereas Tomaj was still confused and therefore a little bored; but Tomaj also knew better than to break off the contest as this was all part of Max's schtick. So he leaned forward, staring soulfully into Max's face.

'Would you like me to fuck you, Max?'

'I can come back,' suggested the waiter.

Max cleared his throat. 'Bring me the egg thing.'

'By which you mean the Spanish omelette, sir?'

'Because it can be arranged.' Tomaj put his hands on the

table. He could grip one of these plates in his open palm, but he simply ran a forefinger over one of Max's forks.

Max was blushing, but he returned the gaze. 'The omelette, yeah, whatever.'

'That comes with—'

'He doesn't care what it comes with,' Tomaj said. 'He's too busy worrying about my cock.'

The waiter faded away.

Max was crumbling. Tomaj twitched his lips just a shade to finish off his opponent, who cracked a smile, then began to chuckle, and finally laughed so hard he was sobbing. Tomaj sat back in his seat and pretended not to know this person.

'OK, OK,' Max said, waving a hand in front of his face to cover his tears. 'Have I discovered how it works? I don't *quite* get it yet. But I'm working on it.'

C was extremely pleased at this news, although Tomaj couldn't imagine why. A second later, Max was all business, wiping his eyes and leaning forward to disseminate his private reek over the table.

'Tomaj, mon homme, this is a very special piece of machinery. It's several levels beyond anything that the—' he grinned, showing fangs, and whispered, '—*Americans* have thought of. It's a breakthrough. Way ahead of its time. But this deal is strictly between friends.'

Tomaj blinked slowly and listened to C's words spilling out of his mouth. 'Twenty-two million dollars between friends. Yes, it's a good thing we're not enemies.' He leaned back while coffee was poured and waited for the server to leave.

'You know as well as I do that this is pocket change compared to what this is worth when it hits the market. I'm helping you out, my love.'

Tomaj moved over in his own head to let C work. '*My love*, under the circumstances you should be paying us.'

'Hah! What a funny thought. You could have a point. Adrien comes bumbling around Moscow thinking he's

85

some kind of spy, flushes out Nikolai who up until now has been a total mystery, and then provides an evening's entertainment for Boris and me. Adrien makes me laugh. You're lucky I didn't kill him and rip out his hardware.'

'If you had, you'd get a personalized bomb from me – not an ax card.'

As Tomaj spoke he took the card out of his pocket and flipped it onto the table. While Max plugged it into his portable and checked the figures, Tomaj continued.

'Surely you've noticed that the interface on the plant has been custom-designed. We can quibble until the cows come home about whether Adrien stole it or had a right to it, but the fact is, I commissioned that piece of machinery and it's been built for *me*. How handy for you that I'm going to be available to test it for you.'

'Maybe so, but there is much to be managed during the course of the launch. You'll need a lot of help, especially in the beginning.'

'I suppose you'll be just the person to supply that help,' C said acidly.

'Now, now, don't be bitter. You're lucky I'm still willing to do business with you, considering how you dissed me going into the Deep behind my back.'

'You killed Nikolai, didn't you?'

'Now why would I do a thing like that? Nikolai is my link to the process by which I was designed. He simply didn't realize the complexities involved in marketing, distribution. And of course, security. Now, we will be a great team.'

Hollow words; terrible words coming from Max. Tomaj might not know what Max was talking about, but it was obvious that C didn't like the idea of Nikolai and Max working together. For his own part, Tomaj didn't feel entirely clear about what it meant to steal from the Deep. After all, the Deep wasn't a person, and it wasn't organized in any official sense. All of the HIT users who interacted through the Deep were anonymous, and they shared cognitive 'space' – therefore how could they believe in the concept of property?

Yet if there were profits to be had, Max Niagarin could find a way to catch lightning in a bottle. He went on, grooming his eyebrows as he spoke: the gesture gave him a vaguely aristocratic air at odds with the rest of his appearance.

'Consider what would have happened if you had used Nikolai for this. Do you think Nikolai is prepared to give you medical backup, psychometric assessment – a shoulder to cry on when things are going wrong?'

'Ah-hah. And what, in your estimation, is likely to go wrong?' There was an air of affront in C's mental tone, but Tomaj didn't allow it to be projected because he knew Max would pounce on any sign of offense. This whole conversation would be a lot easier if C would let him in on the nature of I. C had always been furtive about HIT transactions, but this was ridiculous. World leaders? Assassinations?

'These things are always buggy,' Max said vaguely. The food had arrived and Max began cutting his up into small identical pieces.

'The point is, I'll be there to supervise the situation. I'll be available.' He chewed and swallowed with the speed of a rodent. 'I'm putting all other matters aside to be there for you, sweetie. You know in the end I'm just a regular guy, and I want to see us all come through this together.'

All this with a straight face. Tomaj wondered if Max really believed he *was* a regular guy: he had done everything possible to eradicate his accent, he had smoothed his uneven features surgically, and he succumbed to every fad and fashion to hit the streets in a vain attempt to fit in. Poor Max. He had a dime, he wanted to dance, but he'd step on your toes every time. Right now he was fiddling with the amphora, which looked more like one of those junky old perfume bottles you could get at any weekend antiques fair in Westchester than an eight-figure piece of gray-market HIT.

'OK, I'm going to make this totally clear, Max. You are *not* going to be there. Once I have the plant, it belongs to me. The subject will be made available to you for testing on a *controlled basis*. This is not your pony show, Max, so don't get carried away.'

Max looked at his food for a long moment. He adopted an ultra-polite tone; Tomaj recognized it as a sign of Max at his most dangerous.

'This test is of no use to me if I can't determine how effective the plant is. Therefore, I'm going to need a free hand with the subject.'

Tomaj pronounced every word carefully. 'You can't have a free hand. You're going to turn over the instructions to the surgeon, the specs, *everything* we need to make this fly.'

Max sighed. 'Don't be ridiculous. If I give you documentation, design specs, all that kind of crap, you'll have almost as much information as I do. You'll as good as own the rights to the thing and, let me tell you, if you want the rights well, they're not for sale.'

'Then I'll just take the plant. We'll go this alone.'

Max emitted a cackle and threw his fork down.

'Forget it!' he snapped, anger replacing laughter like a flash flood. 'You're playing my game, or staying home.'

Tomaj gripped the table with both hands, wanting to break it in two and then do the same to Max.

'OK, here's my final offer,' Max said. 'Your doctor gets enough information to do a successful transfer from the, ah, source, to the plant. The plant is then delivered to me. I handle putting the plant into the receptacle. You get no specs, nothing like that, because this is a one-time deal. After the surgery, the receptacle will be returned to you and I'll fade graciously away. This way, C gets to retain anonymity, but I get to know who the subject is, so that I can pursue contact afterward. For the purposes of assessing the efficacy of the transfer, you understand.'

'The subject does not belong to you. I'll give you temporary, limited access. That's all you need.'

An instant later, C was gone, leaving Tomaj to wonder what had just been promised. He had just participated in a huge transaction on C's behalf without understanding what it all meant. Twenty-two million dollars for a prototype plant? Was C mad?

Max had taken out a pen and was scribbling a note to himself on the back of a twenty-dollar bill.

'I have a meeting with AT&T,' he sang, glancing at his watch. 'They want a new spin on the Rosicrucian thing. Got to think of an idea in the cab.'

In another minute he would snap his fingers for the check and be gone. Tomaj thought it was ridiculous that Max didn't hire someone to run around to meetings making pitches; even more ridiculous that he even bothered with the Deep when he made so much money off big corporations – not to mention churches. He found Max fascinating – albeit in the same way as a freeway accident – and he wished he could grasp some understanding of what was happening between the Russian and C.

Tomaj picked up the bottle and held it up to the light. There was a tiny scrawl of opacity floating in liquid.

'I'm sure this will all work out beautifully,' Max was saying, smiling blandly at him and reaching across the table to shake hands.

Tomaj heard the difference in his own voice now that it was just him alone, without C.

'But Max, what the hell *is* this?'

Max drummed his fingers on the tabletop. He obviously sensed the change, too.

'If C hasn't told you, why should I?'

'But it's a plant, right? You're selling a new plant for C to test and you're making us pay in eight figures and you've nearly killed Adrien in the bargain.'

Max grinned. 'C wants to buy it. Ask for yourself.'

He didn't like the look on Max's face.

'I'm not testing it, Max. Whatever it is, I'm not doing it.'

Max batted his eyelashes mockingly. 'Who asked you to test it? You're just the messenger. We don't kill the messenger. This is a civilized business – hell, we're creating a meta-civilization here. Relax. I'm going to be there to take care of everything.' As if that was supposed to be reassuring.

Outside, Tomaj's fingers slipped inside his coat pocket to caress the vial with its minute, semi-organic contents. They parted on the sidewalk; Max grabbed his hand and stood uncharacteristically still looking up at Tomaj for several seconds. Tomaj realized with a shock that the other man had to be well over forty, but until his face stopped moving and gravity overtook his flesh, it was impossible to tell. He seemed about to say something difficult, but at the last second he gave Tomaj's hand a hard squeeze and winked.

'Tell C I'll be saying a prayer. And take care of yourself, kid.'

Then he stood on tiptoe, pecked Tomaj on the cheek with a strangely asexual gusto, and turned away in a garish swirl of color. Tomaj stood staring after him like a lovestruck 1950s debutante, one hand pressed in astonishment to his cheek. He shook his head in denial at the thought: had Max dashed away a tear as he left?

No. Couldn't be.

* * *

Soon it will end – or begin – and then what? What lies over the rainbow for me?

I've been in this particular room for years. Today, of course, most everything in it is 'smart'. The bed adjusts to a variety of positions from which I may choose how best to manipulate this wasteland they persist in calling my body. I can crank its legs up and down individually making a mocking can-can in sluggish underwater time. Using the computer system that's linked to my brain implants I can activate electronic sensors and stimulate whole muscle groups to move in synchrony, causing the legs to flex, the arms and hands to rise in a bizarre, totemic skyshow against what I am told is a bright park view from my windows. Binocular fetishists must take me for a mummy from a 1940s horror movie. That's about how I feel. The computer-driven exercises are futile: they can't return to me the control of my own muscles, much less my own eyes and ears. They can't bring me dignity. I've 'seen' digitized images of myself and I look like roadkill.

Losing Adrien has hit me hard – a high price to pay for I. Everything seems so clear and cold now: so inevitable. I wonder how I can find the strength to go on with this: I'm an aberration, a mathematical oddity. Here in me science falls sobbing on its knees for all it cannot achieve. The straight lines, the prevalence of plastic, the military discipline & *de rigueur* cleanliness, all these form a mere mask for the helplessness with which my people confront disease. Bring me your powders, your ritual fires, your piercèd tongues and headless chickens. For in this way I can pretend at least to be more than a tangle of damp wires.

I fear that one morning in the unspecified past, they unwittingly sucked my spirit out through a catheter and disposed of it.

Nine

The city was bathed in night as the jet came down. Sabina put her hands on her knees because the man next to her was using the armrest. Her fingers crabbed sideways across the arcs of her legs, describing a snatch of a Mozart étude that would not sound in her head no matter how many times she feigned playing it. She was bored. It was ironic that technology could have rendered the action of travelling so passive, such that the definition of making a journey could consist of sitting still and listening to yourself fret. It was like some perversion of Zen.

In her spine, in the grottoes between vertebrae, fragments of desperation whispered obsessively: *this is it this is it this is it.* This is it: compose *now*, produce *now*, or give it up. She had paid rent on her rooms with the last of her money; the selling price of her car had bought drinks for friends on her last night in Zagreb. If she didn't return from New York with something she could use, she would have to sell her equipment and admit that her grand experiment had failed. Leaving University, eschewing work – scorning the middle-class life she was meant to have in hope of finding *something else*, some who-knows-what – all would have come to one more foolishness on her life's list of fuckups.

Adrien's American money swelled her wallet. The plane was landing. She couldn't see how she would ever fulfill the model of the true composer. She could have cashed in the ticket and bought herself a few more months in the studio – surely a real artist would have ruthlessly exploited any such resource in order to push on with the work – but instead she'd come here. The time she'd spent with Adrien had created a window into some unexplored place, a window she could scarcely fail to look out of. And maybe she hoped – but no. It was not a good idea to juxtapose hope with Adrien.

She collected one suitcase and waited at customs, unconsciously grinding her teeth at each delay. His note had charmed her, the burn mark on her arm had healed, and she'd had time to be alone with herself and the inadequacy of the work she'd been doing lately. What was composing experimental music when people like Adrien were experimenting with their lives, with themselves? She recalled the way they had succeeded in exasperating one another – frightening one another, even – and wanted that again.

Outside customs her stomach tightened with anticipation. She scanned the thicket of signs held by yawning hired drivers in dark uniforms and didn't see the unmistakable white head. She felt a pang of worry: Adrien hadn't responded to her phone message by the time she'd left Zagreb, nor had he ever communicated an address to her. She'd simply assumed that, after all the money he'd spent, after his pleas, he would show up to meet her plane.

'Sabina?'

The man who addressed her looked like a basketball player. He was smiling down on her, holding out an enormous hand.

'*Hi*, you're Sabina right? I'm Tomaj. I've been picking up Adrien's messages and I got yours the other day. I figured I'd better come get you, since Adrien's not around right now. Wires must have gotten crossed, huh?'

She took his hand, a little embarrassed because he radiated a kind of kinetic electricity, like a cartoon jumping off the page into 3-D.

'I guess, well … I don't know. You are Adrien's friend?' She had the impression that people were looking at them, but couldn't take her eyes away from him to confirm it.

'Yeah, we work together, he told me you might be coming,' he said easily. 'Asked me to keep an eye out for you. Something urgent came up just the other day, so he

93

had to leave town. He had no way of contacting you – I guess you don't have a phone?'

'What? No. No, I don't.'

He had appropriated her bags and was steering her toward the exit.

'Look, this is really awkward,' he confided. 'If I know Adrien there's probably a lot he hasn't told you. He doesn't mean to be a shithead you know what I'm saying but he's been going through some like *changes* lately. I'm sure you must have noticed that he was working on some things when you met him.'

The sliding glass doors released them into warm night. His smile was conspiratorial, and colored lights gleamed on his dark skin like reflections on water.

'Where is Adrien now?'

He opened the cab door for her. 'Hawaii.'

She paused half crouched with one foot in the cab, stilled by surprise, then sank down resignedly. He slammed the door and skipped around to the other side.

'Not to worry,' Tomaj said as the car started forward. 'He won't be gone long. In the meanwhile, you can stay at his place. And I'll be at your service for sightseeing.'

'Sightseeing?' She was looking out the window at the flat blur of lights. 'OK, I guess. But I don't want to stay at his place. I'm not his … his, you know, possession.'

'I'll take you to a hotel, then. Or you can stay with me. You'd be welcome, there's plenty of room, although if I were in your position I might not feel comfortable with a stranger.'

What a voice this Tomaj had. His speech was protean, slipping effortlessly across cultural barriers almost from one phrase to the next, a slinky bass following its own deep groove going whoknowswhere. She was listening so intently to its shifting tones that it took a few seconds for the words to catch in her mind, and by then she had lost the sense of whether he was propositioning her or not, so she said, 'For tonight, I think, hotel will be fine. You must go to work in morning, right?'

'Actually, I'm just going down to Soho to look at some junk. You're welcome to tag along if you like. Or I can show you around somewhere else. Or not. Feel free to ditch me at any time.' He displayed a regal profile.

'Are you an actor?' she blurted, seeking some distance from which to establish a perspective on him.

A sad smile, lines in the forehead deepening, bittersweet ...

'I used to be,' he said after a minute. 'The world isn't ready for me.'

'What do you do now? You said you work with Adrien.'

'In a manner of speaking, yeah. I'm a collector.'

'Collector? Of what?'

'Obsolescence.'

'I'm sorry, I don't understand.'

Tomaj said nothing. She thought he was silently laughing at her because she didn't know the word, but couldn't be certain.

'Is Adrien ... is he collector too?'

A slow smile. In fact Tomaj seemed to have coined a whole language of smiles. She felt herself warming to him in spite of herself.

'Adrien – well, Adrien is something else, isn't he? How well do you actually *know* him, Sabina?' He inclined toward her, subjecting her to the full weight of his eyes, and she realized she was enjoying the sensation. Then, even as she began to relax and play along, something happened. It happened so fast she could scarcely register the event. It was as if a demon hidden in the interstices of his bones, tendons, and humors suddenly strobed out at her and then retreated. It had no shape or size, but it possessed a purity of intention that was terrifying. She felt its desire like the following moon that sailed outside the cab window, but by the time her body reacted, heart thrumming and adrenaline crackling beneath her skin, the moment was gone.

Tomaj was beginning to look puzzled that she had not responded to his question. He seemed unaware that anything had occurred. Fear crawled in her throat.

'Is none of your fucking business,' she spat, her accent thickening.

'Ooh …' He leaned back exaggeratedly, his head scraping the ceiling of the cab.

'I didn't come here for this,' she said, turning away and pretending to be offended so as to cover her anxiety. She leaned forward and tapped on the bulletproof glass.

'No, no!' He spread all ten fingers to ward off her action. He looked stricken. If he was dissembling, his gaze didn't waver when she challenged it. She was confused.

'I didn't mean any disrespect, Sabina – it was a simple question. You don't have to talk about your relationship with Adrien if you don't want to. Anyway, what were we saying – you were asking me something.'

She leaned her forehead against the murky Plexiglas.

'Never mind.'

Tomaj shifted in his seat. 'Is Adrien a collector, right? That what you want to know? Well, I'd like to explain about Adrien but there are some things that I think he needs to tell you himself. It wouldn't be right for me to say.'

'I see.'

'No, you don't. But you don't have to, not yet. I'm on your side, after all,' he added cryptically.

'My side?' she bristled. 'How do you know I have side?'

'I'm not trying to insult you, baby. Lighten up! No need to be so nervous. We're all friends here. Want to go to dinner?'

She turned to face him but didn't look at his eyes when she spoke. 'Tomaj. Is that your name? Tomaj. I have been flying all day. I'm very tired.' She reached forward again and banged on the glass. 'I get out now,' she called.

The driver turned his head marginally and said, 'No fucking way.'

Tomaj began to laugh. 'You can't get out here, we're on

the expressway. Just calm down, Sabina. I'm sorry you're stuck with me instead of Adrien, but if you'd just give me a chance you'll see I'm not so bad. I've known Adrien a long time, and he'd kill me if I let anything happen to you. Look, let me take you to dinner and then we'll get you set at a good hotel and we'll call Adrien up, OK?'

She made herself look at him again. His expression was genial, open: typical American bonhomie. She wondered what the other thing was, the thing inside him that couldn't be seen now that it had turned sideways against the light but was presumably still there, waiting. She wavered. Whatever she had seen in Tomaj was intangible and alien: but no less real for all that. Was she not now feeling just a touch of what she'd felt when Adrien opened his eyes inside her and came? Had she not already run away from this feeling once, only to sidle back, strangely thrilled, later?

She told herself she was curiosity's kitten. She told herself it was casual.

He took her to a place in the East Village with a garden courtyard whose trees were still strung with white Christmas lights from last year. He told her about New York: what to see, what to avoid. She relaxed a notch or two. They ate. Near the end of the meal he put both elbows on the small table to command her attention. The table tipped toward him and the wine spilled; she caught at the bottle, laughing.

'OK, listen,' Tomaj said. 'I can see there's gonna be like a subtext here, which is that you want to know all the shit about Adrien. And believe me, I know it all. But guess what? I'm not going to tell you. So, the way I see it, you've got two choices. You can go to a hotel and play tourist and wait for him to get back, which should be in a few days. Hopefully he'll still want you for his girlfriend, but you never can tell with Adrien. Or, you can hang with me until then and you'll find out some interesting stuff. But I'm not going to give away Adrien's secrets. I want to be straight with you there.'

'Fine.'

'I mean, I know he's a mysterious guy. I know you must be wondering—'

'Don't strain yourself. I got free ticket to New York. Adrien is not so mysterious.'

'Good! Then we understand one another.'

'I understand you.' She stared right back at him, bluffing for all she was worth.

'So, no more questions about Adrien?'

'Tomaj, what is it with you and rules? Stop making rules for me. It's silly little game.'

'I just want to know where we both stand.'

'Why? We are strangers. What is your rushing to understand me?'

He shrugged. 'I'm curious. You came all the way here from Croatia. Adrien must be cats and dogs for you – he's not usually much for relationships.'

'That's enough for you to know. Stop assuming about me. You don't know me at all. I'm not what you think I am.'

Tomaj took a cocktail napkin and started folding it into the shape of an elephant, looking contrite.

'How old are you?'

She smiled. 'How old do you think?'

'Now who's playing games? Well, I'm thirty-eight. I've been an actor, a gym teacher, a model, and …' he laughed. 'My current occupation.'

'I'm twenty-four.' She glanced at her hands, realized she was shy and off-balance again, and then rallied, making herself look him in the eye. 'I know what your occupation is. Or I can guess. You don't have to make up stories.'

'Whatever.' Suddenly he was looking for the waiter, sitting back and drumming his hands on the table. She persisted.

'I think it is interesting. Don't get me wrong. I just don't see why is such big secret. OK, is illegal, but so are drugs and everybody talks about drugs. Your job, I think it's not so incredible.'

He let out a startled laugh. 'Yeah? Well, I used to think that about sex, like when I was about eight years old.'

Their eyes hooked on that one – she built an image of the two of them in a tangle, trying it on for size—

Tomaj cleared his throat politely. 'There's something I usually like to get out of the way before it can become an issue. Namely, I don't have sex with women.'

She felt herself blush and was annoyed.

'Come on,' he said in a cajoling tone. 'It's still early. Come back for coffee and if you don't fall in love with my apartment I'll escort you personally to the hotel of your choice where you can pay through the nose for the privilege of being treated with indifference.'

As the night went on it was getting easier and easier to accept Tomaj's offers. They rode the train uptown. She liked the subway and the scruffy streets because they were such an unapologetic mess, and she felt the pin fall out that had been holding some emotional fold in check since that scary interlude in the cab. The more she studied Tomaj, the more he seemed to wear Manhattan as a mantle, a crazy quilt of air stone noise dirt people. Especially people. He was on good terms with kids evading citywide curfew, which was more than could be said for anyone else. By the time they got to his apartment, she was beginning to feel like a guest on a tv show hosted by Tomaj.

They stepped off the elevator straight into a living room the size of a cornfield but with the topography of a teenager's never-cleaned closet. In the distance she glimpsed plate-glass windows overlooking the river and the lights of mid-town. A kitchen counter had been erected somewhere on the periphery almost as an afterthought, but otherwise nothing about the place said 'apartment' so much as 'warehouse'.

'It's a little crowded right now,' Tomaj said, 'because I'm still looking for the right space for my museum.'

'Er ... what?'

'It's obsolete stuff. My museum of obsolescence will have only things that are no longer fashionable. In a big way. Actually, my favorites are things that never even caught on. Alternate pasts, you might say. Pasts we don't even remember having. But those are harder to come by. The artifacts get erased if you don't watch closely. Go on, walk around. Touch anything you want. It ain't fragile.'

She drifted through the room, identifying and sometimes puzzling over the objects. It was true that they had nothing in common except for the fact that they were useless. She found herself gravitating to the items she actually recognized. She blew dust off a row of blue-haired trolls sitting on a mechanical bull, jumped when a man-sized Rodan chuckled at her, and squinted futilely at a magic eye poster. Several mannequins an inversion boot rack a Commodore 64 and an entire Le Car (sans engine) later she found herself at the windows. She gazed out on the lights while Tomaj rummaged in the kitchen. A *c.* 1973 ochre refrigerator gurgled sententiously into action.

'What got you started on this?'

'I love fads. I love things that are displaced in time.'

'I've never seen ...' She fell silent. It was occurring to her that in Zagreb she had felt like some kind of freak, but here in New York she was going to have to work quite hard to distinguish herself from even the average lunatic.

'When I was growing up,' Tomaj intoned richly, 'in school we used to do projects about the future. Humans were running out of space. We probably couldn't colonize other planets yet, but in the year 2000 where would we be living?'

She pressed one finger to her lower lip and smiled slightly at the concept of Tomaj at grade school.

'I'm serious! You should have seen it. We would make these dioramas, these things in shoeboxes, of undersea

100

installations, and space stations. "Life on the Moon" we'd call it. Humans would live in these cute little bubbles under the ocean with Barbie furniture and pet octopuses. Whenever I think about the future – which is now of course the present – that's what I think.'

He was making coffee, struggling with the golden innards of some pre-Vietnam electric percolator while over his head throbbed organites, an already moribund fad (Tomaj would explain later) that in California had been briefly as popular as lava lamps, and later as reviled. She gazed at the phosphorescent glow of the biological material hanging in breast-implant pouches as it played over the surface of Tomaj's head and wondered if he was having her on.

'Of course, none of that future-stuff happened,' he said eventually. 'In our present, which was my future, there's nowhere to go but in. To colonize each other.'

He rammed the lid down on the coffee pot and gestured around the room with a spoon. 'Anyway, maybe that explains my hobby. Then again, maybe it doesn't.'

He stood still while the coffee perked, eyes lowered. He was up to something.

'Tell me about Adrien,' she said. 'I mean not HIT. You know. As the person.'

'What do you want to know?'

'Like, what music does he like? What books does he read?'

'Honey, when you've got a body as lyrical as that you don't need to read *books*. You don't need to think.'

'Are you saying he's stupid?'

'I'm saying, I understand why you're attracted to him. That's no mystery. But something tells me he isn't a match for you, intellectually.' There was a trace of cattiness in his voice.

'Is Adrien gay?'

'Don't be absurd. How do you take your coffee?'

'Black. Actually.'

'So you came here to compose. For inspiration. Did you

101

bring any of your work with you? Maybe you're looking for a sponsor?'

She took the coffee and laughed.

'Tomaj, my music is not obsolete. Yet. I hope.'

'Can I hear some?'

'There are some discs in my bag. But—'

'But what?'

'Nothing. It's funny. I'm shy about playing for people, that's all.'

Tomaj said, 'I guess it's like being a trans. Like being naked.'

There it was again. Just like that moment in the taxi: something of Tomaj changed, so fast that her perception of it was almost subliminal.

'What just happened to you?'

Tomaj pulled thoughtfully on his lip. 'If you're talking about what I think you're talking about, the correct answer would be C. My Watcher. Just a little glitch in the connection.'

'But ... what is a Watcher?'

'A Watcher has a special plant that links them to a mainline with software coded to people like me and Adrien.'

'So ... it's a person, right?'

'Yeah, just a regular person with a lot of money. Why – did it scare you?'

There was a silence.

'No,' she lied.

That night she slept on a pre-WWII couch that engulfed her in its swerves and arches. She dreamed about white things: sheep, or maybe the soft and creepy rush of angel wings. In her sleep Tomaj's voice said, *nowhere to go but in. To colonize each other.*

Ten

Normally Tomaj would use a direct feed to listen to music, but Sabina's recordings were on disc. If he put the headphones on, people wouldn't take it amiss if he moved or twitched or closed his eyes on the subway. Whereas without the headphones, he might appear to be having a seizure. So he left her sleeping and made for the street market, surrendering his listening powers to C, who was intensely interested in hearing the Croatian's music. C had not missed a single beat of the evening before. Except for a couple of brief flares, the Watcher's presence had been so subtle that he had noticed it only because his senses had been tuned to an extraordinary clarity, indicating that C was drinking up every nuance of Sabina, physical and otherwise. Now the Watcher rode downtown with him, making him close his eyes and surrender completely to the sound coming through the headphones.

Then, when it was over, C said, *I need for you to give it up*, and he did because it was nothing to him; so afterward he couldn't recall a single tone. He wondered what he would tell Sabina when she asked him what he thought, and then remembered that C would probably have a ready answer in such a case.

In the street market, as always, looking at the junk was only an excuse to enjoy the people. He devoured people like food, did Tomaj: this sallow old lady with the big nose and the crêpe-paper voice, that fat boy shuffling basketball cards and sniffling, the bevy of tourists from Maine that blinked in unexpected sunlight. He preferred his people to be somewhat ugly. Modelling had ruined him for beautiful people; he could no longer tell them apart. So as he was

103

picking up some Nigerian candlesticks and flipping through the jazz cassettes melting in the sun, he also dragged people into his mind as if with a seine, to remember them later, to invoke them when the Watcher left him alone and his soul echoed with abandonment. He took them like potato chips. He would never get enough. He would never get enough of human beings, but he would never look at them straight on: always he would absorb them with his peripheral vision; always he would speak over their voices and suck their voices in at the same time with a separate part of his mind that he had trained to do this. In this way he might possess them without ever confronting them. None of them ever noticed him doing it, but he knew when he had them. He knew. So what if his foraging was no longer a part of acting: so what if he was no longer scavenging for character material? It didn't matter. C wanted everything, and he wanted to give everything he could, and take it all back again refracted by the elegiac waters of C's mind.

In the end he bought nothing, but he stole the smile from a very old Haitian man sitting on a folding chair smoking a pipe. That smile tasted like hibiscus and love, and it belonged to him now.

* * *

Sabina's music is full of subterfuge. She uses computers and digital effects to build a maze of walls between herself and her audience. I use Tomaj to listen to her work. In my judgment, it's as if she is saying, 'Let me make something as abstract as I can; let me be deliberately obscure, so that I can speak without being heard, show myself without being seen – exist without existing. Let me fail as an artist if that is the sacrifice I must make so that the wire between singer and listener is never set alight. Let me frustrate by my absence. I am not here! I am not here!'

She comes close to achieving her perverse goal: she is no

slouch as a composer, and music is the closest thing to an expression of the bodiless as can be achieved in art. Yet all music relies on breath and heartbeat to make itself intelligible to people. Deep within musical conventions are the limitations created by the physical substrata: we resonate to that which calls up the old tides of blood. Sabina can no more escape this than she can escape being human. However hard she works to abstract herself from herself, her sound is rooted in her body. And her music – the music she is so ambivalent about allowing anyone to hear – is all about negative space: silence, privation, and terror.

How well I know her already.

She wants to go away from herself: far far away from her body, her past, her knowledge of death. And at the same time, paradoxically, she wants to go to a neverland where the extreme edge of human madness can be rendered safe so she can touch it, eat it, explore it: conquer it. She wants to understand the wind that blows us out of the world.

I could take her further from herself than she's ever gone.

And she's curious about me. She doesn't know it, but she has touched me through the membrane of Adrien and we have both come away sticky, stamped with one another's scent like a promise whispered in darkness.

* * *

Sabina sat on Tomaj's kitchen counter and ate purple cereal out of a plastic bowl shaped like a canoe. She had resolved not to think about Adrien, but to enjoy being in a situation where she had no idea what might happen next. It was a relief not to be in Zagreb, anyway, obsessing over her music or lack thereof; and although some strange things had been said after a few bottles of wine last night, she was looking forward to getting to know Tomaj better. In the afternoon he returned from wherever he'd been, full of energy.

'Come on,' he said. 'I have to meet someone and, now that I think about it, you might like to meet her, too.'

They took a taxi to the Upper East Side. Tomaj said, 'If you're at all interested in the artistic applications of HIT, Audra is a good person to know. She's a doctor who specializes in using licensed HIT to work with neurologically damaged patients.'

'Licensed HIT. You mean she's not...?'

'A trans like me? No.' He laughed. 'She's got some fancy chair at Mount Sinai and she works part-time at a clinic. I've only talked with her a few times, but she's so smart she scares me.'

The cab let them off in the mid-seventies, and they walked to the brownstone where Tomaj said Audra lived. Two golden retrievers hurled themselves at the door when they rang the bell, and a plump, middle-aged woman hollered at the animals as she let them in through a flurry of tails and paws. She led Sabina into a small study overlooking the garden, ordering her to sit and wait for a minute while she and Tomaj did some business. Sabina played with the dogs, aware of the sound of their voices from the front of the house, and eventually they joined her, the doctor stuffing some papers back into the padded envelope that Tomaj had brought with him. She tossed the envelope in a desk drawer and offered refreshments.

'We can't stay,' Tomaj answered. 'I just wanted Sabina to meet you. She's visiting from Zagreb, and she's become interested in the applications of HIT for music. You know a lot more about it than I do.'

'Have you ever had a plant?' the doctor asked bluntly. Dark eyes scrutinized her as if she were some small animal in a cage.

Sabina shook her head, glancing at Tomaj in surprise. This doctor was supposed to be a *licensed* user ...

Audra laughed. 'What's a nice, upstanding citizen like me doing associating with a character like Tomaj, right? Well, we get a lot of our best innovations from the gray market. I can't conduct this sort of a conversation from my office, but I see nothing wrong with a free exchange of information outside of a strictly professional context. So – you've never had a plant. You're thinking you'd like to try one but you don't want to make a major commitment. Right?'

'Something like that.'

'What about wires? Do you use?'

'I'm not interested in canned experience.'

In her peripheral vision she saw Tomaj smile and then abruptly school his expression.

'Hmm. And you're a musician, I take it? Well, there's a big difference between forming a concept in theoretical terms – that is, *imagining* what it would be like to use a direct feed to make music – and empirical terms, which would be actually *doing* it. Personally, I'm an empiricist, and I believe in getting your hands dirty – but I also understand that the idea of surgical intervention makes people nervous.'

Sabina shifted in her seat. 'I don't know if you understand. I don't care so much about composing music straight from my brain – I mean, I don't have the problems getting a sound out of my mind and playing it. Tomaj, maybe I don't make myself so clear to you. I would like to use HIT to do things that are impossible without HIT.'

Audra leaned forward across the desk, cushioning her plump cheeks in both fists. She and Tomaj exchanged glances.

'Like what?'

'Like … be with someone else, in mind.'

'Telepathy, everybody's favorite party trick—'

'Not the simple guessing thoughts. Total empathy.'

Sabina had a feeling she was sitting across from a snake, which was strange considering she'd never seen a fat snake. The doctor sniffed.

'That's a serious business. It's very dangerous – very difficult. The technology is there, but not many people can do it. Tell her, Tomaj.'

Tomaj tried to hide a smile unsuccessfully. 'It's not easy

being Watched,' he conceded. 'And that's not anything like *total* empathy. I don't think I could handle that, and neither could you.' He looked at Sabina, who swallowed.

'Total empathy,' Audra said cautiously, 'would be more like being a Watcher, because you're on the receiving end of someone else's experiences. It's expensive to be a Watcher, and it takes balls. That's not my game – there are people Tomaj can probably introduce you to who could talk to you about that area. Like I said, I work primarily with licensed technology for patients who *need* it.'

Tomaj looked uncomfortable.

'Like I said, we should go. Thanks, Audra—'

'Hang on, hang on. Let me give you my card, Sabina. I'll be glad to talk to you any time if you need advice. You can come down to the clinic and see what I'm doing with my patients. A number of them who are non-verbal have achieved remarkable things using music and visual art, despite poor physical coordination, thanks to HIT.'

She was looking at her desk, tapping a pen rapidly on her blotter as she thought.

'Now that I think about it, for your purposes, having an empathetic experience with HIT doesn't necessarily mean becoming a Watcher with all the attendant baggage.'

'I never wanted to become Watcher,' Sabina inserted.

'No. I may have jumped to conclusions. Anyway, your timing couldn't be better. I know someone who's having a party tonight – I'll write the address on the back of the card. It's not really my camp – Tomaj, you'll recognize a few faces, I think – but you might be interested because I understand there's going to be some kind of interactive, HIT-based art event going on. I can't vouch for it being any *good*, but it might be a way for you to find out more.'

Sabina took the card. 'Thank you. Thank you very much. You are so kind.'

Audra and her dogs accompanied them to the front door, where Tomaj lingered, as if something still needed to be said. He bent and murmured in Audra's ear. Sabina pretended to be playing with the dogs, but she was listening of course.

'What is it? Did you figure it out?'

'I'm not sure yet. I need more time.'

'What about the—?'

'Don't worry. It's fine. You'll find out everything you need to know, when C's ready.'

'OK, talk to you soon,' Audra said in her normal, strident tones. They left. Tomaj was uncharacteristically silent. They got on a cross-town bus, but once they were on the West Side he said, 'I want to walk. Do you mind? I need to think.'

So they walked uptown for many long blocks; the afternoon scrolled by around them, and with Tomaj immersed in his own thoughts she found herself aching for Adrien to come back. Did he know this Audra? What did he think about licensed use of HIT – what did he think of its medical applications? Did he even care that the technology reached a larger world than was included in the private games of his strange, apparently sadistic Watcher? For that matter, was C in fact sadistic – Tomaj didn't seem to think so – or had Adrien simply been a wreck when she'd met him, blaming his Watcher for everything?

If she could see him again, having had this time to sort out the differences between her interest in HIT and her attraction to him, surely she could determine what those hours in the hotel together had really meant. To her, and to Adrien.

She wondered, also, what lengths she should go to in order to compose again. Was HIT merely a technological trick? Could it really teach her anything, or must she content herself with the music that she, alone, could imagine?

Variations on these thoughts occupied her during the long walk. Eventually they reached Tomaj's neighborhood.

'I'm hungry,' he said, and swerved abruptly into a place called Mama's Fried Chicken. She stood in the doorway while he and the girls behind the counter exchanged insults like old friends. A woman walked by pushing a stroller containing a small child dressed in dirty, ill-fitting clothes and wearing the newest model of Gamebaby visor.

Tomaj came out carrying a paper bag and humming to himself.

'OK, I can talk to you now,' he said genially. 'What's up?'

'This is going to sound stupid,' she ventured, 'but I can't figure you out. You don't seem to belong to any special group. I didn't think there were any Americans like you.'

'What do you mean, Sabina?' She had the feeling he was teasing her but couldn't be certain.

'I can't understand where is your place in the society. I guess you have the money but you live in not-so-good neighborhood. Kids on street respect you, but you are also friends with Audra. You are gay but people are afraid you will beat them up, and you have this whatyoucallit – absence? obsolete? – museum. And then ... there is the other thing.'

'The "other thing"?'

'What you do. The Deep.'

'Sabina, can you understand that the world might be too limited for me? That if I respect its limits I'd never really live?'

'I guess ... I can understand that. But ...'

'I'm not going to be put in a box and categorized. Being a human being in America today is all about eluding identification. Escaping the people out there who want to tell you what to do, pigeonhole you, put their finger on who or what you are. I defy marketing stratification. You've got to stretch yourself, assume multiple identities. Only in that way can you escape the blindness and insanity of the market.'

He was gesturing with his hands as he warmed to his subject, directing his gaze not at her but at the buildings above them.

'You really want the nitty-gritty of this, Sabina? I'll tell you what being a trans is. It's about making a conscious

110

decision to infuse your life with some kind of meaning for someone. Not a traditional someone, like a lover or friend or kid – no, a magical someone you almost never see and know very little about. A spirit guide, of a kind.'

'But Adrien said he was a whore.'

'He is a whore. So what?'

They had reached Tomaj's building and rode the elevator up to his floor. In his apartment the late afternoon light swept over all the strange junk, making it alive with shadows. Tomaj went to the picture window and unwrapped the chicken, setting the open box on a therapeutic nail bed to which spiders had begun to emigrate, and grabbing a bar stool for her to sit on. The westering sun turned the glass and chrome buildings of midtown the color of ripe canteloupe.

Tomaj said, 'What's so bad about being a whore? It's reality. Most people sell themselves to their corporations, or to their notion of family and so become enslaved. Artists, sometimes, are exempt from these things: due to willpower they starve, beg, borrow, and defy ownership – *but*, Sabina, *but* this is false because most of them would gladly sell themselves if only the world were buying what they had to express! Money is the least of it. What does the artist want except for someone else, someone worthy, to get under her skin and take a feel, a taste, a whiff of what she and her world are? Does she do it for the product itself, or for the act of touching when someone really hears her? For the shudder of recognition. For the shudder of the alien. Anything else is masturbation.'

He had said all this without looking at her; she was completely enthralled by his delivery, the mesmeric nuances of his coffee-and-smoke voice. Now he waited a breath, turned toward her, and caught her in a gaze of seemingly infinite understanding.

'A trans composes the whole world for the Watcher. And the Watcher is the ultimate audience.' He turned away and concentrated on eating a drumstick. Gradually the sun disappeared, the patches of gold on the buildings gleamed fitfully and dwindled, and lights came on: the watchful lights inside.

'So,' Sabina said at last, picking at a wing. 'Speaking of marketing: this sounds like sales pitch, no?'

He hadn't turned on a lamp yet, so he was a shadow barely distinguishable from the contents of his collection. 'Let's have a drink, shall we?'

He got up and made noise in the kitchen, but she wouldn't let him crack the mood.

'I mean,' Sabina persisted, accepting a drink, 'why should I want to let someone into my inside thoughts? Why should I want to give away the privacy?'

She was talking half to herself, but Tomaj answered her anyway.

'Most people wouldn't be offered the chance. Most people can't handle the idea of a secret world.'

'But you can.'

He drew a long breath and let it out. She could feel the alcohol softening her beneath her skin. He said, 'Let me tell you a story. When I was in college, I won a scholarship to study theater in London one summer. I rode the Underground everywhere. One day on the Bakerloo line in the middle of rush hour we were riding along when suddenly out of the darkness there appeared this bright golden ... I don't know, this *banquet* of draperies and lights and color and food and gorgeous people – this *pageantry* – just a glimpse of it, though. A lost world. For just a few seconds it filled the carriage windows; then it was gone. The other passengers had no reaction, but I knew what *I* saw. I thought I must've had some kind of vision. For days afterward I thought hey, something mystical actually happened to me! I thought, yo, there's more to life than they tell you in school. I felt this awesome desire to *go* to this place, so I rode that train a couple more times, but nothing happened.'

'A vision.'

'Much later,' he added slowly, 'I found out what it was all about. There was an abandoned station on that line and it was sometimes used as a film set for some historical tv drama or shit like that, which explains why the regular commuters weren't impressed. Seems like there should be some irony there, right? Like the joke was on me. But no. I don't think so. By doing theater we bring to life the unseen. There's a level of reality to these invented worlds that your rational mind can't touch. Imagination adds another dimension to the strictly physical. In theater we create a window between the real and the numinous, and for a minute you can look through. A lot of people in the theater business get focused on the size and shape of the window, the kind of glass used, but I don't care about that. I care what's on the other side.'

She said nothing.

'The HIT scene – and to a large extent the Deep – is practically the same thing. It's self-inventing, self-perpetuating, and mysterious. It's never *there* enough so that you can touch it, but it sometimes comes as close as that three-second glance out the window into something wonderful. So in that sense, the Deep is closer to me than God. In fact, it's more honest in admitting deception as both its *raison d'être* and also its *modus operandi*.'

She mouthed these last words to herself. She had the sneaking suspicion it was all some nonsense he was making up as he went along. He climbed sideways into a recliner and put his feet up on an octagonal fishtank that played 'Jingle Bells'. They sat drinking scotch from beer steins for some time before one of them thought to turn on the old tv held in the lap of one department store mannequin and presided over with feather-duster by another. The mystery of black-and-white instantly transfixed them.

It was the scene in the new King Kong where Kong is trying to peel off the diaphanous white garments of Jessica Lange high atop the Empire State Building. Tomaj had a view of the building from his living room window, and

Sabina kept turning her head back and forth from the tv to the window as if to confirm that the real Empire State Building was there.

'I love this movie,' Sabina said, feeling drunker than she technically ought to.

'Yes,' said Tomaj in a bored tone. 'It's one of the more amusing texts about the racial fears of the white man. But the old version is better. If they were going to make a new version, they could have done so much more.'

Jessica Lange shrieked and whimpered. A scandalous hint of breast appeared under Kong's thumb.

'I would rewrite this movie if I could,' she declared.

'Wouldn't we all.'

'You see,' Sabina went on, only peripherally aware of Tomaj's half-smile, 'they try to make more sexy, but they interpret her all wrong. She is not really afraid of him, but of herself. She needs this big gorilla to make her confront her power, which scares her but—'

'But which can't be denied.'

'Right. So no: it's not rape fantasy, it's about whatsit – you know, the medicine man, what is word – shamanism of power. Her power, her getting off. She can't claim her power by herself, she's got to get fucked with the big gorilla cock first, you know? Here, look, see how coy she pretends to be, but really it turns her on.'

'It does?' Tomaj, mildly interested, leaned closer to better see the screen.

'In my version,' Sabina said, 'her man, her civilization, wouldn't rescue her. She wouldn't stay ... chaste.'

'Yo, I mean, come on, Sabina, you're not looking for some kind of feminist angle here are you because—' His pupils were wide with drink and darkness.

'He's the dumb brute. He's her animal nature, her animus. He's projection of her what-you-call-it, yang part, I don't know. Don't you see it, Tomaj, it's so obvious really.'

'Maybe to you it's obvious. To me she's just supposed to be a possession.'

114

'Not after being with Kong! She becomes something *else*, not white man's toy...'

Tomaj had been chuckling softly. 'So you believe rape can be enlightening?'

They looked at each other. Darkness gathered its veined furry wings in the room, and the fear began to spider across her face. This is where we light our last match in the haunted house and then run, screaming, for the—

'Rape is a door,' Sabina said. She drained her glass and handed it back to him.

Tomaj leaned forward and turned down the sound knob; it fell off in his hand. Silently, King Kong flailed and Jessica Lange shrieked, silently. Sabina watched him look out on his predator city, and back at the bullet-ridden Kong.

'Come on,' she said. 'Is time to go to party now.'

* * *

The preparations have all been made. My haste is unseemly; I know that, but the situation demands that I act now, before matters slide completely beyond my control. I can't wait for my enemies to find out any more than they already know; I've made dangerous slips already. It must be Sabina, and it must be tonight.

Tomaj is unnerved. He thinks Sabina is too inconstant about the idea of HIT: wild one minute, timid the next. She isn't desperate enough to take the plunge, he thinks. If I want her for a trans, she will be more trouble for me than Adrien was. Fortunately, Tomaj has not yet twigged on to the fact that I intend to do more than make her a trans.

Tonight, for the first time, I find a hint of jealousy inside Tomaj – jealousy toward Adrien, whom he senses I am pining for. He shouldn't be jealous: I may desire Adrien, but I respect Tomaj. I hope he survives what I'm about to do to him. In the end, whatever happens to him will be better than, by default, receiving I for himself. If I trespassed on his prized individuality, he would soon hate us both. I tell him to trust me, though I know I must betray him. He falls backward into my strength, and by his trust he makes me even more powerful.

And I need every bit of grace I can get. It's the end of my world, and I can say nothing – not to Tomaj, not to myself. I have watched it approach, closer and closer, with every step Adrien took toward I. Yet I can frame no understanding of what I feel. I cannot fit myself into words; they are too small and vague. Maybe that's why I turn more and more to this young composer: because words cannot save me and I place my faith in her music.

Whatever music it is that comes to enfold me, I am the only one who will not have ears to hear it.

Or will I?

Eleven

With his peripheral vision, Tomaj observed Sabina all the way up the long elevator journey to the penthouse, which was to be the site for this evening of fun & games. Sabina maintained her composure well, the only indication of her unrest manifesting itself in the disgusted, peremptory way she put out her cigarette on the sidewalk when entering the smokeless lobby. She tried to smash it out with her boot heel and, failing, kicked it away sparking. Other than that, she was in control. There were no upraised eyes to watch the floors whiz by, no trembling fingers, no shifting of weight. When the elevator doors opened on the upper level, she smiled.

The floor was polished black marble and stretched out to meet the lights of the city below without any visible barrier between the edge of the building and the void beyond. Only the faint ghost of reflection indicated the presence of ingeniously dark-lit glass walls, so the city itself seemed arrayed at one's feet like mica-lit stepping stones, or perhaps a very complex circuit board. The only obstructions were human, for the intervening walls and architectural structures were made of mirrors, augmenting the feeling of space and complexity. The humans were eccentric in appearance. Fashion in the room ranged from body-paint to rock-climbing gear (Tomaj learned afterward that the latter had been worn because its owner had *climbed* to the party and was now hoping to elude police, who had been stalled in the lobby thanks to an abundance of drugs and the loud whining of a blonde named Lucinda). No two people looked as if they actually belonged at the same event. Indeed, the guests seemed more preoccupied with

117

their own reflections shot back in crystalline shards of mirrors than with one another. Many of them looked too young to be out on a school night.

'Who are these people?'

'Whoever they think they are. Whoever our host has seen fit to invite.' He couldn't keep all the frigidity out of his tone: this sort of thing was too flashy; it made him uncomfortable. 'At times like this,' he added, 'the less you know the better off you are.'

Sabina reached into her jacket and took out a cigarette. She pointed with it.

'Who is the suit?'

Laurence was perched on a plinth from which an alleged art object had been removed, briefcase open on his knees, looking like a travelling salesman who got off on the wrong floor on the way to the lounge bar. People were lined up waiting to speak to him: while they watched, he reached into his briefcase and handed a small object, flashing like tinsel, to a youth of indeterminate gender clad only in *The Adoration of the Magi* and a kilt. The youth brought his/her hand to his/her ear and there was a flash as the wire went in.

'You brilliant cunt,' said the youth to Laurence in a shaking alto. Then s/he walked backward through the room, teeth bared, and was lost to view.

'Laurence is a friend of mine,' Tomaj said in Sabina's ear before breaking away from her. 'I'll bring him over to meet you.'

Laurence stood and closed the case discreetly and shook Tomaj's hand. He jerked his head at the rest of the people on line to get lost. 'I've got something for you,' he said. 'Special courier brought it this afternoon.'

Tomaj set his unfinished drink on the plinth and grimaced, rubbing his forehead. 'I don't like this whole situation, man. What do you think's up tonight?'

C floated hazily through him, strangely out of focus.

'I don't know, but maybe that's why the courier

instructed me to administer Aunt Maurice's Green Silk Parrot Shawl to you this evening.'

'Thanks, but no. I'll have my hands full without any of your wires.'

The courier was from me. Take what he gives you, Tomaj.

Wires weren't C's style, either. Tomaj's uneasiness began to burgeon.

'It's not a wire, it's a drug,' Laurence was saying. 'Hard to come by; once in a lifetime kind of stuff. It's all paid for: I'd think twice about refusing.'

Tomaj glanced back toward Sabina, but she'd moved off somewhere. The lack of boundaries between walls and sky, floors and ceiling, light and dark, made the figures that drifted from one end of the penthouse to another look like exotic fish in a vast tank.

'... brilliant. Not only can it activate these recently repressed transmissions and make them available to your conscious mind, but it also has some very pleasant side-effects. It's going to put you into a state of metaphysical certainty and faith in the absolute that you've never in your life experienced.'

Tomaj paid attention just long enough to realize that Laurence was pitching the Shawl in earnest.

'Really. It's the closest thing to a religious experience I can offer, and without the manic edges of true prophet-hood. It's like a soft, familiar shawl for your brain. You'll be like a babe in the womb.'

He paused and Tomaj held up a hand to stop him.

'Well, not that I don't appreciate it, but there's shit going on you don't know about, Laurence. Or maybe you do. Let me just say: nobody's putting anything in my head tonight. No drugs, no wires, nothing. C is up to something funky.'

C said: *I've transmitted your codes, as well as other information that's vital for your survival. And Sabina's. And my own.*

Every Watcher worth its salt used some kind of a fast mainline system in the bullet-chess of jamming and counter-jamming trans signals; one had to in order to avoid collisions with other com systems and tv and all the rest of the signals that wrapped the Earth like butterfly silk; and to get into that system, to find the individual trans amid all the frequency shifting that went on, a Watcher devised codes for each trans. Well, more than simple codes really – more like pyramids of algorithms and hacker-devouring Chinese finger traps, but that wasn't the point. The point was, Tomaj didn't know his codes and never had. So what the hell was C talking about?

Earlier today I transferred some things to your memory. While you were listening to Sabina's music, actually. I locked your access to this knowledge, but Laurence's drug will unlock it. Take it, Tomaj. Without your codes you'll be dead meat.

What? Was C dropping him? It was Adrien who'd wanted his codes: Tomaj never asked to be set free. What kind of puzzle was this?

'You see,' Tomaj said to Laurence, trying to tease C into revealing more, 'C's into something with Max, something dirty. I'd rather take my chances with my head clear than get involved with some spooky shit I don't even know what it is.'

Laurence raised an eyebrow at such a candid disclosure.

The matter of I is between me and Adrien. Don't be afraid. Take the Shawl – take the codes. You'll need this knowledge.

What knowledge?

About Sabina, and me, and I. So you'll understand something of what's happening. Tomaj, you must understand: I'm going to die tonight.

C cut the link; he didn't notice at first because he was still standing there like a tree, rocking at the blow of its words. The Watcher had hinted at this eventuality; but not that it was coming so soon. Wasn't there a long finity of nights in which C could pass from his life: why did it have to be this one?

Laurence, long accustomed to that abstracted expression so common in the HIT community, waited. After a while Tomaj licked his lips.

'You couldn't call it love, what you feel for C.' He emitted each word discretely, like a magician producing ping-pong balls from his own mouth, his face vaguely surprised. 'But there's a kind of desperation when you think of losing someone who—' His voice caught and he fell silent.

Laurence shifted his weight from foot to foot, looking uncomfortable. He dropped a pen and stooped to pick it up. Tomaj's voice came back to him, gaining momentum.

'All these people, there will never be any way to verify what really happened here tonight, who was here and who was just Watching, what passed through these frames of bone and thought, Laurence. Thanks, man, but I can't take your stuff. C's trying to protect me from the moment of its own death, *maybe*, but what's the point of that?' He bent to retrieve his drink. 'See you later.'

Sabina was nowhere to be found. He strolled across the room and tossed back the drink. It was sweet. After he swallowed, he thought: spiked. He turned to find Laurence again, but the wireman and his loafers had shuffled elsewhere.

'You stupid shit,' he told himself, and made for the kitchen. It was full of servers, steam, and flying olives.

'I need something to make me throw up,' he announced. 'I need to induce some vomiting here.'

A woman who was all cleavage and legs came up to him carrying a tray of frothing blue drinks: she said, 'Get out of the way,' but he couldn't hear her. Instead, he saw handwriting in the air between them: blue longhand, with a European slant he found difficult to decipher.

'Are you French?' he said. She slid by him, turned into a wolf, and went into the mirror maze.

'Oh shit, it's too late.' The words slipped from his mouth and swarmed in the air like flights of insects. Numbers marched from right to left in rows like Space Invaders. The code for Tomaj's plant. He tried to erase them with his hands but they trooped into his pockets. He felt C again. Her words scored the air in jagged black. *I am leaving you now. I am going. Don't forget to learn your codes before the drug wears off. Dying is perfect, Tomaj.*

'I don't believe it,' he said aloud. 'Tricked again. *Part of the drug.* I don't believe it.'

* * *

Someone bumped into Sabina from behind and she turned to find herself practically in the arms of a heavy black woman who smiled at her beatifically.

'—because everyone in this room is a mirror,' she said in a thick French accent, as though already in the middle of a conversation. 'Each of them's an entire culture, colliding with the outside world. But I do find in places like Bangladesh a charming sort of herd-character—'

Sabina stepped around her with effort.

'—not to be confused with Attali's claims—'

She edged away and the woman continued on as if they'd passed one another without speaking. In the mirror she saw herself, looking smallish and rumpled and less convincing than she wanted to feel. She watched two boys cutting each other lingeringly with a scalpel. Somewhere out over the city, near the edge of the terrace, she supposed, although the sound seemed wilder and even more distant, a woman screamed in time with each stroke of the blade.

She drifted skittishly away. As public as this act was, there were no onlookers: the other partygoers behaved as if nothing unusual were happening. She began to feel hot and unnerved and wished for alcohol. Then, as she approached the limits of the room (where the city finally took on some definition and gained depth, becoming itself instead of merely its own image in the mirrors) she saw someone who appeared to be an ordinary civilian, or close to it.

The man was wearing a baseball cap, shorts and a purple smoking jacket. His feet were bare and his thin legs were tan. He had a face like an emaciated game-show host but he was also carrying a tray of drinks, which increased his charisma considerably.

'Hi,' she said, taking one. She lifted the hair off her neck and let the breeze from outside catch it. 'Big crowd.'

'Yeah,' answered the guy, grinning. 'My goal was to get every trans in the Northern hemisphere but I guess that'd be impractical. Still, for every person here, there are several folks on remote.'

Sabina sipped, wondering if this was the host and unwilling to introduce herself as a starving artist and gatecrasher.

'Do you know somebody called Adrien?' she asked.

'Adrien? White hair Adrien? Yeah, I kind of know him.'

'What do you think of him?' Sabina asked.

He looked over her shoulder but said nothing. Then he jerked his head toward the speakers.

'What do you think of the music?'

'Schöenberg is a strange choice of party music.' Another gulp finished the drink. 'Still, better strange taste than no taste. So, tell me about Adrien.'

'I just did.'

She blinked twice and he said, 'Excuse me. I just noticed the natives seem to be getting restless. I'd better go start the entertainment – excuse me, the *art*.'

He darted away before she could ask any more questions.

* * *

Tomaj couldn't seem to find Sabina, although he was too shaken by what C had just said to him to look very hard. He kept leaning on the link, hoping C would return and say it was all just a joke; the code spilled from his pockets and trailed behind him like a popcorn garland for a Christmas tree, or a trail of crumbs left on a journey to a deep cave ... he wanted to have a good scream, but he thought he'd better save that for later in case things got worse. Which they were bound to.

He assumed that the announcement came from the same speakers that released music into the party, because he still couldn't hear anything, but the words flowed out across space in 18-point Helvetica:

THE EVENT IS ABOUT TO BEGIN ON THE DESIGNATED FREQUENCY. YOU SHOULD BE ABLE TO RECEIVE RIGHT THROUGH YOUR CAVALRY-WARE. THIS CAST IS LOCALIZED WITHIN THE BUILDING SO YOU CAN TRUST WE WON'T BE TRYING TO POACH ANYBODY TONIGHT. YOUR CHARACTERS WILL BE RANDOMLY DETERMINED. DON'T MISS ANY OF THE **FUN!!!!**

C wouldn't answer him, but the Watcher was on the link because he found himself homing in on the frequency of Max's artist. He'd heard about these interactive dramas but had never experienced one; certainly he'd never imagined trying to put as many minds as this on the same frequency at once. It did seem a little suspicious: he knew C had good cavalry software which could pull him off the channel if anything funny were uploaded to him, but he didn't much like the idea of Max gathering so many minds in the same place. Max *was* the type to engage in recreational brain-washing, after all. Apparently the others didn't harbor such suspicions, though, for when Tomaj got to the frequency it was already crowded.

—long hair falling down her back. The air was warm and fragrant with the perfume of fruit and flowers. Twilight weighed on all the colors, making them more vivid than at any other time of day. The sand was a deep shade of gold, unlike any earthly sand, and the birds that circled the ocean were all known hues of red, their wings carving wedges in the air like daggers drawing blood.

Everything in the scene was alive; everything was conscious. Tomaj himself had been installed in the body of a lioness, who paced between the sweating leaves and velvet flowers; they shivered sensuously when her fur brushed against them. Even the sand cried out its awareness in the form of sparkling whenever it was touched; but the lioness thought only of the girl, and the old man on horseback who was even now galloping on some distant road from the heights of the palace, carrying with him two jewels and the tiny skull that would change the girl's life. The girl was called Asamariti and she belonged to the lioness. She was a luscious, rounded thing, all come-hither eyes and cinnamon skin, but when the wind lifted the hair from her back it revealed the scars of lion-claws.

Suddenly Asamariti turned and saw the great cat; she hid her eyes from the lioness, trying to pretend that she really did wish to return to the world of humans. But the lioness was not about to give up her prize so easily, and the wind carried with it the smell of the girl's sex, the desire she could not hide. With the enormous smooth patience of her species, the lioness began to creep toward Asamariti, mesmerizing the human with her vertical pupils and gently twitching tail. Surrender was still far away, but the lioness was a connoisseuse of forbidden pleasure, and the night was only beginning...

* * *

Sabina wondered where Tomaj was. She'd had a couple of drinks but was beginning to think it would be better not to have any more. It occurred to her that she had been happier at Tomaj's place, watching black and white tv. What kind of party was this, anyway?

The music stopped and a male voice said, 'The event is about to begin on the designated frequency. You should be able to receive right through your cavalry-ware. This cast is localized within the building so you can trust we won't be trying to poach anybody tonight. Your characters will be randomly determined. Don't miss any of the *fun!*'

Suddenly everything stopped. People stood still, hands lax at their sides, or collapsed slowly to the floor as though practicing some strange form of Tai Chi Chuan. Their eyes closed but they did not seem to be sleeping. The wait staff were nowhere to be seen. Slowly the lights went down.

So this was the 'Event'? Sabina turned in a circle, surrounded by small bits of New York but unable to smell which direction the real city was blowing in from. She realized she couldn't hear the traffic below because the speakers were emitting white noise, not unpleasantly, but at exactly the right level to induce relaxation.

She was not relaxed. She could feel the length of every nerve, from toe to spine to skull: each nerve one fragile cell, a lone archer on the battlements—

'So.'

A man's American voice, out of the dimness in front of her. A shadow moved across a mirror, seeming to glide despite the presence of reclining bodies everywhere.

'Now it's just you and me,' he said. 'Do you know who I am?'

'No,' she answered. Inside the white noise she thought she could hear a Led Zeppelin song as if it were being played through static; she told herself to stop hearing things that weren't there and pay attention to what was happening. She couldn't remember the way to the elevator, and she was surrounded now by comatose bodies. The figure moved toward her.

'Well, I know who you are. You think you're crashing this party but I specifically wanted you here. This is a tremendous learning opportunity for you.'

Sabina looked at the bodies.

'What are they doing?'

'They're experiencing total empathy.'

She shivered. His voice sounded closer, but she couldn't see him.

'You want to do it,' he said. 'But you're afraid. I can help you with that. Laurence?'

Sabina gasped and turned. Laurence had crept up behind her. His lips curled up on one side only.

'Freefall,' the voice said. 'It's very safe. You get a little taste of what's happening here, see if you like it. What do you think?'

'Tomaj was with you,' she said to Laurence. 'Where is he now?'

Laurence glanced at the bodies. But it was the other voice which said, 'In there. With them.'

Sabina took a breath. This was it. Her chance. Courage.

'OK,' she said. She didn't like it that she couldn't see the stranger, but Laurence was now occupying her field of vision, uncapping what looked like a simple felt-tipped pen. He brought it to her forehead and drew something; there was a quick sting like alcohol in a cut, and then a slight numbness and her body became light. The white noise stopped and her hearing went very clear.

'Wait,' she blurted, turning in a circle and raising her hands for balance. 'How does it work? How can chemical connect me to the radio signal?'

Laurence didn't answer. He retreated into the darkness like a good butler.

The voice spoke again.

'Walk, Sabina. Walk toward the sound of my voice.'

She walked forward, stepping over bodies, her blood surging at the idea that she'd actually *done* something and there was no going back. She had reached a mirrored wall, but only realized this when her toe banged into it, because she was unable to see her own reflection. To her surprise, she was able to step onto the wall and walk *up* it. When she got to the ceiling she turned upside down and walked across. The blood rushed to her head.

'Come on, Sabina. Follow me.'

The voice led her to a balcony and she continued to obey until she reached the edge of the ceiling. Then she stepped off into the night. It was overcast, so she couldn't see the stars as she fell up into the sky.

Twelve

The horse was running wild by the ocean; the trees which had been flattened by the great storm stirred their leaves in the dawn; flesh melted into sleep and there was a sound of water dripping slowly. The lioness rolled over and stretched: her belly opened and New York at night was there, whirling closer and closer, its buildings spiking up until—

Tomaj was back at the Party, coming slowly to his own senses as around him people moved and stretched. The music came back on. He was on the floor with someone's slack penis in his hand and for a minute it seemed whole nations were contained in the moisture … he blinked and got to his feet. The Shawl was still working on him because he couldn't hear people talking. He could feel some of its other effects, too: it was subtly oiling hinges in his skull, preparing to open doors.

He had to move. Tomaj stumbled at random through the maze until he came to a door. Inside: two guys, jacuzzi, a friendly Rottweiler. He was welcomed in, all caps sans serif, and invited to join them, but there was a vr hookup in the jacuzzi and Tomaj had always been wary of electricity around water, having had a mother who made him stay away from windows, televisions, and all electrical appliances during storms (especially after she'd seen the movie *Poltergeist* and began to believe in the transmigration of souls). She also kept a file of the weird ways that people died, and her favorite clippings concerned freak accidents in which lightning travelled through phone lines, electric razor sockets, and radios. Tomaj had never quite gotten over it.

The trans in the hot tub took turns tripping with the vr wires. Both were impotent – they said in oblique apology – from a neural fungus they were presently testing ('makes sex irrelevant, sweetie') but this did not stop the dog from briefly attempting to hump one of them while snowboarding K2's south face. Tomaj declined to try the program: the Shawl was phasing him in and out of a reality in which everything was as brilliantly colored as a peacock and the inherent meanings of each object encountered were listed on it like ingredients: wheat flour, aspiration, partially hydrogenated ennui ... The revelatory nature of all this moved him almost to tears.

Around this time the door opened and Lai Fan wandered in, muttering something about espionage. She saw Tomaj and brightened. Her hug felt like a child's, and under the influence of the Shawl she was becoming a butterfly in his eyes. He was glad to see her if only because she was the only person besides Max even close to his age.

'That was such a pretentious story,' she announced, pouting, in a large, childish pink scrawl. 'Ask me why.'

Tomaj, reclining on a chaise lounge, let his head fall back and studied the ceiling tiles, snaky thrills of color whose *spirits* he was beginning to glimpse.

'Why was it pretentious, Lai Fan?'

'Thank you. It was pretentious because that pseudo-fairy-tale stuff is so passé. I can't believe that was Max's idea of erotica. I mean, who is this guy he's paid to do this piece?' As she spoke she was removing her clothes and slapping them down to the floor, but each new word seemed to outrage her more and force her to pause as if shocked by the content of what she was saying. The writing that Tomaj was seeing in lieu of hearing her voice became slowly fluorescent.

'What guy?' Tomaj enquired obediently, knowing from experience that until she had made her point in agonizing detail, Lai Fan would be unable to unwind. The tremolo of her frustration beat the air.

'That stupid artist guy. You know, Max's big Discovery that he dragged us all here to *experience*.'

Lai Fan paused, almost nude, twirling her bra in nervous arcs.

'Oh, that. So what? Max can patronize anyone he wants to.'

She snorted. 'Yes, but why? And why all the hype? Why go to such pains to get so many people here, to get so many Watchers on that channel?'

She kicked her clothes to one side and got in the jacuzzi. Little silver teeth appeared when she smiled; then she turned and kicked one of the jacuzzi guys, demanding a set of wires. 'Move over, guys. What you got booted up for me?'

'Maybe he was trying to distract us from something else.' He wondered exactly what sort of pains Max *had* gone to in order to get people to come. C had made it all sound quite low-key; and if Audra was involved, how wild could it get? Then again, Audra had been overly soothing on the matter of I. She had made it seem as if there were plenty of time to worry about it; but just tonight C had said it was going to die. *Now*.

'Hey!' Lai Fan said, twisting to look at him. 'You may be onto something there. We were out in that goddamn story for a long time.'

Her eyes rolled back: she was conferencing with her Watcher. Tomaj retreated into his own kaleidoscope, thinking that what Lai Fan had said ought to sound sinister ('*We were out for a long time.*' How long had he been 'out' of his own consciousness?) but he was unable to feel threatened by anything, for the world was beginning to harmonize for him, and the snakes painted on the ceiling tiles were mating and multiplying and disappearing in the time-honored waltz of existence. This comforted him, as did the meditative tongue of the dog on the inside of his forearm.

At one point some people beat on the door of the room shouting his name, and then something about Sabina, but

Tomaj didn't recognize her name at first because the door was distorting the written words and making them too puffy to read easily, and he couldn't feel the Watcher at all, so he didn't respond. Then he remembered who Sabina was, thought about how much time had probably passed and the likelihood that she would be given something too strong for her or get freaked out in some other way, and he forced himself to leave the haven of the bathroom. When he finally emerged, the dog trailing hopefully after him, the night was spinning with 'A Love Supreme' played very loud – which is the only way to hear Him, Tomaj thought with approval, watching the ribbons of sound whip like kites through the air. Feeling as gyroscopic and chromatic as the Coltrane, he leaned on the dog's sturdy head and blundered across space.

A young woman in a furry parka grabbed his hand and dragged him to the balcony. He thought she looked familiar, so he said, 'I love you. I love you all.'

Crimson words spilled from her mouth and curled into his eyes, piercing his retina with a gentle hiss but no pain, for the warm&fuzzy feeling was mounting like a slow, high wave.

'Hurry,' her words said. 'Your friend isn't feeling well.'

There were three people standing on the balcony, each holding a beaker filled with lime-colored liquid that steamed impressively as if laced with dry ice. A woman, Sabina – that's right, damnit, he was supposed to be looking out for her – was flat on her back, eyes wide open, talking.

'She's speaking German,' the parka girl told him accusingly.

'That's not German,' one of the beakers said, his neon words coming out of his mouth in elongated handwriting that for some reason reminded Tomaj of Sweden. The city behind the Swede's back had picked itself up and was beginning to walk out into the dawn over the Atlantic with slow, ponderous steps.

'Meltdown is nigh,' Tomaj heard himself say as if from a great height.

'She was out here when we woke up from the story,' said parka girl. She took a cocktail, swigged, and made a lemon-face. 'Except she doesn't seem to be able to wake up.'

The Swede said, 'I can't find a battery on her.'

'That's because she don't got one.'

'Then how could she have been in the story?' asked the Swede.

There was an infinity sign on Sabina's forehead, right dead center where the third eye should be. It looked like it had been done with a magic marker.

'Oh, how *corny*,' Tomaj moaned, and leaned against the balustrade for support. The streets beneath shivered with improbable motion. 'Hey,' he added, looking into their eyes for the first time, 'isn't a swede some kind of *turnip*, or what?'

'Is she one of us or not?' demanded parka girl, whose face was beginning to look like a rabbit's. In his present state of mind, Tomaj loved even rabbits. No – better yet, he respected rabbits. There were too many intertwining sentences in the air, and he could hear nothing.

'I respect you. I really do,' he told her.

'I thought she was with you. How could C make a new trans at this stage? I heard Adrien went over the wall.'

'She's just on a wire, baby stuff. Trans, my butt.'

'I heard C's got a terminal disease.'

'I heard C's the president of Peru.'

'How do you know Adrien left? Did he tell you that?'

'I respect turnips, too, for that matter. I don't want any of you to feel excluded.'

'No but he went to Maui and you know what that means.'

'Tomaj, if she's supposed to be a trans now, something's gone wrong. She's incoherent. Why didn't you supervise?'

'It might mean a vacation. Windsurfing.'

'Yeah, right.'

'She's not supposed to be a trans,' Tomaj said archly, wading through mental garbage to arrive temporarily at his own personality. 'I just brought her along to show her how sick you all are. It's just a joke. Forget about it. I'll take her home.'

'Joke? Don't look like no joke to me, hey.'

'I've already called an ambulance,' remarked the Swede. 'I don't like her color.'

'Ambulance? Ambulance? Are you out of – hey, there it is!' Leaning over the rail, Tomaj could see the ambulance growing larger and louder as it approached, leaping cracks in the pavement engendered by the city's motion toward the Atlantic, and then finally driving straight *up the building*. The spinning lights sank into him like stardust: it was all meant to happen.

* * *

The taste of rubber is in my mouth, and lights are everywhere. Voices, female and male, New York and Spanish, speaking in clipped phrases. Sweetness. I am being propelled too fast through periods of light and darkness. Electronic bells; I am spinning. Someone is talking to me. I know he's talking to me because I can detect his intention, but the words are too garbled for me to understand.

I am falling and I don't want to rise.

I am flying into light.

I—

* * *

The ambulance had dissolved and the Swede was quietly laughing.

'The power of suggestion. Oh, that's all we need – bunch of paramedics nosing around here.'

'Leave her to Max. Max will know what to do.'

A feeling swept through Tomaj then, a nearly physical

133

sensation, like the equivalent of an impending sneeze or orgasm, but associated with some body part that he didn't actually possess. He stood still; his head fell back and his eyes closed; the Shawl swept over him and left a small exploding world in its wake. It opened and opened in his memory, a tesseract – he had a sense of being on the verge of something undreamed-of, something big. His sense of what it was kept morphing and turning inside out, until at last it crystallized and burned down into simple, discrete pieces of information.

NICOLETTE TAZEDAIT 15 rue de l'aguille, Paris

SASCHA MINDLIN Institute for Advanced Communication Studies, Moscow

KANG JUN IL Park Microelectronics, Seoul

I is for Immortality.

Someone shoved an object into his hand. After a while he realized it was his phone. 'Hello, Mom?' Tomaj said.

'Mr Robinson?' He could hear this woman all too clearly. No more handwriting in the air. 'This is Dr Malagon. I'm sorry to tell you—'

'Oh HELL!' Tomaj sobbed, throwing the phone over the parapet before she could finish her sentence.

'Bad investment?'

'Boyfriend cheating?'

'C's dead. Somebody give me another phone.'

'Damn. Free agent now, eh?'

'Where'd you say Adrien was? Maui? Does anybody know his number?'

'Shit, at this rate Queens is going to be completely trampled. I wonder how high the waves are.'

'If he was ditching C he wouldn't exactly leave his phone number, would he?'

'Look out! Somebody grab Tomaj, he's going to jump.'

'Tomaj, Tomaj. Life goes on. You'll see.'

'Try calling what's her name. That chick Yoshimura. She might know where—'

'Someone find Laurence. We've got to get this guy down.'

'I wasn't jumping but I have to join the migration. Look –
sperm whales! We'll be in Europe by daybreak.'

'You're OK, Tomaj. Just sit down here, next to your
German friend. You're OK. Tomaj. Tomaj?'

* * *

The moon is dark, and Adrien's back in a hotel like a
human being, sleeping hard and deep and alone at last,
shiny as a snake that's just shed its skin. He's dreaming of
every move in every kata, and himself free to do them all.
No one will ever control him again.

It's over. It's over.

From the depths of his luggage the phone lets loose a
muffled scream.

A hole in the head

Not I

Samuel Beckett

The geometry of the threshold between sleeping and waking has been flattened and then folded like origami. It has become an invisible country, a blind garden whose topiary is felt rather than seen – it traps things. It has trapped me. The body and all its rivers, its strange and terrifying landscapes, are unwoven and here exposed to their own regard, the tendons cut or detoured to prevent any sudden move: the body stares directly at itself and turns to stone. That magic for which we are all destined but none of us can recognize when it comes for us now dwells in the tyranny of protein synthesis and distant communication. Packed away in the dark interior of stilled muscle a cell among cells within tissue cries out to the distant thunder we call self – and who is there to answer?

No one is there, I tell you: no one. For I am a construct inventing myself at every moment and I will crawl out of her body the way our preconscious ancestors crawled out of the sea to make my fortune in a country undreamed of by the waterborn ones, yet always bearing the sea within myself like misguided hope.

She's dreaming terrible things.

Velvet air; opalescent evening sky; death stench; gibbous black buildings shot through with electric yellow light where their spines have been broken. Careless smoke blows from smouldering debris. Pools of water seem bottomless because light does not penetrate them, but reflects back from their waters the color of shipwrecked gold. There are the remains of cars, turned inside out, upside down. There are people, moving in the darkness, seeking food or, more urgently, each other.

She looks at her hands. They are long-fingered, large, and shockingly unfamiliar. They should be smaller – younger – dirtier. When she tries to remember why this is so, her very sense of having asked a question dissolves and vanishes. She moves forward but her feet are bare, and she struggles over broken ground. Delicate symbols are painted on each toenail. They stir some recollection, tasted on the tongue-tip of memory – these symbols don't belong here, they belong somewhere else, to someone else.

She is looking for the piano. It belonged to a rich widow who failed to get it out of Vukovar in time and was forced to abandon it in the street when the truck that was to have carried it away was destroyed. Sabina last saw it wedged between the wrecked truck and a brick wall, by some miracle virtually undamaged. She played it right there, losing herself for a time in its rich, dark tone – forgetting for a while hunger, the absence of her father, fear – she would have stayed there playing anything she could while the barrage began again, except that Maria came and screamed at her and slapped her face, then dragged her away to cower in the relative safety of the cellars and listen to the ruin of the city.

Now she climbs over heaps of junk, hardly taking in the destruction, searching for the black curves of the trapped piano. She has no reason to hope it has survived this past week, but she hopes anyway.

When she reaches the place, the piano is gone. The wrecked truck is gone. Instead there is a human head as large as a house. It sprouts right out of the street, neckless and listing slightly. The jaw is skewed sideways, lower lip suspended bulbous and fruity, peeling away from the towering, clenched teeth. The upper lip is seemingly drained of blood and tissue; it has been perforated in hundreds of places and stirs sluggishly in the idle breeze. It makes a deep whirring sound when the air moves it. She can see the structure of the tissue.

The nose has been smashed. Flesh curls limp around the

edges of shattered bone and stained cartilage. There is little blood, although long tears score both cheeks from lower eyelid almost to the jaw, exposing ribbons of muscle and bone beneath. It is as if sharp nails had reached up and raked themselves down the face in some last act of shocked, self-mutilating dismay. This impression is reinforced by the raised eyebrows and the lumps of frozen jaw muscle beneath waxy skin.

Of the eyes themselves, one dangles rakishly from its socket, its lid closed belatedly, leaving strings of blood vessels and other ropy stuff squeezing out from beneath juice-stiffened eyelashes. The other eye is absent entirely. Where the other eye should be is utter darkness. Something's moving around back there. Something's going on.

She doesn't want to, but she thinks she has to go inside.

Climb the bones and touch the cells.

Please, not that.

Thirteen

Adrien yawned as the elevator ascended. He'd left Hawaii in the morning; it was now night in New York. As usual his attempts to sleep on the plane had been unsuccessful, and although he was recovering well from the bronchitis and assorted injuries, he felt beat to hell. He didn't feel like seeing Tomaj now. An eerie feeling of responsibility for C's death had taken hold of him somewhere over the Pacific – it seemed a sick coincidence that the Watcher should go and die so soon after his plant had come out. And he had nothing but Tomaj's word for it that C *was* dead: the possibility that this was all part of some ruse to get him back had not escaped him. He would have preferred to stay on Maui until the Watcher had been fully buried and possibly somewhat decomposed, just to be on the safe side. But Tomaj had not sounded so hot when he begged Adrien to return.

The elevator stopped at Tomaj's floor. He pressed the bell, then stood twitching. Training kata on Maui had been good for him; still, he knew he was at the bottom of the mountain. Severance from C had left him a little wild: sometimes he felt ridiculously carefree; sometimes he was paranoid enough to be medicated. Right now he was the latter.

He rang again. Tomaj said he would be here. This had better not be a trick. It was one thing to run away from the government Mitsuko had sicced on him; it was another thing to deal with C. Or Max.

Footsteps within. A woman's voice, foreign accent.

'Who is it?'

He glared into the spyhole. 'It's Adrien Reyes. *Where's Tomaj?*'

Bolts were slid back, the door opened to reveal an almost dark interior.

Sabina.

'Thank god it's you.' She looked tired and spooked.

He slid inside and closed the door behind him. Tomaj's living room contained so many human-like figures, it was hard to be sure she was alone. He gave the room a quick scan.

'Adrien, what are you looking for?'

'What? *Hi.*' His pulse was racing. 'What's going on? How did you get here?'

'You ask me? How should I know? Is your fault.' She was obviously upset about something; her accent was thick and he could barely make sense of her.

'Where's Tomaj?' He strode from one end of the place to the other, half expecting to be ambushed any second.

'I don't know.' She was still standing by the door, her hand rather weakly supporting her forehead.

'Are you OK?'

'I just woke up little while ago. It must have been drug at that party. I was with Tomaj but we got divided.'

'Hold on,' he said, laughing with the air of someone who *really* hopes this is all just a cute mistake. 'I'm a little confused. Since when do you know Tomaj?'

She sighed, shaking her head in exasperation. 'When I get your letter, I called and left message on your phone. Then at the airport it was Tomaj coming to pick me up. He told me you were in Hawaii and so I stayed with him to wait for you. We went to party, but I woke up here, and Tomaj doesn't come back yet.'

'I didn't send you a letter, Sabina.' His smile faded.

'Yes, you did.' She was getting a baffled look, like a beestung dog. 'You wrote to me, *Sabina please come*, and sent the cash, and plane ticket to New York.'

'Shit. Wasn't me.' He found Tomaj's refrigerator by

sound and got a beer, buying time, drumming his fingers on the counter and thinking, *does it never end?* 'Fucking Tomaj. Of all people, I always thought Tomaj – shit. I'm sorry. It looks like you've been tricked.'

She had crossed the room slowly and now stood across the counter from him. Her face was pale and she didn't look well.

'You must have been out late if you just woke up.'

'I don't remember. My head hurts.'

Adrien put the bottle down and scrutinized her face.

'You were drinking.'

'Not so much.'

'Drugs?'

'This guy, Laurence? He gave me something called Freefall. With, like, the pen. He said I could see what being trans is like that way.'

Adrien stared in disbelief. 'Freefall's a stimulant, but it's got nothing to do with – whoa.' He held out his hand as if to push away the thought that had just occurred to him. 'Come here, under the light. Show me what he did.'

She obeyed, pushing the hair away from her forehead. An infinity sign had been drawn there, as if with magic marker. He spit on his finger and rubbed it, but it didn't come off. They were standing close together. He should back away, give her some space, but he didn't.

'Now you will explain, OK?' she said, shifting. 'Stop looking at me, Adrien. I only came here because of you.'

Her eyes looked anywhere but at him; her face was flushed. He knew if he didn't do something, in another two seconds they would be all over each other like a couple of snakes.

'I'll explain later,' he said curtly, snapping his fingers. 'Let's go. Now.'

He wove his way through Tomaj's shit until he reached the door, threw his bag over his shoulder, and gestured for her to hurry.

'My bags—'

'Later.'

She began to scrabble around in the junk, coming up with her jacket and some cigarettes and finally a huge suitcase.

'Forget it, Sabina. It's only going to slow us down. Leave it.'

He hustled her outside and toward the train station, constantly scanning over her head for signs of pursuit. He knew he didn't have a prayer of avoiding being seen if this was a set-up; but he operated this way by force of habit.

They came up from the subway near Lincoln Center; he pulled her across the street, hailed a cab and pushed her in.

'Madison Square Garden.' He turned to Sabina. 'You're sure he said Freefall?'

'I don't know, it was supposed to connect me to art thing, I said, how can this work but he said follow my voice and I did. This guy, he writes me with a *pen*, I mean I can't believe it.'

'No shit. Who was at this party? Did all this happen before or after C bought it?'

'Bought it?'

'You know. *Died*. Are you following me here? C was my ... employer. A Watcher – you understand? It died last night – or so it wants everyone to believe. C was ... with us ... the night you and I were together. If I behaved strangely, that's why. I went to Maui to get my plant removed.' He tapped his head so she would understand.

'Yeah, I'm not stupid, Adrien.'

'Right. Last night I get a call saying C died at dawn in New York. Was this before or after you participated in this ... event?'

'Well ... I think probably at same time.'

'You think?'

'I don't really know when. I can't remember anything ...'

'Short term memory loss. That's Freefall, all right.' Or any number of other agents circulating on the HIT scene. She might have done anything during the black period; best

145

not to tell her that, though. It could have been worse. They could have planted her. C might have intended that, might have died just before it could succeed. He hadn't given much thought to the possibility that C was faking this death, because as long as his plant was gone, C had no hold over him anyway. Now he could see how that might not be true. The Watcher could be using Sabina to play with him. He had to find out for sure that C was really, totally, dead.

'Adrien, if you did not write this letter, who did?'

'You left your wallet,' said Adrien.

'I have here—'

'No, I mean, you left your wallet in my room, and I came to your house to return it. That's how C knew your address. So it sent you the letter, or it had someone send it, of course. You say Tomaj answered my phone? What was the number you called?'

She showed him the scrap of paper that was in her wallet, but she'd left his letter to her in Tomaj's apartment, she said. The phone number was Tomaj's.

'At this party, did anyone say anything about a new plant to you?'

'Not really. I don't think so.'

'Are you sure?'

'I don't know. I didn't talk to many people. I don't remember very much.'

'You have to try to remember.'

'Adrien, why? I thought you said you were finished with HIT. What's going on?'

'I don't know,' Adrien said half to himself. 'Maybe C wanted to get back at me for leaving. Or maybe Tomaj – I don't know. You're lucky you came out of it so well.' The cab let them out in front of the Garden; Adrien paid and dragged Sabina by the hand through the crowd that had just come from a basketball game. 'We'll walk for a while, OK? I just need to convince myself I'm not being followed and then we can stop.'

'Fine, we walk. At least you *can* walk. Your leg – I can't believe it heals so fast.'

He smiled, startled by her concern. 'Yeah. It's coming along.'

They walked in silence for a time, zig-zagging downtown to the Village where Adrien knew there would be plenty of people on the streets all night.

'Why did you come, anyway? What did this letter say?'

'Letter said you wanted to see me, everything would be different now. Come on, Adrien, you're kidding me, right? You did write, didn't you?' She looked uncertain, on the verge of being insulted.

'I didn't write it. If I invited you, I would've had the decency to be here when you arrived.'

But she wasn't focusing on him anymore. 'I am such fool!' she cried, flipping her hair away from her face so that it streamed back into the night. 'I knew it was just the one-night stand. Why did I believe letter?'

She walked faster and he had to skip to catch up, wincing as he threw his weight the wrong way on his injured leg. She was wearing a ratty pair of sweatpants which rode low on her hips. He began to censor his thoughts and then remembered the Watcher was gone. He could look at her. He could touch her. C could do nothing to him now.

He lunged forward and caught her by the shoulder. 'Hey, slow down.' He pretended to lean on her, hissing with pain that wasn't entirely feigned, and eventually she relaxed enough so that he could drape his arm around her shoulders. 'First of all, why shouldn't you believe it, if it was addressed to you? And second of all, I didn't think of what happened between you and me as a one-night stand. There were reasons why I couldn't explain myself to you then.'

'Yes? Like what?'

'Later. First, I need you to tell me everything. Since you got here. Before you came. The arrangements you made. Especially, what happened at the party.'

'And what about you? Don't you have some things to tell me?'

'Sabina, I'm not playing with you. If you just think about it you'll remember I wanted to keep you as far away from this HIT shit as possible. What possessed you to go to that party—'

'Oh, as if you are virtuous one, Adrien?' Her hand slid across his abdomen, coming to rest on his belt buckle. He inhaled sharply and then suppressed a laugh. He wanted to relax and enjoy the unexpected piece of good luck that was Sabina; but he knew better.

'Please. Just tell me everything you can remember, OK? Then we'll decide what to do.'

So she told him about the letter again, about how she'd been restless and needed a change, so coming to New York seemed like the right thing. How Tomaj had picked her up and kept her company, how he made the idea of being a trans seem pretty attractive.

'Tomaj isn't like anyone I know,' she said. 'He reminds me of you.'

Adrien snorted.

'Well, OK – maybe I don't mean you're like him. I mean both of you are not like other people. While I am with him, it's exciting.'

They had reached his new building and he let them in. He had rented the place by phone, through an agency that specialized in placing overseas businessmen: he'd wanted something fully furnished and totally secure, and the transaction was being handled through an alias. When they got inside he went to the phone while Sabina strolled around looking afraid to touch anything.

'So who gave you the Freefall?'

She wrinkled her brow. 'It happened at party. We went because there was supposed to be some HIT art happening there, so I could see what it's like. But I get divided from Tomaj. Everybody else, when performance starts, they collapse, like they are going to sleep except not really—'

'Ah. Yeah, I know what you're saying. They were tuning in to a central source. Go on.'

'Except a few people didn't. Like me. And this guy, this drug guy Laurence?'

'Laurence, yeah, he's a fixture at events like this.'

'Laurence came over with the – what's the word? Like a suitcase for papers, but he doesn't keep paper in it. He says I could try Freefall and I could get a chance to do the art, like all the others, but it's temporary. I didn't want to be the only one awake with all bodies around me.'

'So you took Freefall.'

'Yes. He writes on my forehead with this special pen. And then I close my eyes, and when I open them I start to walk. I walk up walls and across ceiling. Then I fall—'

'Yeah, I get the picture. You trip.'

He dialled Tomaj's number. 'And the other guy, the host of the party. This art patron. What about him?'

'I only talk to him for a minute. I don't know his name. I thought he's a brat. He recognized Schönberg. Not well-dressed.'

Adrien smiled at the kinds of things she noticed about people.

'Did he lose consciousness when all the others did, or was he around when Laurence gave you Freefall?'

'I don't know. I didn't see him after that one time. Someone else was there, I didn't see them, but I think there was a voice.'

He nodded, listened to the phone and hung up.

'Tomaj isn't answering his portable. I don't know what the hell he's been up to,' he said. 'He owes you an apology. But I have a feeling he'll be making himself scarce. The important thing is, no harm's done as far as I can tell.'

'What do you mean, harm?'

'I mean there would be evidence of even a small battery and I don't see that.'

'Battery?' She shivered. 'You mean in my head?'

'You said Tomaj was trying to recruit you.'

149

'He was teasing me and I was interested, but I don't think he would force—'

'Force you into something you probably would have volunteered for, right, Sabina?' He couldn't keep the chill out of his voice.

'Maybe. Don't look that way at me! *You* do it, or you did before.'

'That's just the point, Sabina. I don't want to see you ruined by it. I don't want you to make the mistakes I made.'

'Well, it's over now, yes?'

'I *think* it is. Walking on the ceiling, all that – it doesn't sound too extreme, and I've heard of Freefall although I know for a fact it couldn't link you to a signal. I'd feel better if I knew exactly what was going on.' He studied her closely. 'Is there anything you haven't told me? Are you hearing voices? Experiencing any unusual cravings?'

'No, only usual cravings.' She flopped onto the couch on her back, laying the back of one wrist across her forehead like a fainting maiden. Adrien stood and looked down on her. He picked up her hand.

'You need to know something if you're going to stay here. Look at me.'

The color of her eyes.

'If you came to New York because you're interested in HIT, then forget it. You can't stay with me. No, don't interrupt. I've given it up for good. I don't know what sexy people you might have met, what they might have told you, or what you're expecting from me. But if you want to be with me, you have to forget about all that. I have no tolerance for any of it anymore.'

'I came because I thought you wanted to see me—'

'I *do*.'

'—and it was *your* weird friends.'

'As long as we understand each other.'

Her voice was steady. 'I understand you are finished with HIT.'

He blinked; the air had gone thick as water. He wanted to

bring things back around to the possibility of having sex, but he'd missed his opportunity.

'Go to bed,' Sabina told him suddenly. 'You look exhausted.'

He looked at her hand in his hand.

'What about you?' he said.

'I will sleep in chair.'

'You don't have to sleep in the *chair*—'

'No, I want to. Go on, go to sleep. We talk tomorrow.'

He left her reluctantly, wondering when she'd become so shy about sharing a bed.

Fourteen

Sabina listened to the traffic, the drip of the shower, the ambulances racing down Broadway. She sat upright in the chair, facing the couch. She must have been unconscious most of the previous day – she had only awakened a few hours before Adrien's arrival – yet she felt exhausted. She longed to lie down, but whenever she stretched out a feeling of panic took over and she found herself scrambling upright, heart pounding.

At first she thought her nervousness was due to the after-effects of Freefall; and then she thought the problem was waking up alone in Tomaj's apartment after those *dreams*. Years ago, she had taught herself to forget her dreams: life was simpler if she kept that river dammed. But she couldn't forget the huge, rotting skull, or the old memory of Vukovar in the bombing …

She was angry at herself for trusting Tomaj: she'd blithely gone off without her money or passport and she had been given an unknown drug at a party full of bizarre people – she told herself she was lucky to be alive.

She was alive. But she wasn't the same.

There were oceans of sparkling static behind her eyelids. When she moved she felt the shadows of her own muscles like visitors from some other dimension. There was a synapse of lost hours in her memory: across that gap lay her whole life, intact and complete like a faceted jewel. It seemed to her that she could simply walk away from herself, walk into the future and become … anything.

As the night progressed, she remained awake, wary. She could feel the dream waiting for her, poised to continue if she should only close her eyes. Although she remained awake, she had the sense of listening to a voice from the other side of a wall, where tones and patterns could be heard, but no discernable words. This monologue ran through her mind, indistinct but not random, riding the edge of awareness like an aural ghost.

* * *

If I had a way of thinking about it I might be able to winnow myself away from the cascade of impressions fleeing through her body, replaced all the time by the leading edge of her senses. If I had a niche or a foothold in her I might be able to call myself up, assemble myself from the crowd that roars in her head. But I don't. To slip into existence as I do now is the most supreme act of will, and I am ephemeral. I can't break through: from moment to moment I don't even believe in myself.

* * *

She had been staring at the digital clock. She remembered 2:24. All of a sudden it was 2:51. She was still sitting, but she was no longer in the chair; she was now on the floor. She crawled back into the chair and put her head in her hands. She refused to be afraid.

But she also refused to sleep.

Her eyes were growing heavy.

At 3:59 she began to blink slowly.

By 4:05 she was finding it hard to open her eyes at the end of each blink. She had lost awareness of her breathing.

At 4:14 she shut her eyes and didn't open them. She was now too tired to feel fear; sleep came floating up for her.

She had various dreams: Tomaj was in one of them, and there were taxis, and she was looking for something. But after a while the dreams were eclipsed by a kind of shadow, although there was nothing visual about it. Rather, there was a weight on her, and a sort of reduction *of* her, until her

153

entire being had been restricted to her mouth, which was utterly toothless so that no matter what she did with her tongue, she had no hope of speech. Her consciousness was located at the base of her throat, where the muscles gathered for hot tears from eyes that existed outside her awareness. Gases soughed from lungs that were not in her command. She was a tremendous hollowness surrounded by flesh, unable to grasp even the nature of her own physicality without resorting to memories from a textbook of the developing embryo: the cross-section of the blastula, or was it gastrula, and the little green clusters of cells in the illustration, and how the developing creature formed around this primitive gut, a hole at each end. Topologically the picture made the organism look like two separate fleshes gathered around the white space which ran through it like a road. Now in the dream this frightening emptiness around which any animal is built was made real to her: she was that emptiness, or part of it. She was nothing more than the hole and she had neither the lungs nor the diaphragm with which to draw breath and scream—

'Sabina, stop it. Come on, wake up.' Adrien's voice was low and calm. He didn't touch her but she heard a weird gurgling noise and with embarrassment realized it had come from her. She opened her eyes. She was huddled on the chair in the living room with her knees drawn into her chest in very nearly a fetal position. Adrien was crouched in a parallelogram of sun on the floor. He touched her forearm and his hand was hot.

'You're freezing,' he said, reaching for the throw rug that had fallen to the floor and covering her. He was kneeling beside the chair in his underwear. Pale scars scored the dark skin of his torso. 'It was just a dream. Why don't you go sleep in the bedroom? I was getting up anyway.'

'What time is it?' She clutched the blanket, shivering. He craned his head in search of a clock.

'Almost seven. I wish you wouldn't sleep in the chair ...'

'I'm sorry,' she said. 'I'm sorry. I don't know what—'

'It's OK.'

'Something – something goes wrong with me. Nightmares, usually they mean nothing to me. I never pay attention. Until now.'

He searched her face. 'What kind of nightmares?'

'I can't remember.' His probing look set her teeth on edge. She didn't want to tell him anything. In fact, she felt a sudden urge to strike him. She sat on her hands.

He shifted and sighed.

'I don't know what happened to you at that party. I hate to even think ...' Long pause. 'Maybe you should see a doctor.'

'*No!* No, I—' She had shrunk away, terrified at the concept; she struggled to get control of herself. 'I'm sorry. This isn't me. I can't believe—'

She launched herself to her feet, shaking off dread like water. She went to the window and looked out on the night's stragglers-home, the dog-walkers and the joggers. Fear kept pushing but she pushed back.

'Please, go ahead. Go run. I'm being silly.' She made herself laugh as she turned around into the field of his scrutiny. 'It's just, I don't usually have the nightmares. Remember when I met you, you had bad dreams? Maybe I caught it from you.'

She meant it as a joke but she saw his hand twitch as he began to cross himself. As if to negate the moment, she crossed the room and seized her jacket, looking for cigarettes. Audra's card fell out. She studied it.

'I will go to see this doctor,' she said at length. 'Tomaj introduces us. I like her. She told me to stay away from unlicensed HIT. Like you.'

He took the card from her and frowned. 'Audra Malagon, MD, PhD. Director, Phoenix House. I have no idea who this is. Fancy address.'

'I'm not going to hospital.'

'OK. *OK* – relax. Hey, what's the matter? Who was trying to get *me* to go to a hospital once upon a time?' He came up to her, laughing, and she realized he was about to kiss her. She froze. He put his hand around the back of her head, bending to look in her eyes. But he did not kiss her. His face was troubled.

'Are you afraid of me?' he whispered.

'No. I'm not afraid of you. Why would I be here?'

'Right. Of course.' He moved away briskly, and she knew she'd given the wrong answer. He produced a white canvas karate uniform from his luggage and rolled it into a neat cylinder, tied a frayed black belt around it, and slung it over his shoulder. She looked at his profile, at his mouth which was usually so disposed toward smiling but now showed no emotion, and she wanted to slap herself.

'I will call doctor, make the appointment, OK?'

'If that's what you want. But stay here until I get back. We'll talk about this later. Don't answer the phone or the door. You can order out for food. I would take you with me, but I think you'll be safer here.'

He had a hand on the doorknob as if he couldn't wait to get away.

'Safer? Adrien, why can't I go out? Why do you worry?'

'I *don't know* – that's the whole problem. Anyway, you don't look like you slept very well. You should rest. Just let me think about this.'

She watched him leave the building below, loping off with his right leg still not straightening properly. She thought about her reaction when he touched her. It had not been fear; rather a sensation of displacement, some disassociation from herself that had locked her in place. She didn't like it.

She did not obey Adrien's command to stay in the apartment. After a little while the anxiety about the nightmare wore off; she paced for a long time, and by the time rush hour was in full swing she had begun to feel positively euphoric. She had no idea why. After she took a shower she realized she had no clean clothes because

Adrien hadn't let her bring her suitcase, which irritated her. In fact, his general attitude had been a little extreme. He'd ordered her around, questioned her, and then disappeared just when it was his turn to explain what was going on.

Well, there was no point in being annoyed with him. She would simply remedy the situation. He had left cash; she took it and the spare key and went out. She bought a dress and a pair of sandals and wore them out of the store. The dress was white cotton, and she must have spent ten minutes in the changing room, looking at the way it fell on her body, feeling it slide against her legs, running her hands over its texture. She was conscious that everything she did – every move she made – was a distinct stroke in time, a slice out of a cake that encompassed every sense. The more she noticed, the more she was able to notice, down to the softness of the old bills between her fingers, the mechanical street noise muffled by glass and the mixture of pollution and new-fabric-smell in the air of the store.

She spent an hour in a Greek diner with the *Times* in front of her, drinking coffee very slowly, delighted at the interaction between its taste and the heat of the sun on her face. She'd never felt anything like this before. She knew there were drugs that could heighten the senses, but drugs wore off, whereas she seemed almost to be learning a new skill, and the more practice she had, the better she got. She slipped into a semi-conscious zone, eyes unfocused, and listened. From some great distance within, she could sense the imminence of a music. Whether it was a specific piece of music, or actually a new *kind* of music, she couldn't say; but even from afar she knew it was something she had never before imagined.

She was jostled out of this state by the waitress topping up her cup. The woman caught Sabina's eye and pointed to the folded-over paper, which displayed the day's crossword.

'I wish I could do that,' she said. 'I gave up years ago.'

'Me too,' Sabina answered, and then realized belatedly that most of the puzzle had been filled in. Her left hand held the ballpoint pen she usually carried in her jacket, poised in the act of writing. She smiled weakly at the waitress. 'Practice, I guess.'

The woman gave her a strange look and walked away, but Sabina's heart was pounding. She flexed the pen in her left hand. When she tried to write something in the margin of the paper, it came out as she would expect, wavering and slow: she was right-handed. Yet the strokes on the cross-word were plain and clear. She had no memory of reading the puzzle, much less understanding it. She had been thinking of something else.

She looked at the coffee suspiciously.

Two men had been passing back and forth a mobile phone and some tourist brochures; now they flagged down the waitress and began asking questions in an animated mixture of English and Italian. After a minute it was obvious the conversation was going nowhere; Sabina raised her head and asked in Italian what the problem was. The two wanted to know why no one at the Guggenheim answered the phone and how they could find out what hours it was open: she had no idea, but she translated the waitress's explanation of the vagaries of the museum for them, and they threw their hands up in the air and left.

She finished her coffee, all vestiges of her reverie gone now. She ought to go back. Adrien would be upset if he returned and she wasn't there.

'Oh god.' She covered her mouth, glad the tone of her voice hadn't carried. Written on the newspaper, in the same clear hand, was the following: *Trust no one. P.S. 9 School on 84th and Columbus noon any weekday a message for you ALONE. Trust NO one.*

She whipped around, instinctively looking for the Italians – but that made no sense. They hadn't come anywhere near her.

She left in a rush, the waitress now avoiding her gaze. Out in the light she walked fast, going nowhere in particular, just heading vaguely west feeling bizarre and out of hand. Now the richness of sensory input was like a storm, preventing her from thinking clearly. It was 11:00.

She went back to the apartment, but Adrien wasn't there. She called Audra's work number. Ten seconds after she gave her name to the receptionist, the doctor was on the line.

'Sabina? What can I do for you?'

'I need to see you.'

'You went to the party.'

'Yes.'

'You want to talk about what happened.'

'I want to know about dreams, and why my left hand writes to me.'

There was a silence.

'Can you come to my office this afternoon? It's at Phoenix House on Fifth Avenue between 77th and 78th. Come at three.'

'OK.' For some reason, her voice caught.

'Sabina, where are you now? Are you with Tomaj?'

'No. I can't give you number where I am staying. Adrien will kill me.'

Another silence. 'All right. Never mind. Just get here at three and I'll check you out.'

They hung up. Sabina glanced at her watch again. 11:33. She ought to wait for Adrien. But she didn't. Instead, she responded to a compulsion: it was not rational, but it was highly specific, not unlike the bizarre cravings of pregnant women. She found the 1/9 train and rode it to 86th, then walked across to Columbus and down two blocks. When she got to the school she was afraid to go inside – what would she tell security? She walked past the entrance nervously. It was just after noon, and there were kids running around on the playground. She walked up to the wire fence and looked in on a basketball game among some nine- or ten-year-old kids. She got caught up in the action and pressed her face against the cool wire, forgetting about how strange she must look.

A grey-haired teacher with jowls and a whistle around her

159

neck sauntered up to the fence, and Sabina backed away, preparing to be berated.

'I have two messages for you,' said the woman in a thick New York accent. She took her glasses from their chain and put them halfway down her nose. 'The first is this.' She produced an ax card and passed it through the chain-link fence. 'This is an account at Citibank. I'm supposed to give it to you and remind you that you know the PIN number.'

Sabina stared at the card, shaking her head.

'The second message is from Tomaj.' That name did an odd somersault inside her. 'He wants you to meet him at the sled dog.'

Sabina tried to laugh. 'What? Sled dog?'

'Yep.'

'Where is that?'

'Can't tell you.'

'When? How will he know I'm coming?'

'He'll know.' Spoken with the weary conviction of a middle-aged Jewish New Yorker.

'Who are you?'

'I'm not allowed to say.'

'Where is Tomaj? Why doesn't he talk to me himself?'

'That's between you and him. Oh. I almost forgot. I'm supposed to tell you you passed the first test.'

Fifteen

The dojo looked exactly the same. You'd never know it was there unless you could read the warped Japanese sign at the corner of an alley between a sewing machine repair store and a shop that sold, judging by its window display, nothing but mannequins. At the back of the alley steps led to the basement, where the door to the dojo stood open to the warm breeze.

He was keyed up. His leg was killing him from the run; but it was more than that. The sight of the alley and the door evoked a cascade of memories.

Adrien had grown up with a fascination for martial arts instilled by computer games and movies. He had studied in several schools and watched every instructional video he could find. He had a junior black belt in jiu-jitsu at age twelve and was praised everywhere he went. Then Roger Furuta's name came to his attention. Furuta was famous in martial arts circles for knowing the Okinawa Goju katas with more depth than anyone. He knew secret applications, it was said; he'd studied in Okinawa and China and his knowledge was encyclopaedic. Adrien, technically facile but starved for substance, had begged his mother to let him train at Furuta's Chelsea dojo.

But Furuta didn't fit the bill for a karate master: he was short and plump, spoke in a working-class New Jersey accent, and mangled even the easiest jokes in the telling. His taste in movies tended toward puerile comedy and he had a passion for love songs of the 1940s, which he was apt to sing when drunk. Nevertheless, Adrien studied with him for seven years, occupying the unstated position of star pupil – until Furuta found out about Adrien's 'profession' doing security for a wire crew.

At the time, Adrien had seen the job as a way of testing out his skills. He was proud, in fact, of his ability to subdue opponents without seriously hurting them, and he knew his training made him an asset to his crew. Adrien's associates were all kids he'd gone to school with, the ones who never could quite toe the line, the ones who were quick on their feet or spun a good line of bullshit, but never opened a book. They were his friends. 'Criminal' was a middle-class word, anyway.

Furuta didn't see it this way. He promptly kicked Adrien out.

Not long afterward, Adrien had met Tomaj, and everything changed. He found himself walking out of his life and into the magic of HIT; certainly Roger Furuta had been largely forgotten. So returning to this dojo now was sentimental and unsettling, comforting and freaky: like any homecoming, only more so.

When he walked in, the dojo smelled of faintly stale, salty sweat, just as it always had. Sensei Furuta was sitting on the bare boards rubbing linseed oil into an oar, a traditional Okinawan weapon dating from the times when the Japanese invaders had taken all blades from the islanders, necessitating the use of farm implements and other common tools to fend off the samurai. He glanced up when Adrien appeared in the doorway; Adrien sank to his knees and bowed formally, keeping his head down a long time in a show of respect.

When he raised his eyes, Furuta was still polishing. Unsure of what to do, Adrien didn't move. After a minute, the master chuckled.

'You can't get up, can you?'

Adrien grimaced and got to his feet, tears firing in his eyes from the leg injury. Furuta laughed again – a sound not of mockery, but of genuine mirth.

'Adrien Reyes. Why are you here?'

162

That was a good question. He wanted to be punished, he realized. And as soon as he thought it, of course he didn't want it after all. He cleared his throat.

'I've been doing Sanchin a lot. Every day. Sometimes all day long. It's all I can think about.'

Furuta said nothing.

'And the other katas as well.'

The rag snapped across the oar.

'So why are you here?'

'I want another chance to train with you.'

'Why?'

'Why do you think?' Adrien snapped impatiently, wishing Furuta would stop asking the same question.

Furuta got up and brought the oar back to its rack. He took down a naginata and knelt on the mat with the blade across his knees. Watching him triggered in Adrien a series of memories of Furuta in training. The guy might look like a cupcake, but he moved like something not of this world. Dimples formed in the wide cheeks.

'Just by taking a look at you, I'd guess you finally lost a fight. So what do you want me to do about it? It's a bad world out there. If I were you, I'd carry a weapon.'

Adrien laughed. 'I've lost plenty of fights. It's nothing like that. It's ... I ... I guess you could say I had a life-changing experience. And karate is all I care about now.'

Furuta took this in for a minute.

'Every day at four o'clock I get about thirty kids coming in here. They line up; I teach them; they learn some self-discipline, they learn how to move, maybe some self-defense. Some are better than others. I been teaching twenty years. Over that time I must have had thousands of kids come through here. Hundreds of adults, too. In all that time I never had a student I could teach less than you.'

Adrien tried to figure out how to take this.

'I've been training, you know,' he said. 'Not every day, but I keep up with practice.'

'What for?'

163

'What for? I don't know. Why do *you* do it?'

'Makes me more alive.'

'Yeah, that's exactly it. That's exactly why I—'

'No, Adrien. Don't compare yourself to me. I never touch HIT. Wires make you *less* alive. They make you more like everybody else. Like milk. Pasteurized, homogenized.'

'I've never done wires myself,' Adrien said. And C *had* made him more alive; maybe even too alive – or at any rate, it had made him very much alive but not entirely himself, and the fear of that loss-of-himself was still fresh enough to make him go cold just thinking about it.

Furuta shrugged. 'Whatever you been into, you look like shit. You look like a ghost.'

'That's why I need karate.'

'I'm not going to be anybody's drug.' Furuta spat on the blade and rubbed vigorously.

Adrien was starting to get pissed off. 'What do I have to do?' he demanded. 'You want to play Japanese master, make me camp outside your dojo for a week in formal zazen to prove I'm serious? You want me to carry water up the mountain for five years before you'll teach me anything? Is that what this is about?'

'*Oh*,' Furuta exclaimed. 'You want me to teach you. I see. Maybe I'll teach you. Tell you what. If you can beat me in a fight, I'll teach you everything I know. How's that?'

At first Adrien thought he was kidding: if he could beat Furuta in a fight, what would be the point of studying from him? But the master was putting away his tools to clear the floor.

'Get your gi on.'

When he knotted the black belt around his waist, he flashed the memory of Furuta awarding it to him, shaking his hand. Slapping him on the back.

'OK. Come on, Reyes. Let's see what you got.'

Half-heartedly, Adrien put up his guard. It was Furuta who'd taught him to regard every opponent as the most dangerous man in the world, a lesson he'd never forgotten.

But he didn't want to hurt Furuta. He'd seen too much evidence lately of his own power – and of the fragility of his control over that power.

'You coming in or what?'

Furuta brought his hands up at last and Adrien struck. He unleashed a long roundhouse kick to Furuta's head and rushed in with a fusillade of punches. Some of them landed; but Furuta stepped to one side and closed. He locked up one of Adrien's legs and spilled him on the floor; Adrien managed to grab a piece of Furuta's gi. He pulled the master down into the whirlwind of his fists and feet.

Blows were exchanged; blood flowed.

'You killed someone,' Furuta gasped. Adrien avoided a lock and twisted like an eel. He had forgotten how strong Furuta was.

'Didn't – you. You-don't-trust – yourself anymore. Uhn—' as Adrien's elbow cracked across his jaw and Adrien grabbed for control of the head, thrusting his heel at Furuta's balls but didn't get the angle right and his foot slid off the master's thigh; Furuta bit his hand to free his head, then said, 'You're asking to get killed. You think you deserve it, that's why—'

As Furuta was talking, Adrien had been getting himself set up to apply a complex and difficult lock that would finish the fight without injury; but suddenly Furuta stuck a spearhand into his solar plexus, making him relax his grip. The son of a bitch got loose and was on his feet. Adrien sprang up after him, breathing hard and in pain. Furuta came in to punch and Adrien deflected the strike easily, floating backward, but he had again underestimated the older man's power. Suddenly Furuta was inside his guard; his hands were forced away from him and his face was being pummeled – blood everywhere; he shifted to one side, playing into Furuta's strategy: the next thing he knew Furuta had leaped on his back, there was a lock on his neck, and he was being dragged backward and forced down by a chokehold that threatened to break his neck. He found

165

himself on the floor with Furuta's legs wrapped around him from behind, making his spine arch and delivering him fully into the choke, he could hear his own throat rattling as Furuta crushed his esophagus in the crook of his elbow. Adrien was tapping the floor for all he was worth in signal of surrender and Furuta finished his sentence,

'—you're allowing me to beat you.'

Suddenly he was released. He staggered to his feet, gasping and coughing; in the practice mirror he saw that the choke had turned his face purple. Blood poured from his nose.

'So,' Furuta said, standing and straightening his gi. 'You were talking about kata before. Any idea which kata I just used on you at the end there?'

Adrien shook his head. Whatever the application was, it was fucking sophisticated. Maybe it came from a kata he didn't know: Kururunfa, or Supairenpei.

'That was the first kata, the one we teach white belts. Gekisai Dai Ichi.'

'Don't make me laugh,' Adrien said hoarsely.

'It's true,' Furuta grinned.

'Show me.'

When Furuta did, Adrien shook his head and said, 'No shit.' Resignedly, he walked away and began to take off his gi.

'What the hell are you doing? I didn't dismiss you yet.'

The two men faced each other across the dojo, winded, sweating, blood-spattered. Adrien blotted his nose and smiled redly.

'OK, Roger. Teach me something.'

It was mid-afternoon by the time he got back to the apartment. Furuta had made him work out on the maki-wara and the sandbag, shouting instructions and corrections and especially exhorting the student to let go. Adrien was holding back, Furuta said. He would be better off with no skill and a strong spirit than perfect technique if he didn't have the nerve to carry it out because he was inhibited.

Adrien wondered if Furuta had ever killed someone. He doubted it. Probably Furuta had never been in a real fight.

Still, when he arrived home he felt better. Hitting things, hard, always felt good to him.

Sabina wasn't there. He wrapped some ice in a paper towel and collapsed on the sofa, groaning. For half an hour he waited; then, hungry, he picked up the phone intending to order pizza. Something occurred to him, and he hit redial.

'Good afternoon, Phoenix House,' said a dulcet, female voice.

He hung up.

'El stupido,' he accused himself in the mirror as he went out.

Of course the invasion begins subtly, so that at first Tomaj thinks it's to be an Arabian knight of assaults, 1001 darknesses of veils or is it stories. Plenty of time to plan his defense against anyone who wants in to his mind. He may have been shocked by C's revelations, but that didn't stop him from learning the codes as it asked. Now he walks around with a plant that's as close to impenetrable as he can imagine.

He has no Watcher to act as a sort of feudal lord and patrol the link; no Watcher to warm his mind. It's up to Tomaj now either to have the code altered, or to remove the plant entirely, as he knows Adrien has done. But who to trust, and how to go ahead? If there were a beneficent God, Tomaj would be allowed time to accustom himself to the sheer and screaming void left by C's absence, the sudden and staggering loss of what now feels like the center of himself. Nor does he know how to handle the knowledge C arranged to be released into his consciousness after it died.

Because he knows the truth now. And he's pretty sure

he's the only one who knows the truth. The question is, how to act on it?

He's a stranger in his own home. There's no sign of Sabina; he makes phone calls but nobody's seen her since the party. He has a vague recollection about what happened after he called Adrien. He remembers that Max appeared and told him to cooperate.

'C left you high and dry,' he said. 'I'll take care of you. I'm developing something based on the Egyptian system of magic that I think you might like. I can see to it you feel no pain. Ever.'

Tomaj remembers the Swede peeling his fingers away from Max's throat. He was ultimately knocked out and locked in a closet, whereupon he raised hell until the night porter let him out and informed him he'd lost a whole day.

It's all too messed up. In those moments when the Shawl opened for him, his purpose and how he would achieve it seemed both clear and finite; but he can't seem to hold on to the understanding that was C's legacy to him. To make matters worse, the security code is only partial protection. Someone – or something – is breaking bits of it here and there. Snatches of video test patterns intrude on Tomaj's awareness. Tiny slivers of time disappear for him, making the world jump and blur.

The attacker must be a computer, and it must be at least as good as the mainline C linked him to, because it's outmaneuvering C's system when it comes to jumping frequencies, and it's got enough of Tomaj's code to steal bits of his life. A computer isn't sufficiently conscious to Watch in realtime like a person, but if it can penetrate his codes it can seize his time, storing the data in digital form and holding it until someone who knows how to interpret the data comes along and sifts through it all. Someone like ... guess who?

Knowing what he now knows, Tomaj has little doubt that it's Max who's after his ass. Tomaj has always thought of Max as Adrien's enemy: that was the way C liked things to appear. But it seems as if it will be Tomaj who takes him on, Tomaj who has never killed anything larger than a roach – nor been physically threatened himself (who would attack a giant?). One thing's certain: if he doesn't do something, the computer will come in and suck on his naked brain and spit out anything he can't use.

Tomaj has only one recourse. His biggest pro acting role may have been as a singing construction worker in a laundry powder ad in the nineties, but that can't prevent him from trying to act his way out of this particular paper bag. Except it will have to be the most extreme form of method acting.

He begins by abandoning all his possessions. At the apartment he follows the instructions specified by C's last communication through the Shawl. Then he walks out, leaving everything behind but his ax card. It sits in his pocket like a small security blanket. He tries to forget it's there. If he were a yogi he would now begin to practice his meditations, stretching his being to include all of the city and flowing through it unattached, samsara glitter and pain meaningless to a cerebral cortex programmed to admit only the divine. But his intentions are the opposite: he will go *into* the corruption of the flesh and let anybody who can try to ride along with him – if they can stomach it.

Because Tomaj plans to go mad. He'll do whatever it takes to render his own mind uninterpretable: how hard can it be? It's just a matter of letting the winged things that live in his guts migrate upward, to his head.

Sixteen

Phoenix House was a converted mansion near Central Park. It had its own underground parking garage and looked like every other building on the block: heinously exclusive, forbiddingly expensive. Adrien began to smell the kind of money that Watchers usually had. Furuta was right about Adrien not using his head. He was always one play behind in the action, and as usual he was on the defensive.

'Fucking idiot. I can't believe I let her walk into this,' he muttered as he got out of the cab, tossing a half-eaten calzone into a wastebasket and wiping the corners of his mouth. Inside, the place reminded him of a hotel. There were velvet and brocade chairs, Persian carpets and fresh flowers in an antique vase. The elevator had no directory. He spotted security sensors and no fewer than three camera eyes. The human being who had answered the phone was not in evidence.

'Dr Malagon is in conference,' intoned the automated reception desk when he presented ID and asked to see her. 'You may leave a message here.'

Gambling that the security system wouldn't be on full alert in the middle of the day, he made for the elevator. It didn't respond to his call. The stairwell was unlocked and he bounded up a flight in a rough approximation of his usual agility.

'You have not been cleared by security. Please return to reception,' admonished the sensors.

He grinned at the nearest camera and kept going, annoyed that his leg slowed him down.

'Adrien Reyes, you will not be warned again. Return to reception immediately.'

He got the door to the third floor open and found himself in a corridor. The nearest door was marked simply 'Therapy'. The small window set in the door was dark. He tried the handle.

Something pricked between his shoulder blades and his back went numb. He spun around, but there was no one there. He reached behind himself and tried to grab whatever it was that had stuck into his back, but he couldn't seem to get a grip on it. The floor came closer. He felt stiff and fragile, as if he might literally shatter. Carpet pressed against his nose. Everything swirled.

A woman's fat face hovered over him. She was wearing too much make-up and an expensive, abstract 3-D tattoo on one cheek.

'Just what I needed,' she said, slapping his face. 'What's your problem? Sabina, what's with this guy, does he not understand English?'

Sabina's leg came into view. He grasped vaguely at her dress, his hand unable to do what he wanted it to.

'What happened to him?' Sabina sounded worried – at least she was all right. He tried to smile to reassure her, but it was like being at the dentist. Nothing worked right.

'It's just a security immobilizer. It will wear off in a little while. Serves you right, Adrien. Yes, I know who you are. Cody, bring him in my office.'

Cody was a nurse. He was huge and mean in inverse proportion to his name. He picked Adrien up without effort and carried him down the hall after the two women.

Dr Malagon's office was clean and bare. It had a low, circular couch covered in aqua fabric that looked green in some spots, blue in others. Adrien was deposited here in a stiff heap. The window overlooking Fifth Avenue had been dimmed to filter out daylight, but there were tall steel braziers in which sinuous flames burned without smoke, showing to best advantage the enormous system tank that took up much of the office. The tank was egg-shaped and filled with bright, technical fish. Malagon walked in and addressed the system, her fingers touching the slightly pliant, clear surface of the tank. A string of light seemed to flow from her face toward a flickering window of data deep within the tank, and her eyes shivered rapidly back and forth. Then she removed her finger, the light vanished, and the window was sucked up by a small fish, which then flitted away to hide in a submerged galleon.

Malagon stirred and looked at him.

'Feeling better?'

He flexed his hands, frowning. She sat down heavily and the couch turned slowly to gold in a starburst around her buttocks. Sabina edged closer to Adrien, but he paid little attention to her as he studied the doctor. For all her weight, she was sharp-featured, and her eyes moved fast. There was something familiar about her: he didn't know whether it was her husky voice or some hidden aggression in her mannerisms, but he found himself simultaneously fascinated and repelled.

'So what's your connection?' he said before she could draw breath to speak. 'Where do you fit into the picture?'

He felt Sabina flinch and he leaned forward stiffly, forearms on knees. He was ill at ease on this couch that kept changing color.

Ignoring his questions, Malagon nodded slowly to herself.

'Yes, I see it,' she said, looking vaguely in Adrien's direction, her eyes focusing not on him but on the air around him. 'I can see the appeal. But you're a diamond in the rough, my friend.'

'I'm not your friend.' He kept his voice low, but he was angry and he didn't know why. There was something about this woman, something acute and unnecessarily intimate. His insides began to shiver.

'Dr Malagon,' Sabina said, laying a quelling hand on his arm. 'Maybe you can explain what you find, with my head? Adrien should hear, too.'

'I have a few questions,' Adrien interrupted, again before

Malagon could speak. He had her rhythm now; in fact he could almost hear her heartbeat. Assessing an enemy this way was an old habit from combat, and he thought it was curious that it should kick in here and now, when he was scarcely in any physical danger.

'What is this place? All the expensive real estate, the fancy security. What do you do here, *doctor*?'

Malagon's mouth stretched. Yes, there was something *very* familiar about her.

'Not everyone in the world is out to screw each other,' she said mildly. 'Come over to the tank and take a look at our facility.'

Adrien stood stiffly and positioned himself in front of the tank. Video windows formed inside; he chose one and looked into it. An old man was sitting in a wheelchair staring at a large monitor. Mechanical supports held his head in position; his hands trembled on the arms of the chair. On the monitor an image was developing, colors appearing and disappearing from different sections of the screen. The man's face was a study in tics and twitches, and his body appeared wasted.

'Leon has become an accomplished artist. He sold something to a gallery in California last month. And no – they didn't know he's got inoperable Parkinson's. Leon, of course, is an exception; we've had a great deal of success with Parkinson's recently, but Phoenix House is a facility only for people who would otherwise be hopeless.'

'Very admirable,' said Adrien, not very sincerely. He thought it was a hell of an expensive way to make a piece of art most people would never even see, and meanwhile the emergency rooms of public hospitals were overflowing.

'We're privately funded, of course,' Malagon said as if reading his mind. 'And you'd be amazed how many people we can treat as outpatients now. We can restore mobility where the spinal cord has been damaged. We can compensate for brain lesions. People who would otherwise die in institutions can have lives closer to what we'd call normal.

Anyway—' She cancelled the image. 'You're not interested in any of this. Let's talk about Sabina.'

Her fingers danced and several windows came up.

'This is the data I collected about Sabina earlier, before you interrupted us. The first thing I did was to check for metal. I know your worst fear, Adrien, so I wanted to get it out of the way.'

'I scanned her at home,' he said.

'Those hand-scanners can miss a lot. As you can see, so far I've found nothing resembling a trans battery or plant. I checked the thalamus for any irregular tissue whatsoever, and found nothing. Nothing in the ears, either; nothing so much as a wire. Sinuses are empty ...'

The display showed Sabina's brain with its shifting colors; Malagon kept changing the views and zooming and altering the parameters, so Adrien wasn't so sure what he was looking at. But he knew that anything metallic would have been immediately apparent, even to him: so his earlier scan was accurate. Sabina didn't have a plant.

'Except—' said the doctor, 'this little guy in your molar, Sabina. That's not a plant, just a primitive radio tag. Somebody wants to keep track of where you are.'

'Who? Why?'

'Take it out,' Adrien said.

'I'm not a dentist. Just calm down. Let me see what else is going on here and we'll come back to it. I want to look at the brain waves. What we're seeing now looks like normal beta-level activity. Obviously, if there's a problem with sleep disturbance, I'd need to take a look at her when she's sleeping. The next thing you're going to see, Sabina, is the part where I gave you a piece of soft plastic abstract sculpture and asked you to manipulate it in your hand until it matched the image you saw in the visor, and then there were various verbal tasks, you remember? And after that the sounds? Well, this material I've collected will need to be analyzed. All I've got at the moment is a primitive model of your cognitive pathways.'

174

She brought up a three-dimensional multicolored wave shape that pivoted and moved, changing form constantly.

'This is just a rough sketch, but even from this we can see that there are times when two neuronal groups at once are consuming similar amounts of energy, thereby vying for your consciousness. I'm not a psychiatrist, but I'd hazard a guess that sometimes this secondary, or subconscious, activity is strong enough to poke up and interfere with what is happening consciously.'

Adrien looked at the evolving image but it meant nothing to him. Patterns, Furuta always said. There was a pattern here that reached out to him, but it wasn't in Sabina's brain activity. It was in Malagon. Everything she did, everything she said, the pauses in the way she thought and moved … something inside Adrien pinched him, hard, and he had the sensation of waking from a dream with a feeling of dread.

'You can see it right now,' the doctor continued. 'See how there are several areas lit up? The largest should constitute the awareness that's the most important at this particular moment, but this other one – in this case it's also in the prefrontal cortex – this other one is almost equally large. It may eclipse the primary area from time to time, and a different level of awareness will break through. Let me just cross-reference this and find out what you were thinking about at that moment, Sabina—'

'All right,' Adrien cut in, standing up and putting his hand on the tank. 'That's enough.'

'How am I supposed to help her if—'

'I think you should submit to a scan yourself, Audra. What do you want to bet we'd find a plant in *your* brain?'

Sabina stood up also. 'Adrien, what—?'

'She's a Watcher, Sabina. I'm sure of it.' He turned to Malagon. 'It all fits. The money, the access to HIT equipment, the connections on the scene. The protection of respectability, of being a doctor – the shit you must be able to get away with! But you didn't count on me recognizing

175

you. Did you? It's funny. All that time I was a trans, I didn't think I knew anything about your true identity, but after spending ten minutes with you it's obvious who you are. Did you think you could hide yourself from me? Me of all people?'

Malagon was on her feet and had begun to edge toward the door, her face pale beneath the mask of make-up. Adrien advanced on her.

'You had me,' he said. 'You really fucked me over, C. But you won't do it to her. Don't—' he lunged forward and seized her hand '—touch that security pad. You know I'm capable of killing. You made me that way.'

Sabina's mouth was hanging open. She turned from Adrien to the doctor and back, but Malagon looked only at him, shaking her head slowly.

'I'm not C,' she said in a frightened voice. 'You've made a mistake. I worked with C. Yes, I'll admit to that. But C is dead, Adrien. I can prove it.'

'How? I'm fed up with your tricks.'

'It's not a trick. I can show you the corpse.'

The body was lying in a refrigerated compartment. It was a female, middle-aged Latina. The head had been shaved and was studded with semi-permanent electrodes. She was small; entirely too small to be C, Adrien thought.

'What about the brain implant? Is it still in there?'

'She had several implants, and we've touched none of them. They were custom-designed and would have no applicability for anyone else. Anyway, her will specifies that there should be no autopsy and no tampering of the body in any way.'

Sabina strolled around the side of the body and peered into the face.

'You're showing a lot of respect,' Adrien pressed. 'If I were you, I'd be in a hurry to get in there and see what she was loaded with.'

Malagon looked at him coldly. 'You make her sound like

a sports car. C endured a terrible condition. She had suffered brainstem damage, and for years she was deprived of all motor function and all senses, even though the rest of her brain was in perfect condition. I tried to help her escape. Yes, I've flirted with gray-market HIT; she isn't the only patient I've gone to the Deep for. But don't you dare accuse me of self-interest.'

Sabina put out a finger and touched the shaven scalp, which was speckled with stubble grown, no doubt, in the time since death. Malagon's chin was trembling.

'My whole career revolved around her rehabilitation,' Malagon continued. She gave a derisive laugh but there were tears in her eyes. 'I know exactly what she was loaded with because I put it there myself. You think I'm C? You must be noticing some family resemblance, Adrien. She was my cousin.'

As if on cue, Sabina collapsed like a doll on the floor. Adrien turned to help her but Malagon was quicker.

'Have you seen enough?' the doctor gasped, trying to haul Sabina out of the room. 'I think Sabina has. No, she's only fainted. Bring her in here.'

Adrien picked up Sabina and brought her into an adjacent diagnostic room. He didn't buy this story for a minute. There was a body and Malagon said it was C's – but if C was in trouble with the Deep, what better escape than to pretend to be dead? Maybe even to let Tomaj take the heat for awhile, until things calmed down, which would explain his disappearance. That was the way C liked to play. But Adrien would get nowhere with further accusations – in fact, he should have kept his mouth shut. Now Malagon knew he suspected her.

'I want no part of you,' Adrien said. 'You've done enough damage.'

Malagon's nostrils flared. 'Don't be stupid. I didn't do anything to her. All I did was steer Sabina toward C. I haven't yet ascertained what's happening with Sabina's consciousness. Why do you think I want to look more closely at her? And who are you, anyway? Sabina came to *me* for help.'

'No. No no no.' He put his hand up. So fucking smart; just like C. He couldn't see his way through it. 'I don't want you to touch her. For that matter – if you aren't C, if that body in there is C, then why the fuck is C dead? For all I know, you killed her.'

'Oh, right!' Malagon had regained her former blaring tone. 'Like, first I *am* C, then I murdered C. Do you even have a clue?'

Sabina's eyes opened and focused on the ceiling, the protrusions of equipment hovering just above her. Adrien backed away but Malagon moved closer to Sabina, grimacing.

'Goddamnit,' she snarled. 'I've missed my chance to look at her cognitive activity while she was out.'

Sabina frowned. She flexed her hands. She brought one hand to her face and touched it. She touched Malagon's sleeve. Then she shot up from the unit and bolted out of the room.

'Sabina!' Adrien started after her, but she'd already reached the elevator. The doors opened for *her*, he noticed—

'Adrien, wait!'

He whirled. Malagon stood in the doorway, running an anxious hand through her hair.

'I've handled this badly,' she said. 'It would help if you wouldn't be so suspicious, if you would cooperate even slightly.'

Adrien could barely keep his voice civil.

'I hated C,' he said. 'When you get too close to someone and they trespass on you, that breaking of trust – that's the kind of hate I'm talking about. So, whoever you are, whatever that body is all about – why should I help you? I only care about Sabina now. Not any of this.'

'But Adrien, don't you see—'

'I *don't* see,' he snapped. 'I don't want to see. I don't want to know. You keep clear of Sabina, understand? Or you'll have me to deal with.'

He slammed the call button for the elevator but it didn't respond, so he went down the stairs as fast as his leg would permit. Shit, if it wasn't that same old feeling of being outflanked and outmaneuvered – Furuta was right. He had to do better at anticipating the patterns of things, so he wouldn't always find himself manipulated, jerked around by somebody else's knitting needles. On the sidewalk he bounced up and down on the balls of his feet, agitated, looking for Sabina. He crossed the street and walked north half a block before he spotted her some distance away, ascending the steps of the art museum. He had to leg it to catch up with her. By the time he did, she was inside paying for admission.

'I don't want to talk,' she said, walking past the security barrier fast. She held her head at an angle such that he couldn't really see her face. 'Please. Leave me alone.'

The cool darkness of the museum acted as an anodyne to his turmoil, and he allowed himself to simply follow her and study her actions. He trailed after her through the Egyptian section, stood patiently while she stared at the frescos or whatever they were called: whole walls cartooned with the ancient equivalents of X-Men, cartouches instead of semaphores narrating the stories of gods and kings. It meant nothing to him. At length he followed her into a creepy room containing wooden sarcophagi that were painted in bright, fresh colors but disturbingly small in size; burial shrouds stamped with the secretions of human flesh; jars containing internal organs. A plaque informed him that only the brain was thrown away after death, and he snorted, glancing up to see if Sabina was still upset or if he could talk to her now. She was standing at the coffin of a Middle Kingdom queen, gazing at the blue-winged being painted on its lid.

He approached her and waited for her to emerge from her reverie. He didn't know if he felt uneasy or just bored.

179

'Ma'at,' she murmured. 'Goddess of justice. Tell me about C.'

He glanced at her sidelong but she wasn't looking at him.

'What do you want to know?'

'What kind of person was she? What was it like to have her sharing your mind?'

OK, he was definitely uneasy.

'C wasn't really like a person. It was a presence. Not a voice, not even a personality. How can I explain? It wasn't like C was separate from me and I could recognize it. I knew C was there because I would feel a certain way when I was being Watched.'

'What way? How would you feel?'

Adrien looked at his hands. 'C knew me better than anyone. It could read my mind. It could sense desires I didn't know I had. It could make me want what *it* wanted and I wouldn't even know the difference. It could make me feel exalted, believe in myself and the importance of my life, the meaning of it all. C could do these things any time it decided to.'

'*She*. You keep saying "it". She wasn't an it, she was a she.'

'Yeah. I saw the body, too, remember.' Someone's body, anyway.

'But?'

'But nothing. But nothing, Sabina. There are some things you simply can't understand.'

She looked at him searchingly, finally lowering her gaze as if in acceptance. Then she wandered out of the room, into the huge glass-walled chamber that housed some kind of temple on a stone platform surrounded by water. Adrien tagged behind, depressed. The sight of C's alleged body had brought him no peace. He had always tried not to think of C as human. C had been brilliant, without honor, perceptive, manipulative – and with no leavening of human weakness or vulnerability that he could ever see. And yet the body had been painfully vulnerable: the body had borne all the weakness that the mind flew free of. Malagon was almost certainly lying, for cousin or no cousin, why else would she herself seem so familiar to him? But if there was the slightest possibility that she wasn't lying, that he had seen C, dead, on a metal shelf ... to think that it – *she* – might have been a human being imprisoned in a non-functioning body ... the way he felt about that kept shifting, eluding comprehension.

What was between us? he kept thinking.

Sabina was standing in the entrance to the temple. She glanced over her shoulder when he approached. She said, 'When the people are gone only the structure is left. Only the bones of their world. These things are so hard, so cold. So many lines. Can you feel ghosts here? Can you feel anything?'

'No,' Adrien said. 'Some people think it's scary, but I can't feel it.'

'Don't you see? That's *why* it is so frightening. It's empty. Tomaj and his museum, the same way. Is for dead things. Is a way to look at death. To look at death and feel better. But I don't feel better.'

She slid past him and down the steps. Beyond her, through the glass, he could see cabs gliding from Central Park. If he could just get her out on the street, where the world was moving and breathing and stinking in some way he could comprehend, then it would be all right.

'Sabina, you're in a strange mood.'

'I don't understand myself. Remember when I got in bed with you in Zagreb?'

'Uh, yeah. I think I can remember that.' A halfwit grin found its way to his face from some hiding place beneath grimmer emotions.

'What was I thinking? It's like – how do they say? – catching the tiger by his tail. I was crazy to do it.' She bent her head, looking into the moat surrounding the Nubian temple, the coins lying beneath the rippling water.

'I don't think you were crazy—'

'I was insane.' She paused, licking her lips and breathing deeply, her eyes still fixed on the water. 'In the war, you know, we lived in the cellars for months. Everything in my city, Vukovar, was ruined. In plaza somebody leaving city tries to save the grand piano, but something goes wrong. Maybe it gets stuck in rubble and so it stays there. It got damaged, full of dirt. Sometimes, if shelling stopped, when others are doing washing or looking for food, I go out and play it. I played some Schumann my mother teaches me, a little Beethoven I don't know so well. After one week people take the wire – I don't know what they use for – so some keys don't work. And then the shell lands on it. It's destroyed. But keyboard is still OK. So I go, I went and played the keyboard. I press keys, you know, to hear the music in my head. The Chetniks start bombing again, but I am listening in my mind. The bombs are coming down and I don't hear them.

'My mother. You know, mothers are supposed to send their children away, but my mother she can't go for some reason, and she doesn't want to be separated from me. So I stay in Vukovar, and one day when I am playing piano and the bombs come, she can't find me, I guess. I was playing piano, and she can't find me, and I never have seen her again.'

She took a breath. 'The lady called Maria has to come and pick me up, carry me inside to her cellar to save my life. She slapped my face and later I hear her tell the others, "Poor child, it's got to her. She's—" How can I say it in English? Like, broken. "She's a broken child."'

Adrien kept his voice as quiet as hers. 'You weren't crazy. You were only a kid, that's what kids are like.'

'No, because also after war, never I am doing what I should do. Everybody else go one way, I go another way. I tell myself I have reasons but, Adrien, I don't know *why* am I like this. I think, there is something that everybody else has it, and I don't. I just don't.'

Adrien touched her hair, which fell over her face, obscuring her profile.

'For whatever it's worth,' he said lightly, 'you seemed pretty together when I met you. Except maybe the car needed some work.'

She suddenly looked at him and he caught his breath. He'd seen that look before, in the seconds when they'd been wrapped around each other in bed and he'd felt for a moment … free. Heat flooded him.

She blushed and glanced away.

'I need the cigarette,' she said in a normal tone. 'I guess I can't smoke here.'

He sighed.

'Adrien, you want to know what Dr Malagon said to me when I told her about party? She said Freefall makes people *jagged* after they take it. She said, "it makes the corners of your personality very sharp."'

'The corners of your personality were always sharp.'

She laughed, then cut off the sound. 'It's strange. Seeing that body. At first it made me sick. But now I want to have sex.'

With a mixture of hope and fear, he asked, 'Here?'

He got her into a cab before her mood could change again. But they sat apart, and Sabina neither touched nor looked at him: paradoxically, this inflamed him even more. She was wearing a white cotton shift; he looked at the folds of it, at the floor, at her hand on the seat, his anticipation building to a frenzy. She smoked rapidly and with absolute concentration.

The day's heat hung in the evening, and the air conditioning in the apartment had not come on automatically, so the rooms were stifling. He dragged off his shirt, kicking his shoes out of the way, and made for the bedroom, where he confronted a climate control system he didn't particularly understand. He was vaguely aware of Sabina moving from room to room, opening windows. His hands were shaking and he couldn't think; finally he gave the thermo-stat a slap and thought he heard something break.

'Shit!'

A hand curled around his waist and he felt her mouth against his back. The other hand reached over his shoulder and switched off the lights. Her bare skin was chill with sweat.

'Don't speak,' she said, divesting him of the rest of his clothes.

He turned and flung himself at her, driving her back toward the bed. But at the last minute she stepped aside and he had to follow, coming after her until she stood with her back up against the wall. Beside her the window was half-open, but this was the back of the building and there was no view, only a brick wall a few feet away. She did not seem to be interested in foreplay: the next thing he knew she had slithered up on the sill. He parted her with his thumbs and her legs came around him; his hands spread across her hips to steady her and she grabbed the window frame with one hand. He nudged her belly with the head of his cock, rubbing the shaft against her clitoris. She banged her head back against the glass, gasping.

'I have an idea,' he suggested. 'Why don't we do this in bed?'

Her hand was cranking the window wider. Stinking air hit them with the sound of traffic.

'I said, don't speak.'

So he put his tongue in her mouth, bracing himself against the frame with one hand. But he wasn't prepared for her response when he finally buried himself in her: she released backwards, arching out over the narrow alley with its trash reek beneath. Adrien lost sight of her face and her dark hair was blowing everywhere. He took her hips in both hands again to keep her from falling and a light came on one floor above them in the building opposite. The silhouette of a figure appeared backlit in the window, as near as if it were in the next room. She began to cry out on rhythm.

Alarmed, Adrien began calculating how to get her back inside while still fucking. Sabina managed to reach back and brace herself against the far brick wall with one hand. He felt her abdominals contract as her head came back up and in a fierce tone she panted, 'He has light on. We don't. He can't see us.' Adrien said nothing, transfixed by the lit window and the figure, *just standing there*, and a wave of the old fear began creeping over him...

'Adrien, come on!' she demanded, bucking against him, and he tried to ignore the window and the shadow and the long fall beneath. He gritted his teeth and kept going. Within blessed seconds she came, her feet arching and trembling against his legs, and then she went soft.

Adrien hauled her sharply inside and dumped her on the floor, where she lay apparently oblivious, legs spread, eyes slitted and gleaming in the dimness. He sat back on his heels, his erection harder than ever and sweat streaming down his back. He waited for her to speak, but she gave only an underwater moan and stretched a hand out to him. He fell onto her with his full weight and found himself drilling her into the floor with a kind of vengeance. He thrust one hand into her hair and grasped the back of her skull at the bump of the occipital bone, forcing her head to turn and face him. Her eyes were closed but he felt her orgasm, softer this time but enough to bring him to the brink. He bit her lower lip. She opened her eyes and looked at him. He came.

His heart pummelled both their chests as he gasped for breath.

'Everything,' she said in a soft, thoughtful voice. 'Everything is physical.'

Adrien was too dazed to answer. Raucous night air had flooded the room. Semen leaked onto the floor and pooled. The thump of reggae from a passing car swelled and then went flat in the distance. Darkness exploded with color in his eyes.

* * *

I take down the wall, brick by brick. After she is asleep I uncoil and our body slides away from his. I look down on him. It has been a long time since I've seen Adrien from the outside. He has lost the sleek ease of adolescence – his body has seen too many fights to look young anymore. Yet even in repose, he possesses a quality of arrested motion that seizes the imagination.

I am sore and aching from the sex she had with him. I felt it like a slow wave through sleep: a rumor of pleasure, a certain light in the sky over some distant burning. Soon I will do better.

To breathe; to move; to touch the skin of my own face with my fingertips – I cannot describe the exultation. I feel like a baby taking its first steps. I pick up the dress she discarded and slide into it, find a set of keys and creep from the apartment. I am in the elevator before I realize I'm barefoot. I don't care. I feel giddy, drunk, invincible.

I look up at the sky, breathing. This is life. It's mine. She stirs within me but I can keep her quiet; she doesn't *really* want to know what's going on. She'd rather think of this as a dream.

Someone's looking at me. I turn and see him leaning on the metal grate shielding the pizza place. I know him well. I see his teeth when he smiles.

'C,' he says. 'Congratulations. You passed the second test.'

And I go to pieces.

* * *

Sabina came awake with a start to find herself face down on

cold pavement, her entire body taut and hot as if electrically charged, fear rocketing through her veins like an injection. Her bladder was already releasing and urine streamed across her skin as she rose to a crouch, panting, looking for somewhere to run. Footsteps receded behind her and she had the vague impression she'd been assaulted, although she wasn't really hurt. A block away there were people coming toward her on the sidewalk; there was traffic on the street; but it was dark and she didn't know where she was or how she got here. Laughter, male voices – obeying some instinct for shelter, she shot across the street and rolled under a delivery van parked illegally outside an all-night grocery. She could smell oil, exhaust, rotting food, and her own panicked urine. The belly of the truck quivered and growled over her head.

She was not in a cellar. There were no bombs. She had a set of keys clutched in one hand because she was in New York and she had been with Adrien. Maybe she had been sleepwalking. She'd been having more of those dreams. About cities and canals seen from an impossible height; about geometry.

Yet she couldn't convince herself to move. She had to lie there until the adrenaline subsided and she could come to grips with her terror of exposure. Then, waiting until the street seemed quiet, she crawled out. A woman came out of the grocery store and saw her. Sabina scurried across the street, cutting her feet on broken glass, and ran a short distance before she recognized Adrien's building. She dropped the keys two or three times before she could get the outer door open. Once inside the elevator, her knees gave way.

She was struggling with the alarm code on the apartment door when Adrien opened it. She shoved him aside.

'Sabina, where—'

'Shut up. Don't talk to me. I'm *not* crazy, do you hear me?' Her voice sounded shrill. She got to the bathroom before he could approach her and locked herself inside. She

187

ripped off the dress, stuffing it in the wastebasket, turned on the shower to cover her sobbing, and sat on the edge of the tub, head in hands.

Adrien didn't pound on the door or shout. In fact, she began to think he'd gone away. But after a few minutes a tiny scrap of paper slipped under the door. She picked it up.

She blew her nose and picked grit out of the scrape on her knee. Another piece of paper came through.

ARE YOU OK? KNOCK ONCE FOR YES, TWICE FOR NO.

She chucked a tube of toothpaste at the door for one knock. Her head hurt from inhaling exhaust.

WAS IT ANOTHER NIGHTMARE?

This note had a funny face drawn on it. She unlocked the door and stepped into the shower. Adrien came in and sat on the toilet seat cover. He had put on a pair of jeans, and he picked at the hole in one knee as he spoke.

'Like – this business with Freefall?' he began. 'I'm sure now it's got nothing to do with your problem. Malagon is up to something. If she isn't C herself, she may have killed C. Tomaj might even have been part of it. I don't know where you fit in yet, but I don't want you to think you're crazy. Something's going on, and you just got caught up in it.'

He subsided into his own thoughts.

'It was not really nightmare, this time.' She closed her eyes and surrendered to the water. Even though it stung in her cuts, she didn't mind. It flowed over her skin like a blessing.

'No?'

'I must be sleepwalking, I don't remember going outside, but dream I had was about pictures of something, like diagrams. You know, like architect's drawings, only it wasn't the house.' The recollection flashed into her awareness and then warped into something else.

'How well can you remember? Could you draw them?'

'No. Too complicated, I only have seen them for a

minute.' She was strangely calm, now; whatever had come over her had stopped. She got out of the shower and looked at Adrien, wondering what he must think of her.

He seemed thoughtful and didn't say much after that but drew her into bed and stroked her back for a long time. After a while they made love again, but softly, in a pool of silence. Lying beneath him, penetrated by him, she found herself in a time and place that had a quality of transcendence: it could never be destroyed, not by anything. It was as though their bodies had found some thoughtless state of grace.

It didn't last.

Later, after he'd fallen asleep and she was alone with herself, the urge to panic returned: the bed, the stillness, the surrender – it was all a prison. The very concept of lying immobile filled her with unreasoning terror, yet she didn't want to leave Adrien. She instructed herself to be still.

She was touching the bark of a tree. She could smell pine, earth and rotting wood. There were symbols incised in her fingernails. When she looked at one closely, it reminded her of a maze.

The tree was not a tree. It was a computer, and she was looking at her data. Multivariable functions and charts full of statistics projected into 3-D; it all had to do with the distribution of firing neurons as seen correlated to certain states of mind, characterized subjectively as transcendence, ecstasy, and communion—

She couldn't move. She couldn't move she couldn't move she couldn't hear she couldn't see she was nothing.

Her arm twitched and she realized she'd almost gone to sleep. She sat up with a start, trembling, looking fearfully across the ghostly plane of the bed in the dark. She mustn't lie down. Adrien's hand groped over her leg and he moved closer to her, breathing heavily. She forced down the irrational fear of the bed and willed herself not to move her limbs from his. It was important to her pride that he should not think her weak or hysterical; she must go on as if

189

everything were normal. She wished she could melt with him, could be carried along by him. She wished she could trust him as she dared not trust herself.

You think I am a crocodile that you can hold my jaws shut w/2 fingers, knowing once you permit my mouth to open, I can close it like a drawbridge on you and your optimistic masts, shattering your ability to move forward and harboring you with me here forever. But that is only the shape and nature of your fear, not the shape and nature of truth. For all you know if you will only let me open my mouth I will reveal glittering cities, armies of the faithful and the song, the song you have been waiting all your life to hear. You cannot discover any of this until you untie your terror and set it loose like a dog.

No. No. No.

She was trembling. In his sleep, Adrien's arm slid up to encircle her. She moved her lips against his skin.

'Save me,' she breathed.

Seventeen

Tomaj can taste last night's cheap wine like a failed prayer. Today the people in their green smocks have taken a small amount of blood.

White wine is gold, and blood is blue not red.

That's the way things are: fucked and deceptive. C's little secret, that long string of zeroes and ones, flickers in his memory, switching on and off, on and off, making everything shudder like discotheque lighting. A tease. Didn't C realize keeping this knowledge away from Max would kill Tomaj?

Or was C single-minded enough not to care?

Everything in this room is clean and bright. The demons in his guts exorcise hope, vaccinate him against Max. They call themselves We, as in: We will take you apart such that you can't be put back together.

As in: We will ingest you.

As in: There will come a time when you will have quantified and subsequently shunted on their respective paths all the things in the universe. Then, squeezed out of your space we will exit you and abandon you to the emptiness of your bodies. We will wait until your order collapses in on itself and crumbles, unable to withstand the contradictions of you, its human inhabitants, with your need for cannibalism and love. Then will we return, putrid angels with violent trumpets to tear you from your bodies and free you into glorious inaccuracy, approximation like jazz a sigh of relief after Bach's spiritual superfreeze.

You will be guilty but unrepentant. We will thrive.

You will count on your fingers and toes. The stars unquantified will become beasts of nightmare again. All the world will wake in the light of your ignorance. You will become nocturnal things and you will value blood. Again.

No, no. This is wishful thinking. Satellites rule the earth. The eyes have it. We can never go back. Nothing will ever be as it was.

'Mr Robinson?'

This liddle piggy went to market, this liddle piggy stayed home. This liddle piggy said GETTHEFUCKOUTOFMY-HEAD—

'Mr Robinson!' Shaking his shoulder. 'Are you listening? Your test came back negative! Mr Robinson? NEG-a-tive! Here's some clean syringes and free condoms and there's coffee if you'd like ...'

'Neg ga ga ga. What the fuck you mean negative? I went right through one of those gangs. They *nailed* me with a fucking syringe. I could *smell* the HIV.'

'You'll need to keep getting tested, of course. You may indeed be infected, and we could get a positive result at some point down the line—'

'Don't try to reassure me! I *can't* be negative!'

'Mr Robinson, the virus can't survive long in an airborne condition. A lot of these gangs, they aren't for real. They probably had fluids that were just too old. Or they were ... just playing a game with you. You know how kids are these days. You got lucky, Mr Robinson.'

'Lucky. Yeah I feel like I just won the jackpot. Sorry, baby. You seem nice enough but you don't have a *clue* what I'm dealing with here.'

Tapping the old noggin for emphasis. Ouch. Wishes he could think in Linear B or some similarly obscure language, and let Max's computer try to translate that!

'Nurse, you may not know this, but Max doesn't even need to be a Watcher. No, Shazzam and Isis are *not* a factor. He's got a hotshot computer and he wants my head. Why did C tell me so much? It's a curse. If I try to help Sabina I may bring Max down on her. Do you think I'm going to risk that? Do you seriously think the Mets are going to win another World Series? Huh?'

'Mr Robinson, if you'll just relax for a minute I'll go and make a phone call. I'll be *right back*.'

'Yeah, sure you will, little miz psychiatric evaluation I know what you're playing at but you can't stop me from killing myself, or at least making my body a living hell so he'll stay *away*.'

'Why would you want to kill yourself?'

'Ignorant bitch. Out! Get your hands out of my cookie jar! *Because*. I gotta either get to Sabina or kill myself or both. That's why I'm crazy and they pay *you* the big bucks.'

'Please sit down, Mr Robinson. I don't want you to go. We can *help* you—'

Swinging out into the day, into the signal noise and flashes of desire as that fucking computer chases his code, cutting out snippets of him in the process and fertilizing him with its suggestions and commands. So far the thing can only penetrate his defenses for a few seconds at a time. It can ride him, but not for long: C's mainline will keep whisking him away to a safe frequency. Or so he prays.

To the train station. His frequency yawns open and a big hook grabs most of the sixth grade and everything associated with it, as if a gardener has just tugged a length of vine and all its runners and roots must now follow. Cavalry ware scrambles madly to cut him loose before everything he knows can be snatched by association.

Can no longer remember who wanted what. Did C want him to find Sabina? But you dead, C, and I am not the magnifying glass you gonna burn innocent bugs with. I will not bring them down on her. Let Sabina go free.

Train to 135th Street. Down the big hill over the bridge to the sports park. Kids in fountains. Tennis courts looking ripped up. Inhale: deep deep sewer when the prevailing wind's right. Going down in the works. Home, home. Home is *under* the games now, down where it's nasty. No astroturf for us. We gonna find us some rats, ladies and gentlemen. If

193

the Watchers are still looking, later we might even get ourselfs raped by some Really Ugly Women. Cos as Oscar Wilde once said, *here's a sigh for those who love me/and a smile for those who hate/and whatever sky's above me/here's a heart for any fate*.

Find Sabina. *Help her*.

Don't go near her. She'll only get hurt.

Max Max Max Max Max Max Max stay OUT

Pausing on the sidewalk, laying one hand on the dirty building, its melting essence trying to communicate but don't listen. Don't listen to anyone. Fall but don't break. Stay an individual. Always.

Adrien overslept. When he woke Sabina had gone, leaving a scrap of newspaper on her pillow with the words, *Adrien I am going to buy the guitar. See you tonight, don't worry – Sabina*.

'I don't believe this,' he said slowly. He looked in the yellow pages under 'Musical Instruments – Retail' to see if she'd circled any ads, but she hadn't. He checked the phone log but there was nothing on record for today. She could be anywhere, and she could be behaving normally, or like a mental patient.

Come to think of it, in the course of one day, everything he'd been counting on had upended itself. Tomaj was gone; Sabina was batty; he was sleeping with her and neither of them knew where that was going; he couldn't even be sure C was dead; there was no reason to believe Mitsuko's report wouldn't lead to his arrest, any day now; and if he really wanted to be paranoid, there was no guarantee Mitsuko hadn't stuck a little trace plant in when she took out the one that had linked him to C. He couldn't possibly hope to hold this situation together.

Nor could he simply take off, live on the run, without ever knowing what the fuck was really going on here. There were limits to what he felt able to renounce.

He picked up the phone and called Mitsuko.

'Jerry's truck stop,' drawled a female voice.

194

'Hello? Mitsuko?'

'Honey, you got Jerry's truck stop here.'

'Truck stop? What number is this?'

She told him. It was the number he had for Mitsuko – and he'd used it before. The woman on the phone said that Jerry's was in Idaho.

'Sorry,' he said, and hung up. He tried the hospital in Tokyo but the night staff had never heard of Mitsuko. He called directory assistance in Hawaii and gave them her address.

'Don't have it.'

'Maybe it's under her husband's name,' he said. 'Eugene Ericksen.'

'I have a listing for that address, and the number is published, sir. But the name isn't Ericksen, it's Sanchez.'

'Give it to me.'

Carl Sanchez was not pleased at being woken up at five in the morning, but Adrien pressed him for information.

'You're sure you live there? That place on the mountains with the horse corrals and the big garden?'

'Yeah, like I've lived here six years and in all that time you marketing people have never called at this hour. Never. I want your name, son. I want to speak to your supervisor.'

Adrien put the phone down. His mind reeled. Somebody was fucking with him. Mitsuko said she was scared, but she didn't say anything about joining a witness protection program or some shit like that.

The phone rang in his hand. He jumped.

'It's Roger. Where are you? One session enough to fry your brain?'

'I'm a little tied up.'

'Are you serious or not? Get your ass over here.'

'In a couple hours, all right? I'll be there.'

He wrote Sabina a note ('Stay HERE damnit until I get back'). He packed up his gi, then ran to the subway. It was time to take another look at Tomaj's place.

It was impossible to tell whether anything in the apartment had changed since he and Sabina had left, but he systematically called all of the people listed in Tomaj's meticulously kept personal planner. This yielded up a whole assortment of friends who hadn't seen Tomaj in days, months, years. He became involved in two awkward conversations with jilted lovers, one of whom advised Adrien to take the sex for all it was worth and stop trying to pursue Tomaj because Tomaj was afraid of commitment and one would waste one's time even trying.

After that he brought Sabina's suitcase into the kitchen and upended it on the counter, which happened to be the only uncluttered horizontal surface in the entire apartment. Sabina's passport toppled out, and the letter he had allegedly sent her. It was typed but Adrien's signature was passably forged. He read it several times. It sounded like something he would say. When C summoned Sabina, could it possibly have been doing what it thought he truly wanted? Was this C's clumsy idea of making amends?

If he believed this, then there would be no need to worry about Sabina. But something was wrong with her, and he had the old familiar feeling that everybody knew more about what was going on than he did, and now he didn't even have C to come in and possess him and make him say and do the right things. His connections in the HIT scene were limited, and he couldn't think of one person he really trusted. He'd to have to get Sabina out of New York. If Mitsuko wasn't in the picture, then he'd take Sabina to Tokyo if he had to. He would find someone who didn't have a stake in the outcome, and he'd see to it she was helped.

He began to repack her suitcase. In doing so he accidentally knocked against a ceramic superhero statue on the counter. He reached out to steady it and the superhero's head came off in his hand. It wasn't a statue – it was a cookie jar. Adrien snorted. He picked up the lid, about to replace it, and glanced inside. There were a few crumbs, an origami giraffe, and inscribed in the clay bottom the word 'Shazzam!'

He idly picked up the giraffe. There was writing on the paper. When he carefully unfolded the origami, he saw the following in Tomaj's hand.

NICOLETTE TAZEDAIT 15 rue de l'aguille, Paris
SASCHA MINDLIN Institute for Advanced
Communication Studies, Moscow
KANG JUN IL ?????? Park Microelectronics, Seoul
T.R. May 9, 2011

Adrien put the paper in his pocket and chuckled at his luck.
Shazzam!

Eighteen

It was a weird little Faustian miracle. Whatever fever gripped Sabina and infected her thoughts, it didn't come empty of promise. When she had flown to New York, she'd been almost desperate to be composing again: to be visited by a sound that demanded expression. Now she was losing seconds out of every minute, minutes out of every hour as her consciousness was folded and snipped as though some cosmic scissors were making a string of paper dolls out of her. But the sound! Since yesterday, music had been welling up from some unseen source within; but when she woke this morning it was ready to overflow. In her imagination, the music didn't sound like anything she'd ever done before; in fact, it didn't sound like anything *anybody* had ever done, as far as she knew.

She lay in bed, relieved that she'd managed to sleep lying down, and watched Adrien sleep. In repose his face looked absurdly peaceful. She was ashamed of her weakness in the night. The last thing she was going to do was lurk around the morning after sex, acting clingy. It was bad enough to be going through these fits without putting an emotional stranglehold on him just because they'd shared a bed.

Above all, she must not become paralyzed by what had been done to her. It would be necessary to reach back and find survival techniques she had put aside long ago. After she had lost her mother and was living with Maria in a cellar, Maria had refused to lie to her, even though she was very small and needed comfort. Instead she would say, 'What is happening is terrible, but we'll get used to it. We are humans. We can get used to anything.'

It had been true then – she'd endured the loss of her

parents, of many other people she knew, of her home – so it would have to be true now. She could scarcely refuse to engage with what was happening. Something inside her had a journey to go on, and it had taken her hostage. Whatever the journey was, she would experience it with her eyes open: and maybe, if she could get over her fear, she would get a glimpse of her captor.

She went out carrying cash. Guitar would be best; a piano would be too expensive, and anyway she already had all the keyboards she needed in Zagreb. In the music store she ignored the cacophony generated by amateur musicians with amps turned up too high, playing garbage of every possible style as they tested out the instruments. She headed for the acoustic guitar department and paused before a fairly cheap Yamaha, wondering if it had a decent sound. She reached up to remove it from its hook but her hand stopped halfway.

The guitar was changing before her eyes. The grid made by strings and frets suddenly acquired depth, each rectangle becoming a window beyond which might be found a rainy afternoon; the cellular mechanics of a lymphocyte; the chorus to the song 'Everyday People'; the fajitas at Anna-Maria's bridal shower that made everyone sick; the concept of definite integrals; tea.

And then it was a guitar again.

The strings gurgled beneath her fingers when she grabbed it around the neck, as if it were a living thing that might struggle with her. She sat down, checked the tuning, and began to run through chords. She groped her way along, recalling different fingerings as she went. Articulating harmonic ideas with a guitar was difficult if only because the pitches weren't arranged in a linear fashion: it wasn't easy to find the desired voicings. Keyboards had spoiled her – that must explain why she played the guitar so haltingly.

But there was something more. The fretboard was drawing her in and down; she hunched over the guitar, her hair trailing across the strings. Each note was growing an alternate identity – a smell, or a thought, so that when built into chords the sound's complexity was dizzying.

You shouldn't be here. You should be on a bus uptown. There are reasons, but you don't need to know them now.

So the filler-in-of-crosswords was using more direct means today. She began to play the modes, Dorian, Ionian, the whole slew of them up the length of the guitar, her fingers flying. She swallowed against the nauseating influx of senses other than sound. This had to be resisted, like the dreams. She would buy this guitar, and she would coax from it the sounds she wanted, the music that would give itself to her finally—

I am the sound. I am the music. You are putting the guitar back. You are walking out past the keyboards and sequencers. You are going to the bus stop.

Sabina glimpsed herself in a mirrored shop front as she walked toward the bus, stunned because the voice inside wasn't just a voice. It was determining her actions. In the mirror there was nothing in her expression to indicate what was happening within. She looked ordinary, anonymous, unaffected. She felt bound and gagged.

The bus was pulling up. No. She wasn't getting on. She wasn't going to roll over and show her belly, not like this.

On the side of the bus was an ad for the computer game *Conspiracy*. She tried to focus her attention on the image, but before she could even process its contents, it puckered, swirled like the skirt of a Spanish dancer, and drew her back in time and *in*.

The buildings that are standing look diseased, pox-ridden, waiting to join the fallen. The rubble lies unevenly like a frozen sea, yet strangely pale and insubstantial. She would feel sorry for the windows that are left, forlorn, to survey the destruction, but she is so thrilled about being released from the cellar, even for a morning, that she feels no sadness. She wanders among the ruins, glad of the fresh air and freedom, not thinking of what all this must mean.

Eventually she comes on the piano, broken-legged and foundering beneath fallen stone and glass. The keyboard cover is dented and askew, but the lock is still intact. She breaks it open, hacking into the wood with the kind of efficient fervor the medics use when they cut people's bloody clothes off. The lid springs up and there is the keyboard, undamaged. She puts her dirty hands on it.

You are touching something forbidden. There is blood, white matter, a hole in the skull of the kind ice-fishermen cut in deep winter. You part the tissue, exposing the inner reaches of the cortex to light. The probe touches naked brain and the patient speaks.

'Birdshit. When I was at Cornell I used to take a walk over to the sled dog memorial in Central Park every Thursday and sit on a bench nearby and study. There was always so much birdshit. I hate the city. I wanted to go to the west coast but Cornell had just gotten new funding to become the premier institution for HIT research so I was stuck there.'

She is going to play Schumann, and that's all there is to it. In reality she played Schumann that day in 1993, and she'll play it again now. But what's living inside this piece of music? What's about to come out of the sound and spear her?

Yes, I am cruel. How dare I intrude on your most sacred of memories? How dare I insert myself into your beloved piano, substitute my brain's ruined choirs for its ordered truths? I dare be here because there is nowhere else.

Go on. You touched something: touch it again.

In the black and white keys lies the potential for everything that can ever be expressed. These first notes

201

the aching of unshed tears drawn from the instrument
by her hands ...

*Play on. Play, and listen to the consequences of your music.
The patient is unwinding the idea now, feeling no pain,
forgetting for a moment that her brain is open to inspection.*

'I remember those afternoons in the park, and despite
everything that's happened to me, I remember what I was
studying while I was there. The physical basis of consciousness.
Recent technological advances had brought an explosion of data
and I threw myself into it. My cousin was already involved in the
surgical side; we'd open an HIT practice and the two of us would
be pioneers. I was young and I thought of nothing else. Food was
to keep the blood sugar steady and sleep was an inconvenience.
That's just how I was, since I was a child. I never knew how to
stop; I never knew when to say, "Enough!" I took the figurative
at face value; I couldn't separate the abstract from the concrete.
Ideas had more substance for me than substance itself.*

'If you would have told me in those days that I could get rid of
my body and get by just as well using my brain and a computer,
I probably would have gone for it.*

'As it happened, though, I wasn't actually given a choice.'

Sabina the child kneels in the rubble and pulls from the
crippled Bosendorffer a threnody for a fallen city. She is
disappearing in her own sound.
    For there is another child, a briefly sketched child:
intense and precise in all the ways she is not. Focused.
Obsessive. And in another moment, if she isn't careful,
that child will wipe her and her Schumann away as if
they never were.

*You need not be destroyed by her. Listen. Listen. Is there
nothing familiar? Is there nothing for you here? Don't forget –
the patient has been to all the places you want to go.*
    And I've left a trail of blood behind me.

The chords are soaking the air; a shell rends the sky; the piano is a life she clings to—

'My ambition had no end. I possessed all the characteristics of a fanatic, I believed only in empirical truth, but I believed in it big. I was looking for the thing beyond consciousness. I believed consciousness derived from communication, and I was living in an age when communication was recodifying itself again and again. Seeing the world through alien eyes with all the intuitive power of one's own senses, limbic colors, associations – this was on the brink of becoming possible. A direct interface between minds would mean understanding more nuanced than anything permitted by the dumb toy blocks of language.

'I believed that, by deep-sensing through other people's minds, we might arrive at a deep-language also, a level of consciousness where no earthly grammar could take us. A place more precise than math and more beautiful than music.

'This was what I had in mind when I joined the Deep.'
But I get ahead of myself.
Where am I now? What am I now?
Let's just say there are a lot of places to hide information in human consciousness. The brain's a forest of redundancies, and, Sabina, yours has one tree you've grown big enough to hold me. Music. That's where I'm going to unzip myself, map myself into you, and mate you.

Get off the bus, Sabina. We're here – aren't you paying attention?

After two or three blocks it became obvious to her where she was going, but she didn't protest – not at first. It was broad daylight, and Central Park was full of people. She cut into the park near the south end and began to walk north, because she was guided that way. Now that she was on her way, there was no particular impetus to go fast, so she went slowly. At length she arrived at a bronze statue of a sled dog set on a plinth. She circled the area.

This was where she was supposed to be. But she didn't

know what to do now. She found a bench and sat down. There was indeed birdshit.

'Is this what you want?' she whispered. 'You want to sit on this bench again? Well, I'm here. On your bench. So tell me who you are.'

A passer-by glanced at her and glanced away. The pressure from within had gone. There was no answer to her question. Yet she felt she couldn't leave. She had to wait, to keep waiting, as long as it took.

Time passed. She turned the music over in her mind, trying to examine it objectively. She was annoyed that she hadn't succeeded in getting the guitar, and resolved to pick one up somewhere before she went home. She was tired; she hadn't had nearly enough sleep lately, and this constant struggling with herself was wearing her down. At length, a grayness overtook her and she nodded off where she sat.

She must have slept for a while; the shadows had moved some distance when she woke up. Nervously she patted herself down to be sure her wallet hadn't been stolen. She was just counting the bills when a shadow fell over her.

'I've been noticing that when you walk on it now, the sidewalk comes close and recedes with every step,' Tomaj said. He was standing like someone on a ship stands. He wore torn, dirty clothes and his skin shone with sweat. 'You notice that? It must be a consequence of the melt, like in grade school when we learned about tectonic shift by putting graham crackers on top of a pan of jell-o. It's finally really happening. And I'm here to see it.'

He began to walk rapidly away, still swaying drunkenly. He smelled very bad, but there were no alcohol fumes. She leaped up and went after him.

'Are you feeling sick? I could hardly recognize you.'

'I can't win now. Whatever has attached itself to me, it won't let go until I'm dead. The end will probably be violent, which is too bad. I would prefer, like the city, to simply melt. Melt into the dirt.'

'You shouldn't say this,' Sabina said. 'Are you upset about C – is that why you run away?'

Tomaj looked down at her. He had acquired some kind of facial tic. She also had the impression he was slightly cross-eyed, but he didn't look at her long enough for her to be sure.

'You ever watch nature films, like you know Mutual of Omaha's *Wild Kingdom*, shit like that? You ever wonder how the zebra feels just when it's getting caught? Like, one minute, it's running and it might get away, and the next minute, the leopard is ripping up all this red flesh, yum yum, right? But in that second or so that it's going down, it's *being killed*, what does it feel like?'

'I think it surrenders. I think it gives up itself to death.'

'Nuh-uh, baby, that's where you got it wrong. I been *living* that second for *days*, and it ain't no surrender. It's a constant *fuckyoufuckyoufuckyou* on the part of the zebra to the leopard. It is for this zebra, anyway.' He paused, brushing at the dirt on his pants, which were beyond salvation.

'If you could tell me what's wrong, I could get Adrien, we could help—'

'I don't want to talk about me. Let's talk about you. I've been watching you, since the change. I saw you fucking Adrien – what are you trying to do to that boy?'

'In the window opposite, it was you …?'

'Of course it was me. And you came down later, looking for me, but as soon as I started talking to you, you lost the plot. And I can see where you went wrong so clearly.'

'See what? What can you see, Tomaj? Please, I'm lost, I'm struggling. Tell me.'

'I look at your face and I can see it's wrong. You're doing the wrong thing, pursuing this course. To be alive should be enough for you now.'

She backed away, flabbergasted.

'Enough? Enough? I don't even know what I am.'

He rounded on her, his face savage.

'Hey, kid, you think it's easy from my end? Let me tell you—' he broke off, his eyes rolling back. He stopped walking and his body began to quiver and jerk. 'You live in boxes and dream of a life in which you might set us free.'

He was talking so softly she found herself leaning forward and blinking, just to follow him. But she couldn't follow him. Every few words his speech was broken by a kind of hiccup or speed change or alteration in pitch, so the sense of what he was saying was lost. Not that the words themselves were especially coherent.

'Oh, you can't imagine **an** existence without us: you crave **your** drugs and alcohol for we ride them out of the dark and febrile past **into** your now thereby endowing it with **THE** validity you are in such need of. We inhabit your cartoons and archetypes. You   have carved avenues to us in opium, in wine and now in direct neurostimulation. You are relieved when we come and baffled when we leave you, dry-mouthed, confounded,   awakening to strangers and their body fluids clotting on the sheets. But neither do you **wish** for us to stay. For we CANBEQUITE AUTOCRATIC, quite insistent, and we have an imperial bent. When we come we will conquer. We will rule you in your **boxes** and control your controlling and you will walk the earth   as soldiers in our army, and be glad.'

He paused for breath. She reached out and shook his arm.

'Tomaj, stop it! Stop it!'

He pulled away.

'Sabina, I have to. If I don't fill up the channel they'll raid my memory, don't you get it?' His shoulders sagged. 'It's stopped now, for a second. I don't know how much longer I can keep this up. It's not safe for us to talk.'

Sabina steered him toward a bench and made him sit down.

'Please could you make sense? Tomaj, please. How did I get here today? What about the messages? How are we communicating?'

'I followed you,' he said. 'I had to be careful. I followed you and Adrien so I knew where you were staying. I been living by the sled dog, for reasons of my own. To keep myself as crazy as I can be. But the messages, your coming here – don't you know that's all to do with you? Look, it's getting to be too much responsibility for me. You didn't anticipate the kind of weapons they'd be using against me. You didn't even prepare me—'

It happened again. This time he froze in place and did not move, didn't even blink, for what seemed like many minutes. Sabina fidgeted and looked around. No one who walked by seemed to be looking at them, although she felt sure that Tomaj was as much of a spectacle as a person could possibly be.

This time when he spoke his pace was sluggish, as if he were sleeping.

'The forces of history are not what they seem. Some say … history lies in personalities, others in technology, but we … say it lies in the subjective nature of reality.'

Sabina said, 'Yes, that's maybe true, but—'

He raised his voice to drown her out, his face suddenly animated, his tone clear and expressive.

'You want to step outside and define once and for all: what the fuck's happening on this planet? In what terms can consciousness and its objects be explained? But you will ever filter the world through yourself, as Walt said.' He laughed. 'And you are only as big as the holes you will let us carve in you so that starlight shines through you like swiss cheese and limns the atomic letters of a new history.'

Sabina ran her hands through her hair, tugging it by its roots, willing herself to figure out what to do.

'Oh, god, Tomaj, I think you should come back with me. You need rest. I was maybe mad at first about what happened at party, but I don't want to see you like this.'

His face had become warm and unclouded again.

'Mad at me? *You* were mad at me? *I'm* the one who's going to die. For you. Don't you get that? I'm going to die

207

for you, because you wanted Adrien. Of course, I'm always there for you: good old Tomaj, right? And I'd die for you because, because of what – because of what you've been to me.'

Sabina felt cold and hot and cold again.

'I have to go.' She stood up and began to edge away.

'Don't.' His voice was soft; his bloodshot eyes were turned inward. 'Don't run away from it. You can't. It will get you in the end.'

He got to his feet and moved jerkily after her. It was too much.

'What do you want from me?' she shouted, backing away from him. 'What am I supposed to do?'

'Listen!' he said, raising one finger and cocking his head. 'Just list—'

Two cops on bikes came around the corner of the path at speed.

'Hold it!' one of them yelled at Tomaj, who responded by spinning in a slow, confused circle, looking at the sky.

'Do you think it will rain, grandma?' he asked.

'Put your hands up. Move away from the woman.'

'What are you doing?' Sabina demanded while Tomaj was being frisked.

'Is there some trouble here?' asked the second cop. 'We got a report of a woman being harassed by a vagrant. He harassing you?'

Sabina looked on, horrified, while Tomaj was handcuffed.

'He didn't do anything!' she protested. 'Is the misunderstanding.'

The cop had noticed her accent, and he narrowed his eyes at her. 'Yeah, right, a misunderstanding. Let me give you a piece of advice, all right?'

'No,' she said angrily. 'I never have asked for your help. Let him go!'

Using the bulk of his body, the cop was driving her back away from Tomaj. She tried to dodge around him and was caught by the waist and stopped; in the same moment, Tomaj broke away from the other cop and leaped into the bushes, hands still bound behind his back. The police charged after him on their bikes, and Sabina was left standing, dazed, while people went on their way, the incident already forgotten.

A few yards away stood a slender man with a phone at his ear. He was looking at her. The wind caught the edges of his coat, and he held out a hand to catch a drop of rain. Their eyes met, and she recognized the host of the party: the player of Schöenberg. Fear engulfed her without warning or explanation. She turned and ran.

Nineteen

His teacher was working out on the makiwara when Adrien
arrived. The ricochets of his fists off the bare board sounded
like firecrackers. While Adrien stretched and warmed up,
Furuta syncopated the blows with syllables.

'I been thinking about you. You know how to move like
an animal. This is what makes you good in a fight. But
you're lazy in your head. You think you can use your mind
like an animal, but you're not an animal. You're human
and you gotta be able to make complex judgments. It's not
enough to see and react. You must see and understand
patterns. Be able to predict, anticipate. Know your fucking
enemy – then you're acting instead of reacting. Then you're
leading instead of following.'

Adrien's nostrils flared. He felt a surge of energy at
Furuta's words.

'It's true,' he said, thinking of C. 'I've been a beast of
burden. I haven't been free.'

'Lose that,' Furuta said. 'It's got to be all you. I can't even
teach you. I told you that before. It has to come from you.'

Adrien took a deep breath and let it out.

'How?'

'The meaning of an action is contained in that action.
There: that sound funky and Eastern enough for you?
Patterns are there all around you. If you can see them, you
can take advantage of them. Let's see your katas.'

Furuta watched silently while Adrien trained. When he
finished, hot and pleased at his performance, his instructor
chuckled. 'You're doing everything bass-ackwards.'

Adrien, stunned, could think of no reply. His katas were
perfect. He had fine-tuned every move, every nuance...

'You have to do them from the inside out. Who cares if you know the moves? Give me a professional dancer and I can teach him all the Goju katas in a week. Doesn't mean shit. These katas are martial forms. When you're training them, you have to activate the opponent in your mind. You have to create your opponent, and use the kata to beat him. You have to see the applications and work them for yourself. They aren't obvious. It's like they're written in the kata in invisible ink. You need to get a fire going to see them, yeah?'

Adrien nodded.

'OK, let's try something easy. We'll do Saifa applications. I attack you. You use the kata on me. Go.'

An hour later, Furuta at last acknowledged that he was doing slightly better. Then he took himself off to get lunch; Adrien suspected he just needed to catch his breath. Physically, Adrien was recovering fast, and he'd put Roger through his paces just now.

Mentally, he had a long way to go. He knelt in zazen facing the mirror, thinking. When the moves for a given kata were thoroughly learned, they seemed to be absorbed by the very tissues: the mind seemed irrelevant. And yet, Furuta's constant talk of strategies and patterns beneath the surface made him feel ignorant and blind. He stared at his reflection until his mind quieted; then he let his eyes close to meditate.

When he heard the slight sound in the doorway he knew it was not Furuta even before his eyes floated open.

'I was hoping I would find you here.'

Max stood in the doorway – he made a mocking bow when he saw Adrien's gaze reflected in the mirror. Adrien didn't hesitate. Any attempt to prolong the silence or stare Max down or even think would backfire. His body answered Max for him, whirling and charging across the bare floor to leap the low wooden railing that separated the training area from the lobby. He pounced on the slighter

211

man, spinning him half off his feet and applying a half-nelson before his victim could so much as squeak.

He was relieved Sensei Furuta was not there. Max was panting, his distressed face rolling and wrinkling like a manic clown's.

'Adrien, what the fuck?' he bleated. 'This is not a way to get on my good side. And here I am trying to help you out.'

The last word trailed off into a soft scream as Adrien grabbed the tender skin of Max's neck between the thumb and forefinger of his free hand and twisted, hard.

'What would I do without your help?' he said into Max's ear, patting him down for weapons and chucking out of reach a .38 special and a whipknife. He almost missed the whipknife because it was lying quietly along the inside of Max's left thigh. Max got a scratch while Adrien was extracting it.

'Hope that wasn't poisoned,' Adrien said cheerfully, chucking the weapons out the door.

'You are unamusing and predictable,' Max gasped.

Adrien walked Max outside, into the alley, and pressed his face into the cement wall.

'What was it you wanted to discuss?'

'Sabina.'

'You have no right to even speak her name. Forget her.'

'Adrien, Adrien, Adrien. Do you think I'm not aware how possessive you Latin types are? And look how violent you've become. Don't you think you could let go of me now? You have my weapons.'

Adrien leaned on Max's shoulder a little; he wasn't trying to dislocate it, merely to inflict pain. 'That's a nice whipknife you've got. Maybe I should carve a message in your skin and send you home to your mother.'

'Stop … trying to be … like me. It's … unbecoming.'

'How dare you even mention Sabina's name.'

'I'm trying to give … you … an opportunity … to be part of … something … big.'

'Shut up, motherfucker!' Adrien changed the half-nelson

212

to a full nelson and gave Max a taste of the pressure that could be exerted.

'You don't have the balls,' Max said in a hurry, as if sensing this might be his last chance to speak. 'I already know that. What do you think Moscow was about? If you were strong, like me, you would have strangled the kid Nikolai the first time you met him and taken the next plane with the plans in your greedy little fist. But you missed your chance. I'm giving you another one. If you were to help me out here, I'd be in a position to do a lot for you.'

'I'm not interested.'

'I've been making a real effort to treat you as an equal. I didn't have to let you live in Moscow. I like you, Adrien.' Max tried to smile at Adrien over his shoulder but could barely move his head. 'With no effort at all, I could remove Sabina from your world entirely. I have things to offer that you can't possibly compete with. But I'm not saying I'm going to do that. I'll cut you in. I'm trying to give you a chance to have a life after C. What else are you going to do? Make martial arts videos?'

Someone was coming along the alley whistling 'And I Love You So' as found on the 'Perry Como's Greatest Hits' CD. Adrien let go. Sensei Furuta sauntered toward them, bag of gyros and soda in hand, applying a poignant tremolo to the long notes.

'Fuck your favors, Max, and stay away from Sabina. You better go before you piss me off.'

Max shook himself like a dog, managing to cast resentful glances at Adrien and smile at the approaching master all at once. Then he turned to face Adrien and for the first time Adrien noticed that Sabina and Max had the same sort of vampire canines. Max was displaying his now.

'I wouldn't try to restrain Sabina. Remember, it's unhealthy in a relationship for one partner to exert control over another. You of all people ought to know that – *ueunghh!*'

He cried out as Adrien feinted at him. Sensei Furuta slipped past them in the alley and went in the open door, bags rustling. Max shrank against the wall as he passed. Adrien saw the beads of sweat on Max's face and suddenly he was disgusted.

'C went and died at a convenient time for you, huh, Max? Not much competition for you these days. I begin to wonder more and more whether you had a hand in it.'

He picked up the gun and took out the bullets, then tossed it at Max's feet.

From within came a burst of song: *'and yes I know how lonely life can be ...'*

'I neither confirm nor deny,' Max said, bending to get the gun. 'Keep the whipknife. A gift. Well, I should be going.' He started to turn. 'Oh – I almost forgot. I have a friend in the NSA. It seems your name's been cropping up on their to-do list. My friend could easily prevent your name from being released to the Secret Service, but as you say – fuck my favors.'

'... but I don't let the evenings get me down ...'

Adrien's blood surged toward the surface of his skin. Max began to back down the alley, raising his voice over the noise on the street beyond.

'If you were smart, you'd kill me right now. Keep Sabina for yourself, stay out of jail. Right? Only I know you're not a killer. That was C, wasn't it? Nasty piece of work, that one. Give my regards to Sabina when you see her.'

At the end of the alley, he turned and darted away as if he expected Adrien to attack him. Adrien went back into the dojo.

'What an asshole,' Furuta remarked, handing Adrien a Coke.

Adrien looked at the floor. 'Sensei ...' he began heavily. Furuta chewed.

'... I came back too soon. I thought I left all that shit behind me. People like him. I thought I'd be able to pick up with my life. I'm sorry he came here.'

'He doesn't worry me,' Furuta said.

'You don't know Max. He knows I train here, and he's

not going to let the thing drop. I'll be drawing down trouble on you.' He sighed in frustration. 'I just wanted to be able to go back to like it used to be, not complicated ...'

Furuta pushed a sandwich at him. 'You can't separate training from life. Everything's a fight.'

Adrien gave him a startled glance. Those had been C's words.

'Yeah, I know, in theory...'

'Never mind theory, I'm serious. You need better tactics, Adrien. Use your mind, that's what it's for.'

Adrien bit into the gyro. Funny, he'd gotten in the habit of thinking his mind was incidental, just an annoying middleman in the pure flow of sensation from the world to C.

'You may not see me for a while,' he said with his mouth full.

Furuta shrugged. 'I told you, I got nothing to teach you. It's up to you. Practice your kata. See the inside of stuff.'

*　*　*

After calling the apartment and getting no answer, check-ing unsuccessfully with Phoenix House, then returning to Tomaj's place to see if Sabina had turned up there; and finally after unsuccessfully attempting to ascertain where Max was staying, Adrien gave up trying to find Sabina. Disquieted, he headed back to his empty apartment. The city was roaring with heat and a capricious southerly wind had begun to gust. He opened the windows and let the evening blow through. There was a sound of thunder. Adrien leaned on the sill of the living room window and looked out. He thought about Max's threats, Mitsuko's disappearing act.

Tactics. He ought to be thinking about self-preservation, and tactics. That was how to survive. But his emotions ran in all directions, flying with the wind among the bricks and streetlights and windows. As he gazed over the gray and red

215

city waiting so eagerly for its storm, it seemed to have displaced itself in his memory. This city was supposed to be the place of his childhood: a spiked pit to be escaped from, to be survived. You could not have love in New York City, any more than you could have mercy or silence or beauty, because its opposite would always be springing up to taunt you. And that, thought Adrien, would be unbearable.

Yet now New York of the stench and contradictions, the hype and the glory, the bickering and the unapologetic self-obsession, New York the Illusionists How-To Manual was to be the setting for what he feared was becoming a love affair.

This was unacceptable. Had it gone on in Paris or Hong Kong or even Nairobi, he might have been able to convince himself that his feelings for Sabina were romance, a response to the local color – something that could be separated from reality. But New York was inimical to these finer feelings. Therefore, stripped down to the bone, what was happening between him and Sabina must be something far more brutal. It was the gazelle gone limp in love's jaws, dragged through the dust by the weary lioness. The gazelle and the lion, the lion and the gazelle. It was not romance. It was the real thing, made of blood.

The first lightning was an inhalation. It rendered the city like an etching. Drops flew in his face and settled on the sill. He watched people scurry below, whooping; watched cabs plow through the water smugly full, and the rain came down harder. Lightning came again – definitive, repeated lightning giving lessons in architecture that were not meant to be forgotten. He felt the thunder groaning in the walls of the building. The rain was making incredible sounds and it actually hurt his face, but he didn't move. It hit the windowsill like a barrage of artillery.

Then he saw Sabina. She was running down the sidewalk toward the building, not the way people run in the rain because they don't want to get wet – she was already soaked. No, she was running as if her life depended on it.

* * *

Run Sabina run. See if you can escape me.

I had to seize control in the park. If you would only cooperate you'd understand why it was dangerous for you to be there. The question is, was Max following Tomaj, or following me? I thought I could finesse them both but now I'm not so sure.

I don't think Max was able to track us. Still, if he knows about Tomaj—

Get down! Stop struggling. You're running too fast; you're going to fall, and you're making it impossible for me to think. There's no reason to get hysterical. Get your breath back, or I'll have to restrain you again. I need time to work this out, and I can't have you fighting me at every turn.

Yes, I know. You don't understand.

Share with me. I can give you everything you ever wanted. It's simple, isn't it? All you want is to be seen. To be seen by someone who knows the meaning of you. By someone who will hold you in their hands like a bird and feel your fast heartbeat and breathe on you their love. What else is there?

Are you deluded enough to think you can find this through sex? In one man, or a thousand? Is that why you slipped between the sheets with Adrien?

Human beings are programmed to have certain kinds of relationships: the parent-child bond, the more general familial or tribal tie, and the male-female union which has been elevated to such unrealistic status. But there are other ways of being together, and these are only dimly understood. Much is mistaken for sexual love that is something else. What's happening among jazz musicians? Or children deep in play? Are these activities just sublimation of some basic drive, or are we capable of more?

I say we are. You knew this when you signed on; it was

why you signed on. But now you're not listening to me because you're afraid of transcending yourself.

Back when God was the hottest act in town, everybody got offended at the idea of science discovering the prime cause of life. Imagine decoding God in the form of DNA! Blasphemy! Now we think little of it. Now, of course, our hubris is much more personal. For though we've objectified our bodies, we remain infatuated with ourselves. How dare I decode *you*? How dare I *change* you? How dare I tell you that you never even existed except as an abstraction?

I dare because I can.

Get out of my way, Sabina. I'm going to take you and make you something else.

Twenty

Adrien stood by the elevator. When the doors opened, she fell into his arms. She was laughing edgily.

'Where the hell were you all day? I've been going crazy!'

With a blank smile, she wiped rain from her face and shook her head in his direction so that droplets flew. He stepped back, annoyed.

'I'm sorry. I lost track of time,' she said woodenly.

'I saw you from the window. Why were you running like that? I thought you were in trouble.'

He held the door open for her and she darted inside, kicking off her shoes and leaving a trail of water on the stripped wood floor as she sailed into the bathroom. She came out naked, towelling her hair absently, and went to the stereo where she proceeded to study the menu.

'Ooh, Quadrophenia!'

Adrien winced as the speakers roared on, the music jerking as she flipped through tracks. He crossed the room and turned down the volume. She avoided eye contact, spinning away to the window, where she looked out at the rain.

He decided to say nothing about her behavior. He began to pack. Bass and drums beat the air.

'I saw Tomaj,' Sabina announced in a strained voice. 'At the park. He is sick.'

Adrien couldn't see the expression on her face. She was gripping the window frame so that the tendons on the back of her hands stood out. Her shoulders were elevated protectively.

'Sabina. Don't try to pretend nothing's wrong.'

She gave no sign she heard him. He took a shirt out of his

bag and brought it to her. The streets outside were a mess; it wasn't going to be much fun getting a cab to the airport tonight.

'Love,' she said, 'reign o'er me.' She sniffed and wiped her eyes with the back of her wrist. Then she pulled on the shirt, visibly struggling to get a grip on herself.

'Why are you crying?'

She buttoned the shirt, fixing him with an odd bright smile.

'I'm not crying.'

'This has gone far enough. I don't know why C brought you here, beyond using you as a weapon against me, but right now we have to—'

She turned into him and pushed until he broke off speaking and let her pass. She stumbled across the room, bumping into the sofa.

'I have to tell you something, Adrien.' Her hand went suddenly to her throat, and she stood for a long moment in the dimness, silent.

He waited for a few seconds and then circled the room, gathering what few possessions they had and stuffing them into their bags. Sabina wasn't moving.

'Get dressed. I'm not messing around anymore.'

'I have to tell you,' she repeated. The music had stopped, and the storm reasserted itself. He tossed the bags toward the door.

'We're going to the airport,' he said. 'We're getting out of the city. Tonight. I don't give a fuck what happens to me. Max is on the prowl. I'm taking you to Tokyo and we're going to find out what was done to you.'

'You can't!' She flew at him, falling to her knees beside the bags and ripping his open. She started hauling clothes out.

'Cut that out, Sabina.'

'I won't go to hospital! You can't make me. And what about you? They arrest you.'

'Stop it.' It was futile trying to return the stuff to the bag as fast as she removed it. He grabbed her wrists. She was panting slightly, mouth slack and eyes shining with a kind of unreality.

He said, 'Why won't you talk to me? You think this is your fault? It's not. I brought you into trouble. I didn't mean to. I tried not to. But now you're being used to get at me, and I won't have that. Not for anything.'

The muscles in her legs went lax and she sank onto the floor. She searched his face. 'You know about C? You know? Tell me what you are saying.'

He took a deep breath. 'I can't figure out what Max is up to, OK? Or if C's dead or not. All I'm saying is, nothing anyone can do to me can hurt me the way it will hurt me if they get to you.'

Her eyes closed. '*Adrien.*' Her anguished voice. 'You don't know me.'

He held on to her hands but she wouldn't look at him anymore. She was becoming so fucking elusive – why? He ought to be direct but he found himself talking in circles.

'I don't know what this is,' he said. 'I don't know how deep it goes. I'm afraid I'll reach down and hit the bottom of it. I'm even more afraid I'll reach down and there won't *be* a bottom.'

She sounded hoarse. 'Bottom of what?'

He was going about this all wrong. It was the wrong time, the wrong way of doing it, but it was too late to stop now.

'In Croatian, how do you say, I love you?'

She was shaking all over. 'You can say more than one way. People say *Ja te voljeti.*'

'*Ja te voljeti.*'

'Please, Adrien, you're making it so difficult.'

'It doesn't have to be,' he said. He caught at her over the bag and they went down among the strewn clothes. Her limbs wrapped around him and he could feel in her body that it was right, even if her face showed the effects of an internal conflict.

221

'I'm trying so hard,' she whispered. 'But I can't. I have to and I can't …'

At this moment there was something frail and luminous about her; it made him feel incredibly protective toward her. Her hands on him were desperate.

'You must trust me,' he told her. 'We'll go to the airport.'

Her manner shifted yet again, turning sensual this time. 'I hate airports,' she drawled, and kissed him. 'The rain. Not tonight.'

'I know, but it's important. It's what you need right now.'

She was flushed; feverish, almost. Maybe that explained the preternatural brightness of her gaze.

'I need you,' she insisted. 'Not doctors. Not machines. All I ever wanted was you.'

A soft smile lit her face; it sent a current through him. There was something to be said for being in deep water, he thought. Had he ever needed a Watcher to feel alive? It was hard to believe.

He forgot about the luggage.

Twenty-one

In the morning he left her sleeping and went out for food and coffee. He'd been up since four, making phone calls and leaving messages, trying to arrange things so that he would appear to still be in New York for some days after he'd left. Sabina slept like the dead. He knew he shouldn't have caved in to her pleas last night, but with the rain and her state of mind – and the fact that in the afterglow of sex the idea of going to La Guardia of all places seemed absurd – he had let his resolve slip. This morning he was apprehensive. He walked back from the deli flicking nervous glances in every direction. He noticed a panhandler on the corner, started to glance away, and then turned and stared.

The beggar had been a big man but he was stooped almost double, his vertebrae protruding through the damp t-shirt. There was blood rippling openly from cuts on his bare legs. Track shorts were stuck to his crotch, encrusted with excrement and black, dried blood. The power in his torso and the grace of his frame had not yet been taken from him so he looked like an actor portraying a prisoner of war. If you cleaned up the body it could still belong to a Greek statue. But the face was entirely new to evolution. It was neither animal nor human; organic nor machine.

The face had many obvious things wrong with it. Yes, the eyes were bloodshot. Yes, the teeth were fouled and broken. Yes, the lines of pain were laid down as exquisitely as the drapes surrounding an artist's model. Taken as a still photograph surely this could pass as the face of a common madman or generic sufferer of any time on Earth. But in motion it became truly unreal. It jerked, twitched, grinned, garbled its expression beyond comprehension and went deliriously blank, all in the video-scrambled time of a subliminal advertisement. It was a face that seemed capable of uttering whole messages in the microtic pauses sandwiched between tics. It was overly dense with data; and moreover, it was an *it*. It was not a he, not anymore.

The tongue panted slightly as if in concentration. The knees buckled, the body moved always toward the point of greatest stress, ever collapsing in on itself, torquing away from the direction of nature as if to wring itself dry of life. An alien might be inhabiting it, abusing the body the way a three-year-old mangles Barbie.

Adrien stopped in his tracks. '*Tomaj?*'

Gibbering, the face with its hyperdriven patterns of movement yearned toward him and the rest of the body followed slo mo like a model brontosaurus from a Japanese monster movie.

'There you are, Adrien, how is sh-sh-she-Sabina?'

Inadvertently he took a half-step back. All that blood.

'It's OK. I'm fighting it. I have to … keep it out.'

'Keep what out?'

'I can't let the machine have me. It wants – no, I can't. Where's Sabina?'

'Don't you have any money? What are you doing out on the streets, you look like a mental patient …'

'Aha, it's my strategy, if I go low enough, they won't want me. I'm not giving them no fucking caviar and Matisse paintings, Adrien. They gonna feed on my head I give them some shit, know what I'm sayin'?'

He could see and hear Tomaj in there, for a second.

'Yeah, is it working? You look like hell, what are you doing to yourself …'

'Some computer, I guess it's Max's – they can't get me but they're *bombarding* me, they're dumping weird data bombs on me looking for the holes it makes – never mind. I can't explain. I gotta find Sabina. I can't stand—' He put a shaking hand across his mouth and staggered sideways as if he had just witnessed some awful event.

'Why the fuck did you call me on Maui and then disappear?'

'Isn't she with you?'

'Never mind. What's going on with her?'

'I didn't know, man. Adrien, I swear I didn't know what C had in mind until it was too late.'

People were giving them suspicious looks. Adrien tried to steer Tomaj toward the awning of a closed shop but Tomaj reeled in the other direction, toward a bus shelter.

'It's not a world for me, my friend. We're all becoming each other. I won't survive the melt. I'll become extinct.'

'You wrote that letter, didn't you? Why did C want her in New York?'

'Thought it wanted a trans. You left C, shithead, and then it died. Who are you to ask me questions? Where's Sabina, I wanna talk to her.'

'You can't.'

Suddenly the face stilled and Tomaj's eyes focused on him. 'Do you have I? Who has it? Did they read the will?'

Adrien stood shaking his head, unable to follow this train of thought. 'I. What does I have to do with it?'

'C wanted you back,' Tomaj mumbled. 'The plant was supposed to be for you.'

'What,' said Adrien carefully, 'do you know about I?'

'Nothing. Want to see Sabina. I want to see her.'

Words would not form in Adrien's mind; sensible thought was impossible. Something evil had sprung into his mind.

'Tell me,' Adrien said, trying to get Tomaj's eyes to focus on him. 'Tell me C didn't get hold of it after all.'

'We bought it from Max. It was in a little glass jar. Tacky.' Again for a moment Tomaj appeared within the machine face, grimacing with distaste. 'I gave it to Audra.'

No way. The Watcher had let him walk into a deathtrap in Moscow to try to get I and then turned around and bought it from Max after what Max had done to Adrien. Unbelievable.

'And then what?'

'Don't bug me, Adrien. Hey, I might have AIDS. Do you really want to fuck with me? Take me to Sabina so I can see with my own eyes if it worked.'

'Forget it.' Adrien was shaking. He did not like this. Tomaj gave it to Malagon and Malagon said an unspecified procedure resulting in C's death had been performed the night of the party.

Tomaj reached out to grab him and he danced away. Coffee leaked through the bag. Tomaj lunged forward again but was too slow and seemed to be having trouble moving his legs. Then he paused, and for a moment he seemed completely lucid.

'You know why C was obsessed with I? Because it could transform life. I doesn't have to receive input, that's the beauty, so there's no need for wiring or batteries. It's an extremely tiny synthetic chip embedded in neural tissue, and as it degrades it functions like a time-release capsule. It's a new delivery system for data – but I can't tell you too much. I'll be getting myself offed soon enough – I just want to see her one time. I want to see if it worked, and give her one last message. Please, Adrien.'

Adrien began to back away, too shocked to answer.

'Rape,' said Tomaj to the sky. 'Is a door. Rape is a door. Becomes a mantra a fugue a door to where?'

He had a beautiful voice and a couple of middle-aged women stopped. Tomaj seemed to have forgotten Adrien was there. He spread his upturned palms toward the sky. 'It's a door standing alone on a blank hillside and the sky's beginning to rain, you open it, you walk through, and when you turn around the door is gone and everything's just the same as it was.'

He moved his head from side to side but he wasn't seeing his audience, which now grew warily outside the deli, afraid to walk past him or else momentarily entranced by his performance.

'Right? Everything is the same, except you can't go back

to check and your memory in which the present is a very brief time, neurochemically a few seconds or maybe less what do I know, cannot be relied upon, so how do you know it's the same? Simon says: I is for immortality. A b c I is for immortality.'

A van pulled up to the curb. The pedestrians suddenly managed to disperse, to be looking elsewhere, to have urgent business in another direction – and the door slid open. Adrien saw the flicker of a barrel, the glint of the dart, and Tomaj sagged to the ground. He checked his avenues of escape, wondering how fast he could manage to run on the bad leg, but he was unable to wrench his eyes away from the scene. Three men shot out of the van, picked Tomaj up, and dragged him inside. The vehicle pulled away, accelerating even as the door slid shut.

He walked away quickly, automatically – a van abducting Tomaj had already become the least bizarre of the morning's events.

C had liked Sabina. Sabina had been curious about C.

Adrien paused outside his building for a minute, looking at the traffic. There wasn't much on a Sunday morning. Up and down Broadway lights drifted from green through yellow to red. Between the shapes of passing cars streamed much emptiness. He could feel everything changing.

The rhythm of her breathing filled the apartment. Even as he rode the elevator his head filled with fire and it seemed to him that the elevator swelled and sighed with her exhalations and he was surrounded. He put the bag in the kitchen and went into the bedroom where she was lying in the white bed. It was sickeningly obvious now. He was hard just looking at her, and even the thought of the corpse and its attendant machinery – gleaming plastic tubes, gas cylinders, the frizz of computer relays – could not make the erection go down. As she stirred in her sleep, maybe sensing him standing over her, she sleepily groped toward the empty place where he'd been in bed beside her.

The morning had ceased to be something he could cope with. He was outside himself although he was fully aware of taking off his clothes without a thought in his head as to why he was doing it.

He got on top of her and the living qualities of her skin puzzled and angered him, as did the shifting of her body, soft and inexorable as the sea. She was a threat, a personal tornado. She had to be dealt with but he didn't know how. He threw off the sheet and moved into her. Her body welcomed this. Her hair fanned across the pillow, tenebrous and lush, her arms stretching to either side to grasp the edges of the mattress as she surged against him. Her legs wrapped around his back. He lowered himself to his elbows, his face scant inches from hers, and she opened her eyes.

'It's you, isn't it?' he whispered. His throat felt like a column of stone. He was being drawn into C's sickness and he couldn't help it.

Her eyes weren't focusing on him. She was panting. He continued to fuck her – distantly, but she didn't notice this. It was like grinding chemicals with a mortar and pestle in order to get a scientific result.

'It's you. C. Isn't it.'

She wrung the sheets in her clenched fists, the bed was a pane of glass, the white folds radiating from their bodies were stress marks describing an impact zone. The bed was transparent. Sabina was transparent. All could be seen. Collision.

'Isn't it.'

Here we go. Her head thrashed from side to side, her feet curled and flexed, her mouth trembled.

'Yes,' she breathed. 'I am here.'

He grimaced as she came. He let her experience the full arc of it, her pelvis flexing slowly in the aftermath, her eyes finally closed. He stroked her neck with his thumb. How pale she was. He laid his hand along her throat. A swan's neck. He put the other hand beside it and gently curved his fingers around behind her cervical vertebrae.

She sighed.

'What's wrong?' she murmured, shifting against him and divining that he was no less hard. He didn't move. There was only one way to make this end. She opened her eyes, startled.

'I know what you are.'

She blinked slowly and smiled, thinking she was being teased. 'What am I?'

His thumb was right beneath her chin. A quick break, or a slow strangle. If C had been here, it would have gone for the slow strangle. But then – C *was* here. He felt nauseous.

'Adrien, do you mind?' There was a wariness, a quick side-to-side of the eyes. She tried to move her head, swallowed in his grasp, took a nervous breath.

'I know what you are,' he whispered. 'When I said I loved you do you think this was what I meant? Is this your idea of love?'

Fear became panic almost instantly as she realized she was completely trapped. Her hands pushed and scrabbled at him. Her pelvis twisted.

He was on top of her. For once, he was on top of C: he had C here in his hands. He was calling the shots, even if everything he did cut him open as sure as Max's whipknife, for what could he do to her? If he killed her Sabina would be dead, but wasn't she worse than dead already, for she'd been corrupted, eaten out from within …? Could he play C's game and succumb to the thrill of killing? For there was a certain frisson now, a certain righteous anger that made any action seem justifiable.

Her pupils were dilated, the bitter smell of fear mixing with sex and last night in the white bed and her rapid breaths blew in his face while her muscles and bones knotted beneath his weight. This helplessness struck at him and turned his own energy back on him, especially because of the small ugly noises she was making and he let go in disgust.

It took a few seconds for her to realize she'd been released and she continued to flounder while he backed away. He was perturbed by the sensation that she was growing smaller and smaller as if every inch he retreated from her had been changed to a mile in some funhouse distorting glass: vertigo and camera tricks. He moved away shuddering with horror and shame. She slithered up the bed to brace herself against the headboard, drawing her knees up to her chest. Somehow in the brief struggle he must have ejaculated, because saltwater glistened on the dark hair between her legs and he was ebbing, no doubt about it. He couldn't remember even the faintest tremor of pleasure.

'Don't start getting into some psycho shit, Adrien,' she warned, and her accent sounded less pronounced.

He heard himself laughing sardonically, knowing he sounded like an asshole but unable to stop himself.

'Yeah. Freefall. Yeah, sure.'

He put on his clothes: jeans, boots, a jacket though it was hot out. He looked around for something to throw but there was nothing breakable in the room.

'Now I understand,' he said. 'Why you couldn't remember what happened at the party. Or maybe you could remember, but you just wanted to keep it secret long enough to fuck me. I hope it was satisfying. I hope it was worth destroying Tomaj.'

Her expression was dark and frightened. It did not show understanding, but she knew. Down there somewhere. O, she knew.

'You little conspiracy.' He had the presence of mind to go for his passport. Ax cards. 'You sellout. Rapist. Whore.' The crucifix his grandmother had given him years ago. 'You're everything. You're the willing victim *and* the murderer. You *are* the crime. And for me – why me?' Some coins left over from his last trip to Okinawa – good luck charms. They sang and were muffled in his pockets. 'I'm more important to *you* than I am to myself. It's sick. And to think I was afraid you'd been murdered. To think I felt pity for you.'

He had spoken the words but they did nothing to explain

how he really felt. The woman's bluefire eyes followed him as she got her back to the wall and edged toward the window, her face white, her feet tripping over themselves.

'I don't know what you're talking about ...' Her voice was low, jagged with morning.

'I'm talking about I. Cute, huh? Ring any bells? I, a little piece of living organic tissue. I gather it's configured to override your immune system and mesh in with your brain, grow into you, download its contents and basically make life hell for those of us who thought you were *DEAD!*'

That had been a shout. Not a good idea. Saliva had flown from his lips and he'd lost track of his breathing. He was quivering. She had reached the window and was clutching its frame, her eyes darting wildly from the outside to the inside.

'Go ahead,' he told her. 'Scream for help. Maybe you'll come to save yourself.'

'Adrien, please ...'

He passed a hand across his eyes. Violence must go now. He couldn't permit. 'It's just too twisted,' he said. 'Even for me, I can't take it. I can't help you, I can't ... I can't believe it.'

She had folded her arms across her breasts and pressed herself into the wall.

'Tell me it's not true, Sabina. Can you look at me and tell me it's not true? You're her now. You are.'

She said something in Croatian.

'No,' he said, shaking his head as if to convince himself. He said, 'No. Don't look to me for pity. What you did to me.'

She said it again. He recalled the phrase this time. I love you.

'No,' he said. Turning, he walked out of his own apartment and closed the door.

Twenty-two

He had run out of ideas, so he got drunk. In an anonymous, seedy neighborhood bar he slumped in a red vinyl booth feeling as light as an insect corpse, and as insignificant. Shadows intersected and moved across the floor. Black shadows and their uneven false penumbras rippled over his shoes as a result of the peculiar angles of the buildings across the way, muddying the winking rose of neon that splashed into the midst of the shadows and vanished, again and again: the backwards 'R' from CARWASH.

He couldn't make up his mind who he hated more: C, or himself.

At the bar were two weary transvestites. An old guy in a waistcoat held court in the far corner, supplying ad-stripped Freex™ and Mandarins to a steady stream of college kids while his associate flexed silently nearby. The tv was broken: no baseball, no horseracing.

If he hated himself for involving Sabina in this mess, then he would play right into C's guilt trip.

The transvestites became couples with shopping bags and later, some beery Teds. At long last it grew dark.

If he hated C, then he would have no choice but to despise Sabina. He'd already showed himself disturbingly capable of such an emotion.

He went outside, regretful that he could still see. A Vietnamese girl with gang scars on her face and her hair in Pippi Longstocking braids offered him head, heroin, and Sonic in that order, but only alcohol could properly go together with lost love. He couldn't imagine that anything else would do the job as well as the bottle of JD he carried away with him. He walked north.

His life was all rhythms: heart beating, lungs shifting, feet hitting the pavement at a steady clip while the lite-brite city sparkled around him, a mockery of the children's peg-board toy. If he still had friends, how would he find words to talk about this with them – even drunk, even with such mad friends as he'd usually surrounded himself with – what use were friends? He had been spoiled by perfect empathy, understanding without language – the Watcher had ruined him for the foolishness of human discourse.

Was this how Sabina had gotten so close to him, so easily: by slipping under the language barrier?

No. No, it was not quite so easy to explain how he had fallen for Sabina.

He went down by the river in the dark, emboldened by the fact that in all his years in this city, no one had ever jumped him. He lived under a charm. Though he'd fought for a living almost since childhood, whether for his old crew or for C, he had never had a problem with muggers or gangs in his native city. When he got to the water's edge he began to throw stones.

Would Sabina go back to sleeping in the chair?

Sentiment. Setting in like the flu, fluttering in the bones and stealing over the house, knocking you flat on your back. You had to fight it.

He stuck his finger down his throat and vomited.

Everything he was doing and had done was predictable. *Be capable of surprise*, he could hear Furuta saying. *Surprise even yourself and vex the enemy.*

It was too late now. He might have done many things. He might have bundled her into a cab and taken her to Columbia Presbyterian. He might have taken her back to Hawaii and Mitsuko – but no, Mitsuko had disappeared, hadn't she? Then, he might have tied her to the bed and kept her prisoner in his apartment until he sorted out how he felt. But no. The betrayed lover had to walk out and go get shitfaced.

Well, now that he was drunk, he had a valid excuse do

something stupid. The way Adrien saw it, he had nothing to lose. His relationship with Sabina was a shambles; he would be arrested any day now for information crimes and possibly murder; he no longer even had a plant to set him apart from the common man. About all he had to look forward to was a life of leisure in Bolivia.

So what the fuck, right? What the fucking fuck.

He threw the bottle into the river and walked over to Broadway, where he got a cab to Phoenix House. He stood outside, trying to remember all he could about the layout of the building. The security system was state of the art with respect to anticipating every possible subtle, diabolical, sneaky form of electronic infiltration. The front door was bulletproof Plexiglas. The ground floor windows were elevated from the sidewalk and covered with iron bars.

He was going to punch through the glass of one of the lower windows, but he could hear Furuta laughing himself sick at the blood running from Adrien's hands after he got cut, so he went across to the park and found a big rock. He waited until the block was empty of pedestrians; then he leaped from the sidewalk, caught on to the iron bars of the window farthest from the front door, and pulled himself up until his knees were on the window ledge. He pounded the rock against the glass until it broke.

He jumped down, brandished the rock and made faces at the niches where he suspected the security cameras were, then ran away. It felt good to run, and he circled the block with pretty decent speed considering that the alcohol hadn't left him with much control of his legs. When he came around to Fifth Avenue again he slowed and ducked behind a large party of well-dressed, tipsy people. There were two security guards on the sidewalk examining the damaged window and talking on the phone, and a third standing in the room inside. The front door appeared closed.

Adrien waited until the group came abreast of the security guards and someone said something like, 'Can you believe these kids' – then he darted up the steps and to the front door. It was ajar; a flashlight had been put down to hold it open. He closed it, shot the manual bolts, and lurched toward the stairs, unable to stop himself giggling.

'Intruder! Intruder! Intruder! Intruder!'

Glinting camera eyes spun to track him; the speakers spewed warnings. Instinctively he caught the rhythm of the darts and dodged them until he was in the stairwell. He raced upstairs.

Malagon's office was open plan: everything worth stealing was in the system tank, and that wasn't going to be easy to break into. He sat down on the carpet with the tank between himself and the door and leaned his forehead against its side. The surface yielded slightly to his touch. Starbursts went off inside.

'Your gesture can not be interpreted by this system. Please articulate.'

'I can't.' Fuck was he drunk.

'Your voice cannot be recognized by this system. Please seek assistance.'

'I thought it was you.' Dr Malagon appeared on the far side of the room. 'Here to burn the place down, or what?'

'Something like that,' Adrien said listlessly.

'Where is Sabina?'

'I don't know, and I don't care. When I think of what you've done—'

'What I've done? What *I've* done? Let me ask you something, Adrien. Who got Sabina into this? Who abandoned C in her hour of need and forced her to take Sabina, when we both know it was someone else she wanted?'

Adrien stood up.

'You don't know where she is. You're not tracking her.'

'No. And before you start asking me offensive questions, I don't know very much about C's plans.' She took another step into the room, raising her hand to stop him from speaking. 'I'm about two seconds away from calling the cops. What exactly the hell do you think you're doing?'

The alcohol was making him honest. 'I'm trying to find out about the Deep.'

Malagon snorted. 'Adrien Reyes, pursuing the Deep! It's like Flipper the dolphin going Nazi-hunting.'

Adrien laughed. 'I'm glad you don't like me, either. That way I don't have to feel guilty about wanting to—'

'Don't say it. Adrien, we need to find her, you and me. Sabina trusts you, and C trusts me – without that trust, there are going to be problems. I'm worried Max could get involved.'

'He already is. Look, Audra – you aren't the only show in town. Why should I bring Sabina to you? As far as I can tell, you're her enemy. You helped C do this to her.'

'There are things you don't understand about C.' Her voice was strained, and her fleshy face looked strangely hollow in this light.

'So tell me. Tell me the truth about C.'

'The truth about C.' He had said it sarcastically, but her response was sincere. 'Sit down.'

'No.'

She ran a hand through her hair, which was looking unwashed.

'You may know more about that than I do. C was a physician, not a surgeon like me, but a researcher. She became a specialist in HIT in the days when it was all new and the Deep was just forming. I knew she was flirting with it, but in those days the name wasn't synonymous with danger; it was just slang in the field. The technology was ahead of the theory, and the hottest place to be was in the Deep. My cousin was eager to capitalize. She was young. She was going to catch up with me, she said, and then we would be partners.'

Malagon had been pacing as she spoke; now she stopped by the system tank. Its oval bent the misery in her expression to something almost comical. Adrien looked away.

'Well, she went to a conference in Brazil one weekend

and never came back. Two years later she turned up in a hospital in Rome, comatose. She went unidentified all that time, until someone got around to checking her DNA against the physicians' database and came up with a hit. She was brought to California, where eventually they figured out that even though she appeared unresponsive, she was actually conscious. Some of the nerves in the reticular activating system of the brainstem had been damaged. This caused a condition where her cognitive function was OK, but she couldn't move – she couldn't even sense anything. If you try to imagine this, you'll find it very difficult, but in a nutshell she was trapped in a kind of sensory black box.'

'Sounds like being dead.'

'Can you think when you're dead? If you want to know what I think, it's probably a little worse than being dead. Anyway, I was a fellow at Seiroka HIT at the time. Yes, sound familiar? In those days, Mitsuko Yoshimura was head of the department.'

'Did Mitsuko know?' He pounced on this information. 'Did she know who C was?'

'Of course not. I don't think she ever made the connection between Conchita Malagon, her tragically ruined protegé, and C, monster of the Deep. She felt too guilty to suspect. Mitsuko tried to forget, but she was never the same. She helped me get set up on my own, but after that she ignored my work. I could have blown Seiroka out of the water years ago, but I've kept a low profile.'

'Because C was your ticket. C was the one who trawled the Deep for you.'

'Yes.' She went to her desk, rummaged, and came up with a package of cigarettes, which she ripped open almost savagely. 'You're not quite as stupid as C made you out. Smoke? No. I forgot. The precious body. Well, as you've guessed, I brought my cousin back to New York and began working with a plant to connect her visual cortex directly to a computer. For a year I fed her optical data. I told her

237

what happened and what we were doing about it. I built up research contacts and put all my time into her rehabilitation. My surgical work went out the window. In time, with every new advance in HIT, I brought her closer to being what you could call human, until at last she was fully interfaced and could manipulate the system using brainwaves. Once she was surfing, she didn't need me anymore.

'I was pleased with myself. I had really accomplished something. But C refused to give me permission to publish. I probably would have overridden her wishes, but right around that time she found her way back into the Deep. As you say, Adrien, she trawled other minds for knowledge. She made huge sums of money as an anonymous consultant for corporations and universities, then pumped that money back into my research on the wetware side of things. So I guess you could say we were partners of a sort, although not in the way we originally intended. I had to give up having notoriety in the world of licensed HIT; I kept a very low profile so as to protect C. When we set up Phoenix House, she wanted her legal status to remain that of a patient. As far as the world was concerned, Conchita Malagon was one step from being a vegetable.'

She fell silent and he studied her. She still radiated something that reminded him of C, and he was finding it difficult not to think of her as a kind of surrogate.

'You were dependent on C. Dependent enough to kidnap and headrape an innocent like Sabina.'

'I did nothing to Sabina but try to help her. I gave her the information about the party – C wanted her to have that – but I didn't know what was going down. I didn't put it all together for myself until the day Sabina showed up here, and it was too late by then.'

She leaned against the tank and blew smoke through her nostrils.

'I don't believe you.'

'I don't care what you believe!' The doctor smacked the tank with an open palm; the digital fish scattered. She talked faster. 'I get a plant she says she wants to use. C gives me less than twenty four hours to learn the procedure she wants done. She says she wants me protected in case of legal problems. That's what she always says. It takes almost twelve hours with this plant working in her head before I'm allowed to remove it. When I do, she stops breathing.' Malagon took a tissue out of her pocket and blew her nose.

'That sounds awfully tidy.'

'You always act like a bastard when you drink?' She tapped her ash on his shoes; he backed away. 'I'll tell you what. I think she figured out how to get control of her autonomic nervous system. I've seen her do that kind of thing before. This time she faded away, and there was nothing I could do. Just before dawn I sent a courier to deliver the plant to a designated drop, and that was it.' She laughed and blew her nose again. 'You didn't believe me when I told you I didn't touch her body. You were right. I did a post-mortem, and I found a tumor. Probably caused by the hardware. I think she knew she was dying.'

'I'm sorry,' he said, mindful of not being a bastard. Malagon ignored him; her eyes were looking far away.

'I had her body on my hands, and no explanation. Until Sabina wandered in here complaining that her left hand wrote messages to her.'

Sabina. He covered his eyes. The room swayed.

'Why couldn't you have said this before?'

'I didn't want to shock you. So I obscured certain facts. But I did try to talk to you, Adrien. You guys high-tailed it out of here so fast you left burn marks on my carpets.'

'Can you take it out?'

'What?'

'The plant. Can you take it out? Can you bring Sabina back to normal?'

'I don't know. It's already at work on her.'

'Stay here. Just stay here, will you?'

'You *do* know where she is! Adrien, let me come with you.'

239

'Forget it. You'll only be in the way.'

'I've already made arrangements to leave Phoenix House. C left instructions for me to shut down the whole operation. I gather she was afraid of reprisals from her enemies.' She was getting in the way, blockading the door; he stepped neatly around her and swung into the hallway.

'Yeah? That's because she ripped off Max Niagarin, which is never a good idea.'

But the doctor didn't seem to have heard him. 'Most of the patients are already gone, and the few remaining will be transferred out in the morning. Everything we worked for is dissolving, and I can't do anything about it.'

He was striding toward the stairs. 'Just wait here. I won't be more than an hour. You fucked up, doc – you know that, don't you? If you want to make up for it, you better be here when I get back with Sabina.'

The cab shot downtown, slowing only at Canal Street where the traffic was perpetually thick. He had a bad feeling the second he opened the door.

Silence. He turned on lights.

'Sabina?'

He went through the rooms, unable to decide which he was more afraid of: her absence, or her presence. At last he arrived at the bedroom. The door was ajar and a breeze was blowing through. The window where they'd had sex was wide open. He turned on the light.

On the floor beside the bed, in a pool of dark blood, was a human head.

Emergence

Stars, hide your fires
Let not light see my black and deep desires

Macbeth; Act 1, Sc. 4
Shakespeare

Twenty-three

She bit her own hands and arms as far as she could reach to prevent herself screaming. Squatting in the bathtub slick with sweat she watched the blood, skin oil, semen and tears mingle and slither toward the drain. A feeling of guilt as deep as a black bird cut out of the sky had become the gravity inside her. She wanted to destroy herself.

What have I done?

She turned on the water and it came gurgling reluctantly out of the tap. For a while there had been hope. Adrien had been holding out the promise of a future whose possibilities shot out like rhizomes into the unknown; yet he also offered shelter. What would it be like to live intimately with him – to have a home in him? For hers had been taken from her, once at Vukovar and again at seventeen when her grandparents, who had brought her up, died. There would be no more shelter now. She was in New York and Adrien really had contemplated killing her – that's not the kind of thing she's prepared to accept – this is not her idea of life, do you understand?

Who was she talking to? There was no one there. There had never been anyone there. It was all a cruel hoax.

For a long time, possibly hours, she crouched in a stupor. Out of boredom, finally, she washed herself. Mechanically she put on her clothes and ate the food he'd brought without thinking of what had changed between last night and this morning, how had I love you changed to I hate you. She was scared. She felt exposed, vulnerable, stripped of her very skin. As she moved about the apartment she found herself shrinking against walls. She had the feeling of being *seen*.

Adrien had called her C. But C was dead. Something was playing her mind the way she played piano. She had wanted to see what being a trans was like, but not if it meant this.

Please, she said. If I am a trans, help me, whoever you are. Tell me what to do.

She was standing in the middle of the bedroom. There was a full-length mirror in the corner and a compact home gym, complete with speed bag. She looked at herself in tights and t-shirt and bare feet, the circles under her eyes bleeding sad darkness into her cheeks.

There was a crash and she jumped, ducking into the corner. Through the open window thumped a round dark object about the size of the proverbial bomb in the Roadrunner cartoons. It rolled unsteadily almost to her feet and stopped.

Don't look at it 'cause it's not nice. Don't look.

It was a head.

I said don't look.

Was it? Was it? Not Tomaj ...

Tomaj's head came through the window. Tomaj's head came through the window. She stood there on the brink of hysteria for a few seconds and then she tried to look at it again to confirm its identity but she couldn't. It was just like the head in the dream: she could look at it, but her eyes wouldn't admit the sight.

Running from the room, one hand over mouth, gasping, clutching stomach almost-choking.

This isn't the head in the dream, remarked a small objective aspect of her memory. *That was a female face, with the breeze blowing through the skin like Navajo flute music. But not Tomaj.*

Something's getting control; something's pulling herself together, but it isn't Sabina.

Don't think. Don't ask me how I know these things. Just go.

She took some money and stuffed it in her bra. Passport. Also – what's this? The ax card the schoolteacher had given her. She stayed away from the windows. She went to the front door and closed it and locked it from the inside. There was a security monitor that showed the halls and stairwells. In the stairwell was lounging a big, blond male, smoking a cigarette.

Sabina ran back into the bedroom, shut the door, and stepping over Tomaj's head climbed out the window.

* * *

When he got back to Phoenix House, the front door was ajar and all the lights were off. Adrien crept inside, wondering what it meant that the security system had been deactivated. A dim yellow emergency bulb lit the stairwell, where the air already was beginning to seem warm and moist; the air conditioning was off.

He ascended to Audra's floor, where he found the corridor dark. A bluish light shone from the open door of her office. He slipped along the hallway and looked in, but the room was empty. The system tank was utterly dead; the only light was generated by an electric wall sconce. The hum of some kind of generator came from farther down the hall, so he continued on until he'd reached one of those doors marked 'Therapy'. He remembered now that this was where Malagon had been examining Sabina. He tried the handle, but it was locked and the small window was dark.

The next door opened to his touch. He was at one end of a long room which seemed to be constructed entirely of galvanized steel. There were several horizontal platforms on which bodies rested beneath tents of plastic and wire, surrounded by monitors and other equipment. The nearest of these supported Audra Malagon, fully clothed but prone, motionless. Her head was enveloped in a net reminiscent of the kind used in beauty parlors of the previous century. Her eyes were closed but her mouth was open. Speaking.

And sitting nearby, leaning over her like a worried dentist, was Max. He looked up and saw Adrien. He smiled.

245

Adrien froze. Max's smile waxed.

'A rabbit in the headlights. All that training, and for what? Sit down, Adrien, and listen. Some fascinating insights are coming from our doctor ... right, Audra?'

The doctor had been mumbling in a low voice the entire time, but at the sound of her name, she fell silent.

'Audra, what were you saying about the foreign body you found attached to Sabina's brain?'

The doctor wet her lips and said softly, 'It's not the same object I transferred from C. Already it's changed; it's grown. I don't know how to evaluate this. I don't know what this *is*.'

Max spoke over her. 'You see, Adrien? What help could you get from this amateur? Sabina will be safe with me. I'm the only person on the planet who can put the resources together to cope with what she has inside her.'

He gestured to the other patients who silently inhabited this room.

'... glial cells in the auditory cortex are metabolizing an unusual ...' said the doctor's voice.

Max chuckled. 'C thought that after the surgery it could slip away from me – it concocted elaborate plans to evade my attention. Oh, there have been all kinds of things going on behind your back, Adrien. Secret messages, assignations in the night, all kinds of good stuff. Sabina's been a very busy girl. But she can't escape me, and therefore neither can C.'

'... expect to indicate hemianopia but instead ...'

He paused, making a show of pursing his lips to think, then pointed a long white finger at Adrien. 'However, you, my friend, have one last choice to make. Do you want to go free, or do you want to end up like say ... Tomaj?'

Adrien swallowed, regretting the JD that was still in his bloodstream. He wasn't particularly listening to Max's words; rather, he was watching the way his eyes moved, the way he gestured, the balance of his body. Max was playing the heavy with too much camp even by his own standards;

in fact, there was a sense of rising hysteria about him right now that didn't make sense. Max was on top; Max was in control. He wasn't in a full nelson now and nobody was going to break his neck. So why was he acting like such a wreck?

Adrien said quietly, 'This is a spooky room, isn't it?'

'... more than a simple anomaly in the decussation,' the doctor whispered. 'If you look at the language function, it's turning up in the wrong *place*—'

Max flinched as if an insect had just crawled up his spine. 'What? Shut up, Audra.'

The doctor fell silent.

'So you've learned C was a patient here, right, Max?' Adrien said. But he could see from Max's face that he had not. 'Dr Malagon, tell us about C's condition. Why was she here?'

He was improvising the hell out of the only thing he had to go on – namely, the fact that Max seemed uncomfortable in this room – but he had gotten lucky: Max was acting genuinely creeped out by the presence of the insensate bodies – what else could explain the sudden anger on his smooth face, the sort of cardboard expression that would inspire mockery if it weren't already associated in Adrien's mind with danger?

'... damage to the reticular activating system appears to have been deliberate ...'

'It's almost worse than death,' Adrien murmured.

'... extremely delicate procedure ...'

'Especially if it happened suddenly, without warning,' Adrien said. 'If suddenly you woke up to find out that you – well, you *couldn't* wake up. That you couldn't communicate with anyone, or see anything. You couldn't scream, or cry.'

He couldn't be sure Max was even listening to him.

'... presumably to produce a specific effect, as the autonomic functions were deliberately unaltered. Unfortunately the severed nerves are irreparable, meaning the condition is ...'

Max leaped to his feet, his rubbery face seeming to peel away from itself and become a different face, distorted by extreme emotion. He pointed a finger at Adrien, who knew instantly there was someone behind him. He struck out with his right leg, automatically spinning around to follow up the kick. His hands reached out to grab anything that came near him, until at the last instant his eyes fell on the glimmer of light catching on the tip of a hypodermic needle, where a single drop of fluid quivered. He withdrew his hands before the needle could touch him, yielding a few feet back into the room. The needle-bearer was big (of course) and had a rapt look on his face, as if about to apply the final card to a house of cards. Adrien recognized him at once.

'Hi, Boris,' Adrien said, and kicked him neatly in the balls.

Boris folded over, the needle wavering between his fingers; Adrien bent and thrust the tip into Boris's palm and depressed the plunger. He whirled to ward off Max, but to his surprise, Max had slipped through a door at the other end of the room. Adrien pursued, but by the time he got into the stairwell, Max was already exiting two floors below. Adrien watched him running across Fifth Avenue.

It was the first time he had ever seen Max make such a mundane and uninspired exit. Adrien didn't even know what had set him off. Why was Max so freaked out by C's condition?

He knew he didn't have much time. The police and private security might be late in arriving, but that didn't mean they wouldn't come. And he had no idea how to revive Malagon. He returned to the room where he found her still mumbling away. He looked at the contraption on her head and concluded that Max had been intending to save to disc every bit of Audra's memory he could get. Adrien wondered how much had already been sucked from her.

It took him a few minutes to figure out how to stop the

program and get the disc out. He took it, and a portable reader – a brand new model, as pricy as a car.

'Don't worry – the insurance will cover it,' he said to Audra, and switched off the system. She began to stir, and he fled.

He had to take the disc to a wire pilot before he could understand any of the information on it. Luckily, he had connections in the business from way back, and he found a guy who called himself Xtreem and claimed to be swift enough to do more than simply take the ads out of general release wires so they could be sold on the street as bootlegs. Xtreem said he could actually translate a chunk of raw experiential data using his own personal interface, which would enable the pilot to go through Malagon's head and come out the other side and talk about it.

Guys like that didn't come cheap. Xtreem said he'd do it if he got to keep Malagon's new data reader afterward; then he instructed his crew to stand around Adrien with baseball bats and shock rods and to kill him if Xtreem went to the zoo.

'My 'face better be just as pretty on the way out as on the way in, you hear me, Reyes? I get just one blown connection, you gonna pay.'

It took a day and a night, and Xtreem's crew had several debates about whether to kill Adrien anyway, because although Xtreem didn't shock out, he was obviously on no joyride, and he came out the other side of Malagon with bloodshot eyes and gray skin.

'What a flight!' he said. 'Never a-fucking-gain.'

'Just tell me what you remember. Omit nothing, even if it doesn't seem important.'

He had to ply the pilot with food and cigarettes all day long. Xtreem talked and talked. He gesticulated; he made noises intended to approximate what he'd heard; he broke out in sweats and got chills; he *faded* into trances from which he emerged talking a mile a minute. Then he asked for cash on top of the reader, and Adrien gave it to him just to get out of there because Xtreem's kids were still looking vicious.

He found another place to stay and holed up there for a while. He needed to think about everything he'd heard.

It seemed C had confided quite a lot in Dr Malagon – it was only natural, Adrien guessed, since they shared common blood, similar professions, and Audra had saved C from a life of total sensory deprivation. There were a great many things Audra didn't know – she hadn't been lying about that – but there was plenty she did know, and even more that she'd tried and failed to understand.

Years ago, before Tomaj or any other trans had come along, C had tried to slipstream Audra into the Deep. The experiment was not a success – Audra couldn't hack it, and this was why Xtreem had such a bad time deciphering Max's headsuck. Max had asked Audra about the Deep and I, and Audra's impression of the Deep was one of chaos: disassociation, loss of self, madness. It was the noise of thousands of unintelligible voices all talking at once. It was all the material of thought without any organizing principle she could grasp.

But C's experience of the Deep had been entirely different. C had tried and failed to convey a sense of it to Audra. What emerged from Xtreem's ramblings was the fact that, unlike the relationships C would go on to form with Adrien and Tomaj, its involvement with the Deep was not primarily sensory; nor was it unequal, as the Watcher/trans relationship inevitably was. The connection between minds in the Deep was closer to old-fashioned telepathy, except that there could be several minds on the same link at once. Nor were the connections entirely conscious.

'Remember the old idea of the collective unconscious?' C had asked Audra. 'Remember how it turned out to be nothing more than the mutual substrata of human cultures, the basic boilerplate human being? But the Deep is an *artificial* collective unconscious, and it *can* be tapped into. It's a pool of selves, endlessly changing; a resource of memory and knowledge; a collection of skills that can be exploited by any user at any time.'

And C had exploited it. For the most singular aspect of the Deep had to do with its complete and utter separation from the waking world of names and addresses and credit card numbers. Anonymity was sacred in the Deep. Real-world consequences of the Deep's activities were inevitable and indeed desirable, but its members were always protected by secrecy. They learned to guard their true identities from each other very early on; later, of course, when trans began to grow on the periphery of the Deep, those Watchers who kept them became vulnerable through their trans. However, despite the perpetual intrigues that brought the Deep to the notice of ordinary people like Sabina, its purposes were very often connected with real discovery – not sabotage and destruction.

As for the plant I, Audra was convinced that it had been conceived by the Deep. Its basic intent; i.e., to re-construct one personality within the brain of another, was so far ahead of what the HIT field could currently do that Malagon could scarcely believe it had worked on Sabina, even in part. She privately maintained that such a technology was twenty to fifty years away, if indeed it could be done at all.

So if I was working, it implied that the minds of the Deep were capable of something qualitatively different than any individual, or team of individuals, could accomplish on its own. There was no other explanation for the rapidity with which they'd developed such a plant. C had never discussed I with Audra, but it had said that the Deep had transcended communication.

'Within your mind,' C told Audra, 'there is no need for communication as we know it, because your mind *is* communication. A kind of magic is at work: things simply *appear* when needed. If you imagine this kind of process

251

going on *across* minds, then you have a kind of shadowy idea of what the Deep is like. The only thing that slows us down is the speed of radio transmission; if the Deep ever gets off the satellites and finds a way to work as fast as neurons in the brain can fire, then watch out!'

What role Max had played in the construction of I, Audra didn't know. She wasn't even sure if Max was really Deep: if he was, he'd be the exception to the rule of anonymity. She also didn't know how C had gotten itself into such an untenable position in Moscow, or why it had chosen Sabina – or what it had intended to do after the download. Audra was upset, in fact, that she had been excluded from so many of C's plans. Even if she believed C had been trying to protect her, she was hurt.

Malagon didn't think Sabina was strong enough to cope with C. Malagon didn't think C was a person anymore. She, like Mitsuko, thought that C's interface with the system and its involvement with the Deep had rendered it somehow multifarious and fluid. As much as C might want another chance at life, Audra didn't think it could ever fit into an ordinary walking, talking human body again.

None of this boded well for Sabina. The knowledge needed for the safe removal of the plant didn't belong to one person, or even to a group of people associated in the real world. To get to I, Adrien would have to get to the Deep. His only link to the Deep, now, was Max.

Unless he counted those three names Tomaj had gone to some pains to hide.

They had to be important to have been hidden in the Shazzam cookie jar. Right?

First he got on the phone to Gigi, a systems snoop he'd often used in the good old days with C, before everything had gotten so complicated. Gigi was an expert at gathering dirt about people and organizations. When Adrien gave her the list of names he'd found in the cookie jar and asked her to find out who they were, what work they did, and their contacts with the Deep or HIT in general, she sounded disappointed.

'Is that all you want?'

'Yeah, but I need it in six hours. I'll call you back.'

Then he crawled into bed and passed out. Six hours later, Gigi fired back the answers to his questions.

'Nicolette Tazedait is an Algerian national living in France. She's a biosynthetic engineer. That means she builds artificial tissue. Her specialty is neural tissue, human and animal. Until three weeks ago she had a position at the Institut Pasteur in Paris. She's married to a painter called Christina De La Russo. She has no HIT contacts that I'm aware of. Clean as hell.'

'What's she doing now?'

'She's in Morocco. Sunbathing. Picked up and left her project, just like that – people on the team aren't saying much, but the impression I got is that she had a nervous breakdown.'

'Hmm.'

'Next: Kang Jun Il. Thirty years old, a senior engineer at Park Microelectronics. Educated at MIT. He's twice tried to go out on his own as an inventor and consultant, but the company lured him back both times. I gather he didn't make very much money as an entrepreneur. He's widely believed to have a great head for technology and no business sense at all. Wife and kid in the suburbs, uses recreational wires, but he's strictly a commercial HIT user. No Deep connections.'

'But what does he actually *do*?'

'Job involves scaling down circuits – I gather it's a premium market. Shit's expensive to make and as you know, the demand for nanotech isn't what everybody hoped – but there's always someone somewhere who needs something done really small and is willing to pay for it.'

'OK. What about Sascha?'

'He's thirteen years old, his father is Sergei Mindlin, a cable tv executive in Moscow. His mother is a software consultant. Boy's precocious. He's a former chess champion, started work on his PhD at eleven and writes code the way you write checks. Definite links to the Deep: if he's not actually one of them, he's within smelling distance. His father's a powerful figure, politically. Got where he is by ... uh ... taking advantage of the currency situation in the early nineties.'

'Do you mean what I think you mean?'

'Let's just say, there are relatives in Brooklyn, you know?'

As soon as he cut off her call, Adrien began making travel plans. It was strange to be going off this way on his own initiative; but he kind of liked it.

He would decipher the bunkai of the kata. He would untangle this knot C had tied him up in. There was nothing left to lose – right?

* * *

I take her down the side of the building. She is all but paralyzed with fear anyway – of me, of the people who killed Tomaj, of herself – and she needs my help. Her body isn't as responsive as Adrien's, for she hasn't trained it to obey her, but the descent isn't physically very difficult. The walls of the two buildings are only about three feet apart: I can brace my back against one and my feet against the other, and simply inch down. I am not afraid of the height, so I push Sabina's terror aside and do what I have to do. I don't have much time. At the bottom, the alley is empty, but I encounter a blood trail that must have come from Tomaj's head.

I slip out of the alley and start to walk, not too fast, ignoring the pain in my feet – to be truthful, I am probably revelling in it a little. The ax card is sweaty in my hand. I look for any sign of police cars, or anyone who might be connected to the man waiting for me in the hall of the building. He will wait a little longer, and then he will break in, I think. At least I have a head start.

I confess, the thought of physical danger thrills me. It has all been too theoretical for so long. If only I didn't have to steal her body to get this sensation; if only she could be counted on not to return and demand control. I badly need more time to feed Sabina the memories she will need to elude these people; it doesn't help that she is so resistant and will only receive me when in a semi-conscious or unconscious state – or when I force her, like now. I guess I have Adrien to thank for that. He's made her believe I'm some kind of devil.

Two or three blocks away from the apartment I get in a cab. I want to let her out but I can't risk having her make a scene when she comes to her senses barefoot on a crowded sidewalk when the last thing she remembers is opening the window.

I get the cab driver to take me to a bank in midtown, well away from Adrien's neighborhood. I put in the ax card, enter the PIN number, answer the second-tier security questions I programmed, and find the balances I expect. I take out cash, pay the driver, and take another cab to Times Square. See how easy? I get a room in the Marriott among the businessmen and tourists, and lock myself in. I order clothes to be delivered by phone, using Tomaj's credit card number because Audra might have cancelled mine by now; then I send out for lunch and, because I know Sabina will be needing it, a bottle of vodka.

I sit down on the lid of the toilet and start picking pieces of gravel and glass out of my shredded feet. This barefoot thing is becoming a problem. I find myself hissing as I clean the cuts. I was so excited to have control of the body that twice now I've forgotten to think about shoes. The pavement was filthy and I'll be lucky if I haven't picked up an infection.

Room service shows up with the food and drink. I pay cash, shut the door, and a split second later it's as if someone's kicked me in the stomach. I put my hand over my mouth. My heart is beating double-time. I feel dizzy, and I'm suddenly overcome by a wave of uncontrollable nausea. I go dashing into the bathroom, where I begin to vomit so violently my diaphragm feels like it's up in my tonsils. Tears flow; heat rushes through my body; remnants of coffee and bagels shoot through my nose as I retch repeatedly, then begin to spin and grow small; another spasm grips me and—

* * *

Sabina flushed the toilet, washed her face, and rubbed her aching midsection apologetically. She hobbled wincing into the living room, where the food was waiting in covered dishes. She flushed it down the toilet and ordered something else. She ignored the vodka: she knew it was only an invitation to surrender.

While she was waiting for her food, she found some stationery and wrote:

I am not afraid of you.

All right – maybe that was a lie, but…

Fear won't stop me. You can't control me with fear.

Yet here she was, skulking in a hotel room because she was afraid to walk out into a world in which she was not herself.

I'm going to go to hospital. Not Phoenix House – not where you can have your way. I'll walk into major teaching hospital and let them decide what to do with you.

It was a good idea, in principle. But then what? It didn't change the fact that Tomaj was dead and Adrien reviled her.

She dropped the pen, curled up on the bedspread and let the tears flow. The rhythm of her sobbing triggered the music. It was in C# minor, a snatch of some shape so perfect she must have heard it somewhere before – yet at the same time she was aware of herself creating it, deciding where it was going and how … She stopped crying, enthralled by the imagined sound.

There was a knock on the door. Wiping her eyes with the back of her hand, she got up and let in the room service cart. The man pushing it was not dressed in a hotel uniform. In fact, from his Nike basketball sneakers to his plastic hair, he looked completely out of place here. Had he been following her since the park?

Not now. Not this.

'Allow me to give you this,' he said gravely, handing her a business card. She knew his voice immediately. 'I won't interrupt your meal, but I'd like you to call me if there's anything you need. Or call me just to talk. You'll find me very supportive.'

Sabina whispered, 'Walk toward the sound of my voice, Sabina.'

He smiled. 'Yes. And you did. Come to me again, Sabina. You won't be sorry.'

He backed out of the room. 'Enjoy your meal.'

The card in her hand said, 'MAX NIAGARIN. Under the Deep.'

Twenty-four

He had hired a translator called Kim Moon Kyung from the same company he had used on previous 'errands' for C. She met him at the gate and took him to Park Microelectronics on the twentieth floor of a high-rise in downtown Seoul, where she chatted with the personnel secretary while Adrien stood around yawning and jetlagged in the background. He was wearing a suit, and every time he glimpsed himself reflected in the dark glass that predominated the decor, he wanted to laugh.

Moon found out that Kang Jun Il was an engineer in their plant outside the city limits, but he was on leave of absence at the moment.

Gigi, thought Adrien in annoyance. This is the shit I pay you to find out ...

'He has come down with the sickness, I'm sorry I don't know the English translation, it's a virus that makes you very tired all the time? People who work too hard can be very ill from it.'

'Chronic fatigue syndrome? Job stress? Mono?'

'Ah, yes.'

'*Mono?*'

'Yes, that's it, I recognize the word. Jun Il has mono.'

Adrien groaned. 'Well, how sick is he? Can I talk to him on the phone? I only need a few minutes of his time.'

There was a good deal of hushed talk and fluttering of hands. Finally Moon took his arm and led him out of the office.

'Sorry, so sorry about that,' the receptionist called after them.

'They won't let us see him,' Moon said in a low voice as

they waited for the elevator. Before he could express his frustration she added, 'I saw the address on his file. I can read upside-down.'

She drove him to Jun Il's house in the suburbs. At Moon's insistence, they staked it out, waiting until the wife left ('It's better this way,' Moon said. 'Trust me.') which took some time. Adrien fell asleep until Moon shook him awake.

'The coast is clear,' she said, and marched right into the back door of the house, which was unlocked. Adrien made a mental note to tip her well if this worked out, and to fire her if it didn't, as she slipped into Kang's darkened bedroom. Suddenly there was a thud and a shriek.

'Mr Reyes!' Moon said in a sharp voice. 'I think you better come in here.'

If Kang Jun Il had mono, it sure was a funny strain of the disease. He was standing stark naked on the bed, and his entire body was covered with markings similar to tattoos. He looked, in fact, as if he'd been run through a printing press. He took no notice of the intruders, as he was busy writing something on the ceiling with a ballpoint pen.

Then Adrien noticed that Moon's attaché case had spilled out on the floor.

'He stole my pen!' she said in an outraged tone. She began berating him in Korean, approaching the bed and holding out her hand demandingly. He saw her, made a low noise in his throat, seized her hand for a second and scribbled something on it.

Moon snatched her hand away and stared at it. Adrien turned on a lamp and looked at what Jun Il had done.

It was a tiny drawing that looked like a scrap of circuitry. In the lamplight, Adrien suddenly noticed that what he'd taken for black and white wallpaper was in fact white wallpaper with Kang's drawings all over it. He had made elaborate, detailed diagrams covering the entire room.

Moon had been trying to get him to answer her all this time; at last she despaired and said to Adrien, 'I think he's insane. He won't answer me.'

259

Adrien took his scanner out of his pocket and gave it to Moon.

'I'm going to hold him down. I want you to turn it on and wave it all over his head. OK – ready?'

He caught hold of Kang and knocked him down; Kang didn't fight – rather, he went suddenly limp and lay there with his eyes moving back and forth as though reading something written on the air in front of him. Moon scanned his head twice, but nothing registered. Then Adrien reached behind each of his ears and probed. Behind his left ear was a slight indentation and a scab.

Adrien shuddered. It was finally occurring to him how lucky he'd been to get rid of his plant so easily, while retaining all his faculties. He might easily have ended up like this.

Or might he? What had Kang been up to with C that he could now do nothing but draw these diagrams?

A woman's voice snapped something at them in Korean. Adrien turned to face Kang's wife, who stood in the doorway holding a bar of soap and a towel.

'I thought she went out!'

'So did I ...'

Moon was getting to her feet and talking rapidly to the wife. Adrien released Kang slowly, and the engineer got up and resumed his activity on the bed. At length Moon turned to him. Jun Il's wife had burst into tears. She approached Kang and began to sponge off his body.

'She says she's furious with herself for ever letting him get involved with these mind-games. He told her no one would ever come to their house. He told her they would be rich. Now he can't speak, he can't work, and great shame will be on them if the company finds out what really happened.'

'Ask her what all this writing is about.'

'It's something he designed for a person he met in his head? I'm sorry, that's what she said.'

'Did he know who this person was, in real life?'

The wife shook her head and added a few words, sniffing.

'No. She doesn't think he knew. She says there was a lot of money involved and she even thinks he might have been paid, but he can't speak and she doesn't know where the account is or how to get it.'

'Does she know what it is? The thing he designed?'

Moon frowned as she translated.

'She says it's a very tiny version of a larger idea the person gave him. In order to make it small enough, he developed a new technique – I'm sorry, I don't understand everything she says – that he hoped to patent, I think.'

Adrien took a deep breath.

'Are we the only people who have come around here to see him?'

'Yes,' Moon translated. 'Thank god. He built the chip using company time and resources, in secret. If the company found out...'

Adrien said. 'Tell Mrs Kang that she should go straight to her husband's firm with a photograph of part of this diagram he's drawing. She should tell them he's developed this new technique and she knows it's worth a great deal of money. She should bring a lawyer with her when she goes. I don't think the firm will be mad at all. I think they'll be ecstatic.'

Moon relayed this information and the wife's face brightened instantly.

'She's invited us to stay for tea,' Moon said.

'Sorry, no thank you,' Adrien said to Mrs Kang. 'And, Moon, tell her to get her husband to a good neurologist.'

'I don't think she cares about him at all,' Moon said disapprovingly. 'She wants money.'

He turned to leave, wishing he could get the image of Kang's vacant face out of his mind.

'Wait!' cried the wife in English. She went into another room and came back with a small envelope.

'She says she doesn't want this in the house. It has brought nothing but bad luck. She wants us to take it away.'

He waited until they were in the car before he opened the envelope.

It contained a disc, a magnifying glass, and a tiny plastic bag holding three bits of what looked like glitter. The label was handwritten in tiny, precise Korean characters that could be read only with the magnifying glass.

'FAILED SAMPLES,' said Moon.

Adrien swallowed. Moon started up the car and pulled away as if she thought she was in a James Bond film.

'That was weird,' she said, and began fiddling with the stereo. 'You like Louis Armstrong?'

He put the disc in his portable. About half was code and the rest schematics. The only text was in Korean, and the code was written in the SHATTER language and meant nothing to him. He was disappointed. He didn't know much about the technical aspects of HIT, but he was almost positive there was no way you could implant a simple chip like this and get the effects of I.

It was not as if he had anything else to go on, however. He should have exhorted Mrs Kang to inform him if anyone else came looking for this data – Sabina in particular – but he had been eager to get out of there.

He rubbed his eyes, looking away from the screen. Tomaj had had Kang's name. Kang's Watcher had given him data to build a component, but there was nothing spectacular about that component that he could tell.

The car careened toward the city center.

What if Kang had been C's trans? C had expected to download into Adrien, but was forced to change plans at the last minute. So it gave the contact information to Tomaj – why Tomaj? Why not Sabina?

Because I might not work? Because Tomaj might have to track down the people who actually built the I prototype to iron out glitches?

It would be just like C to distribute the tasks among a variety of people. That way, it wouldn't have to trust any one person. He had been assuming that Nikolai merely stole the plant itself from the Deep and then sold it to C. Now it was apparent that the only thing stolen had been information. The actual building of the thing had been under C's control all along.

No wonder Max was so pissed. C had gone over his head. Adrien could feel a subtle electricity charging through his limbs, just as if he were C's trans again. He glanced down at the screen once more.

'Shit!' he cried.

Moon jumped in her skin and swerved. 'What? What?'

'It's a virus. This disc's protected. Fucking thing is self-destructing!'

'Ohhh, ... too bad you didn't think to read it at Mrs Kang's house. I bet it was set up to read only on their computer, you know for protection, or—'

'Moon, shut up and drive.'

He sat there fuming for awhile, looking at the nonsense characters on his screen and wondering what, precisely, had been lost. Did it really matter? He was trying to find Sabina, and unless this information led him into the Deep, or to someone who knew what had become of her, what good was it really?

When in doubt, rationalize.

Twenty-five

Max's box was behind home plate. The day was blazing hot and the plastic seats smelled of beer and felt furry against her legs. She was wearing a skirt selected from the clothes delivered to the hotel on C's instructions, shorter than she would have chosen for herself. She hadn't slept last night, and she felt tired but proud: nothing had broken through. There were no gaps in her memory, no unexplained actions. She yawned. The clouds over the outfield were a sickly yellow.

She had picked up the phone this morning and dialled Max's number. Partly she did it to take revenge on C after what had happened with Adrien. The more she thought about what C had done, the angrier she got. C had briefly tried to manifest in the shower but Sabina had fought her back. C didn't want this meeting to take place, but Sabina had had enough of being in the dark. It was obvious Max could follow her anyway: if he wanted to harm her, he could do it the minute she set foot outside her room, if not before.

Anyway, he might not be so bad. He had been gracious on the phone and suggested they meet at his reserved seats: her ticket was waiting for her at the box office. And now here he was, like a recurring dream. This time he was wearing a baseball jersey, and he chewed gum. He grinned and waved at her.

'Is this OK for you?' he asked. 'I thought you might like to be out in the open.'

She nodded and he sat down.

'Before we go any further, I just want you to know that we're immensely pleased with the progress you're making. I say this without making any formal assessment, but just based on what I've seen of your recent actions. You're right on target.'

She fixed her eyes on a couple of Toyotas that were being driven around the outfield as part of some kind of advertisement.

'What do you mean by "we"?'

'What do you think I mean?'

'You are actually … member, then? Of the Deep?'

'Well, if the Deep were a company, I'd basically be their deal man. I would do PR and handle the interface with the rest of the world.'

'But you know who they are, yes? They are not secret for you.'

He hesitated. 'Like I said, *if* the Deep were like a company. But it isn't.'

'Yeah, OK. Maybe I accept you are the important guy. So what?'

He smirked. 'That's where you come in. Would you like me to explain your situation?'

'Yes.' She didn't look at him. She looked at the fans and the ads on the scoreboard. She wished the game would start. All this waiting was making her nervous.

'OK …' Max said at last. 'You are pregnant with a dead woman. Unlike an embryo, the dead woman within you is already developed, a fully realized personality eager for life. And, unlike an embryo, she will never depart from you. She will become you.'

It occurred to her that she didn't really want to be hearing all this. She looked across the diamond. The Toronto Blue Jays were coming out of the dugout and no one was paying attention as the lineup was read. She wished for something to concentrate on so as to shut out what he had just said. What she had made him say.

Jorgé Torres! said the announcer as if he were declaring the discovery of radium. *Ben McCloud! Terence Goralski!*

'Baseball is a fucking boring game,' Max remarked in an

off-handed tone. 'It's one of the few things about this country I really hate.'

'So why are we here?' She began to get up, but he pulled her down.

'We can talk. We won't be observed. The middle of a crowd is the best place to be if you don't want to be seen.'

He waved to the ESPN camera as it panned across them.

'I knew you would never work as a trans,' he said. 'You have no aptitude for games. Everything is either/or for you. You have no sense of grayness. It's better for you this way.'

He snapped his fingers and waved money at a hot-dog vendor, acquiring two hot dogs and beer. He offered some to Sabina but she shook her head.

'It's all right,' he said. 'You think I'm full of shit, but you'll see. I know you better than you think. But I didn't bring you here to tease you. I'm the only one who can help you, so you've got to trust me.'

The national anthem began and he abruptly got to his feet, juggling hot dogs and hat, and sang in a surprisingly supple tenor. He knew the words.

When they sat down she said, 'Tell me how. How did you do it?'

'It's a new technology that has an organic component. It can integrate with your tissue and teach your brain how to accept the patterns stored in the inorganic segment of the plant. We used Freefall to relax you and make you more receptive to the data generated by the plant. Among other things, Freefall speeds up your ability to process information, and we needed that so that we could coordinate with the surgical team on C's end. C had been busy downloading itself into the plant, and we were operating within a narrow window of time.'

'Uh-huh.'

'I'm sorry,' Max said. 'It must sound macabre to you. The implantation process has caused memory loss on both sides of the transition phase. That's why you don't remember the process, and I assume you don't remember going back to Tomaj's place afterward, either. Do you?'

'No,' she said warily.

'You were perfectly cognizant when you left the party. We trailed you to Tomaj's to make sure you'd be all right.'

'But I don't know the codes to get in Tomaj's building.'

'No. But C did. We were encouraged by this early positive result.'

'Adrien hates me,' she said suddenly. 'He told me not to see you. What kind of person are you? You put a thing in my *brain* while I was on Freefall? What kind of sick—'

'Hey.' Max laid a hand on her forearm and stopped her gesturing. 'Let's get one thing really straight, OK?' He squeezed the two bones together. 'I am in control. Not you. Me. Want to go to the cops? Be my guest. You'll end up in a mental hospital – or worse, a real hospital. You don't really want that, do you?'

The very thought of it made her want to bolt from her seat – but he was still holding her arm. She heard herself whimper.

'Shh. I understand. One lifetime spent trapped in an institution is enough. You're free now. I gather you're free of Adrien as well, which is a very good thing for you. He left you, didn't he? He got scared or pissy or whatever and he left you to cope with this alone. Didn't he? Aha. I knew it. You're better off without him, believe me. He's a coward underneath it all.'

She said: 'You're afraid of me, Max. Aren't you.'

He seemed to get something stuck in his throat. A bat cracked on the ball with that unmistakable homerun resonance and the crowd shouted. Number 27 of the Yankees sprinted for the wall, jumped, and caught the ball. Max stood up and cheered, dropping one of his hot dogs.

She stood up and shouted in his ear.

'There must be truth between us, Max. Or there is no trust from me. You understand this?'

The transformation was remarkable. He looked sheepish,

confused, benign. He blinked at her like a favorite uncle suddenly accused of paedophilia.

'It's not you, Sabina. I swear it isn't you.' He wiped his sweating forehead with a paper napkin. 'I've known *of* C for a long time. I've had dealings with C. It's just that I only recently learned what C really was. And every time I look at you, I can't help feeling ... strange.'

'You feel strange? *You* feel strange? How do you think I feel?'

'Right. You're so right. I'm sorry. Please – have patience with me. Understand this: you are the only thing in my life now. I am at your service, night and day.'

If she hadn't been quite sure about this, she was sure now: she despised him.

'What is it you want, Max?'

As soon as she said it she knew she'd spoken the magic words.

'Very simple. First, you stop climbing buildings for fun or profit. It is not funny to scare Brother Max into thinking you might fall and kill yourself. Second, you call me daily with a status report. Third, you need to complete a series of instruments designed to measure the success of I.'

'Instrument?' It made her think of torture chambers.

'Just a test, an oral exam, if you will. It's an important part of the process for you, and it will allow us to monitor your progress.'

'Who's "us"?'

'You know. *Us.*'

Somebody from the Blue Jays popped up a foul ball over the stands nearby and everyone leaped to their feet to try to catch it. There was a minor skirmish below them and the people waved for the cameras.

'But what if something goes wrong? What if there's a problem?'

'Well ...' He faltered a little. 'Well, then of course we'll go straight to the experts. I have many contacts. Anyway – everything's going brilliantly.'

'Is it?' She was thinking of Tomaj again, but she wasn't going to say anything to Max because she couldn't bear the thought of what he might tell her about Tomaj, and she didn't want to cry or anything like that in front of him.

They watched the game in silence for a while.

'What are you going to do with it?' she asked. 'After you test it. I mean, what's it for?'

Max smiled. 'The possibilities are endless. We can make one person into another person; we can inculcate people with desired characteristics or knowledge. We can teach people to interpenetrate each other.'

'And there is market for this? I mean, why do you care?'

He snickered. 'Is there a *market*? It *is* the market, as far as I'm concerned. HIT is changing the whole character of human relations, and you and I, Sabina, are sitting right in the middle of it making it happen. Can't you feel the power of that? It's huge, it's divine – and it's ours.'

He is crazy. 'You think people will want to feel like I feel?'

'You can't see farther than an inch in front of your face. That's why you need me. Don't you know you're the embryo of the next stage?'

'Next stage of what?' she said in a hard tone, but he didn't answer her question directly.

'Listen,' he said. 'I know I'm not doing very well at this. I feel like I'm a little bit over my head, you know? If I'm rough around the edges in the charm department it's because I'm nervous. It's as new for me as it is for you.'

He was lying. He had to be.

'I don't trust you, Max.'

'OK, maybe not right now you don't, but give it time. These next few days will be a crucial period. And you can't go it alone.'

She laughed. 'But I'm not alone. Am I?'

* * *

There are voices in your head and then there are Voices in

your Head. The problem is that Sabina can't be sure which is which. The voices are ordinary, internal: they speak her language, operate on her with her own tools. They use her memories and reference points as a child uses colored blocks, to build arguments urging her to action – these are the tricky voices, because they seem to be her own.

The truth is, she doesn't know if she's alone here. It feels obscene to think that what Max says is true. But she has said and thought and done things she couldn't explain afterward. Sometimes she has the feeling of being on a threshold. The place beyond is like a white room with many windows all flung open and a polaroid blue sky beyond: an aerie of purity, a time-pool of absolute stillness in which to immerse this grimy confusion and make it come clean. Who would not want to come here?

But maybe it isn't what it seems. Maybe it's a trap.

Equivocation, again. She can't escape it, being of two minds.

I find it easier and easier to empathize with her. I didn't expect it to be like this. I thought I would move in and rearrange the furniture to suit myself; but the furniture is alive.

Up in her room overlooking Times Square she feels trapped. She wants to fling away introspection, put on a catsuit and go out into the throb. The streets look like mechanical blood vessels in some titanic genital. They get hard and soft at prescribed times of day. They pulse. This makes a sound, and it's not the music you hear coming from the ghetto-blasters, not the brazen beat-driven frenzy imported from the motherland, cranked up on amps and digitized for machine digestion: no. The sound of the streets of blood has all the density and richness of ocean noise, the chaotic complexity of the curling village-eating tsunami; but it's black noise, pitches found way out there in left field on a piano, timbre squeezed from the guts of earth and hung out to dry in the weightless air that hawks and dives through these staggered geometric canyons.

At first she was captivated by the sonic potential of subways but now she knows you've got to go deeper than that. You need a subway so deep it's hot, you need a sound that's blown with magma breath right into the ears of the dying, who are in the best position to hear it and know what it means.

I say this from experience.

Strange that the insect frizz of humanity scooting around down there 1 2 1 2 on their little legs could build something that requires a music so deep.

This is what she means by voices. Does she know what I'm talking about? Does she believe in me, or does she still think her brain is generating this stuff to amuse itself?

Hey – what's the difference, after all?

There is no such thing as the self, Sabina. Learn it once, and profit from it forever after.

* * *

She had parted with Max, promising to meet him that evening so he could administer the instrument. But she fell asleep in the cab on the way back from the game, and when she woke up she was in Queens.

C had taken her to this street in Far Rockaway, to a neat yellow house in a row of identical houses. Sabina stood on the sidewalk and studied the house. Why had C brought her here and then fled? What did it want? There were roses in the front yard, heavy lace curtains hung from the front windows, and a painted sign above the mailbox read, 'Malagon'. While she stood there, a hand parted the lace curtain and she glimpsed a rocking chair, a white-haired face.

She turned and walked rapidly away, aware that tears were streaming down her face but not understanding them, except in an abstract sense. She found a subway back to the city, and puzzled over the incident as she rode. Had that been a grandmother? An aunt? Was C trying to teach Sabina that it had been human, also?

Or was she merely being manipulated? For when she got back to the city, C had a new desire. It didn't force its will on Sabina; it simply spread a hunger all through her until she could think of nothing else but finding what C wanted to find. Even though Sabina didn't know what it was.

She went to Tomaj's apartment with a crowbar and bolt-cutters. She smiled sweetly at the kid in the hardware store where she bought them. The worst that could happen, she told herself, would be getting arrested. How bad could that be? Maybe the police would believe her. Maybe they had heard of trans and Watchers and plants. New York City cops were supposed to have seen it all, right?

But it was easy to break in: she knew the security codes, after all. Upstairs, the hall was deserted. Adrien had already undone most of the locks. He had closed up after himself and then damaged the security system so it remained permanently locked. She got quite a bit of pleasure out of forcing the door. Only two splinters.

She didn't know exactly what she was looking for, and she wasn't going to let C suck her up and use her. No – C was going to have to learn to *ask*.

She wandered the huge living room, touching the objects: Already they were collecting dust. In her own cells, her own bloodstream, driven by her heartbeat, things were happening that she could neither hear nor understand. The other consciousness was alive all the time now, making neurochemical sweeps. It could see her. It could feel her right now, and her questing fingers, and her uncertain breath, pacing the floor. It was patient.

Those things which seem blurry from a distance require only closer scrutiny to render them in all their harsh & livid detail. Distance grants romance. Distance transforms the object as time transforms memory. I have made the mistake of thinking I could get in close and scrutinize without penalty; I have made the mistake of thinking I could step back and acquire perspective. O

I'm in close now but I no longer know the names of what I see, let alone their values in relation to a world that is only shamming with respect to its own coherence.

What kind of world is this? Anything can happen in it. For all the rampant paranoia, politicking and brainwashing that live as greenly in our era as in any other, it is a world with nobody at the wheel.

Imagine if ordinary people went around in this fashion! one is tempted to cry out, dismayed by the disorder of the world. Does not the typical human seem sane enough that, added up, a group of humans should equal a sane society? Yet even the simplest man is divided within himself. Take any human being with his multipartate brain and question him. He believes 'he' is studying math, cooking an egg, flying jetplanes! How can 'he'? It's ludicrous! If nothing else his brain's a closet of approximations and guesses, a compost of evolution's excesses – badly in need of cleaning. But he persists in believing that 'he' exists. Just as the world – whatever that may be – gets away with calling itself a world even if it's a mass hallucination from billions of perspectives. The chaos within and without: how do we carry on? Who, in the end, is in control?

As if I didn't know my own name. As if I weren't master of myself.

I do not exempt myself from these judgments, for I am worse than any human, and to boot I've got delusions of grandeur. These must be carefully noted and recorded and considered when assessing the final outcome. $1+1 \neq 2$. Rather, $C+$ Sabina$=?$ There are far more than two of us in here, like a gospel choir feeling funky as hell on a Sunday morning, whether or not God's listening.

She had to get a hold of herself. The apartment looked sad. It needed dusting, and she found tears in her eyes when she thought of Tomaj and also of Adrien. There was a deeper resonance in her whenever she imagined Adrien now, another remembered lifetime surfacing at whiles and throwing him into new perspectives.

And the sandpapered, anguished, hyperactive nerves. She

started so violently when someone knocked on the door that she fell sideways into one of the mannequins supporting the tv, and caught herself just in time to prevent the whole setup from collapsing.

'Who is it?'

'Sabina? It's Max. I've been looking for you everywhere.' She let him in.

'Tomaj is still missing, is he?' he asked, his brow furrowed with concern.

'Tomaj is dead.' It was an open challenge, but he smoothly sidestepped it.

'I'm sorry,' Max said solicitously. 'Did you want to be alone? We can talk another time. I was concerned because you missed our appointment last night.'

'I wasn't feeling good.' She turned her face from him, hiding tears and thoughts.

'Let's sit down.'

They went to the kitchen counter and Max, with what Sabina thought was stunning disrespect, rummaged through the cabinets until he found glasses and a bottle of Scotch. He gave her a drink and poured one for himself.

'You look like you need something to steady you,' he told her.

'I'm all right.' She sipped, though, and it did help. 'So ...'

'It's time for the assessment of your progress,' he said. 'I don't want to pressure you, but we really need to do it as soon as possible.'

'I don't know ...'

'It will be easy. I promise.'

She was staring at Tomaj's Shazzam cookie jar. The urge to open it and look inside was almost unbearable. Max, watching her, said carefully, 'Are you hungry?'

He seized the lid of the cookie jar and looked inside. He frowned.

'Sorry. It's empty. Look, I'll take you out to eat after the assessment, OK? There's a good Thai place just down the street.'

He was grinning at her so hard her legs trembled. What did this mean? C wanted to flee. The empty cookie jar – Max's face – the residual Tomaj-smell in the dead man's apartment—

Sabina realized she was taking a perverse pleasure in C's distress.

'All right,' she said abruptly. 'We do it now.'

'OK ...' He took a photograph out of his breast pocket and showed it to her. 'What is it?'

It was a piece of industrial equipment, a metal cylinder with a glass top and some kind of control panel on it labelled in Cyrillic.

'Security thing. HIT storage system.' She reached for the bottle and filled the glass to the top this time.

'Do you know how to work the controls?'

Her hand trembled and the brimming glass spilled over when she tried to bring it to her lips. 'Maybe, I don't know. No. I don't remember.'

Max glanced at her shaking hand.

'Let's try a different one.' He took a business card out of his pocket, turned it over, and made some geometric shapes on the back of it. He put the pen in her left hand. 'Can you please complete the diagram?'

Her hand began to fill in lines, tiny abstract forms, almost before she knew what she was doing. At the same time a swell of voices rose in her, all talking at once. She dropped the pen, spilled the drink, and backed away from the counter.

'No. I'm sorry. I can't do it, Max.'

He smiled reassuringly and put the stuff away. 'It's OK. Maybe tomorrow.'

She flared at him suddenly, because she was frightened. 'No, maybe not tomorrow. I don't like this. I don't want to do this anymore.'

She was breathing hard, but Max sat calmly and mopped up the spilled drink with a potholder. 'We talked about this yesterday. And you knew what you were taking on.'

'No I didn't.'

'Yes you did.' He put his hand on the counter emphatically. There was reason in his tone, but also a certain hardness. 'You knew. You asked me. You paid me money. You arranged your life to make this possible.'

'You're lying.' She felt her nostrils flare, and a wave of heat rose in her torso. 'How dare you say I did such things?'

'C, you did. You may not remember, but you did.'

'Stop calling me that,' she snarled. 'I'm not C. I'm Sabina. C may have asked you, but I'm Sabina.'

'I want to speak to C.'

'Stop it, Max. Stop pushing me.' She was shaking her head rapidly. 'This is ludicrous.'

'You just don't get it, do you? This is the real thing, kid. It's not *art*. I'm sorry if that's harsh, C, but—'

'Goddamn you! *Izgubi se!* Can C speak my language? Can C play Bartok?'

'*Touché.*' Max got up and walked into the living room, as if trying to muster distance around him to his advantage. 'Still, you can't ask to have a transcendent experience and then start whining when it gets scary. If it was easy to arrive at, it wouldn't be transcendent, would it? Sabina may not have consented in so many words. But you two must work that out among yourselves.'

'*What?*' she spluttered, following him. 'Don't deny your responsibility, Max. You are party to this.'

Max narrowed his eyes. 'Are you *sure* you didn't ask for it? In your heart of hearts, can you look at me and tell me you didn't want the Watcher inside you? You must be truthful, now. As I recall, you came to my soirée for a reason, even if you didn't fully understand it yourself.'

She sent her mind back to that day, her talk with Tomaj, the feeling of being right on the edge of something astonishing; but it was like looking at herself through a thick lens. She couldn't even *remember* her own feelings or her rationale – she had changed too much already. She might well have been holding in her hands a set of tiny clothes belonging to a child, knowing she had worn them only yesterday – realizing that something was terribly wrong. She began to shrink away, wounded and vulnerable, but then rounded on him suddenly, inhaling with a snarl. Startled, he backed away.

'It was rape,' she said, forcing him past the mannequins and the electronic birdbath and the magnetic sculpture. 'You know it, I know it, C knows it. I was asking for it, and it was still rape. But that didn't matter to you, did it? You knew you had the higher purpose in mind. Whatever that means to you. So you felt free to play god.' She drove him back and back, until he tripped over the psychedelic rug and stopped with his back to the plate glass window, the city smeared behind him. 'You are the master of religion, yes? Let me ask you something, Max. Whose voice calls you in the night? Who watches over you?'

She waited, breathing too loudly, while he fixed her with a cool snake eye and seemed to take her measure. He made a sound like a laugh.

'The age of individuals is over.' He spoke in a monotone as if reciting a magic spell. 'It was historically brief and now it's over. The only role left for individuals to play is in surfing the big mudslides of mass desire. Charisma is created in the eyes of the people, and the people have become one giant, ciliated organism ruled by the objects of their desire – unless they have gone underground, become Deep, to escape the mass hypnosis. To be of consequence, all an individual can do now is seed himself across the species, multiplying and therefore, paradoxically, ceasing to—'

'You want I for *yourself*.' She discovered it with a sudden disgust. 'You're halfway there already, with your Army.'

He shoved her aside and strode to the couch. He picked up her cigarettes and lit one, speaking through it as he puffed.

'No one's voice calls me in the night. No one watches

over me. Everywhere I look for a sign, but everywhere I find nothing. My capacity for faith has been destroyed.'

At Max's words, C released a rush of terror and guilt beneath her skin. Something was very wrong.

He sat down on the sofa and crossed his legs. He looked like a fashion ad.

'Why are you doing this to me?'

His smile said, *don't you know?*

She stared at him and he calmly set down the cigarette in an ostrich ashtray.

'Because I can.'

Sabina let her face fall into her hand. She could feel herself breaking.

Because I can. C had used those very words toward Sabina – but now they were coming from Max. He was looking right through her; he was looking into places within her she hadn't known existed. Between the two of them, C and Max, they were ripping her to pieces. She was being drawn beneath the cape of C's will, into its hypnosis.

Girl: you wise and sentient thing. You know when to give it up, don't you? You don't suffer from that hyperinflated rational penis they'd like to strap onto you. You know when to let go. You know when to change the focus on the world because it really is a womb painting, diffuse light playing out oh so softly through the delirious trees. In that redness somewhere ghosts a sun, coyly disguised behind the many veils of age and experience. She haunts your painting but does not inhabit it. She is a lamp shone through from another dimension, rubbed on by hope, and producing this arrangement of color and texture which gives you such peace, now, looking upon it.

You will give it up, won't you? Give it up to mama. For it's a slow and lush river, a serpentine of gentle potentials but none of them will harm you, provided you stay close by me. For I have eaten all the beasts of the jungle, they are all under my command. And they bring me offerings in the form of flowers and dead men.

Sabina was shivering. She could feel Max watching her

but she looked concertedly at the floor. 'Please excuse me,' she said in a faint voice. 'I just – I need to get some air. I'll be right back.'

'Go.' He was cold and polite. 'I thought – I hoped – you might have the courage to face up to the consequences of your own actions. I thought you might have something to say to me, you who have made the journey no one has ever made.'

The door was far away; she was stumbling toward it through a graveyard of lost potentials. Her breathing was loud; her throat was closing as if she'd walked out into a frigid wind.

'There's nowhere you can go where I can't find you. I'll get what I need from you.'

She glimpsed him taking a long drag on the cigarette as she slipped out the door, casting a last glance at the six-foot-tall stuffed Barney in the corner. She ignored the elevator and flew down the stairs pell-mell. On the street she sprinted for the subway and pushed her way through the doors just as they were closing. She was soaked in sweat and shivered in the air-conditioned car. No one looked at her.

Twenty-six

There was a plane: it passed through the night sky. Let us not yet speak of who was aboard. Let us not speak of which person sat in first class, face covered by a hot towel, remembering the sound of a Mozart piano étude but unable to make the fingers articulate their counterpoint on the tense knees. Let us not consider who eschewed the headset designed to remove all awareness of hurtling in a hollow tube on the business end of a controlled explosion 34,000 feet above the dark sea, preferring to shift in the seat and listen to the engines, inhale the dead air, and imagine vast schools of krill in the phosphorescent ocean so far below – who attempted to embrace the seemingly impossible.

Let us not think of the shedding of cocoons.

Wars are comprised mostly of waiting. This is a waiting moment, of cigarettes and card games. We cannot speak of who was on the plane due to a problem of pronouns. The being flips over and betrays itself incessantly, making 'she' and 'I' about as effective against the terror of multiplicity as a cardboard box against sub-machine gun fire.

She cannot be objective, or even pretend anymore.

She wants to inhabit my eyes and fingertips and I give these up as reluctantly as a child gives up its most ragged doll. Partly it's because, when she is the full master, it's not clear to me where I go. I don't think 'I' 'go' anywhere. I think rather that I dissolve or disintegrate and cease to be myself and that's a notion which doesn't appeal, for I am already tenuous even at the best of times.

What is who, here in this pocket of warm damp air, up high where the world is supposed to be rare? She won't be content until she has engulfed me. She's quite the Napoleon – or am I? I capture her memories like armies – I'll make them my own. I don't think I'm being unfair: if she would settle for it, I would allow her enter into me as a man enters a woman – that is to say, not at all. But that's not enough, not for her. She insists on possession of her own cell tissue. Which one of us does it belong to?

Analyze these words and you will see that I am profoundly involved with my own body. I won't let it go. When you have survived a rupture in your universe it is difficult to explain what happened even to yourself. You can never be sure what you are from moment to moment & so you hesitate, waiting for knowledge to catch up with experience but, alas, knowledge is doomed forever to cling to experience's coat tails.

Do not make the mistake of thinking that because I say 'I' I mean 'I'. I am only the local territory embattled in a much larger campaign. It is for all of us that I speak when I say: I am not myself. Quick, tell me who do you crave? Marilyn Monroe? That boy dancer in the cage with the tiger's body and the abandoned eyes? Or is it some piece of meat you tasted on a wire and found to your liking? O – you say – 'he feels this' or 'she wants that'. You identify, you sexualize, you caress the object in your warm regard.

Don't be coy. Don't pretend you don't. Everybody has somebody, usually many bodies, upon whom they prey in this manner. You suck them into yourself. Also, furtively, you take the villains, so that you can make them fight and squabble and kiss each other in your head just as once your toy action figures did. You have constructed yourself out of these things. You are an entire culture.

Only now you're playing with somebody else's toys, and your hindbrain knows by sense of smell that they aren't yours. You wish you could put them back in the toybox.

Stop. Stop.

It can't go on like this. If my insides are made of the outside is made of my insides, if subject and object are going to persist in fucking each other this way, what hope have I got? How do I know that even now she's not subverting my senses?

I'm falling into her ...

Max is terrible. Max is danger. There are obvious reasons to be afraid of him, but crawling beneath those, wrapped up in its own darkness, is something infinitely worse. We heard it in the emptiness of his voice in Tomaj's apartment: a voice calling and echoing up the walls and into the high spaces of a cathedral; a voice unanswered. We both heard it, but one of us won't acknowledge this.

Things have changed. We may fight for control, but we are equally petrified now. So we run – into each other. And the plane vamps sideways across gravity.

* * *

When at last I made my way back to my country, I drove up into the hills, to the house where I used to live with my grandparents and the place in the wood where I've buried my parents. I don't mean this literally, of course: my parents died when I was just a small child – my father early on in the war, my mother some time after we were separated the day Maria dragged me inside from the piano. When I'm feeling really awful I tell myself she probably died looking for me. Anyway, their bodies were never found and I imagine they ended up in a mass grave. But I don't like to think of them being there. Maria found a woman who shared a cellar with my mother after we were separated, and she gave me a plastic barrette that my mother wore, and the wire frames left from broken glasses that had belonged to my father. I should have kept these things, of course: cried over them, held them as talismans all my life to invoke the spare handful of memories that have not faded: the way my mother held the bread loaf against her chest, for example, gripping it with her firm tan hands while she drew the knife calmly toward her to split the loaf; or the black stubble, seething with life, that sprouted from my father's cheek where I would nuzzle every morning and then sit back to watch, fascinated, while he shaved. But I found I couldn't keep the objects. These things were too pathetic, and after a time looking at them I became angry. No person should be reduced to this sightless bit of twisted wire, this cheap plastic hair fastener. It isn't right.

At that time I lived with my grandparents on their land in the mountains of Istria, in a cottage that is now occupied half the year by holiday-goers and empty the other half. I went to the clearing in the fir wood which had become a special place to me. From a very young age, I was accustomed to going there whenever I could sneak away. I loved the forest because of the darkness beneath the trees, which must have made existence impossible for other plants, for the fir trees reigned in solitude. The lower branches of the trees themselves had died away, leaving long avenues open. Even in the middle of the day there was a crepuscular stillness in this wood: it frightened me a little, but naturally that was part of the appeal.

I was only about four the first time I got lost in this wood. It's amazing how foolish you feel when this kind of thing happens, since it's exactly what you've been warned against and everything you thought you were clever enough to avoid. Children of this age are not supposed to have a fully developed sense of the self, but I can clearly recall feeling as much embarrassment as fear, as if God were taking a look at me and chuckling to himself, saying, 'I told you so. I told you to stay in the garden where Nana can watch you.' Nana was snoring in a plastic lawn chair under the shade of the pea plants, her schnapps bottle tilted dangerously against a small hummock of grass. As I grew more and more confused in the wood I began to ache with guilt for the worry she would suffer when she woke up and I wasn't there.

I wasn't concerned for my own safety in the slightest.

I remember after some time wandering, the sound of my own breath distressingly loud in my ears, I came upon what seemed like a mountain of rounded earth in the midst of the trees. It was perfectly symmetrical, pointing up like a very large, mossy egg. Feather ferns grew on the top; it was nearly noon, so a thread of light speared down on the ferns and they glowed with the diffuse brilliance of undersea plants in sunlight.

This was my island in the wood: I waited here to be rescued. I climbed to the top and sat cross-legged, becoming quickly absorbed in the activities of ants and the shifting patterns of light through the incandescent fronds. After a time I saw my mother in the distance, and then the red of my father's shirt flashing between the dark trees from a different direction. They were shouting for me, and then to one another, 'She's not by the brook,' or 'I'm going to check by the fence.'

I must have been hypnotized by the quiet of the forest, because I didn't respond right away. I merely sat watching and listening as they moved farther away and then closer. Finally my mother was near enough to me that I should have called out, I should have done something. I remember her clearly. She was wearing a purple ski shell and jeans, with only sandals on her feet. I thought she was very beautiful, with her short, dark hair and her eyes the color of a woodland pool in summer, and the softness of her voice. She was walking through the trees, unaware of being observed, her face turning this way and that, her hands reaching out to part branches sometimes. I was above her looking down, and she seemed vulnerable and alone. I didn't move as she walked right toward the mound, looked up, saw me, and stopped still.

'Sabina, what are you doing?'

I burst into tears. She began awkwardly to climb up the sides of the mound, but she had only sandals on and there were vines everywhere. She struggled; her feet slipped on the loose stones thinly covered with earth and vegetation:

she fell. I made no effort to move, but sat there sobbing and watching her awkward attempts to reach the place it had been so easy for me to come. Within moments my father had arrived and climbed up to seize me with a matter-of-fact grunt. They were angry, although they didn't scold me until later, and I was confused. I didn't know why I behaved that way – what kind of an explanation is it to say for those few minutes they seemed like strangers to me?

My mother wanted to know about the pile of stones with its egg-shaped central pillar, where it had come from and what it was. She looked at it with accusation in her face, as though it were somehow to blame for what had happened.

'It's a cairn, I guess,' said my father. My mother crossed herself. I learned a new word that day.

That, of course, is where I eventually buried the barette and the wire frames. I thought my grandparents would own the land forever or that some cousin would inherit it, but after their deaths I learned they had twice mortgaged the property to continue sending me to University for a second year after I had failed out of my original scholarship, and now my cairn belongs to an Italian tour operator who rents out the cottage and the land to harried executives in the summers.

In my visits over the years I have made various offerings: music, chiefly – I play it for them in my head. Poetry I sometimes read aloud, but other days I just sit beneath the trees and breathe. I have seldom thought of that first time I came there, lest my parents revisit me as spirits still looking for me: *Sabina, what are you doing?* They agonized over me, wrung their hearts for every tiny thing I did, and yet they were the ones in danger, not I. The strange part of it is, they had *always* been like ghosts to me: when they were killed I had not yet grown out of the stage of fearing they would die and leave me. When my fears came to pass it seemed like the fulfillment of a prophecy. The war was irrelevant to me, merely a fluid, phantasmal arm flung out from the amoeba of my own internal destiny.

Since it was summer now and the cottage was occupied, I had to park along the road and walk back through the woods, and it took me a long time to find the place. As I walked I kept telling myself to calm down, to allow the beauty of my surroundings to capture me and soothe me, but it was no use. I must have walked quite close to the cairn three or four times before I actually saw it – and then I was startled to suddenly *see* it, as if it had some power to become visible and invisible, some ability to act on my senses without my knowledge.

I sat down at the base of the mound. To look at it I would have to crane my head back, like a supplicant at a temple. Suddenly I realized I didn't want to be here after all. There was a trembling in my stomach: audition fever or some other high-pitched emotion, the rising Richter needle of C's imminent arrival.

It is difficult to dig up the dead things. C does not wish to talk about the Deep but I will make her. The Deep is a kind of scaffold built between a group of people. It is not merely a collection of people; nor is it merely the relationships among them. It is not one thing and it is not many. It is a meta-consciousness that derives from its members but is neither included within them nor separable from them.

Your mind is a collection of neurons; your mind is an organ; your mind is a quantifiable series of electrochemical events; your mind is a system of logic; your mind is the entire world and everything in it. Which of these is true – are they all true in some way?

Like most things which bear weight, the Deep is hard to explain but simple to experience. The thing that hurts most is what happened there.

I stood up. I walked to the cairn. I picked up one of the stones and hurled it into the woods. Worms and things shone beneath. I took another and did the same. Years of leaves, brittle needles ground to a paste, cemented the stones together. Vines were among them, and spiders.

Systematically, breathing hard and beginning to sweat, I began to dismantle the cairn.

She's looking at a radiographic image of her own brain. Wide awake, she watches the tiny plant, guided by magnets, navigate unerringly toward its destination. The surgical team talks about last night's hockey game; nobody makes the mistake of asking if she is scared. For they are all Positive Thinkers; they are all Explorers; they don't acknowledge the concept of failure. And after all this is the high point of her life: soon synergy will cease to be a cliché. She will *be* synergy.

Are these the last moments of her life as a natural being? Or is the whole braid of her development, from a baby learning the most fundamental communication, to a young doctor eager to find the subtlest logic of the body, to the enacting, here, of a process that will expose her directly to other minds – is all of it a continuum, and does it lead somewhere, and if it does where does it go?

'Conchita?' says a surgeon. 'Do you notice anything different?'

'I smell … burning hair? Ugh.'

'Good. We're in the process of slipstreaming you with your sponsor. Mitsuko will help you to stabilize once you're in. Stay with her until you've figured out how to go on your own. You may get flashes of sensation, but they're temporary.

'I am now required to recite to you the following disclaimer. Ahem. Do not attempt to ascertain where you are: this can endanger you as well as the rest of the Deep. Respect anonymity. Leave things the way you find them: information is communal, but emotions are not. Also, please remember when you are in the Deep, you are tapping the subconscious abilities of the other members. They may be driving a car or cooking a meal, so be inconspicuous. Do you agree to respect these guidelines?'

'Yes, of course. Is *this* Mitsuko?' Something's climbing all over her like some psychic grease monkey, dropping images in her mind, inciting feelings … teasing. How icky. Is this what a human being feels like, on the inside?

'Sure as hell hope so!' the surgeon laughs.

'Mind like a pinball machine,' she says sleepily. 'Can we turn down the bells and whistles?'

She ought to be more respectful. Mitsuko Yoshimura is a bigshot; she's brought Conchita into the Deep as a research assistant for her new project in building a paradigm for consciousness based on the direct observation permitted by HIT.

'Pick a problem,' she has told Conchita. 'Pick some aspect of higher thought, design some experiments. I want you to develop a general methodology for studying consciousness through the Deep.'

It's an opportunity whose scope she can't even begin to grasp. If she could, maybe she wouldn't be so sanguine about taking this step.

'All right,' says the surgeon. 'We have contact. It's up to you to develop from there.'

'What about the Deep? I don't see anything. How am I supposed to find it?'

The surgeon sniffs.

'Like it says in the brochure, we don't sell roadmaps to the Deep, sugar. So, Jerry – you going to the Devils game on Friday?'

That was how it began. But it had not ended that way. Yes, it is difficult to dig up the dead things.

Each stone made a bassy thump as I pitched it to earth. The egg-shaped rock was damp where I exposed its lower areas. I was becoming filthy and overwrought. I threw myself at the central rock and tried to move it. I looked up at it from beneath, the stones shifting and rattling around my ankles, and tried to see it as a child had seen it. How had I ever climbed up there? I pushed at it again, not expecting it to move and it didn't. I stepped back and surveyed the results of my excavation, baffled with myself.

Father. Mother. What is happening to me?

The Deep isn't a place, but a kind of time. She can tell herself apart from everyone else only by speed: techno-logical restrictions mean that the thoughts of others come to her slowly: like a sweet, thick syrup. She learns to relax into satellite time, to ride with it. Sure, the Deep is 90% garbage – the noise of everybody's subconscious going full blast – until she starts learning how to use it. To find the paths; find the strong signals.

Go: let the eyes go let the hand go let sequence go let—

She is incandescent, in a fever of thought. It isn't difficult: it's easy. It's the easiest thing she's ever done. Ideas hold their places, bend when asked, do her bidding. Information sought comes flying at her. She lets an idea loose in the Deep like a boomerang, watches it cut a swath through first-class intellects of every stripe, and catches it when it returns. There are no abstractions: everything is real. The very *ness*-ness of the mind of humanity is there for her like a sky that comes but once—

It's even better than she hoped. Gone are the restrictions of science which dictate that problems must be small and mechanical; that the big questions can't be looked at head on.

Not that she abandons scientific method. Not entirely.

By the second or third time Conchita has entered the Deep, Mitsuko has revealed herself as timid and limited. Mitsuko's the kind of person who skis with perfect stem christies, feet one inch apart – never going too fast, never falling. Conchita is the kind of person who attacks moguls and breaks her bindings and receives warnings from the ski patrol.

Fools rush in.

289

Conchita does not tell herself it is an accident. She acts deliberately; not maliciously, but deliberately.

She selects her research problem based on how easy it will be to study. Some aspects of consciousness are more discrete than others. One reason the Deep will ultimately become so effective at developing technology is because the common language of mathematics makes it easy to communicate ideas. In the Deep, mathematical thought runs clear.

So does music, as a matter of fact.

And so does prayer. Very early on, she locates something she comes to think of as a prayer-well. Here, she can see and feel and hear the act of spiritual communion as a concrete, measurable thing, generated by the handful of members of the Deep who engage in such practices. This region is a natural area of the Deep that's never been looked at scientifically, as far as she can tell.

Well – here's something that could put her on the map. Not only can she fulfill Mitsuko's objective of developing a way of studying the Deep; she can actually find out something that people might want to know. How about finding the source of the religious impulse? How about finding the location of the God-potential in the human psyche? How about identifying its size and shape and relationship to the rest of the person?

Conchita Malagon is a rational being. She isn't intimidated by the emotional content of her chosen field of study. She picks it because it's big, and impressive –and ambitious. She's built for speed, and she knows it. So she goes for nothing less than uncovering the biological basis for spirituality. She intends to untangle it from the knot of personality: take a sample, put it on a slide, have a good look. If her experiments work, she'll find out empirically what it is: what is belief in god made of, and why does it persist across cultures, and what purpose does it serve in the survival of the organism.

Of course, the easiest way to accomplish this will be to see what happens if faith is altered or subverted.

She halted there: she actually choked on her own memory. I felt momentary relief. In my heart, I knew this wasn't going to be a happy ending. What did I think I was doing? I was a madwoman in the forest, tearing to bits one of the few things I hold sacred. I had not found any bones here. Birds continued to move unseen in the trees.

I wanted to leave, but I had to finish what I started, and I couldn't let C stop just short of the truth. I took a deep breath and it continued: she becoming part of me, forever.

A long time is spent gathering data and determining the parameters of her work. The task is overwhelming. She ends up deciding she'll learn the most by doing a close study of a single individual; but she doesn't tell Mitsuko this. It's considered suspect to pick on individuals within the Deep.

She traces the strongest prayer signature she can find and begins recording information about it. In time she is led back to a person. She explores, but she never touches the senses, nor the details that establish identity. She takes a guess at gender and comes up with male, but she can't really be sure. All of this is part of her rationale that, provided she protects privacy, anonymity, she won't really be violating the rules of the Deep.

Then she designs her experiment, just as Mitsuko suggested.

Thoughts have a kind of power in the Deep. She doesn't have to do anything physical to anyone. No lab animals; no amputations with whiskey as anesthesia; no playtime on desert atolls. Nothing so crude. She simply wanders into her subject's mind, finds the box where he keeps his god, turns it upside-down, and shakes it. Thoroughly. She watches what happens. Then she dissolves back into the Deep, surfacing with her data.

A doctor who had been a friend of my father's was involved in the Croatian summer offensive a few years after my parents' deaths, the beginning of my country's inconclusive but bloody revenge for Vukovar. I remember what he said about it – something along the lines of: We are a civilized people. We don't like to see the bodies everywhere in the villages when we take them. It hurts us to see this human suffering that we have engineered. Can we stop? No, we don't think we can stop. But it hurts us nevertheless, you see.

There is something of this false yet inexorable logic in C. It came very close to crushing me as I stood over the cairn with mud on my hands and tears plastering the hair to my face. At that moment I did not want to be a human being.

After Vukovar I was afraid of the dark for years and years. I can still see the many layers of darkness in our hiding place. It swirls with phantom lights and shapes, figments of tired eyes. There is a little grayness when it is midday outside. I can see a piece of timber slanting against concrete, covered with dust. When a shell hits the street, the dust jumps ecstatically. I am already small but I make myself smaller still, shutting out the moans and the stink around me. I think: *I am not here. I am not here.* If I am not here, I cannot be hit.

And now war comes to me. It doesn't kill me: it just tells me I don't exist. My old strategy of disappearing in the face of danger will not save me now: it will destroy me. So what position shall I take? If I fight I am the battleground. If I lie down I am the booty. Either way I will never be free of my invader. And secretly, I revel in the suffering … isn't that what's required to make the music by which I define my self?

Her soldiers are raping my women and seeding them with their own sperm. They are burning the fields of memory so I choke in the fumes. Her will to live moves everything – and *she is dead.* 'My mind' – it's a contradiction in terms!

This guilt is going to be mine to bear. It is as if I did these things. She will lay on me all the karma for her crimes; all the weight of her genius; all the guilt she was incapable of feeling in her own heart. I no longer have a choice about who I am. Either I find a way through the maze of her past, or I must retreat completely into unconsciousness and let her live my life.

Surrender, submission, dying. It happens all the time. Why can't I do it?

I went back to the car. The roads were clogged with families, trailing five deep in their swimming costumes, the children carrying giant inflatable animals and the parents, some of them, wearing absurd hats. I had a sudden longing to go with them, to their ice-cream destinations, their lumpy holiday beds, their mosquito-bitten sunsets. Instead I drove to Rijeka with a lump in my throat, fueled the car and, sleepless, started down the coast with the sun to my right melting to rose over the water. The road sprawled before me, the land siphoning color from the sky until – suddenly it seemed – both were a resolute black. I pressed on, glancing occasionally at the hands on the steering-wheel and trying not to ask myself if I recognized them.

Twenty-seven

Gigi had traced Nicolette Tazedait as far as a real estate agency in Morocco; she and her partner Christina had rented a small house on a hill overlooking Tangier. Adrien arrived in the middle of the day, but constant travel had worn him down and he had to drink several coffees before he could make his way to the house.

The woman who answered the door was not more than thirty, beautiful in an off-handed sort of way: she was barefoot and wore only a man's shirt, which reached to her knees. She gave Adrien an odd look when he introduced himself in English and asked for Dr Tazedait.

'She is resting.'

Adrien's thoughts flashed to Jun Il and his dark bedroom; he wasn't sure what to do.

'Christina, *ça va.*'

A small figure appeared silhouetted against light from the back of the house. Nicolette Tazedait came forward haltingly. She was dark-skinned with a mass of gray-streaked, curly hair that she brushed away from her face so frequently the gesture had become unconscious. She was very thin. On her head, left hand, and right leg were large white bandages, and her lower lip was swollen. Her left arm was covered with scratches, some healing, some fresh.

'She should not see anyone,' Christina whispered to Adrien. 'Don't upset her.'

Nicolette studied Adrien.

'I know your face,' she said. 'I have seen it in the Deep. Come in. Sit down. Christina will bring us *café.*'

Adrien cleared his throat. 'Have you been in an accident?'

'No.' Nicolette reached up and ripped out a handful of hair

with a sharp jerk. Tears shone in her eyes. She dropped the hair on the floor and continued speaking as if nothing had happened. 'C told me about you. It said that the Deep must always have connections with the daylit world, and that you were one of them. C said we might meet someday, and here you are.'

'Did you invent something for C?'

'Invent? No. C gave me something. It gave me an idea, and a set of procedures. C asked me to grow some tissue.'

'And you did this.'

'Yes. Neural tissue – it was an extraordinary thing. C said I could take credit for the development of the technique. And I will. As soon as I can understand how it works.'

'You can't understand it?'

'I can follow the recipe to do it. I can't explain it. As soon as I understand the technique a little better, then I can publish. But I must wait—' she grabbed the skin of her own face and began pulling and tugging at it '—until I know what I am talking about.'

'Nicolette, why are you doing that?'

'Doing what?' She stopped. 'After I turned over the product to C's messenger, I began to have terrible problems with the Deep, so I left.'

'What kind of problems?'

Christina walked in carrying a tray.

'First it was nightmares,' Christina said. 'Something in the Deep was attacking her. She was flooded with meaningless information until she couldn't work.'

'I had to have the plant removed. I didn't like the Deep, anyway. It is a very murky state of being. I won't even call it a place.'

'Do you know Max Niagarin? Ever work for him?'

'I never heard of him. Have some *café*.'

Adrien suddenly glanced up and saw that Nicolette's fingers were immersed in her own coffee, which was scalding hot. He caught Christina's eye.

'Nicolette, *non*!' Christina ran into the kitchen and came

back with ice, which she pressed to the older woman's hand. Nicolette appeared unconcerned.

'You know why she does this?' Christina demanded. 'Can you help her? She'll kill herself. She destroys her own body. I must watch her all day. She tried to set herself on fire the second day we were here.'

Adrien looked at Nicolette. 'Why?'

She shrugged. 'The body. It is disgusting. I cannot think with the body all the time, always the body. If I could get rid of it, maybe then I would understand this new theory.'

Adrien said carefully, 'I would like to see this technique you speak of. Do you still have the information C gave you?'

'No!' Christina said sharply. 'You can't see it. Now you must go.'

She ushered him to the door, but shut it behind herself and walked with him toward the road.

'I destroyed the information,' she said in a low voice. 'It was making her crazy. Did C send you to help her? If so, I can drug her coffee and take her to hospital. That is the only way. You must—'

'C didn't send me,' Adrien said. 'In fact, I think C drove Nicolette out of the Deep, maybe to protect her – I don't know.'

'Why *are* you here?'

'I have to get closer to the Deep, and I found Nicolette's name.'

'Nicolette told me the only way to get in the Deep is to be approached by a member. They have to volunteer to … *initier* – I think in English it is called slipstreaming. Once you're in, you can't be traced. I don't know who slipstreamed Nicolette, but she cannot induct anyone else because she has left the Deep for ever. You are wasting your time with us.'

'You're sure you destroyed everything?'

She looked him in the eye. 'Everything. It was like poison.'

'Then I'll go.'

'Tell C that Nicolette needs help. It's only fair. C should not use people and then just vanish into the Deep again.'

'If I ever find C again, I'll give it your message.'

She turned and went in, but Adrien stood there in the heat for a while before returning to his hotel.

About a year ago, driving through Ireland on some obscure quest of C's, Adrien had gotten really lost for the first time in his life. He was a seasoned international traveller, but the rural road system of the Irish Republic had defeated him at last. The signs had consisted of boards nailed across one another at angles, with the destination of each road printed (ostensibly) on that board which pointed to the corresponding road. In some cases there were several choices of road, all hiving off in different directions. After driving around in circles for some time, Adrien had twigged on to the fact that someone must have amused himself by taking the signs for a whole series of intersections and rotating them by a single increment, so that no matter what road you took, you became lost – and went on getting more lost with every choice.

He had that feeling now. That night, in the air-conditioned sanctity of the hotel with all of Tangier cast out alight before him, he began to practice kata. There was no point in analyzing. You didn't understand the bunkai of a kata by objective analysis. You understood it by performing the kata; and you understood it best of all if you performed the kata while your enemy was trying to kill you.

He was beginning to get inklings of a pattern, but he didn't have enough of a grasp of C's plans to see how everything fit together. If I had an inorganic component that was used to store data, and an organic component meant to mimic the host's own tissue, then he had already met the two people who had built the parts of I. But someone had to put it together for C. And someone else, presumably, had to invent it. There was only one more name on the list, and from the way things were going Adrien had a pretty good idea that Sascha Mindlin was Nikolai the little-shit-who-double-crossed-Adrien at the deal point.

Max never let himself be bothered by international boundaries; still, if he called any place home, it was Moscow. If Adrien was going to find Sabina or the Deep or both, all roads seemed to lead back to the place where he'd nearly gotten killed in April. He didn't really know what he was doing, but he'd have to try – or forget the whole thing and go home.

He sat down at the table with the complimentary hotel stationery and pen, and began to write a letter.

Twenty-eight

I drove to Split.

None of it made any sense to me. C's research problem was stupid and I could see no value in her precious experiment. I thought, if faith was a thing in its own right; if the capacity for believing in god could be isolated from the rest of the personality, then why did some people need religion more than others? Why did some people see spirituality as an explanation for the unexplainable while others saw it as a source of moral behavior? I didn't see how the experiment could work.

And if it did work, what then? What would become of the subject?

The more I thought about it, the more it bothered me.

Not that I had nothing else to worry about. I had two major, concrete problems. The first was the tracer that had been embedded in one of my molars: it had to go. Bleary-eyed, I went to the first dentist I could find in Split, paid cash, and demanded immediate help. The dentist was puzzled by the X-ray which showed up the location of the tracer, but I refused to take no for an answer and in the end, he pulled the tooth.

I felt slightly better, but Max must have tracked me this far: even without the radio tag, my actions in coming here had been entirely predictable. If I was already being followed on the ground, removal of the tag would probably not help me, unless I could find some way to disappear. I couldn't think of one. Maybe C had omitted all the skills I would need to elude pursuit, thinking that it would be Adrien who received I. But I wasn't Adrien, and I didn't know how to tell if I was being followed.

The second problem had to do with the fact that C's plans for our survival and the continuation of her work lay in ruins. I had gradually come to understand that there was some information that Tomaj was to have kept for – me? her? whatever – given to him by C before she died. She told Tomaj to keep the emergency information safe in his own memory; and if he was in trouble, he was to switch to low-tech mode and leave it in the Shazzam cookie jar in his apartment.

As far as I can determine, C obliterated this information from the scan which transferred her essence to I. She retained no memory of it. Working through trans had taught her that by breaking down data and scattering it, leaving one piece here, another there, she reduced the chances of anyone putting together the whole picture. If I worked right, everything necessary for survival should be *here*, in this body – so why was there was something else, hidden away deliberately? I couldn't answer this, and that made me unhappy. There was too much I still didn't know.

She hadn't reckoned on Tomaj being broken – presumably by Max. After his death, despite C's best efforts to get me to the cookie jar first, someone else had gotten hold of the cache. That someone appeared to be Max.

It was impossible to know what the information was, so I had no way of evaluating the danger to me or to anyone if it had come into Max's hands. C had carefully cut around the edges of the memory when designing the transfer, and there were few associations for me to follow.

On top of these two problems, there was the fact that all I wanted to do now was make the music that had finally come to me. I didn't want to think about Max, or I or C or the Deep or even Adrien. I just wanted to let the music out.

I was virtually paralyzed with indecision. In the end, exhaustion took over. I got a room in a guesthouse at Split, crawled into bed, and slept.

Conchita wakes up. Only doesn't.

She can't see.

She can't hear. Even her heartbeat is gone.

She can't feel anything.

She knows she's awake, because she is thinking. She is aware of herself. She is simply unaware of anything external to her.

She can't dream.

There is no time.

She has some vague memory of being in an airport. It was a conference. She's supposed to be presenting the results of her work in the Deep to a group of colleagues. It's supposed to be her moment of triumph.

Yes. She recalls the hotel now. She arrived in the middle of the day. She lay down for a siesta. Now this.

She tries to use her plant but it doesn't seem to be there. She can't get to the Deep.

Unmeasured, dead time stretches into her and empties her.

At first her mind manufactures sensory images out of memory to replace the ones she has lost. She is at sea in the dross of her own life. Tv. Lecturers. Memory on memory, until nothing retains meaning and her life has been eradicated by repetition.

Then comes the silence.

And the slow realization.

The Deep.

She has been punished. Someone has discovered what she's done. She can't imagine how. She was careful to detach herself from her subject once she had the data she needed. And the Deep is unregulated – or so she thought.

What have they done to her? How long will it last?

There is a premonition of endless time, infinite entrapment, the shrinking of the self down to almost nothing. She can feel it bearing down on her, nullifying—

I woke up screaming. The landlady beat on the door; I

stumbled out of bed and reassured her I wasn't being attacked. She informed me it was the middle of the next day and asked when I intended to come out of my room.

I ended up paying double.

To settle my nerves I went to a local café where the tables spilled onto the street. As I was finishing my coffee, a woman stopped beside my table. She was carrying a clipboard and I thought she was going to ask me for some kind of donation; I hesitated. She addressed me in German.

'I am Lieutenant Schutz. I am doing a survey. If you could absorb the personality and experience of any person, who would you choose?'

'Leave me alone.' I looked around for a waitress.

'My God is the God who sees you, Sabina. You cannot go on running from him forever.'

I stood up, too angry to be frightened.

'What's all this?' Having overheard, a young waiter sauntered over and winked at me as he said, 'Anyone in history.'

'For the sake of argument, yes.'

'Why do you want to know?' he demanded. I began to edge away.

'We are trying to establish a market.' She reached out and grabbed my arm. 'How does the tooth feel?'

A second waiter arrived, removed her hand from my arm, and gave her a rough shove into the street. 'Christoff, don't let these people harass the customers.'

'In China they say the ancestors are watch—'

'Get out of here before I call the police!' screamed my champion.

'Sorry,' the young waiter said to me. 'I've never seen that one before. Usually they just ask if you want Head.'

I paid my bill and fled.

I decided to take the Dubrovnik ferry and try to lose myself in the islands. I had to have time to work on the music. As I stood on the deck of the ferry gazing down at the faery-green froth of its wake, I knew I had to capture it soon, or I might lose it. I wrote down bits of it on the travel brochures I had gotten at the ferry dock, using a modified notation I'd developed while at University. Some of the chords had distinct images attached to them, and when I concentrated on the music I also saw things. Superimposed on the world, *ghosted* as photographers say, were diagrams that looked like maps of cities from 1,000 years in the future, and minutely crenellated flowers that had evolved from circuit boards, and the same cuneiform language that had been haunting the undersides of my eyelids when I was waking from dreams.

I slipped off the ferry at Korçula, getting myself mixed up with a large party of Austrian students. I wended my way through the symmetrical streets with their pale buildings and red roofs, drawing strength from the fact that this town's history stretched back in legend to the time of the Trojan War. However unreal my life seemed now, it was still somehow connected to the past, to the boats on the azure sea and white stonecraft that had been here since the beginning of Western civilization.

I did not want to be accosted by Max's army of believers-in-Max. Not here. I decided to hire a boat and go to the volcanic island of Jabuka with enough food and water to last while I composed the music. No one would find me, I was sure: the cliffs rose right out of the sea like an irregular pyramid, and nothing lived there but birds and black lizards. Compasses went funny due to some magnetic property in the rock. It was my kind of place.

And then what? I didn't think further than that. The music was becoming everything to me. All I had ever wanted was to be taken over by my music – now that it was really happening, nothing else seemed so important.

I hired a car to drive to Vela Luka on the other side of the island, where I knew I could get hold of a boat quietly and quickly. My plan was to put a brick on the gas pedal and send it into the sea near Vela Luka harbor – this should put

Max off my trail just in case I had been followed from the ferry.

But several miles out of Korčula a motorcycle began to tailgate me. I was already driving too fast, so I pulled over to let it overtake, but the rider simply skirted my car and came to a stop beside me on the shoulder. I cursed and stepped on the gas, planning to steer around him, but the rider pulled out a very big pistol and blasted out both tires on the driver's side. Then he pointed the gun at my head.

'Get out of the car.'

I did. I had already put my hands up.

He took off his helmet with one hand, the gun still pointing at me.

'Let's take a walk,' he said. 'You go first.'

Abandoning both vehicles, he directed me through a field of high grass. The hills were dry for this time of year, and the land was wild and uneven. I began to think about death as he walked behind me. For a while he whistled. Then he said,

'So, let's chat, shall we? What would you like to talk about? And what would you like to be called from now on, by the way?'

I said nothing.

'OK. I'll pick a topic. The meaning of life? No, that's too trite. How about the existence of God? What do you think, C?'

I looked at him sharply.

'What are you talking about?'

His face was sweating and flushed, his plastic hair melting on the edges from the force of the sun. I couldn't recall *ever* seeing Max looking like this.

'You know,' he said, 'the temptation to blow off your head and then my own is almost irresistible. So: is there a God? Tell me what you think, you with your understanding of the human psyche.'

I stumbled on the rugged ground. We were out of sight of the road now – not that there had been much traffic. 'I don't know why you're asking me. You are the one who sells people gods. Why don't you ask your own followers if there's a god?'

He laughed.

'You don't get it, do you? And here I thought you understood what I said at Tomaj's apartment – I thought that was why you ran from me. I mean, imagine us meeting for the first time in person back in New York, and neither of us recognizing the other at first. And now I've seen your old body, and you've seen my old soul.'

The bottom fell out of something inside as I realized what he was saying. I held my breath.

'I was in the Deep before you, C. I was the one you experimented on. And you ... you ... Well, there really is no word for what you did to me. Is there?'

I said, 'I didn't know. I swear. You've changed so much since ...' *Since what? Since I turned your mind inside out?*

He gave a bitter smile.

'I didn't know it was you, either, until Audra started spouting off about the handy job that had been done on your reticular activating system. That's a piece of work I'm truly proud of. You know, if I hadn't had to find you through the Deep, to track you down in the flesh and take revenge on you, I never would have learned to manipulate the Deep the way I did. The vengeance I dreamed up for you was my first great act.' He directed me down into a dry streambed. 'As a matter of fact, the same surgeon who sabotaged your RAS inserted I into your head – Sabina's head, I mean. I didn't know it at the time, but what symmetry, no? What beauty.'

I felt strangely calm. It's amazing how, when the very worst thing that could happen, happens, all the worries just fall away. What more, after all, is there to fear?

Max was on a roll. 'We have made each other, do you realize that, C? When you robbed me of my soul, you taught me where it was located and how it worked. I've made my fortune out of what you destroyed in me. And you … I'd thought I'd gotten rid of you forever. I never imagined you'd find your way back into the Deep. Now it turns out you've been one of the most dangerous members of the Deep all this time, and you succeeded in hiding yourself from me. I may have separated you from your senses, but you fought back and now you've defied death. Who knows? If I hadn't been monitoring the borders of the Deep so carefully, I might never have noticed Nikolai. You might have gotten away with it.'

I could see the ocean now, down below us at the end of the watercourse.

I said: 'Whatever I did to you, and whatever you became as a consequence, is over now. C is dead. She lived through hell and then she died. I am not C.' I tried to sound as though I believed it. 'So what do you want from me?'

'You misunderstand me,' Max said. 'Revenge is finished. I don't hate you anymore. I truly think the whole thing is rather funny.'

He laughed again, as if to prove it. I could sense the gun above me as we descended a steep, rocky slope above the ocean. There were fishing boats out there in the distance, and yachts; people were playing pop music and soaking up the sun. I was no longer convinced I'd be getting a bullet in the brain; I was no longer calm.

'You know by now that I don't know where in the Deep I came from, so therefore you must know what I want. I want I, and I'm going to take it because I've checkmated you – like I said before: because I can. I'm really not capable of anything more passionate than that, thanks to you. You're going to tell me how I was conceived, and where, and by whom. You'll tell me how it works, or as much as you are able to understand. You'll help me get one of my own.'

We were on a cliff just above a small natural harbor. Tied to the rocks was a speedboat. Where I was standing now, if I slipped, I would fall half a dozen meters to the rocks below. I might die. Or I might just break every bone in my body and end up where I'd started.

'I can't.'

'I think you will, when you consider the alternatives. Go on. There's a path to your left.'

We scrambled down; he ushered me on to the boat and handcuffed my wrists and ankles. I sat on the floor of the cockpit as he cast off, started the engine, and turned in a neat circle in the harbor. Then he accelerated to the open ocean.

'I'm listening,' he yelled over the noise of the engine. 'Start talking any time you want.'

'No. I mean I *can't*. I don't know. I get flashes of memory, but it's like in a dream. It falls apart before I can get hold of it. Everything C knew is all mixed up with this music I'm writing. It makes no sense to me.'

His face looked unnatural in the sunlight. He didn't know whether to believe me; neither did I. What I said was partly true: I *didn't* know where I had come from, and there *was* something lurking in that music. But I could have answered some of his questions already. I didn't want to. I wanted him to think I was weak and confused, and maybe he wanted to think that, too, because he said, 'I can remove the plant any time I want. The Israeli surgeon who put I in your head is back in Jerusalem now; I can take you to him very easily. You understand this, don't you?'

I was so angry I'd begun to cry.

'Go ahead!' I said. 'Take it! That's what you'll do anyway.'

'I'd rather have the means of contacting the designer. Why reinvent the wheel?'

'I told you,' I said wearily. '*I don't know.*'

'You will,' Max assured me. 'If it's worth a damn, you will.'

Twenty-nine

It was a wet spring in Moscow, and the snow had gone. As before, he parked the car some distance away and continued on foot. This time, though, he was operating purely on a hunch – a glitch of the memory that he hoped would reveal to him one of the patterns he was seeking.

Long before he reached the lot he saw the cranes and earth-movers in tropical fruit colors soaring overhead. The slaughterhouse was half-razed, its rain-tarnished walls torn raggedly like a crumpled paper bag. Within, a fluorescent lemon mechanical tower posed like a praying mantis studying its food, dangling the wrecking ball. Adrien stopped in his tracks, crushed.

Why now? Why, after all these years of being allowed to stand, was it being destroyed now when he needed to see something? He broke into a run. To his left, across the road, rose the tiers and tiers of the new tv station, a white ziggurat with satellite dishes mushrooming from its levels at unlikely angles. Antennae laced the air above the roof, the largest dish of all basking in their midst like an occluded moon.

A wire fence had been erected around the site. Workmen were attending to their tasks in a desultory fashion; they seemed primarily engaged in removing the rubble they'd created, which struck Adrien as absurd since the job was only half-finished. The extant half of the building was ignored. As he got closer, he reckoned that some small bit of luck dogged him: the metal door he remembered kicking in was still there. Of the interior ... he would have to see. He skirted the fence until he was shielded from the workmen's view, then vaulted over it and dropped to the ground beside the abattoir. There were orange plastic nets and ditches everywhere he looked, and a profusion of flies. Adrien darted around the crumbled edges of the wall and found himself in a huge, half-open space. The roof was mostly collapsed but in places the steel frame was intact and he could see a cross-section of floors stacked against the outer wall nearest the road. From the splintered wood and plasterboard it was clear to see that this section had been constructed long after the original building. Adrien found himself bending halfway over, subconsciously expecting the remainder to collapse at any moment. The metal door came into view – only half of the room it accessed remained. He splashed through puddles and stood on the spot where he'd lain shivering, waiting to be flushed out by Max's army of believers.

There was too much debris to see the original holes in the plaster, but he remembered that the wires had gone through the ceiling. Now the only way up to the next level was via the twisted cords of steel that emerged from the concrete like frozen veins, as well as the heavy wall-studs that had fixed plasterboard to the wooden frame constructed when this section was renovated. He grimaced and gave the wall a soft kick. It seemed solid enough ... Grabbing hold of the metal, he swarmed up, hanging onto a piece of broken two by four once he'd reached the next floor because he didn't trust his footing there.

There had been electrical outlets in this room. The cables were gone, but fitted against the wall were Formica cabinets which appeared to have been custom-designed. All had holes in the back to permit the passage of wiring. One surface, sheltered from above and on two sides, still bore the imprint of whatever equipment had rested on it, written in grease and dust on the smooth surface.

Something had been going on here. But now, conveniently, the evidence had vanished.

Shouts from below. Adrien took a last look, spat, and scrambled down, dusting his hands on his jeans and whistling. His hand was bleeding where he'd scraped it on the stone. Two construction workers approached him, gesturing and yelling.

Adrien grinned and greeted them in Spanish, edging toward the metal door and noticing that it was blocked by pieces of rubble. Changing tack smoothly, he smiled and stepped forward, extending his hand and continuing to chatter about the latest soccer results while their expressions changed from angry to baffled. They pointed to the roof over his head and waved their hands expressively to indicate the danger. Adrien took off his cap and wiped his forehead. '*Qué?*'

He wished he could have laughed, for they were forced to resort to picking him up bodily and carrying him off the site, while he asked questions about their sexual preferences in a language none of them understood. They dumped him in the road and aimed a couple of half-hearted kicks at him to bring home their point. He rolled away with just a touch too much agility, so that they didn't go back to work right away but watched him until he had jogged several hundred yards down the road, a big wide grin on his face.

Not that he had anything to laugh about. If those wires had led to some kind of hideout, its occupiers were gone and someone had gone to some trouble to make sure no evidence remained. It could hardly be a coincidence that 'Nikolai' had met him here; that Sascha was a precocious boy answering to Nikolai's description; that Sascha's father worked at the tv station. It could hardly be a coincidence that Max had broken in on C's deal with Nikolai.

He walked around the block to the front entrance of the cable tv headquarters. At the reception desk he showed his trusty press credentials from *Newsweek* and said that his translator would be joining him shortly. A phone call was made; after a brief exchange in Russian, Adrien was told politely that there must have been an unfortunate oversight. Mr Mindlin had no appointment to do an interview with a *Newsweek* reporter, but he would see Mr Reyes tomorrow at two p.m.

Adrien tried to look aggrieved. He ducked his head as he walked past the security cameras, hiding his pleasure at getting a crack at Mindlin so easily. He decided to go back to the hotel and get more information from Gigi. This 'family in Brooklyn' business sounded kind of ominous, and it would be best if he knew what he was up against. Gigi said she would dig and get back to him. He went out to dinner. Halfway through the main course, he began to feel drowsy. He stopped drinking wine and switched to water. But what he'd taken for jetlag turned out to be something a bit more sinister.

He felt rubbery and uncoordinated as he got up from his table and wove across the room. A waiter grasped his arm and suggested something in Russian, but Adrien shook him off. Desperate for air, he stumbled out into the cool evening and fell at the feet of the ones who were waiting for him.

Thirty

Max enjoyed taking over my life. He told me he was giving me one week in my studio – a week in which I could try to integrate my memory with C's. At the end of that week, he would question me; and if that failed, he would headsuck me; and then he'd take the plant. I felt sure the plant itself wouldn't help him much once removed from me – otherwise, why bother to give me a week or even a day?

No: there was something he needed from me.

I tried to objectify myself; I tried to be only Sabina, if only in theory. I knew that C would never give it up to Max freely. She had not been in control in New York, so she had been tricked into revealing herself in Max's presence, but that had only happened because she'd just begun to wake up. It wouldn't happen now. I could try to make her give up the information he wanted – it would be for her own sake, I reasoned, because it was C who would be destroyed if the plant came out, not Sabina.

Anyway, considering what C had done to Max, why should I be so protective? But it wasn't that simple anymore. I was no longer a separate person. What she wanted, I wanted. What she feared, I feared.

I didn't know what I was going to do. I had to compose – I *had* to, like I had to breathe. Beyond that, I was stuck. Max took me back to my house in Zagreb, bribed Philip and his friends from downstairs to leave for a week, ripped out Philip's phone line, installed a supply of food and drink, put an assortment of locks and alarms on all the doors and windows, and confiscated my mail. A pile of bills was later deposited at my workstation. There was also an airmail letter. The first night we were back, he cheerfully read it aloud to me.

> Dear Sabina,
> You know by now not to trust letters from me, so I don't expect you to take this very seriously. I'm not right on the other side of the bathroom door this time, passing you notes.
> I came by some information that was entrusted to Tomaj. If I can follow it to its source, I may be able to help you somehow. Or I hope so. Meanwhile, if you're reading this, you're in Zagreb. Get the hell out of there.
> I keep asking myself why I don't just go home and forget about it. I think the answer is you.
> I was in love with you. I won't say any more now. It's hard to write this knowing you probably won't read it.
>
> Adrien

'Give me that!' I snatched it out of his hand. No one else knew about the notes under the door. The handwriting was Adrien's. It had been posted in Korea. Adrien must have found the cookie jar! Adrien Adrien Adrien. Not Max. I could hardly conceal my elation.

'Information entrusted to Tomaj, eh?' Max said, giving me a keen look. 'Son of a bitch. I wonder what it is.'

So did I; but I was busy coughing and blotting my eyes and shaking like a fucking flower. If Max didn't have the cookie jar, he didn't know shit – he might suspect things, but he didn't really have anything solid to work with except my own guilt.

I said, 'Don't look at me. If I knew that, I doubt I'd be here.'

He laughed.

'What would you have done with it?' Max asked me. 'If I weren't here, what would you be doing with I?'

'I don't know,' I said honestly.

'You told me you wanted it only for yourself. Remember? The day I had breakfast with Tomaj.'

'Yes.'

'So why are you fighting me now? You have I. You have your new identity. All you have to do is cooperate. Turn me on to the designer, and I leave you alone. Why is that so hard?'

He was smiling at me. What could I have been thinking, letting Max into my house? Adrien would have run him over out there on the road and never looked back.

The whole situation had spiralled too far out of my control. I was supposed to be responsible for things that had been done in another lifetime, by a person I wasn't anymore. At the same time, I found myself back in my own home. The studio reminded me of my old, unsuccessful efforts to work. The disc of recordings from the train station was still lying around. It didn't sound any better now than it had at the time, but at least I'd been making an honest effort then.

Max had installed himself on a small couch in the corner of the studio with a handheld and a visor. I crumpled up the letter and threw it into a corner, furious with myself. He raised his eyebrows.

'Listen to me,' I said. 'The deal is, I have a week, right? And you don't have anything to say about what I do during that week—'

'As long as you don't leave this house or attempt to contact anyone, no.'

'—so sit there and shut up, Max. I'm going to work now. This may be the only chance I ever have in my life to write something really good, and I'm going to do it while I can hear it. If you know what's good for you, you'll stay out of the way.'

He spread his palms out in my direction as if to ward me off.

'Forget I'm here. I'm just a fly on the wall.'

I turned my back on him and wiped the dust off the sequencers.

When I think of myself, I think as much of my small boredoms, stupid fixations and trivial habits as I do of any higher aspects. When someone makes a piece of music, it's said that they 'pour themselves into it' – and I'm no different. One reason I compose is to temporarily banish all my follies and be transported as some pure essence into and through the work. But what has C done here in me? Has she given me only her deepest yearnings, her most distilled powers of mind – for I don't find that the trivial parts of myself have been altered, much. Has she stripped away all but the most select memories and characteristics, thereby passing on to me that most ambitious of compositions: a person? A distilled person. Imagine that. A person abstracted from time. Her time superimposed on my time, so that everything about me is subtly twisted.

Compose yourself: then die and infect another human. At first I feared her, because I thought she was some kind of power fiend, some devious controller as Adrien would have had her. But no. She was only an artist.

In my abandoned studio, the irony lay thick as dust on keyboards and computers. *Only* an artist. Max sat, watching me, as I picked up my guitar and touched the deep frets. There's a reason why this thing is called an axe. I plugged it in and powered up the system.

If C was the artist, it must be my turn to be the fiend.

Thirty-one

The most dedicated of bondage enthusiasts would have been hard pressed to come up with a collection of restraints such as those which bound Adrien in the back of the van. His circulation was unimpaired, but about the only things he could move were his nostrils. There were two guards, both booted and armed with pistols; one of them used Calvin Klein's Eternity. That was all he knew about them because he was blindfolded.

At some point during the night he had been put on a plane, but he'd been unconscious for that part and only awoke on landing, when they'd loaded him into the van. A long journey followed; then the van stopped. There was no sound but the wind. They opened the doors and hauled him outside. When one of them removed the blindfold he saw that it was either early morning or evening, and he was surrounded by empty grassland for miles and miles. The guards wore masks and spoke only Russian.

His hands were unbound and it was indicated to him that he would be permitted to take a piss. He stood there, buffeted by a hot wind, and looked across the expanse of land and sky, feeling inhibited. He was afraid – not simply for himself and his skin, but in some larger and more diffuse sense. The winds of HIT were demons like Mongol horsemen. They would fly over these plains and everything would be different. Sabina with her altered memory, hiding djinns of every description in the soft bloodlace of her cortex, the notion of her was as incomprehensible to Adrien as the galloping hordes had been to their earth-bound neighbors. What is it that comes with these hooves, this cry of muscle and bone, come to sweep us away and render us as if we never were?

Sometime during the journey he had fallen asleep in the back of the van, tossed about like a sack of coal. He dreamed that he found her. He was to enter a room where she would meet with him, she said. He opened the door. In a puddle on the bare floor was a small human fetus, covered with dark blood but still moving.

'Adrien,' it said. *'Ja te voljeti.'*

He woke up choking, and one of the guards kicked him in the back.

He replayed his actions on the last morning he'd seen her. Had he witnessed something waking in her eyes at the stimulus of his accusations? Had he seen her shadow self rouse and stretch there in those long seconds as she dragged herself from the bed along the wall like a blind thing grabbing for what was solid and straight behind her? Might she not have lived with him, slept in his bed all her life maybe unwitting of what she had within her? But – he told himself, but – a person cannot be separated that way. The mind is the map of the world is a map of the mind, like an endless promenade of imperfect mirrors but in Sabina's case a new distortion had been added. At what point could he consider her to be C? And where was she still Sabina? No, no. They were both gone. There was no more C. There was no more Sabina.

So what existed instead – whose pulse had beat beneath his hand as he cradled her head, her vulnerable neck? Why had he wanted to kill it?

The horsemen, wind incarnate, had run like dread over these plains. He thought of the Watcher's cold thirst for knowledge, the infection of its desire. To think what C was doing to Sabina chilled him, no less because he had turned from this very prospect himself and cowered on the sands of Maui. He had turned down the mountain journey, the travel beyond death that would have been the absorption of his own Watcher. Seen from here under the ragged blue sky it became evident that, given the opportunity to enclose and possess the thing which had been possessing him – to eat his personal god, maybe – he had turned aside in abject fear. Eat or be eaten: a familiar enough credo. But to look at the victim or the aggressor in isolation was to miss the true story. The real interest lay in the dynamic between them and couldn't be captured in their respective forms.

Now he saw what he might have done. He might have closed that circle. Had he not fled C he might have become the horsemen, the vanguard of the next wave to challenge and aggress upon humanity. He might have taken the firewalk to a condition of mind never known before. But he had chosen instead to shrink from the horizon, to be only himself.

The question that he must answer was: was it a coward's choice? Or merely the only choice? For here in the uncertain body of Adrien Reyes there was no sense of harmony with the world, or the self. The world was unlike its description. He could not have appreciated this while he was a trans, for however literally the camera captured the messiness and stupidity of life, the outcome in the form of image was inevitably romantic. By the mysterious process of watching and paying attention, people conveyed meaning to the inherently empty. Now there was no one to impregnate his existence with meaning – no one but himself and he'd already seen how unreliable he was as a guide to his own life. Even when he was trying really hard, his own behavior was full of futility and scattered thinking. He simply didn't know how to handle life. Tomaj could have done it. Tomaj, through sheer will, would have seen what he needed to see in order to live. Adrien could not. Doubt had colonized him, and now it was too late.

The guards had finished their cigarettes. He pissed in a long arc and thought, *What the fuck? My hands are free. I should try for it.*

But he didn't. He was too unsure. He let them bind him

and blindfold him again. They put him back in the van, and he sat brooding until he was let out in the middle of an encampment on the plain.

The place looked like an archaeological site except for a row of vans with satellite dishes sulking dustily in the sunset. Tarp-covered ditches cut lines in the earth; among them were tents, metal-bound black trunks, and video equipment. There were people in T-shirts and jeans bending over and conferring, or arguing heatedly, or lounging drinking from thermoses. Adrien stood blinking and licking his cracked lips while the driver conferred with a short, dark man who had a phone on one shoulder and another in his hand.

Presently the phone man came over and gave orders to the guards. They unbound him and stuck their pistols to his ribs and head, respectively.

'I'm Sergei Mindlin,' the man said. 'I believe you were looking for my son.'

'I need water,' Adrien said.

He snapped his fingers and one of the guards dashed off.

'As it happens, my son also wishes to see you. That is why I have brought you here. I do apologize for any fright or inconvenience we may have caused you. However, I cannot be too cautious when it comes to my son. He is precious to me.'

The guard came back with a bottle of Snapple and gave it to Adrien. It was lukewarm.

'Come.' Sergei Mindlin led the way through the camp.

'What is this place?' Adrien asked after quaffing the Snapple. 'Or am I not allowed to ask?'

Mindlin laughed. 'We are filming a nature documentary. Nothing more sinister than that, I'm afraid. It will be shown in the autumn.'

He gestured for Adrien to precede him toward one of the vans. A door on the side was open. 'Go in. Sit down on that box right there. Don't move from that spot. The guard is covering you and if you move—'

'I will be shot.'

'When you are ready to come out, put your hands up.'

Adrien ducked his head and climbed into the dim interior. He sat obediently. Outside, leaning against another van, were Mindlin and the guards with their patient guns. Inside, the van was lined with softly humming electronic equipment that bristled with wires and colored tags made of electrical tape. The place smelled faintly of ozone and fresh plastic. In the middle of it all, crammed between computer monitors, stacks of processors and a tangle of colored wires, he expected to see the boy crouching, but there was no one. Adrien looked quickly around but there was no room for a person, even a child, to hide.

'Where is Sascha?' He wasn't permitted to move from this spot, or he would have gone over to take a closer look at some of the stuff. He turned his head toward the men outside. 'Am I supposed to wait for him?'

Sergei Mindlin said, 'If you wish to speak to my son, you must go to him.'

For a wild moment Adrien had visions of himself barrelling across the plains in this van with all its juicy equipment. Then he saw the head mesh lying on the crate beside him as if it had been casually tossed there. He winced at the idea of something so valuable being treated in this manner, then glanced at Mindlin, who nodded.

The wires weighed nothing in his hands. They were light as silk and surprisingly untangled. Some wise-guy had designed the mesh in the shape of a very large and wicked-looking spider. A psychosomatic throb began in the scars on his head as he began rearranging his hair to accommodate the mesh.

'I've never used one of these,' he said without looking at the men outside. 'Is there anything special I need to know?'

'There are alarms all over the system,' Mindlin said after a pause. He gestured to the monitor banks and their colored displays. 'If you set one of them off, don't expect to live.'

Adrien allowed himself a grim smile. 'Thanks.'

The spider crawled onto his head.

His body became a cartoon blob with a loud heartbeat. It responded to his presence hesitantly, as if it could no more accept that he was its mind than he could believe this was his body.

'Sascha' had done Adrien the courtesy of appearing in a virtual form resembling Nikolai. He reclined in a black leather armchair and looked at Adrien through half-lidded eyes. Adrien was sitting on a three-legged stool. The room was small and white. There was a closed door in the wall to Adrien's left, and a high window above Nikolai's head. Blue sky had been painted in it. The room contained nothing else except for a clay flowerpot with a geranium in it.

Adrien groaned.

'Isn't this kind of ridiculous? I mean, first you double-cross me, then you have your father kidnap me, and now this?' He gestured around the room. 'What's this supposed to be?'

'I like simplicity,' Sascha said. 'It helps me think.'

'Where are you?'

'I didn't trick you, that night. It was bad luck. I didn't know Max was following me. Although he interrupted our transaction, fortunately I was able to prevent him discovering my larger and more important project, which he would have done if you hadn't been there to distract him.'

Adrien straightened. 'The slaughterhouse.'

'It used to be my base of operations. I had feeds running from the tv station so that I could analyze the signals I was picking up from the Deep.'

'What is your father's involvement? Don't tell me he's in the Deep, too?'

'Would I tell you if he was? My father has taken an interest in my work, and because of his position, he is able to avoid some of the pitfalls that Max has created for others pursuing this path.'

'What path would that be?'

'I'm a kind of anthropologist of the Deep. I am studying it.'

Adrien threw back his head and laughed. 'You've got to be kidding! Max – men with guns – a technology that nobody knows where it came from – and you're sitting here in the middle of it all playing archaeologist?'

'Anthropologist.'

'Whatever.'

'Try to understand,' said Sascha, 'what the danger is really about. Max is not a threat to society. Nothing he's doing is different from the kinds of scams going on all over the planet, throughout history – selling salvation is part of human nature. And the Deep is not about human nature.'

Adrien tried to lean back in his seat with an air of amused, adult tolerance for this youthful philosopher, but he found the chair wasn't programmed to move from the floor.

'So what, in your view, is the danger in the Deep?'

'It violates all the ideas we have about ourselves. It violates the divisions between people; it violates the special-ness, and even the actual existence, of the self. People are perfectly happy to enjoy the fruits of scientific theory when they make life easier and richer; but alter the fundamental rules, and it gets ugly. You know, Adrien, if anything, Max is serving the purpose of holding the world at arm's length from the Deep. People are wary of organized crime and they don't want to inquire into it too closely. Even governments share this outlook. So it's easier for the Deep to go about its business, doing what it does, while Max runs around intimidating people and throwing money around.'

'So is he in the Deep, or not?'

Sascha smiled.

'Max is a master of hiding in plain sight. Yes, I think he's in the Deep. I think he's been a part of it for a long time, and I think he's a master of its currents. How else would he have got the ability to create these religious wires of his? He's no designer. The Deep must have helped him acquire the understanding of the human spiritual impulse that lets him exploit this impulse as he does. Did you know that his men, his servants, actually *worship* him?'

'This is not the point—'

'This is exactly the point. The Deep is something that is only dimly understood, even by the people who are a part of it. You've been a part of it, Adrien.'

'No, I haven't,' he said vehemently. 'I was a trans. I didn't have direct access to the Deep, even if C did.'

'You got rid of your plant. Why?'

'I'd rather not discuss it,' Adrien said, irritated because he sounded prim even to himself.

'So if I said that your Watcher had become too intimate with you; that your Watcher had started to light up areas of yourself that you wanted dark – would it be fair to say that?'

'I guess.'

'Don't you see what was happening? You were being absorbed into a Deep. C's own, primitive Deep. I didn't understand it fully until I learned C had no body of its own, not really. C may have used Sabina for a receptacle, but it was already in the habit of spreading itself around among many people. It was comfortable being in more than one body, in using you and others in a coordinated manner, the way you use your hands and feet. You of all people, Adrien, should have some idea of what the Deep is and how it works, because you've surely touched something close to it.'

'I don't know about that,' he said slowly, still working on the idea that he had been, maybe, only one of C's *feet* ... 'I was a trans for C, and there were things going on I didn't understand, but I was always myself ...' Except for the odd millisecond in combat, but he already knew that physics didn't permit a satellite to control his muscles, so that couldn't be what Sascha meant. Unless – unless C had been *changing* him; gradually, until he became capable of things that were formerly unnatural to him.

Sascha folded his hands and leaned forward, faintly condescending.

'OK. Let's look at it a different way. How many people were involved in the smuggling of the technology I? Several that you know of, and presumably some that you don't, since you haven't yet discovered who really conceived of the idea or provided the original plans that C distributed among its helpers for construction. In any event, an elaborate plan was conceived to build the plant secretly and to wield it, if you will. In you. You were chosen.'

'I know.'

'If you had gone ahead with it, Tomaj would have run interference for you. He would have helped you elude Max; but as it was, Sabina was playing your part and she didn't have a clue. So Tomaj got stuck in the middle of you and Sabina and Max, to his misfortune. Now that Tomaj is dead, we assume Sabina is vulnerable to Max—'

Adrien clenched his fists.

'—but if the plan had been executed as it was originally conceived, you and C would right now be integrating into one another. You were already familiar with one another, you had established means of communication and understanding, so it would have been relatively easy for C to use I to transfer its most important cognitive habits, its memories and the other psychological patterns that form what they used to call personality. Presumably you would have retained your contact with C's various trans, in one form or another. And, gradually, all of you would have been exchanging knowledge and information and identities. Sooner or later, you all would have become a Deep. A kind of bud off the main organism. So to speak.'

Adrien thought of Kang and his empty eyes; of Tazedait and her bandages. He thought of C and its ability to insinuate itself into him. And he shuddered. He didn't want to be Deep; not that Deep.

'Of course, Sabina is taking your part now.'

'Wait a second,' Adrien said, not wanting to deal with

that particular guilt trip. 'Back up. You say you don't know where the design for I came from. I know for a fact that C passed on the specifications for two separate components to specialists who built them for it. The next thing I know, you're getting ready to give me the finished plant. What exactly did *you* do?'

'I put the pieces together. I collated information on surgical procedure. I followed C's instructions.'

'But you didn't invent the thing.'

'I assume it came out of the Deep. Something that sophisticated would almost have to, by definition.'

'It came out of the Deep? How? Why? What do you mean by that?'

'That,' Sascha replied, 'is partly what I'm trying to find out here.'

Adrien frowned. He didn't know what to believe. 'How did you meet C? Were you her trans?'

'No.'

'You're Deep yourself, aren't you?'

Sascha smiled again.

'Did you know C left your name with Tomaj, so that it could find you after it was transferred to Sabina?'

'I tried to get Tomaj to give up that information, but he refused. The most difficult thing in the world is erasing evidence of yourself.'

Adrien went cold.

'Your computer attacked him? You helped kill Tomaj!'

'I had no intention of killing Tomaj. I simply needed to be taken out of the equation. If Tomaj would have let me erase my own name from his consciousness, he would never have had to drive himself mad as he did. Max only caught him because he was acting foolishly.'

'It wouldn't have done any good,' Adrien said. 'He wrote your name down. How do you think I found you?'

'Yes,' Sascha drawled. 'And here you are.'

Adrien could feel himself wanting to panic. Had he been lured here for the purposes of erasure?

'Why do you need to erase yourself? What difference does it make? You're obviously protected, wherever you are.'

He had to keep Sascha talking. Outside this simulation, guns were waiting for him. He studied the virtual room. The fact that it had a door struck him as a singular detail. A door to where? An escape route?

'I don't want to be embroiled in a grudge match between C and Max.'

'That's pretty lame.' The door wasn't merely sketched: it was rendered with some élan. The resolution of the visual would only be this good for a reason – the flowerpot, after all, was obviously hastily coded, suggesting he couldn't pick it up and throw it at Sascha, much though he might like to.

'You think so? They've fought before – but let's not go into that. What do you want from me, Adrien?'

'I want to know where Sabina is. And I want to know what I has actually done to her.'

'I can't help you find her, because she isn't in the Deep. I've developed the ability to match members of the Deep with their real-world identities, and to track them – but it only works on some of them some of the time, and anyway it doesn't tell you much about what's really going on. When you break down the Deep it's no longer the Deep, it's just a bunch of signals in the atmosphere.'

'I know she has a radio tag.'

'Do you know the frequency?'

'Well, no. But what about Max? I'd settle for finding him.'

'I wouldn't mess with Max again if I were you. I've never seen him crack under stress. He's unshakeable.'

Adrien suddenly grew tired of this kid's smug posturing.

'Oh yeah? If I could get in a room with him now, I'd shake him so hard I'd make pineapples fall out of his branches. What's behind that door?'

Sascha looked at the door, and back at Adrien.

'That's my access point to the Deep.'

326

'I thought you had to have a plant to be in the Deep.'

'Naturally I have a plant.'

Adrien found himself rocked by this. He still considered himself young; but here was a thirteen-year-old boy who took it for granted that one could move from individual to collective consciousness like changing channels on television ...

'Where we are now is something different. I've built a computer environment to trace the signals and try to untangle them, so I can parse the Deep, if you will. I have a whole system of satellite receivers mainlined with a program I adapted from the military. It tries to figure out the dodging patterns used by individual members to avoid detection. It also tries to decode the data in the signals.'

'You mean, you're actually spying on the Deep? You can tap their activity?'

'Well ...' Sascha hesitated. 'I'm working on it. It's a difficult problem.'

'Right. So you go in there and find Max for me.'

'Even if I could, I would risk revealing myself to him if he caught me. And I've already gone to great pains to avoid being found by Max.'

Adrien lunged for the door.

Sascha, of course, beat him to it. The boy floated from his seat in a streak of light, leaving behind a neon trail of smile like the Cheshire Cat on LSD. Adrien continued to hurtle forward, barely able to coordinate his limbs. He anticipated the inevitable collision and struggle, but to his surprise the boy seized the knob, opened the door, and stood politely aside. Adrien saw all this happen, powerless to stop, as momentum propelled him toward the threshold.

Beyond the door was a black pit, and beyond the pit was a wall of screaming data, sound and vision whitely incoherent and pulling like a horseshoe magnet: Niagara Falls in a box. Adrien extended his arms in a last-ditch effort to save himself, grabbing for the doorframe as the hot lubrication of adrenaline penetrated the simulation to electrify his veins, a telegraph from reality. His fingers caught the wood. He flashed the memory of years of training his hands: the *nukite* or spear-hand strikes practiced in pots of sand, then pots of gravel, and then against rocks, all to develop the ancient techniques that were said to enable the dislodging of internal organs. He could hang by his fingers indefinitely. They would not fail him.

But these were not his fingers.

The soft wood (pine? cedar?) felt eerily real, its grain and texture minutely articulated against fingertips made sensitive by the simulation only in these last quarters of a second. He clung, pectorals clenching as he tried to pull back the weight of his body, which had already crossed the threshold – one leg in fact dangling over the abyss – and he looked down in spite of himself. Predictably, there was darkness and more darkness, just the sort of thing that would appeal to a thirteen-year-old kid's aesthetics. The depths were dusted with fireflies.

His fingers found purchase. The body began to cooperate, but it was slow – he gritted his teeth in frustration because it would not do what he should so easily have accomplished were he only in his own skin.

'You see?' Sascha chided. 'You are like a child who must burn his fingers before he believes the oven is hot. You don't want to go in there. You cannot interpret the data. It's all coded. You will be nothing but stray noise, and the chaos will overwhelm your senses.'

Sascha held out his hand.

'I won't have you killed. Come. You don't belong here.'

Adrien was struggling so hard his real body twitched; ruthlessly, he got himself under control. He *didn't* belong here. He never had. But when he'd tried to get away from the Deep and be normal, he'd gotten entangled even further. Now that he was here, he didn't intend to lose.

Sensei, how can I fight when it's not even my own body?

The treacherous fingers began to release.

'You stupid fool!' Sascha shrieked. 'You'll bring my system down.'

Yes, Adrien thought. *I'm just a stupid fool. Stupid, stupid fool. Now everybody just shut up and get out of my way.*

Sascha grabbed for him; Adrien caught the boy's hand and *pulled*. They both spun away, and spray from the falls slapped Adrien's face and blinded him, sharp as acid. He clawed at his eyes and let go, somersaulting into the pit with Sascha trailing behind him like a kite string. Falling into the fireflies might not be too bad – it was probably his only way out of the simulation, but in the struggle he had drifted too close to the water, which now seized hold of one foot and pulled him toward it as he tumbled. Adrien flipped over; the foot was gone, and the waterfall was still pulling. The pitches numbed his mind. No. Raw data. No. Get away from it.

Too late.

He was inside some abstract creation phantomized within his own brain using a satellite link and a spider. He could feel Sascha but he didn't know how; nor did he know how in the span of an instant he had become a being of pure will. Thought, intention, and action all catalyzed one another and he was the smoke that went up. He enveloped Sascha and rode him through the chaos.

Sascha had a plant. He could interpret this deluge of information, or some of it; Adrien reached into the abstraction that was Sascha and thought: *Max*.

Had Sascha not already succeeded in pinpointing Max's signature in the Deep, nothing would have happened. Had he not previously begun the process of translating Max's transmissions through his own plant and re-digitizing them into computer storage, nothing would have happened. If Sascha had been able to resist the force of Adrien's will, nothing would have happened. And, had Adrien stopped to think, even for an instant, how very nearly impossible it was to drag information straight through the Deep without a plant, into a computer, and then into his own cortex and expect his brain to make sense of it – nothing would have happened.

But Adrien, for the first time in his life, had reached out into the unknown and caught hold of that ineffable combination of opportunity, trust, willpower and synchronicity that can turn a fighter into a force of nature. For just a second, he got hold of what Furuta had been talking about; he got his teeth into it. He saw the Deep and knew what it was all about. He saw right through Nikolai's carefully articulated simulations into Nikolai's head, and past that into the ocean of the Deep, and into one of its big fish, and out its unblinking Max Niagarin eyes. Just as the Watcher had done to him so many times, he took Max's senses.

He recognized the room: it was in Zagreb, destination of the wrong train for Adrien Reyes. But the black plastic bags had been ripped from the windows, revealing dirty glass, and now all the equipment was up and running. A scant four feet away, staring down at a musical keyboard, was Sabina, frowning in concentration. She looked just the same.

He must have made a sound because she glanced up at him. He looked into her eyes and moved Max's lips. 'Sa—'

From somewhere on the forgotten physical plane, acute and sudden pain shot through his head. He had one rueful thought: security systems might fail and alarms could be bypassed, yet there was nothing like a good pistol-whipping to bring a man back to earth.

Then everything was gone. He went away, to someplace where none of this had ever happened nor ever would. It was quiet there.

The sky had clouded over. Thunderheads so grey they were green mustered on the horizon. There were great pillars and marching statues of vapor too solid to punch through: cloud-bellies pregnant with deep lightning sound, growing heavier and faster with each mile of momentum as they

330

tumbled toward the place where he was lying. The barometer must be falling fast, because he woke with his ears ringing and sat up to the spit of windblown dust and a premonition of moisture. The grass bent over. Adrien got to his feet, the Deep forgotten, rubbing a bump on his head and wishing for aspirin.

No camp. No jeep. No sign of … anything.

No wallet. No passport. No rubles.

Ha-ha. Ha.

Ha. You sneaky devils. Now what?

Thirty-two

When I first began to work on the music, I thought it was going to be mainly a question of taking dictation from the sound in my head.

No.

It was nothing so simple. For one thing, every sound I uttered carried with it resonances, associations to things from C's life. Those few moments playing scales in the guitar shop had been disorienting, but now the sound was full of intention and passion, and it threatened to over-whelm me even as I tried to articulate it in an expressible musical form. It evoked the four-dimensional cities I had started seeing on the ferry to Korčula: gorgeous, Byzantine. Stamped on the undersides of my eyelids, the images became a kind of wallpaper for my studio, and I forgot, sometimes, that Max couldn't see them too.

Max was less of a problem than I expected. I hardly noticed him. In my efforts to stay with the music, shape it and bring it out of itself like a flower opening – to make its focus perfectly sharp – I walked around half in a trance. I thought C and I surrendered to each other when I left New York; but the final integration happened in that studio, and it was embodied in the music that came from both of us.

I still had two days to go in my contract with Max; I didn't know what I was going to do when the time was up. C was part of me now; I had no intention of giving up the plant. Yet I could think of no way out, so I became almost fatalistic in my devotion to the music, thinking, even if only this survived, it would have been worth it. I had to finish it.

Max turned out to be one of those people who only

needs a few hours' sleep in the dead of night, and when he does sleep he's like a cat, the tip of his tail always twitching. The rest of the time he watched me, usually from the couch, where he sat with his system and a phone that was security-locked; he needn't have bothered. Who would I have called?

One night I was sitting at the keyboard listening on headphones to a passage I'd just finished. I didn't like playing my music on the speakers, and anyway there was a loud party going on two houses down, and the headphones shut out the noise better. I thought I was totally absorbed in what I was doing; but out of the corner of my eye I saw Max give a little jerk as if he'd been shocked. I glanced over. His face was strained as if withstanding g-force acceleration. He stared at me. 'S—'

Instinctively I drew back in my chair; an instant later he leaped up and came at me. His hand closed around my throat and his spittle flew in my face as he gibbered.

'What do you think you're doing? How dare you?'

I got one foot wedged against his stomach and kicked him off me. He landed back on the couch where he'd started and sat there wearing the most flabbergasted expression I've ever seen. He looked at the floor, frowned, cleared his throat and composed his face. Then he stood up.

'Excuse me,' he said. I heard him descending the stairs. I got to my feet and followed him out to the landing. I could see him in the hall below, pacing. He lit a cigarette. He paced more. Then he glanced up and saw me.

'You will tell me everything you know about I. Now. My mercy toward you is contingent on how much information you can supply.'

'We agreed that I had a week.'

'We also agreed that you would attempt to contact no one.'

'I haven't.'

A faint breeze from an open window flared the end of his cigarette.

'Adrien Reyes is in the Deep.'

My hand went to my mouth. With a defiance I didn't know I had, I said, 'You'll never succeed in headsucking me. I know every trick there is. You'll get nothing from me.'

Max charged up the stairs like a bull in rut.

I reached into the studio and snapped loose a speaker cable. Then I threw the speaker at his head. It missed, gouging the ceiling and then crashing to the steps and bumping down like a domino. Flattened against the wall, Max was breathing hard. I grabbed a steel-cased effects processor, ripped it from the rack, and hurled it. Max was struck a glancing blow, but he had raised his hands to protect his face. Head down, he resumed his assault on the stairs and I seized the Telecaster, thrusting its pointed head toward his midsection like a spear. He caught hold of it and wrenched it away, grabbing my wrist at the same moment.

'I think we can come to terms, Sabina, don't you?' He pulled me down the steps, forced me against the wall, and twisted my hand back painfully.

'No.'

'Your resistance would be admirable if it weren't so stupid.' He was whispering against my face. I could feel the moisture of his breath. 'Give me what I want and I'll go away. I'll take it on disc, I'll take it on paper, as long as it's the real thing. Shall we go upstairs and I'll have a cigarette while you get it ready for me?'

I ducked under his grasp and threw myself down the stairs, stumbling and falling into the entrance hall. I clawed my way to the door and got outside, shouting, grateful that I was fully dressed and even had on my boots, which I wear in the studio rather than sweep the floor. But I barely reached the sidewalk before Max caught up with me. Something hit my face and I became dizzy and confused for a time. The next thing I saw was the ground.

What do you do in such a situation? A man is on top of

you, your jaw's probably fractured from the force of the punch that put you here, you are dizzy, he is stronger. Your flesh is soft against his. He has an erection no doubt brought on by the thrill of the chase and he's grunting with the effort of holding you down. You bite. The rain is still falling, you can hear the party nearby. Music, shouts, squeals. You go limp a moment, thinking, maybe he will spare me. Surely he doesn't expect me to fight ... for you know you need only a moment's relaxation of his guard, a quick twist and somehow you will inflict pain.

Submission is a fair option here. A man wouldn't have this choice, not yet: a man could not go limp, cry, beg mercy and expect to receive anything but contempt and possibly worse injury. But it is an option for me. He has my wrists trapped in one of his hands, forced over my head, pressed back as far as they will go. I try to slither out with my hips, get a knee in there somehow, but he's quick. He grabs my hair and I bite again, lunging for his neck. My teeth catch something but he cries out and throws his weight on me hard, knocking the breath out.

I find myself pushed to the edge of the curb, my head hanging in the gutter, my hair trailing in the rainwater. Using his right hand he shoves my head down and back. I bite at him and he forces my face in the water. My neck cannot resist him long, but he shifts grip, holding my hair now and using it to jerk my head from side to side, up and down. He bangs the back of my head on the pavement, twice, three, four times. My nose has blood in it. My ears ring. Into the water – can't breathe.

'Be quiet,' he said. 'Be quiet and very still, and if you're lucky, you'll live.' With his free hand he's groping for something.

I open my eyes and see the weapon, delicate, slender as a circus wire, curving in the yellow light of the streetlamp: a whipknife. He brings it close to my eyes. He raises it above my forehead. This is the end it's over no going back no other chance this is it.

I hear the deep scream – where did I get the breath for that? – black deathsound coming up the chromatic scale raggedly but with no diminishment in volume. I can see the rage on his face, but I wouldn't have believed his bland features capable of such savagery.

'*Shut up!*'

His hands, both of them, on my face and head, my face in the water, his hand in my mouth, covering my nose. The whipknife singing in the air between our faces. My hips to one side and kick, my back arching, legs scrambling for some purchase and my hands grabbing at the street to press myself up out of the water. The whipknife moves; sound of my boots on the stone and try for another breath but suddenly upper body free – he's rearing back, I try to crabwalk away but one hand on my belly, my legs are still trapped, he holds me, my boot comes up to kick and he snakes the knife up along my thigh, cool and like butter, I wait for it to stop but it doesn't. I don't feel it at first, no pain at first for it's so slender, so sharp – then it pierces something inside and he starts to carve with it, my uterus maybe or something deeper, he's turning the knife inside, his face serene with method—

I threw myself backward into the street, breathing fast with shock like a small animal and he stood up. I remember the dark faces of the houses behind him and the uneven paving stones at my eye level, and the light coruscating through the rain drops as he stood over me, the whipknife still pointed at my head like a wand, and I was silent.

Thirty-three

Adrien kept thinking of Roger Furuta and how he would approve of the virtues of this situation in which Adrien now found himself. Furuta would probably call it something ridiculous, like 'reality training'. To Adrien it was an exercise in thirst and frustration. He followed animals to water, grateful for the recent rain that meant, at least, he wouldn't die of thirst in an otherwise desiccated region. Food was out of the question, and as for direction? He only knew he went west, sort of, following the sun. Since he didn't know where he'd started from, it wasn't until much later that he figured it all out.

Later when he had occasion to consult a map he estimated that he had run and walked some sixty miles over two days before he came to a road. Not surprisingly, there had been a road less than ten miles from the place where he'd been dumped. But the rain had soon obliterated the tire tracks of the vehicle that brought him there and he had nothing to follow. Deprived of landmarks, he must have turned astray and walked far wide of the highway.

When in the end he reached the road, he got a ride to Ozhezkazgam on the back of a coal truck and called American Express. It was three more days before he reached Zagreb, beginning to feel like a civilized person again but only barely: the itch to do something unpleasant to Max had returned like herpes.

He went straight to Sabina's house with a six-inch length of lead pipe in his back pocket. There was no answer at the front door, or the back door. He climbed over a garden wall and broke into a back window.

There was a feeling of emptiness in the place. A stereo

speaker lay on the stairs; a broken guitar was in the front hall. The studio was full of dirty coffee cups. Nothing to indicate where she'd gone. Until he noticed the fingerprint-dust on the speaker and the guitar.

'*Madre de dios*,' he said.

For the first time in ten years, he was in a library. He had balked at the last second when faced with the prospect of entering a police station: he was simply too paranoid. The chief problem with the library was that he didn't know the language at all. Still, he managed to find the newspapers and looked back through the last few days' worth of local news. He had just come to the conclusion that he was going about this all wrong and needed to hire a translator right away, when he saw the photo.

It was on the front page, four days old. He stared at the picture until the image broke down into its constituent fibers.

Max's photograph. A blurry shot of a crime scene: a body awash in blood, nearly beheaded.

He thought his heart had stopped. He looked closer. It was a bad picture, but the head had short hair. The shoes on the body were men's shoes.

He sprinted to the reference desk and in frantic whispers begged for help. The librarian seemed delighted to practice his English. He said Sabina Lazarich was mentioned in the article and was being treated in the hospital. He opened his mouth to comment further and Adrien cut him off, demanding directions.

As he had ever been, he was too late now. But she was alive, and Max was dead. He could have leaped for joy. He burst out of the library and it suddenly hit him that he was going to see her.

Smoke, the artefact of fire. Flame can be described but not captured, identified but not defined. When he saw her, would he know her?

Thirty-four

They had to drug me heavily for the first few days: when I woke up in the hospital bed I immediately tried to leap up and run away. I resisted everything, fighting like a cat whenever an IV was put in and spitting at a neurologist who attempted only to look in my eyes.

It didn't help that I couldn't speak. I could understand words, but I couldn't seem to reproduce them. My head hurt most of the time. The spat-upon neurologist was very kindly. He told me that I had brain damage in the language areas – he actually put it that vaguely, as if he were talking to a two-year-old. I wanted to demand real information, but obviously I couldn't. I had to be content with his assurances that similar cases had been rehabilitated with some success.

Gynecologically speaking, they had put things more or less back together. There was no infection, despite the fact that my intestines had apparently been damaged as well. But I wasn't feeling much below the waist, and I didn't care to look. It had been pure spite that had made him do this to me; but I wasn't surprised.

I knew the plant was gone because I had seen Max take it. He pulled it out with a sodeyama grip – a piece of HIT surgical equipment I was all too familiar with. When he held it up to the streetlight, he forgot about me for a second or two. Adrien was right all along: I do have within me a capacity for violence, a kind of joy in it. But I had only ever practiced it vicariously – never with my own bare hands, so I had never really known what it meant.

Watching Adrien through all those fights, I'd learned a couple of tricks. I lay there bleeding in the rain, and for a few seconds the pain just didn't come. Probably I was in shock; I don't know. I remember rolling to one hip, scissoring my right leg over my left with Max's shins caught between my legs; then I snapped my feet together and he went down. The sodeyama flew out of his hand and he immediately scrambled to his knees and began to crawl after it. I picked myself up and threw myself on him. The whipknife was still lying nearby. We struggled – he was trying only to get to the sodeyama grip with the plant – I got the knife.

The rest is described in detail, I'm sure, in the coroner's report.

Our blood was all mixed up. When I saw what I'd done I was sick. Then people started coming. Even with the noise of the party going on, someone must have seen or heard something, because there was a crowd in no time. I remember seeing the sodeyama grip go spinning across the pavement and into a storm drain. After that I passed out.

The first few days in the hospital were the worst. I wanted to communicate but I didn't know how, and the feelings of helplessness and *déjà vu* were no less for the fact that I knew it was different this time, that I still had a body. They gave me some paper and a pencil to see if I could write (I couldn't) and I found that I could manage musical notation without much difficulty. My concentration was poor, but I put that down to the drugs. I wished I could have had the score I'd already worked on, back at the apartment, but there was no way of making this desire known. In truth I was a little afraid to start over. What if I couldn't call up the music? I didn't know how much of me was left, and I didn't want to look inside and find holes where only recently there had been an entire lifetime's history.

In the end it was boredom that motivated me. I began with the first sound of the piece, and when I invoked it, everything was there. I could no longer hear it as vividly. I heard it the way you hear memories when you recall them in a conscious state; not the way you hear dreams when you are dreaming them. It would have to be enough. I began to write.

I couldn't believe it when I heard his voice outside. What threw me off was that he was attempting to speak Croatian. He sounded frantic. First he said he was my boyfriend. The nurse on duty primly informed him that only family could visit me.

'I'm her cousin!' he yelled at her in English. Then: 'It's incest, OK?'

He didn't get in.

Neither did the police, or the media. The neurologist had been strict with his instructions, and Carmina, the head nurse, was very effective.

It took him two days to figure out who Carmina was, and another day to figure out how to charm her. By then, they were getting ready to let me out of intensive care, and I was halfway through the score. He walked in five minutes before the end of visiting hours. He had a paper bag cradled in his elbow.

'I brought you some vodka,' he said shyly. 'I hear they have plenty of morphine here.'

We had started out being more intimate than any natural human relationship could permit. Now I could not even say hello. Maybe it was better this way. I couldn't have put it in words, anyway. Not any of it. I was happy to have him sit on the edge of the bed and complain about Croatia. How come he was constantly being cheated on his restaurant bills? How could they let people smoke so much in public – even in a hospital, for godsake? He was thinking of changing his hairstyle, he said. Something more mature. He liked Albert Einstein's hair – what did I think? Would it look good on him?

I knew he was terrified, and he knew I knew. And yet he was here. He never once brought up I, but it was always present in the silences – and there were many of them.

Adrien isn't clever enough to keep up a one-sided conversation for long. He talked about wanting to live a quiet life somewhere; wanting a chance to step back from everything that had happened and let it sink in.

Silence.

He talked about martial arts, and how it was all making sense to him now.

Silence.

He talked about wanting to hear some of my music.

Silence.

I pointed to the score. It was lying near the bed, weighted down by a vase.

'I can't read music,' he protested. 'All I remember about music is in fourth grade we learned the notes. All Cars Eat Gas. And what was the other one? FACE.'

I laughed.

The question he most wanted answered, of course, was the one I was least capable of answering – with or without language. The question in his hands and back and throat was always the same: *what are you?*

I'm an exponent now. I'll never be solitary again. I'll never live only within the walls of myself. And I don't even know what that means.

We could say that **I** delivered its information, but that's a false conceit left over from the computer paradigm of consciousness. Information doesn't exist. It's an interaction, not a thing. The information I am made of now is animate. The plant may be gone, but we're still growing. We're still going … somewhere.

I don't know what C wanted to do with **I**, ultimately. Maybe she truly did want it only for herself. But that was then, and this is now. It's a different world already, just because I'm in it. And she was right: it's also a world with no one at the wheel. Reality's inventing itself, and anything *can* happen.

Considering what's gone down so far, I'm not sure what I think about that.

I had been out of intensive care and in the neurological ward for about a week when he showed up with a wheelchair and announced he had a surprise. By now I was walking, although I still had abdominal pain, but he said where we were going was too far to walk. He was right. We went across the hospital and down to the basement, where Adrien had found a small, little-used chapel. It gave the impression of being a place where people prayed silently for the dead and dying, and it seemed very old. However, there were altars for several faiths set side by side, a place by the entrance for shoes, prayer rugs, holy water, incense, and books. Fading paintings from different traditions decorated the walls. There were folding chairs stacked against the walls. And, toward the back, there was a piano.

He wheeled me up to it, and I hoisted myself out of the chair and onto the padded bench. I didn't have much hope of the instrument being in tune, but when I struck A440 it was close enough.

I hadn't noticed him take it from my room, but now he put the score in my hands. I had only finished it yesterday; he must have noticed. I had become obsessed with it, going over every little detail with great care. Now Adrien unfolded a chair and sat to my right, beneath a Tibetan mandala. He clasped his hands together and leaned forward expectantly.

I handed him the score, shaking it at him to make him take it. I didn't need it. I knew exactly what I was doing.

He looked down at it and I gestured that he should read. He made a face, then sighed and addressed the first page. There was no title because I still didn't have the use of language. I watched his brow wrinkle and he glanced up at me.

My stomach had gone tight.

He so much wanted this to be over.

Didn't he?

'What are these decorations in the margins?' he said. I shrugged. He turned the sheet over and stared wide-eyed at the back. The drawings had been very difficult to reproduce, even using the finest pen, but I had had a lot of time on my hands lately. Adrien rapidly flipped through the pages until he came to the end of the score. As an end marking, I had been unable to resist drawing a single, half-lidded eye.

He let his hands drop, and the pages fluttered from him like tame birds. His gaze tracked them as they settled on the floor. I held my breath. Adrien said nothing. His head came up, and those green eyes fixed me across the room. We sat looking at each other, absolutely still, in the room that smelled of incense and old carpet and mold.

Slowly, as if he couldn't believe himself, he smiled.

It was the best thing that I ever had. I spread my hands across the keyboard and began to play.